Praise for
BEAUTIFUL SERPENT, RESTLESS EMBERS

"Plummet over the garden wall with Laurel; follow her into the woods where the dead speak and secrets come alive."

-Shannon McRoberts
USA Today Bestselling Author

"An impressive debut by a talented new author, this epic tale follows the trials of a young woman learning to harness her gifts—both the light and the dark. It blazes with a fierce power and is written with a poetic force that digs deep beneath your skin."

-Georgina Key
Phoenix Prize for Best New Voice Winning Author

BEAUTIFUL SERPENT

RESTLESS EMBERS

BEAUTIFUL SERPENT

RESTLESS EMBERS

YNES FREEMAN

Content Warnings available at the end of this book.

Published by **MEMENTO VIVERE PRESS**
www.mementoviverepress.com
First Edition, July 2024

Line edits by Kathy Riggs Larsen
Proofreading by Erin Elyse

Cover art and design by Eben Schumacher
www.ebenschumacherart.com

Pendant design by Robert Carl Ruble
Emberwynter – Dark High Fantasy Jewelry
www.emberwynter.com

Chapter headers by Elisha Bugg / Inkwolf Designs
inkwolfdesigns.wixsite.com/inkwolf-cover-design

Publisher's Cataloging-in-Publication Data
Names: Freeman, Ynes (Daniela Ynes), 1983- .
Title: Beautiful serpent, restless embers / Ynes Freeman.
Description: Green Bay, WI : Memento Vivere Press, 2024. | Series: Beautiful serpent series ; book 1.
Identifiers: LCCN 2024942358 | ISBN 9781964501000 (pbk.) | ISBN 9781964501017 (ebook)
Subjects: LCSH: Empathy – Fiction. | Bildungsromans – Montana -- Fiction. | Boarding schools – Fiction. | Visions – Fiction. | Man-woman relationships – Fiction. | Politics and war – Fiction. | BISAC: FICTION / Gothic. | FICTION / Fantasy / General. | FICTION / Coming of Age.
Classification: LCC PS3606.R44 B43 2024 | DDC 813 F—dc23
LC record available at https://lccn.loc.gov/2024942358

DEDICATION

For my Roland

CONTENTS

PART ONE

"You're gentle as a lamb, aren't you, cherissima?"

I did not have the heart to tell her she was wrong—so wrong—about me.

A TASTE SO BITTER

It was not the first time I had seen Her. She had appeared plenty of times in the gardens, before I had come to this place. When I walked under trellises, rays of her light peeked through tangles of wisteria vines, and I imagined She was speaking to me, punching a message in bursts of light and darkness in an ancient language, even older than the old tongue. I had believed that perhaps, if my legs carried me fast enough, I may be able to decipher Her meaning.

Tonight, She was a small white semicircle, the fullness of her shape obscured by clouds. A faint glimmer of light illuminated the sharpness of the mountain below Her, running along one edge of a jagged slope. Gripping the stone edge of a window, I watched Her as my fingers turned cold and white and the night breeze pockmarked the flesh on my arms.

"Well? How is it?" Suzette asked from behind me.

I turned and her gray, inquisitive eyes met mine from beneath a sprig of her dark curls. Two thick black droplets ran from her eyes, streaking her fair skin with bands of darkness. They were more than shadows; each was a stream, an expression of the desperation and fear Suzette held in her heart. As I was a Lunare, her feelings manifested in me as a waltz of empathy and madness.

Ilex and litha.

The darkness clung to the curves of Suzette's cheeks and dribbled to her chin, a drop splashing onto her neck. A blotch of shadow stained the ethereal spring of lace at her throat, spreading down her bodice and to her skirt. The darkness pooled at her feet, flowing across the stone floor in heavy, viscous spatters. A dark drop unfurled into a ribbon beside me, crawling across the toes of my slippers before I could sidestep it.

I was unsure if it was truly happening, or if it was my mind.

Scratches of worry appeared in a crisscross at the hem of my skirt, blotches soon appearing like ink stains: saturating my waist, darkening my bodice. I reached to my lips to stifle a scream, but the shadows rose quickly, spilling into my mouth. I grimaced at the taste, as though I had taken a bite out of a bar of soap.

"Is it working? I heard that the moon is supposed to calm the litha."

I closed my eyes and turned away from Suzette's distorted form.

"Ilex is the gift. The moon is supposed to draw it forth," I whispered. "It does nothing to calm the litha."

Suzette bit her lip and I felt the shadows in my mouth shift—Suzette's bitter desperation turning a sour flavor. I rolled it on my tongue.

Impatience, exasperation.

"The litha is still here," I said. "I can feel it. I can taste it . . ." A shudder ran through me and I thumbed the pendant at my throat to calm me. My gaze turned to the window and I stared into the sky: a sprawling veil of darkness. There were no stars winking encouragement; a hazy cast of clouds smudged the moon's only light, the tops of mountains wafting in and out of my sight. The curtains shuddered, the night breeze flowing freely, needling at my hands. I felt the shadows burrowing into me: thin braids of darkness wrapping around my chest, the blackness in my mouth crawling down my throat—all hope, warmth, and breath squeezed from me.

I turned and gazed longingly at a small teacup perched on the nightstand beside Suzette. It beckoned me to hold its warmth on this frigid night. After gripping the windowsill to stare at the moon, I welcomed the pinpricks of heat that would shiver through my fingers, the promise of peace: even if for a short time.

If I drank it, I could forget this night.

Suzette caught my gaze and scowled. Bunching her skirts in her hands, she stamped her foot on the stone floor.

"No, Laurel!" she huffed. "You must try harder to master your gift."

I folded my lips in disagreement. Suzette did not understand: it was not that I could not master the ilex. It was simply that I could not separate it from the litha—the madness that came with it. I opened my mouth to tell her and the shadows reached further into my body, darkness seizing my lungs. Struggling for breath, the room began to spin beneath me. I held tight to the window's ledge, lowering myself cautiously to the floor.

"Shh." Suzette's heels clicked behind me. I felt the weight of her hand on my shoulder and she coaxed me to face her. She raised my chin and smiled calmly, sweetly. A small brooch on the collar of her gown caught a ray of moonlight. Sweeping away one of her thick, black curls, Suzette's fingers passed over the hematite stone at the center of her brooch, tracing an arc.

"It will get better, cherissima," she sang. She made another pass at her brooch and the taste of her distress dissolved from my tongue.

Suzette was not supposed to use her gift on me. We were not even supposed to be here, tucked away in the unoccupied bedchamber at the end of the hall, away from our headmistress and her vedovas—but Suzette had never been one for following rules.

Suzette d'Isparza was the youngest of her bloodline, and

the only daughter. She was the descendant of great women, exalted women: Damica. We were both born to Damica: thrust into a long, proud tradition of women with gifts: the ability to feel—as I could—or to speak—as Suzette could—certain truths, matters of the heart that others were not privy to.

Suzette was a Verdetto: a class within the Damica that allowed her to command words with ease, bending them with an arc of her finger. With her gift, the linguina d'argent, she could twist words tight as a cord and release them when the moment was right.

I was not clear how Suzette discovered she could use the linguina d'argent to command the litha. The litha bent easily to her gift, bowing in submission and releasing me from the shadow-hold: but it was a violation of our headmistress's rules to practice our gifts on each other.

For as long as I had known, the Damica were put into service in the Localita di Fiore, destined to become wives and advisers in the high court, yielding our powers to lords, generals, gentries—so that they may never worry about losing their wealth, their honor.

Suzette was fated to become Damica. I, too, was fated to become Damica, the same as my mother.

I was eight years of age when my gift blossomed—a proud, white rose sprouting under my sternum, and I shall never forget the first morning it blossomed. It embraced me while I lay in a quiet cocoon of quilts that held me, like a cherub's arms, before dawn. It tickled the back of my neck when I planted my toes on the cold, wooden planks of my bedchamber; it smiled upon me while I dressed, carrying the scent of jasmine across my terrace, kissing my nose and cheek with the final breaths of night.

I felt it in the deep thrum of my Papa's hymns—the

notes that guided me, upon waking, down the corridor, and I heard it in the tired groan of our stairs bending under my weight. I felt it when I silenced my toes on the fibers of the rug at the bottom of the steps, and I felt it in the warmth I held in the soles of my feet. I was frightened to reveal it to my Mama, for it was no secret that filia like me were sent away—our travel-trunks packed hastily, a carriage soon awaiting us at the threshold to usher us to the Accademia Marl.

It had been mid-morning and Mama was sitting in our entryway, statuesque, her hands resting in the folds of her skirt. I approached her with caution, mouth dry, pulse rushing through my ears.

"It happened, Mama. I feel it."

Mama's delicate brows wrinkled, forming a narrow line on her forehead. She lifted her chin and the soft sunlight caught in her braids. She smiled at me, the creases under her eyes folding joyously.

When she smiled, I saw my reflection in her: her eyes the color of moss, her shoulders thin, her face framed by dark blond hair, the hue of a wheat field blanketed in sunlight. She was a frail creature with a pallor to her skin like a gardenia shorn from the bush, her cheeks sculpted like marble. She brushed my hair aside and kissed my cheek.

"Do not be anxious, filia. It is a proud tradition to carry. Come!"

Within the Damica, Mama was of the Fortuna class—and her gift was called suerradio. While Suzette could command words with her linguina d'argent, Mama could twist fortune, alter its course so that it may bring blessings to some, sorrow to others. Mama bore a silver bracelet on her left wrist made up of chains and hooks: two intertwined serpents, each with an emerald eye: one representing fate, the other, chance. She kept one long, ivory finger perched on them most times.

Mama smoothed her skirt and rose, beckoning me to follow. "Let us read your leaves."

I followed her across the room to our hearth, the scent of wood hanging heavy in the air. Her hands were like marble as she clamored about, her fingers moving in and out of shadow as she gathered a kettle and set it over flame. When she practiced suerradio, she always began with a reading—a check on fate, the way a sailor may check the winds by licking his finger and holding it to the air. She sometimes used a divining bowl, a deck of cards, or even simply tapped her bracelet to perform her reading. Of all her methods, though, she preferred tasseomancy: the art of tea reading. I felt that it had something to do with the stars. On the nights we sat in the garden, she gazed past the moon with indifference, her attention instead captured by a twinkling net of stars. She pointed, drawing lines between them, her lips turned up in contentment as she spoke stories about them.

While the water for my tea boiled, Mama instructed me to sit at the counter, and she lay a small cup and handkerchief before me. Her slippers clicked in excitement across the floor while she twirled around the room, and with a flourish, she added a sprinkle of leaves and a ladle of water to my teacup. Forcing a weak smile, I positioned my hands around the cup as it cooled, and then I drank deeply. Mama rested her wrists on the table, folding one hand on top of the other, tapping at her bracelet. She stopped me before I finished the tea and she took my cup in her left hand, swirling what liquid remained counterclockwise. Fate and chance. Balance and adjustment. Small details, to a Fortuna, could mean the difference between wealth and starvation, joy and lovelessness: life and death.

Mama inverted my teacup suddenly, allowing the liquid to seep into the handkerchief before me. She allowed it to soak for a moment before raising the cup, and I felt a stone of apprehension at the center of her chest. To my eye, the leaves were little more than a scattering of ants, gathered in bunches on the side of my cup. They meant nothing to me, but Mama peered at them with an intense focus, forming delicate, invisible threads to connect them. While I could not read the shapes and meanings of the leaves, I could read feelings. Her worries lifted away and she smiled.

"Laurel, you are Damica, indeed," she beamed. "You will bring fortune to our family!" She pressed her palms against the cup, her green eyes brimming with pride. "Men of Trionfi will pay a high price for a Damica bride." A peal of her laughter rang throughout our home.

She perched a finger on the rim of the cup and ran it along the edge. The mirth fell from her face.

"What is it, Mama?" I asked thinly. Her dismay was impossible to ignore; her laughter had flowed between us like the tea itself, swirling in the cup: rich, honey-colored, full of contentment. And it had stopped suddenly, become still. My skin felt cold, my toes restless from the silence.

Mama reached for my handkerchief, smudged the leaves, and pressed the cup face down on our table.

"It is a quirk; nothing more. We will speak of it to Headmistress Elan soon. Do not concern yourself with it." The corners of her lips fought to uphold a smile, and she rose quickly. "Come! Let us celebrate! We shall buy roses for the table tonight."

She rushed me through the entryway and I scarcely had time to reach for my day-bonnet before rushing out the door in pursuit of her.

We lived in the Localita di Fiore in the kingdom of Trionfi, and our home sat at the edge of the marketplace beside two domiciles with which we shared walls—each with the same arched roof as our own, all our weathered walls joined by beams crossed with beams, rectangles and squares.

Though our home was small, humble: Mama walked with her chin held high, squeezing my hand in hers, the chains of her bracelets pressing into my wrist. The marketplace was like fire, but it never disturbed my senses—I welcomed the bubbling, aureate roads, the clamoring hooves of horses and donkeys. There was music sizzling within the voices of merchants, beauty in their multicolored blouses and trousers.

As we walked hand-in-hand, my Mama captured the attention of everyone we passed. It was curious to me how the locals flashed her a longing gaze as she moved past their stands—while the wandering tradesmen looked upon her with fright—a glance at her bracelet sent them shuffling past with hurried steps.

She was Damica Clare Aleandri, the Fortuna—blessed with the gift to dance with fate and chance. She could wrap each around her wrist and choose to stretch it into rays of gold, spreading bliss through the marketplace—or she could inflict sorrow, sparing no merchant from trouble and woe. Although travelers feared her, she had always chosen to sun the marketplace with good fortune. I did not know at the time that she was not supposed to use her gift in this manner—for all gifts of the Damica carried with them a duality: a blessing and a curse.

Fate and chance.

Ilex and litha.

Perhaps it was Suzette's disregard for the rules—much like my mother's—that drew me to her. She struggled to balance veritas—truth—and her linguina d'argent.

We had all studied mercilessly under the tutelage of Headmistress Elan and her vedovas. I had been at the Accademia Marl for eleven years, and Headmistress Elan had warned me about Suzette early on, steering me clear of her company. I was quickly approaching my twentieth birthday and Suzette—my senior of a year—had just celebrated her twenty-first. While we flourished in our gifts, we had both failed to secure a betrothal. We were the only two among the Damica our age, and Suzette was already one year past marriage age—

and I soon would cross that threshold.

With her enchanting smile and soothing voice, it was not her looks that had driven Suzette out of favor. Suzette had gained a reputation for being troublesome—a touch wicked.

"You have mastered your tongue too well," our headmistress had lectured. "Your temperament is too sharp, and your speech is too pointed for your suitors to desire you as a bride."

I, on the other hand, was altogether unfit for suitors.

Even as young as eight, it was common for the Lunare to begin to stir in our sleep. The vedovas were sent to watch us at night, to sit in our quarters and report to Headmistress Elan, in the morning, which of us were being haunted by night-whispers.

It was all part of the litha. Night-root eased these maladies, and, after our supper, we were made to drink a tea of its extract. It gave my sister-Lunare long, tranquil slumbers so that they could channel their ilex, unperturbed by the litha.

It had never worked for me.

During my first year in the Accademia, while I sat in the dining hall with my sister-Lunare, each of us with a cup of night-root tea before us, I felt a light tap at my shoulder.

I turned to find it was a vedova placing a quiet hand on me. Her rose-colored sleeve brushed my neck as I turned to her. A ring with a tiger's eye stone rested on her index finger, a symbol that she was of the Vigore class of Damica—a woman with exceptional muscle memory and movement.

"Filia Laurel," she said, "Tonight you will share tea with the Vigore."

My sister-Lunare cast a perplexed gaze in my direction, and I felt their curiosity at my back as I rose. I followed the sway of the vedova's hair past the dining tables of the Verdetto and the Fortuna classes, every inquisitive gaze itching on my back as I shuffled past. The vedova seated me at the Vigore's table beside the daughter of a gentry named Riognach. Her russet-colored hair matched the striations of the tiger's eye stone she wore on her index finger. Her gaze was not a light tickle like the others; it was sharp, a sting of disdain.

"What is *she* doing here?" Riognach whispered to a filia beside her. The two exchanged a look and the vedova pushed a cup and saucer in front of me.

"Enough, Riognach," she warned. "Like it or not, the Lunare are your sister-Damica. It is your duty to protect them."

"Yes, Vedova Oriana," Riognach mumbled, dipping her head in deference. Even at age nine, my ilex came to me with such clarity that the falseness of this acceptance shone through, glinting at me like a coin in the sun. I did my best to look away from Riognach while the vedova filled my cup with a cloudy, olive-colored tea.

"The Vigore drink vendrake to balance our brutavis," she explained. "Headmistress Elan believes it will help with your problem. Drink deep, filia. I will be by to take you to your chambers. May you find rest."

I peered into the liquid; my bewildered reflection stared back at me. I questioned how the vendrake would help me, as the ilex was anything but brutavis. Brutavis was a Vigore's gift: the force within to stay in motion always, moving with a forward momentum.

Riognach chuckled while I brought the rim of the teacup to my lips and the putrid liquid rolled into my mouth. I winced trying to swallow, and Riognach twisted her lips into a smirk.

"You Lunare are as fragile as feathers."

Brutavis.

For Riognach, it was the need to prove her strength above all others.

Any memory beyond her quip was lost to me: for that

was the purpose of the vendrake. To snuff out experiences, like a glass over a candle, to turn them to smoke and watch them perish.

I awoke the next morning in the Lunare quarters. My arms and legs felt heavy, my mind filled with cobwebs, leaving me to stare vacant at the floor during my lectures.

Vendrake.

For years, I drank deep—and it had turned me entirely numb. While my sister-Lunare blossomed in their gifts, some of them weaning from the night-root and sleeping through the night without the litha, the numbness of the vendrake spread through my body: my tongue slow, my limbs weary. My eyelids always felt heavy; many mornings, I could hardly muster the power to lift them.

I lurched into my adolescence in this manner—the vendrake clouding my mind, my stupor making me unfit for suitors.

"Laurel!"

My attention snapped to Suzette. She was holding me by the shoulders, caressing her brooch in the moonlight. I could feel she was afraid—it manifested as a light hum buzzing through my ribs. When she smiled, her eyes became two gray half-moons, her teeth hiding behind her lips. She wondered, in this moment, when our headmistress would tire of us—Suzette and her spiteful tongue, my catatonic state with the vendrake—and my unbridled madness without it.

"We are not meant to serve men. Pah!" Suzette sneered. "Terrible, foul-smelling clods, hair everywhere!" She wrinkled her nose. "I prefer the company of women. But—as we cannot court who we wish to, freely—it is simply my wish to quell your litha so that Headmistress Elan might keep me in the Accademia as a vedova. Away from my family—away from all men."

"I do not think it is our fate to remain unwed," I whispered, bowing my head.

Suzette snorted. "Maybe not yours, but I would be glad to be free of men and marriage. And I would like to see you free of that which vexes you, cherissima."

I wished it were so, but Suzette did not understand that there was no escaping fate. I rose and walked to the nightstand, reaching for my teacup.

"My litha is too strong, and Headmistress Elan will never approve of you using your gift on me. I will take my tea, now, and return to my chambers," I said to Suzette.

She balled her hands into fists, pushing them onto her hips. "We have to try, cherissima! *You* have to try. Just give it a chance."

Fate and chance. It always came back to fate and chance. I swirled the tea, watching the cloudy texture spin, circling the cup like the chains of my mother's bracelet. I felt pity for Suzette for coming to such a hapless Damica as myself for help.

Suzette frowned, and though our headmistress had warned me that she was selfish, cunning—with the ilex and the moon, it was not difficult to pry back her exasperation and feel in my heart that she cared for me. Her concern washed over me in the dull silver light, a sprinkle of tenderness like a light snow, kissing my cheeks, my eyes.

I tried holding the emotion on my skin for a fleeting moment before allowing it to melt away. Lowering my teacup, I looked to Suzette, trying my best to will my eyes to reflect my compassion for her.

Suzette approached me slowly, cautiously, and plucked the tea from my hands. Her heels clattered across the stone floor and she tossed the liquid out the window, relinquishing it to the moon and the mountains.

PAIRED WITH DEATH

"I have five brothers," Suzette told me, just before supper and tea. "The eldest is a baron with a vineyard in the hills. He has not lifted a finger in years! The second is an artist. He paints like a child; the only reason he has seen success is because of the d'Isparza name."

I thumbed my pendant as she spoke, watching several vedovas whirl around the dining hall, placing plates and cups at our tables. Their pale pink robes blended with the white stones of the walls, the light reflecting off pillars—everything bright—too bright, dizzying. I wanted to rest: to retire to my bedchamber and cover my head with a pillow. All sight and sound felt heavy in my mind—the murmurs of my sister-Damica, the clanking of plates, the clicking of shoes. Try as I might, I failed to wrap my mind around why Suzette d'Isparza had pulled me aside, why she was talking to me. Her words swam in my ears, and I struggled to make sense of them. With the vendrake dulling my body and mind, few of my sister-Damica ever spoke to me—or perhaps they did, and I simply could not recall.

On my steadier days, when the vendrake did not claim the entirety of my mind, I took notice of Suzette; she was difficult to ignore. Ribbons decorating her black curls, she dressed impeccably: a lace collar accentuating her bodice, her waist cinched, languid skirts falling to the floor. She carried herself with such poise, her shoulders squared, her neck elongated as she peered into others' eyes, rather than bent and bowed like my own. Despite our headmistress and the vedovas reprimanding her for her brashness, she never became demurer, and my ilex told me she was brave: even more than my sister-Vigore, brutavis and all.

Her crimson lips continued to form words. "My third brother is a layabout," she said. "He dreams of being an actor, but he has no skills, save how to feed his addiction to opiates. My parents have sent him to live with his uncles twice, and he has even seen a curandria to break free from his habit. Useless man! Terrible waste of space.

"My fourth brother has just been appointed as an apprentice-at-law—he is the first in the d'Isparza family to branch into the justice system. We shall see how long he lasts." Suzette giggled into her gloves, then tossed her head back. Her hair sparkled as she laughed, and my head pounded as the vedovas bustled about, laying forks and knives on the tables. I struggled to stay focused; my gaze wandered around the room, and I noticed that my sister-Damica had begun to form a queue. I folded my hands together, twisting my arms in discomfort.

"Suzette?" I whispered.

"Let them wait!" She waved a dismissive arm. "You've yet to hear of my youngest brother."

My stomach lurched and I felt I may bleed into the colors and lights soon. I breathed a small sigh and threw my shoulders back, trying my best to mimic Suzette's posture.

"My youngest brother calls himself a 'hero of the people,'" Suzette rolled her eyes. "He has dabbled, somewhat, in politics—and has found little success in gaining the love of others. He has come to the Accademia to ask Headmistress Elan to release me into his care—to return me to my family. He says they have great need for my linguina d'argent—but with the way he looks at me, I believe he desires more than just my gift."

I lurched forward, catching myself with a clumsy step. I was stunned, disgusted. Had I heard correctly that her brother wished to take her to his bed?

"Pah!" she exclaimed, her fine features wrinkling together. "I have not been driving away suitors, only to be claimed by a man as insipid as my brother! I need you, cherissima. You must help me."

I blinked, the clatter and her words rolling into a searing pain behind my eyes. Suzette d'Isparza asking for my assistance? I could not fathom why this was so, what I could possibly do for her. I pinched the flesh between my brows and tried to untangle her words from the pain. Her gaze traveled toward the dining hall and the vedovas moving tirelessly about.

"Your mother, she nearly became a vedova, did she not?"

"Mama?" I whispered. My voice caught in my throat. She was gone from this world, buried, with her serpents, years before. I felt a welt of grief in the back of my throat as I tried to keep the room from moving in circles. Draping a hand over my face, a hazy memory of my mother swirled behind my eyelids, her fragile fingers poised around a teacup. I uncovered my eyes and turned my gaze to the arches above me, searching for my mother's calming smile.

My eyes stung with tears and I squeezed them shut, opening them again to see Suzette heave a sigh. She rubbed her thumb on my cheek, smudging a wet droplet across my skin.

I had not realized I was crying.

Suzette dabbed at my eyes with the corner of her sleeve. "Look at what they've done to you."

The day I left for the Accademia Marl, Mama dressed me in a gown that fell past my ankles and covered my shoes. My heart raced as I flounced around the entryway, twisting my hips to rustle the hoops around my torso and legs, my hair thick and free of any bonnet or veil; I imagined I was not just a filia—I was Damica—generous and proud, spreading good fortune, just like my mother.

Our coachman soon arrived to drive us through Localita di Fiore to Cortellion, our capital—where the Accademia Marl was situated. He extended a pristine glove and took my Mama's hand, lifting her into the carriage. I caught a glimpse of the insignia on the door as he took my hand. It was emblazoned with a curious emblem: five stones, situated in a semicircle like a cat's paw: at the top, a tiger's eye, to its right, the mischievous twinkle of hematite. To its right, I found a smooth cut of emerald—beside it, a milky, opalescent crystal. At the bottom of the paw, a stone of pure black stole the light of the day.

We settled into our seats while our horses' hooves clicked, our carriage wheels turning upon a stone road. Gentle rays of sunlight passed through the window, and I imagined they were wishing us well on our journey. We passed through the bustle of the market until merchants, shops, and stands fell away, transforming into rows of tilled earth and wheat—and when I believed this was all I should see for the remainder of our journey, a field of violet blooms opened before us, stretching like a royal carpet.

"Filia, look!" Mama tapped the carriage window. Squinting, I could just make out the shapes and colors on the horizon—a still life captured by the soft brush of an artist's hand, broad, gold strokes peppered with short, staccato clusters of wisteria blossoms. As we drew nearer, the shapes grew into enormous estates—our own home trifling in comparison.

I gasped, awed, and Mama squeezed my hand. "We are passing the tenutas of the Localita di Fiore. You and I—we shall call them home, someday." White florets and plum-colored trumpets crawled up the walls of the grand buildings, their petals reaching toward the sky like butterflies. Mama continued to stare out the window, pressing her palm against the glass—and in this moment, I felt the ilex. Mama's restlessness swelled within my chest, buzzing like a cricket's song—she had hope for a life bigger, grander than the one we had. When the estates faded from our view, the vibrations in my chest quelled. Mama slumped back into her seat, tapping at her bracelets listlessly.

At the gates of Cortellion, wisteria trees greeted us, their dark-and-light clusters drooping under the weight of a recent rain. They shed their petals—and as our carriage ambled past, our wheels kicked up a pink-and-lavender trail, giving it the appearance of a marriage cart. Gusts of wind swept through the roads, carrying the wisteria to rooftops and scattering them about.

We reached the Accademia Marl in this manner, as though we had entered a dream. The sun spilled over the building's spires, turning the white walls a soft gold. I watched our window in wonderment, wisteria blooms swaying like clusters of grapes. Our wheels began to slow, pulling to a stop in front of an arched entryway.

The coachman helped me down from the carriage and I took Mama's hand. Together we descended and passed through the Accademia's gates. A group of smartly dressed men with books tucked under their arms stared as we walked by.

Inside, I looked up at the ceiling. A prism of light spilled through mosaic tiles—my dress painted, momentarily, in a rich purple hue, the color of an iris. The colors faded as Mama led me down a long, windowless corridor, her heels thundering across its stone floors, the patter of my own shoes following behind hers with flighty, uneven clicks. We arrived at an oak door that did not match the newness and polish of the rest of the Accademia; its wood was blistered and cracked with age. At the top of the door, I had my second look at the cat's paw with its brightly colored stones; my chest hummed with nervous energy as I stared up at it.

Mama reached up to rap on the door. Her knuckles had but grazed the wood when the door creaked open, a smooth, gloved hand peeking through.

"Laurel." A blue eye—sharp as sapphire—peered through the crack in the door, scanning me from the crown of my head to the hem of my dress. I bit my lip and curled my toes inside my shoes.

"Headmistress Elan." My mother bowed deeply. Always tall and statuesque, I had never seen her bow to anyone before this moment.

The door swung open and I marveled at the woman standing before me. Her skin was wrinkled and fragile, and a damask cloak weighed on her shoulders—scarlet in color, shading the pattern of the flowers on her gown. Her pale hair shone despite the dim light. A few hapless golden tresses had survived the days of her youth, and they were swept into the torrent of snow pinned atop her head. Her gaze fixed on me; she did not give my mother but a glance.

My cheeks warmed instantly, a surge of anger rising through me at how dismissive she was toward Mama. My mother—Damica Clare Aleandri, the beloved Fortuna of the market, bringing smiles and blessings to those she passed. How could the headmistress treat her with such disregard?

"I've been expecting you, Laurel," she said. "I am Headmistress Elan. You will come with me. You too, Clare."

Before I could speak, Mama tugged at my arm and we followed Headmistress Elan down a white-walled corridor, passing, on occasion, several filia in dresses finer than mine. The headmistress's heavy skirts brushed the floor as she guided us into a private room. Quiet and dim, a floor table sat at its center with several plush pillows arranged around it.

"Be seated, Laurel."

My mother took a step forward and Headmistress Elan held up a hand. "Not you. Tell me, have you already performed her reading?"

"Yes, Headmistress." My mama wrung her hands, worry written in every fold of her face.

"And?" the headmistress asked impatiently. "Speak,

Clare."

"Her gift was paired with death."

Paired with death? I chewed my lip and plucked at the pillow I sat upon. I did not know what this meant, but my mama's apprehension whipped through my ribs like a cold wind.

Headmistress Elan folded a brow. "You believe she is a *Catene?*"

"I . . . was frightened. I did not read any further," Mama stammered.

"You should have come to me immediately," Headmistress Elan scowled. With a sweep, her cloak came free from her shoulders and she turned to my mother, who rushed to take it from her.

Headmistress Elan spun to face me, revealing a brooch on her gown. Five stones—the same as before—were arranged in the shape of the cat's paw. The headmistress lowered herself beside me and peeled off her gloves one at a time, draping them tenderly beside her as if each were a snake's skin. She removed the brooch and placed it on the table.

"Have you ever killed anything, filia? A plant, a rodent? Even by accident?"

"No," I whispered.

"No, headmistress," Headmistress Elan corrected. She shot my mother a look of disapproval. "You should have taught her this by now."

I despised the way that she spoke to my mama. My nails dug into my palm, but I drew in a sharp breath, holding my tongue.

"No, headmistress," I breathed.

She extended her arm and stroked my cheek with the back of her hand. Her skin was like parchment and I felt the sapphire-steel of her eyes peel my flesh, whittling me to the bone. She clucked quietly to herself, forming assessments and opinions that I could not decipher.

"She is not a Catene, Clare. Be glad for that, at least."

I drew my fingertip across the cheek on which the headmistress's hand had rested. The sensation haunted me, ruminating across my flesh like the hum of a tuning fork. I recognized it as a feeling.

Disappointment.

It was one I would come to know well.

Headmistress Elan's eyes flared. "Concentrate. Place your hand on the brooch."

I felt a swell of darkness from within and my eyes grew wide. Within my ear, a quiet buzz stirred. It was like no sound I had ever heard—a surge, and then a lull—a frothing wave shifting between inner darkness and luminance. Without giving it thought, I extended my index finger, fixing it upon the milky white stone on the brooch. The rock stared at me, vacant, like a blind eye.

"Moonstone. It is as I thought," the headmistress declared. "Filia Laurel is a Lunare."

I glanced, wide-eyed, at my mother. Her lip quivered, and a sob escaped her mouth. Alarmed, I called for her, but she turned away from me.

"You knew this was a possibility," Headmistress Elan said. Her words carried a heaviness to them—an intonation I did not understand. "You could have prevented this outcome, if you had done what I instructed with your suerradio."

"I could not," my mother choked.

"Then you should have avoided marriage and returned to me. I would have had you serve as a vedova."

Mama shook her head vehemently and Headmistress Elan rolled her eyes, muttering under her breath. She turned her attention to me and she stroked my hand, the aged pads of her fingers causing my skin to crawl.

"Lunare is the class I was born into, she of the moon, who can see into the hearts and minds of all." Headmistress Elan smiled and it was awful. Her teeth flashed like the foreboding gems on her brooch. "Your pairing with death means you will pair well with a general—serving our kingdom as a military adviser—perhaps a war scribe."

She took my hand and I squirmed, a rush of blood in my ears deafening me to her words. A strange sensation washed over me, a poison. I did not know what I wanted to be—but it was not *that*.

The thought of taking a husband made my hair stand on end, my skin crawling with flickers of dying hope. War, blood. Death. It did not sit well in my stomach. If my Papa had known, I was certain he would have snatched me from the Accademia and brought me home, never to return to this place. But he had deferred to my Mama, trusting her to tend to my rearing on matters relating to the Damica.

Headmistress Elan reached under the sitting table and retrieved a small chest with a moonstone setting. I bit my lip, a stone of dread rumbling in my chest. I did not wish to see what was inside. I wished to jump up and run—past the wisterias and the tenutas—to return home to the corner by the marketplace, and hide in the familiar comfort of my bed.

From the box, Headmistress Elan retrieved a pendant on a silver chain: a decorated crescent moon with a small, white stone set in silver, dangling.

"The Lunare wear pendants to help with the litha," she said. My mother sobbed while the headmistress slid the chain over my head. I lifted the pendant and it jangled in my hand, like a chime.

"We are finished here," Headmistress Elan said, snapping the chest shut. "Clare, see yourself out. I'll escort Filia Laurel to her quarters."

My quarters! The words sent a pang through me. I would not be returning home. *This* was my home. I was to remain here in the care Headmistress Elan and her windswept hair, her hideous smile. I ran toward my Mama to embrace her, burying my face in her dress. I could not imagine being left in this place, away from the warmth of our hearth, our assortment of pots and pans hanging beside sprigs of herbs—and the scent of bread. Papa was traveling at the time of my departure, and I sobbed into the folds of my mama's skirts. I did not even have a chance to bid him farewell! What would be think when he arrived home, only to find my empty bed, a vacant seat at our table?

"My cloak, Clare."

My pendant clinked against Mama's bodice as we exchanged tearful kisses on the cheek. Mama helped Headmistress Elan into her cloak, then scurried to retrieve her gloves, kneeling as she slid them onto the headmistress's arms. I wanted to rush back to Mama, hold her hand and feel the weight of her serpents against my wrist, but Headmistress Elan shot me a stern look. I was fearful of what she might do should I dawdle. Wiping my eyes, I followed her out of the room, glancing back at Mama through the corridor—her face buried in her hands.

"Come along, filia."

Headmistress Elan motioned with her neck for me to follow and she led me up a spiraling set of stairs.

Arrivederci, Mama.

I should have run back to her, taken her by the hand— and never let her go.

"The Damica is comprised of five classes: Vigore, Verdetto, Fortuna, Lunare, and Catene," Headmistress Elan chanted the names in rhythm with each step she took, and they echoed in my ears as I followed her up the stairs. When we reached the top of the staircase, she swept her arm through the air, gesturing toward a row of doors.

"You will each be taught by the vedovas of your class in separate rooms in the learning hall. You sleep in separate quarters, and your bedchambers are marked with the stone of each class. The Vigore sleep by the stairs." She pointed up to the first door, the warm striations of tiger's eye resting above the frame. "They have sharp eyes and ears. You would do well to remember that, filia. The Fortuna sleep in the next room. They spread fortune throughout the hall. Very good, to get a blessing before you sleep." I glanced up at an emerald, and Headmistress Elan ushered me down the corridor. She halted at the next door, a pale orb of moonstone above the frame.

"We have arrived at your quarters, filia. Come." Headmistress Elan opened the door to a plain room—much simpler than even my bedchambers at home—with bare stone walls. A row of six beds decorated in black sheets lined the room. There was a window covered with a thick black curtain, and my lip quivered. *Dreadful.* I could not imagine this somber place as my home.

The headmistress's hand came down on my shoulder. "It is not so bad, filia. You will see. The darkness will help you sleep without worry of shadows haunting your dreams." She moved forward and patted the bed closest to the door. "This is yours. Your trunks will arrive soon. Sit, filia. We must speak of your first night." I took a seat beside her on the black sheets, spreading my fingers wide, anchoring my arm against the bed frame to keep myself from crying.

"In these early days, you will be visited by the litha. You may hear words, voices—which are not of this world. It will take time and practice to separate your gift—ilex—from the litha. This is where we end today. It is best to keep you from too much excitement, filia, until you begin drinking your tea."

I twined my hands deep into the folds of my skirt. I had many, many questions. When would I see Mama again? Why was I not a Fortuna like her? Why did Headmistress Elan treat her with such contempt, as though she were a speck of dust on a bookshelf? What feat had she asked Mama to perform—and that she refused?

"Listen to me closely, Filia Laurel," Headmistress Elan murmured. "A Damica must do what she is instructed—even if it brings sorrow to herself or her loved ones. Do not follow your mother's example. You must trust that I know and will do what is best for you."

"What lies they have told us, cherissima," Suzette said. "I saw it in your eyes—just now. They have wronged you. Hurt you."

I grasped my pendant, the memories of my Mama and Headmistress Elan spinning with the vedovas and the dining hall. I fantasized often about running away, daydreaming what it would be like to abscond into the night, to truly be free. A quick spin on my heels and I could slip out of line, or flatten my back against a thick, white pillar at the end of our lectures, waiting for the corridors to clear. But there were so, so many eyes in the Damica: vedovas, roaming the halls—and Headmistress Elan herself, thumbing her brooch. She would sense my intentions immediately, as if she could hear the thump of my heart against my ribs, pounding—pounding—

Suzette grasped me by the shoulder, shaking my thoughts into even more of a blur. "You feel it—do you not?"

My head whirled with anger. I winced, disgust instantly plaguing my tongue as I tasted the indignities of my youth. Betrayal cracked between my teeth like sparks, and darkness filled my mouth, a sticky clump spilling over my chin.

Litha.

I pawed at my lips, trying to stop its spread.

"I feel it," I whispered. The litha dripped down my chest, while vitriol churned in my stomach, bubbling, bursting—

I squeezed my head between my arms and my legs sank beneath me. The dining hall fell into silence—the vedovas, and their plates and cups and forks at a standstill. All eyes turned to us.

"Oh, cherissima!" Suzette cried.

I opened my mouth to apologize and the contents of

my stomach spilled onto the floor.

Suzette wrinkled her nose and I was sure she would sidestep me, leaving me in filth on the floor. But she stayed with me, instead, kneeling beside me, gathering my hair in her hands. She swept it over my shoulder and ran her fingers over my forehead, stroking the crown of my head.

"Shhh, shhh, there now, be still, be calm. Look at me." She coaxed me to my knees and made a pass at her brooch. Her voice a nocturne. "Be still, be calm. Let your mind be at ease. I am with you."

She lay her hands atop mine and I felt the darkness begin to recede, the litha slithering away. The throbbing in my head slowed, and I exhaled, long and fluid, my stomach calming.

She used it on me! The realization was abrupt, cutting through the placid waves that lulled me. She used it—her linguina d'argent. *She is not supposed to do that!*

But it had worked.

A crescendo of footsteps rattled toward me, rose-colored robes.

"*Diosemma!*"

The vedovas began to shout, to call my name in a panic. Suzette made another quick pass at her brooch and her voice was no longer a soothing murmur, but an ember in my ear.

"Meet me in the Catene chambers after this debacle is over."

She stepped back as the vedovas encircled me.

DEMON WHISPERS

The litha did not wait long to disturb my slumber.

My first night in the Accademia, it came to me in the form of demon-whispers. They passed through the cracks of light at the bottom of my bedchamber door, stretching like ribbons across the floor, and climbing into my bed, they grinned with black teeth, snapping at my memories. They mocked my longing to be in my own home, to see my Mama and to feel the weight of her serpents when she took my hand. They tore pieces from her voice, grinding her words like pulp and spitting them back at me as grunts. Their words scratched my ears. I twisted wads of sheets in my hands, pulling at them until my knuckles ached.

"*Daremi pacce.*"

Bring me peace. In the early days, I was so young, tender-hearted, and helpless. Far from home and hearth—shivering, alone, paralyzed with terror. *What do they want from me?*

"Please. *Daremi pacce.*" I squeezed my eyes shut and pushed my hands against my ears.

"*Daremi pacce, daremi pacce.*"

I lacked any skill beyond prayer to banish them.

The words spilled from my lips—again and again—until my voice grew pinched, my throat clenching shut from my fear. *What will they do to me this night?* The possibilities rose like bile in my throat, and I could no longer speak. It was all I could do to rock myself back and forth, trying to find a calming rhythm.

Daremi pacce. Daremi pacce. I may die in this place. *Daremi pacce.* I may die in this bed. Blood rushed to my ears and my heart felt as though it would burst through my chest. And then I remembered—my pendant.

I reached blindly across my nightstand, fumbling for it. My fingers trembled as the demon-whispers jarred my resolve, but the cool chain of my pendant brushed against my hand and I drew it to me. My palm swallowed the moonstone as I squeezed my hand around it.

Daremi pacce.

Ahhh! The wind returned to my lungs. I slumped back into my pillow and watched the shadows begin to recede into the rafters. They stared down at me, but with my pendant in hand, they did not fall from the ceiling and burrow into my sheets. I bit my lip while they studied me, praying they would vanish entirely.

"*Daremi pacce,*" I said, with a quivering jaw. "Do you hear me? *Daremi pacce!*"

The moon. I did not know why the thought occurred to me that She may help drive the demons away, but I felt it vibrate in my heart. I kicked the sheets from my legs and climbed out of bed. The room was dark—everything black— beds and sheets and silhouettes. I dragged my hand against the wall as I crept to the far end of the room, the rough texture of stone soon giving way to a gap. *Daremi pacce.* A window frame. I pressed my hand against it and drew back its black curtain, eager to bathe my troubled body in the moon's silver light. What I found on the other side of the curtain caused me to gasp.

There was no moon. There was no sky. I was met by splintering boards and gray nails that looked to have lost their sparkle years before.

I let the curtain go and slumped to the floor. The

demon-whispers slithered all night in the rafters while I gripped my pendant. I shivered each time they shifted shape, against my will. My toes turned numb against the cold floor as I waited—waited—for the morning light.

Moonstone, Lunare.

Litha. Madness.

It was what defined me.

My first night in the Accademia—and every night since.

Over the years, I became acquainted with my sister-Damica and even came to learn some of their names. There was Bethany, a Lunare who arrived the year after I did; she slumbered in the bed beside mine. Her skin was as blanched and bloodless as mine, although her ash brown hair made it look even paler. We did not spend much time outdoors, unlike the Vigore, who received nearly all their lessons in the courtyard. Among the Vigore was Riognach—who, at sixteen, had dramatic green eyes, free-flowing auburn hair. She carried herself with an arrogant stride imbued by the fact that her family owned one of the largest *tenutas* in the Localita di Fiore. Though she needed no fortune, I usually found her keeping company with Maialinne—a Fortuna with a plump face and bright locks.

They were not my friends. Not truly. How could there be friends in the Accademia when we were all competing to be betrothed, to live our days with wealth and luxury at our fingertips—and live out our days fanning ourselves in the shade, while other women toiled until their knuckles became raw?

Even if there were friends, the vendrake put me in such a stupor that it cast me out of friendship's favor. From the filia to the vedovas: the Damica all knew that the litha was rooted most deeply in me—twined like a stubborn weed that continued to come back, no matter how many times it was plucked from the earth. They all knew that there was something wrong with me, something deeply disturbing. I heard fervent whispers about me pass between Maialinne and Riognach often, and the rumors spread among my sister-Lunare. On occasion, Bethany probed me with an accidental brush of my arm as I passed her in our quarters. While I stood in queue with my sister-Lunare, their eyes probed me, searching for some gruesome detail with which they may entertain themselves. But with the vendrake numbing my senses, I had little to offer by way of entertainment.

Suzette did not see me as a blight or a spectacle. Perhaps it was because she was a persona non grata—like my mother, like me—cast out of fortune's favor. I continued to meet her, following the night she tossed my vendrake out the window. It was not as difficult to sneak out of my bedchamber as I had imagined: I lay in bed, feigned sleep, watching for the flicker of the Vigore's candles in the hall—bands of darkness and light passing under my door. I waited until they floated past, and I would rise, pressing myself to the wall, clutching my pendant to steady my pulse. The Vigore talked in bored voices, yawning as they performed their perfunctory watch—and I waited until their voices tapered into silence before I sprinted down the corridor on raised toes, slipping into the unoccupied chambers at the end of the hall—the Catene chambers.

In all my years at the Accademia, I had never known a Catene, and no one—not Suzette, nor Bethany, nor Riognach and Maialinne—had ever crossed paths with one. From what little I gleaned during my lucid moments, it was rumored they could control life and death.

I began to speculate whether the Catene had ever existed, since their chambers looked to have been vacant for quite some time. There was only one bed, barely more than a roll—no sheets nor blankets nor pillows decorating it—and Suzette had struggled to open the window, pushing her shoulder into the frame, and gritting her teeth before the shutters finally cracked apart.

The linguina d'argent made it easy for Suzette to leave her chambers without scrutiny, and she waited inside the Catene chambers for me—with open arms, she pulled me into an embrace.

Sometimes I questioned whether her voice was madness or panacea. It was impossible for me to tell; but I did not concern myself with it. The nights I spent with her were peaceful, free of demon-whispers and shadows, and that was all that mattered. I felt happier, lighter, and my fantasies of running away from the Accademia came to me less often. I could not imagine leaving Suzette's side, to never again feel her squeeze my hand in reassurance and speak her beautiful words.

After a fortnight in the Catene chambers, my sister-Damica began to take notice of me in new ways. Riognach and Maialinne stopped to gape at me as I passed them in the corridor, even footed and with my chin steady. Even though they were scheming and foul, I felt like I was like them—with their glittering eyes full of energy, life, youth.

The vedovas soon took notice of me as well.

I had been put through the Accademia's courtship conscription a handful of times. It began with the vedovas lining us up by class, measuring our bosoms and hips and tilting our heads back to examine our skin in the light. I had seen a similar practice in the marketplace when my Mama picked through fruit, giving it a small squeeze to determine its ripeness and weight, turning it over to survey its skin for any blemishes. So, too, we were all put under the same scrutiny, and I was consistently passed over.

I could almost taste my mama's disappointment—if she had still been alive, she would have been so ashamed that I was rejected every time, while filia younger than I flounced in their gowns, hugging each other in excitement when they were chosen, eager to unveil their gift to their suitors: for the Vigore, a dance to display their flawless movement; for the Verdetto, music to sway and enchant hearts. The Fortuna would perform a tea-reading for their curious suitors—and the Lunare would simply plant a kiss, carefully on their suitor's cheek, to reveal truths and intentions that lay beneath their skin.

I did not expect to be called back to this conscription, but after weeks of deep slumber without vendrake, I found myself once more in a queue with my sister-Damica. I quietly took my place beside Bethany. She was focused on straightening her skirts and did not pay me any mind until she brushed up against my arm and, without looking up, muttered a quick apology. After a moment, she whipped her head up, no longer concerned with her skirts.

"Laurel!" She placed her hand at her heart and let out a breath. "Ah! You surprised me! You are not supposed to be here."

"I was told to come," I uttered.

"No, no. That can't be right. Who told you to come?"

I motioned toward a cluster of vedovas measuring the filia at the front of the line. Bethany shook her head.

"You must have been listening to the litha again. The vedovas would not call you here. This is the line for courtship. Do you understand?" She enunciated each of her words slowly, deliberately, and I blinked—unsure of what to say. A tingle of spite crept through my wrists. Was this how the filia spoke to me daily? Perhaps it was appropriate, as the vendrake slowed my mind, but the hairs on my arms stood on end, and I felt that there was something cunning, deceptive lurking under Bethany's skin. She had seen me in our quarters, in our lectures, in the dining hall over the past few weeks; she had witnessed the color returning to my cheeks, my eyes no longer dull like unpolished stone.

She knows I am supposed to be here.

And she does not want me here.

"Let's return you to your bed. Quickly, now." Bethany curled her fingers around the back of my arm and she coaxed me out of line. We had only shuffled a few steps down the corridor when a voice thundered at our backs.

"What is the meaning of this?"

Headmistress Elan!

Bethany froze in place, her fingers tightening on my arm. She pursed her lips and released me, reaching for the moonstone pendant at her breast. It all seemed so odd: Bethany and her falseness, the headmistress—present at the courtship conscription. Usually, this was a task she left to the vedovas.

I could not make sense of it, any of it, and I bit my lip, calling upon my ilex. Under the headmistress's wary gaze, Bethany flinched, and I felt it in her veins. *Resentment. Panic.* I felt them cycling through her body, rushing from her chest down to her legs. Her knees were beginning to quiver. It was not an uncommon reaction for a filia to have when Headmistress Elan addressed her.

"Forgive me, Headmistress. Laurel was wandering the halls again. She got lost and I was just returning her to our quarters." Bethany's elbow jabbed my side, and I cast my eyes to my slippers, bowing to the headmistress.

"Lost?" Headmistress Elan raised an inquisitive, white brow. "What makes you believe she is lost, Bethany?"

"Because . . . you know how she is." I felt Bethany's pulse beginning to surge—her panic rising—and she squeezed her pendant.

"Go on." The corner of the headmistress's lip curled upward, and it was clear to me—and likely Bethany—that she was finding amusement in the exchange.

Bethany released her pendant, looked down, and curled her hands into fists.

"It isn't fair!" She threw her arms open wide. "She doesn't deserve to be here!"

She has such pretty eyes, a small nose! Ugh! With my ilex, I heard Bethany's thoughts seethe between her teeth like dragon's breath. *Why has she stopped being slow? They are going to choose her—and leave me behind.*

The filia standing still against the wall began to shift and fidget, buzzes and whispers passing between them. To speak with such defiance to Headmistress Elan! Bethany was truly perturbed by my presence, and I could not help but feel guilt. Talking back to a vedova resulted in punishment—perhaps we would miss our next meal, or if it was repeated, the punishments could increase in severity—a filia could have her wrists bound and be left blindfolded in the corner of the courtyard for a time. Once, when I was lucid enough to be aware of my surroundings, I had seen Suzette endure this punishment. I could not imagine what defiance toward Headmistress Elan would bring Bethany.

"Fair?" Headmistress Elan chuckled. "Do not be naive. There is nothing fair about courtship. It is all about who shines, and who . . . fades." Headmistress Elan's coat flared as she turned to the filia on the wall. She paced down the corridor, each of my sister-filia straightening her posture, bowing her head, as the headmistress passed.

"Filia! All of you!" Headmistress Elan called out. "What is the most desirable trait in a Damica?"

"Obedience," one of the filia answered.

"Loyalty," another said.

"Allegiance to her headmistress," a third one called. "Through courtship, marriage, motherhood—always."

"Good." Headmistress Elan reached the end of the queue. She did an about-face, the train of her gown slinking past each of the filia as she made her way toward Bethany and me.

I did not know what she was thinking, feeling, or planning in this moment. And I dared not try to listen or peek into her heart just a little, like scratching the paint from glass. She would feel the intrusion instantly.

Headmistress Elan held Bethany in her crosshairs. From the shadows, I sensed two vedovas flanking Bethany from behind.

"Filia!" Headmistress Elan cried. "Has your sister, Bethany, proven herself to be obedient? Loyal? Devoted to her headmistress?"

"No, Headmistress." A chorus rose from the wall.

"Let's use her word, shall we? Do you think it's *fair* that Bethany be chosen for courtship?"

"No, Headmistress."

"Good, *filia*." Headmistress Elan tipped her head, and the vedovas emerged behind Bethany, each of them taking her by one arm.

"Please, no! I'm sorry, Headmistress Elan!" Bethany cried, her green eyes brimming with tears. "You must choose me for this! Riognach told me you are taking us to the palace—"

The palace?

A frenzy of whispers ignited on the wall.

"Why her?" The desperation rose in Bethany's voice, pinching it, turning it shrill. "I am loyal! Obedient! All I wanted to do was help you. Laurel has been such a problem, and—"

"Quiet!" Headmistress Elan's command echoed across the stone ceiling. "*You* are my problem, Bethany. And you have stirred up enough trouble for one day." She nodded to the vedovas, and they nudged Bethany forward, forcing her down the hall. Echoes of her protest faded as she disappeared into the darkness.

Headmistress Elan pulled at the front of her coat, straightening it as if she were casting off an unwelcome mist of rain. "It is so ugly to see you filia fight. Wouldn't you agree?"

"Yes, Headmistress."

"Ugly, yes. But understandable. What Bethany said is true. In two days, I am visiting the palace for the end of estival festivities. And I have an opportunity to take some of you with me. There will be sovereigns. There will be royals."

The filia stirred, restless with excitement. The palace! Signors and Signoras! Surely, the filia who attended would come away with suitors; or, if they were truly fortunate, an offer of marriage.

"This is an important event—and not all of you are ready," Headmistress Elan said. "It is only natural that you will want to turn against your sister-filia, undercut them for the opportunity to shine. But you must resist the urge. It is most unbecoming in a Damica. What we witnessed Bethany do to her sister-Lunare is tragic. But let us turn our attention to that which is even uglier than her behavior toward poor Laurel—her attempt to conceal her heart from her headmistress. This is deplorable. Shameful. And it will not be tolerated. Do you understand?"

"Yes, Headmistress."

"Good. I do my best to protect you, filia. To nurture you, train you, so that you may use your gifts to serve the kingdom, and live comfortable lives, free of poverty and hardship. All I ask in return is your allegiance." Headmistress Elan cast her gaze in my direction. "Laurel, come."

Obediently, I bowed my head and approached the headmistress.

"Kneel, Lunare."

I fanned my skirt and lowered myself in front of her feet.

"It seems you have finally rid yourself of the litha. We've all noticed, and we feel great pride to have you among us. Your mother would be proud of you, as well."

I twisted my hands around my skirt at the mention of Mama, wrapping my thumbs in its folds. The desire to leap from the floor and run—run anywhere!—flashed through me. I closed my eyes and drew in a deep breath, allowing my mind to drift to Suzette: the timbre of her voice and her sweet words filling my ears until the sun poured through the window and the night was no more. The urge to escape passed through me, shrinking into the corridor until it was consumed by the walls.

"Tell me the truth, Lunare," Headmistress Elan said. "Have you been drinking your tea?" Her eyes glittered, sharp and inquisitive.

I lowered my head and plucked idly at a loose thread. There was no use in trying to hide. *She already knows.*

"No, Headmistress."

The Headmistress raised her chin, a sweep of her snowy hair bounding down her shoulder. "Ah, yes! You see, filia? This is loyalty—devotion! There should be no secrets between you and your headmistress."

Headmistress Elan smiled at me and placed her hand on the crown of my head. I felt a love—like a mother to a child—in the entanglement of her long, elegant fingers through my hair.

In a sentimental haze of allegiance and fear and haste, I cried, "Suzette calms the whispers!"

Ah, how I wished I had not spoken such foolishness.

I felt a chill pass through me, and Headmistress Elan coaxed me to rise. Quickly, her jeweled hands snatched at my chin, and with a swift jerk, she lifted my head. She studied my face with her sharp blue eyes. In a whisper, she said, "Take heed, filia. You should not spend so much time with such an ill-fated Damica."

"She saved me from the litha!" I gasped. "Is that not what you wished for me?"

Headmistress Elan's cheeks creased, deep lines forming with the sprout of her frown. She narrowed her eyes and the bite of her fingernails sunk into the flesh of my chin. She released me and touched her knuckle to her lip, tapping it a fingertip's breadth below the opening of her mouth.

Yes, it was what she wanted.

It was not what she wanted *Suzette* to do.

Headmistress Elan's lips wrinkled and she waved me away.

"I will see to it that Suzette receives her due. You are dismissed, filia."

TENDERNESS IN TATTERS

The litha had earned me a moniker: Viper.

When I was not in my catatonic state, I was prone to violence.

It was what Riognach and Maialinne called me when they whispered among themselves. Secretive, deceptive, malevolent: I detested the name and all that it implied. It was how Bethany spoke of me when the headmistress and her vedovas fell out of earshot—my sister-Lunare, always attempting to pluck the memories of my violent outbursts from my mind: the shame, seeping from my pores, in fat, black ribbons of shadow.

Litha.

My relationship with my Papa had been mangled by it. During my first summer home from the Accademia, the litha had torn apart our affection with its teeth, leaving it in tatters, a trail of heartache stretching between my home in the Accademia and his residence in the mountains.

I wished with all I was that I knew how to pick up the pieces, to make amends with him. I imagined, sometimes, that I might climb the window in the Catene chambers, planting each foot on the stone sill and holding the frame. And there—framed by the arch and the moonlight, I could dive into the night and become a lunar moth fluttering among the stars. I would be drawn to each thread like shards of light, and holding them upon my back, they would no longer bring pain. I would gather each piece, weave them into my wings, while the moon coaxed me onward to the mountains—and I would arrive to greet him with a complete tapestry of our hearts.

I was in the Accademia Marl only one season when my mother fell ill and passed. The last time I saw her was the day she took me to meet Headmistress Elan, my last look at her was through the corridor after the headmistress waved her away. I left her standing alone, with nothing but sorrow to keep her company.

I imagined her disappointment as she sat, slumped, during the entire carriage ride back from the Accademia, her beautiful, wheat-colored hair shrouding her face in shadow. She would not have looked up while the carriage rattled past the tenutas; she simply would have continued her journey through the rows of farmlands until she reached the bright, trumpeting colors of the marketplace and arrived home.

My mind was consumed by pangs of guilt: the images of my mama in the hall—and the headmistress's contempt toward her. I could not shake them from my thoughts. As much as I tried to occupy myself with other matters—the images continued to vex me.

When Headmistress Elan told me she had fallen ill, my ilex stirred immediately, telling me that it was my fault. Somehow, I was at the center of it—and so new at my gift, I could not decipher why, or how, this had come to be.

Nevertheless, it was my fault. But not mine alone.

I did not know how, but Headmistress Elan had something to do with it as well.

The memory and the feelings, however, were all cloudy. It was as though I was trying to view them through a haze; time kept slipping away. At some point, Headmistress Elan told me that Mama's illness had worsened and she could no longer emerge from her bedchamber—and after hearing this, neither could I. I stayed wrapped in my sheets and let the litha take me at night, their whispers louder now, cleaving at me, breaking my body to pieces.

One morning, I awoke to find a fresh cut rose from the courtyard on my nightstand, and I knew Mama had passed.

I had little memory of the days that followed. I watched the rose wither, its parched petals straining to quench their thirst through a cracked, dry stem. When the rose's head dropped and its petals began to shed, I believed that I, like the withered rose at my bedside, would fall into a permanent silence.

But this was not so.

After Headmistress Elan dismissed me from the courtship conscription, I returned to my quarters and sobbed, clutching my pendant with such force that it left a trail of pink marks in my palms. Red-eyed, I looked up from my pillow at the neatly pressed bed next to mine. Bethany's. She was likely already undergoing her punishment—whatever it may be—for her disobedience. Whether they blindfolded her left her in a corner of the courtyard, or forced her to pen an apology a hundred times—whatever whim the headmistress had concocted.

It was both odd and terrible to think about the two of them. They were alike, both liars—treachery staining their hearts, bleeding black as the shadows and demon-whispers that tormented me. I yearned desperately to leave this place—to grab Suzette and run, never to give the Accademia another fleeting glance or thought. I questioned where we would go, what we could do if we were truly free. Clearly, we could not return to Suzette's family: to return to her estate would be to shuffle from one prison to another.

My father belonged to the Order Umbilicus. Their monastery was nestled in the mountains, the ones I had viewed nightly in the Catene chambers when I sat with Suzette. I had not seen him in years, but in daydreams where I successfully escaped the Damica, I always sought him out, searching the mountains for his warm brown eyes. If Suzette and I ran, we could find sanctuary in the Order; we would find peace with my father.

But I was what I was: Viper.

And I was where I was.

I looked from Bethany's bed to the window at the far end of the room. No light peeked through the curtains, and if I pulled them back, they would be sealed with planks and wood. No way out.

Never a way out.

In the weeks following my Mama's passing, my Papa sent a carriage for me. I had peeled myself from the shrouds of my blankets, packed my smallest travel trunk, and sat at the edge of my bed, waiting for one of the vedovas to call for me. I studied the rose. Its shed petals formed a sad, dry arrangement by the bottom of my vase. I wished the carriage would hurry and arrive. I was eager to pull away from the Accademia Marl, watching it fade in the distance, withering and turning to dust, like the rose.

I kicked my legs impatiently and waited for a knock at the door. When it finally arrived, it was not a vedova who came for me, but Headmistress Elan herself. She swept into my bedchamber with a furrowed brow, her crimson coat brushing the floor. She extended her arms to me and folded me into an embrace and I felt queasy, the scent of flowers pervading my nose. I squirmed against the itchy fibers of her gown, the cat's paw brooch on her bosom pressing uncomfortably against my collarbone.

"Oh, you poor filia," she crooned. "Clare's passing is a tragedy. Such a waste." The headmistress breathed in and sighed, releasing me from her hold. Between the cloying scent of her cloak, the anguish of my Mama's passing, and my impatience to be out of my quarters and out of the Accademia, I felt a scream rising in my chest.

Litha.

I drew back from the headmistress and clasped my pendant, rolling it across my throat. I tried desperately to hide it, to quiet it with silver and moonstone. Ahh, but my efforts were futile—like always, I could rail against it, but there was no way to triumph over the litha.

My actions did not evade the headmistress's watch.

"Filia, what is this about?" Her expression twisted into one of concern. She took my fist in her hands, coaxing it open to let my pendant fall loose. Headmistress Elan touched the back of her hand to my throat and her eyes widened with alarm.

"You are not to leave this room," she commanded.

I pulled away from her, my eyes wet with grief and bewilderment. "What?"

"The litha is too strong in you. Under no circumstances are you to be released." She rose from my bedside, her heels clicking quickly across the floor. "I'll notify the vedovas. You will be under watch at all times."

I felt a swell of resentment rise through me then, so quick, so powerful, it was like poison running through me. I forced myself to swallow. The air tasted like petals and I tried to keep my nose from wrinkling, but it did me no good.

"I despise you," I seethed, my lips, my words bathed in darkness. "I hope your heel catches on your coat, and you break your neck tumbling down the stairs."

"Filia!" Headmistress Elan placed a hand over her heart. A look of pity crossed her face. "The litha has taken you. I cannot let you out in this condition. I know you wish to grieve your mother, and it seems unfair to remain here. Cruel, even. You must trust that I know what is best for you."

Her decision filled me with more hatred, a wretched contempt. I surrendered to the darkness in my heart and permitted the scream I had been holding back to pass through my throat, but it came through my lips as no more than a sigh. My legs twitched in frustration, my limbs restless. I felt the darkness buzzing from within like insects, a legion of twitching legs scratching at my skin from the inside. Unable to contain myself, I swept my arm across my nightstand, knocking the vase to the floor.

It shattered into shards: hundreds of glittering fangs.

I had not felt the litha so strongly in years. In my bed, in my quarters, awaiting my fate, and Suzette's, I was fearful that it was once again rising in me. I imagined the vedovas whispering among themselves about Bethany's disastrous exchange with the headmistress, my calamitous admission: throwing out my tea and taking direction from a Verdetto on the cusp of exile. The rumors would be spreading like specks of dust: weightless, invisible to the eye, and everywhere. If I pressed my ear to the door, I was certain I would hear them.

I wiped my sleeve across my eyes, drying my tears. Yes. Perhaps if I listened in the halls, I could hear what the vedovas were scheming. Maybe I could extract from them some way to save Suzette and myself. I had to try.

I planted my toes on the floor and the chill of stone penetrated them. Thumbing my pendant, I tried to keep my nerves steady so I would not succumb to weeping. When my breath slowed enough and I felt ready, I dropped my heels to the floor and willed myself to stand.

It was too late. No sooner had I steadied myself than the door to my quarters cracked open. My heart sank, and I lowered myself back onto the bed. I bowed my head, waiting for vedovas to flood my chambers, to take me by the arm and lead me to my punishment. I felt no sorrow for myself, but deeply regretful for the pain I had caused Suzette.

She had counted on me—and I failed.

"Cherissima?"

I thought I imagined it. Suzette's easeful, melodious voice—whispering sweetly, calling me. I raised my chin. It was no illusion: Suzette stood at the doorway, her spiral curls tied neatly with ribbon, her gray eyes holding a heaviness, a weariness. I leaped from my bed and rushed to embrace her.

"Suzette, oh! Cherissima!" I threw my arms around her and hugged her, the bodice of her dress crinkling as I held her. Suzette returned the embrace, and half-smiling, she swept a lock of hair behind my ear.

"Mind yourself, cherissima," she whispered. "We are not alone."

She pulled back from our embrace and, tossing her curls over her shoulder, revealed her brooch. I wanted nothing more than her fingertips to pass over the surface, to hear her soothing, silver words. She shot me a sharp glance and clasped her hands in front of her. I mimicked her stance.

Headmistress Elan's crimson coat darkened the doorway behind Suzette, announcing her presence. She swept into my quarters with a proud, dignified gait and nodded approvingly at Suzette and myself. She situated herself in front of us.

"Bethany will be spending the night elsewhere," Headmistress Elan said. I caught a spark of curiosity in Suzette's eye, as if she wanted to ask, "where?" But we both knew that the question would earn us trouble—more trouble than we were already in.

"It has been many years since I've seen such subversive tendencies among my filia," Headmistress Elan said. Her eyes fluttered closed. "The vedovas and I discussed the possibility of sending all of you home to your families. I have half a mind to do so, but . . ." she sighed, rubbing her temples. "The vedovas are truly to blame. They should have stamped out the flames of insubordination years ago. So, here is what I am going to do.

"Filia Laurel, I have decided to take you to the palace. You *and* Bethany both will be representing the Lunare in the court. I expect that during this trip, you two will make amends. I expect you will smile, be pleasant, and charming."

I stifled a gasp. The palace! I was going—even after the tension in the courtship ritual. At last, I would be leaving these four walls, traveling somewhere new, experiencing fresh, unfamiliar sights and scents, and seeing new people beyond my sister-filia! My heart vibrated, a shiver of excitement running through my spine.

"As for you, Verdetto." Headmistress Elan took two pronounced, deliberate steps, and faced Suzette directly. "You accept that there will be consequences for your actions. Severe consequences. You'll be made to sweep chimneys and wash chamber pots for weeks to come. And I'll be taking that brooch of yours so you will not be tempted to talk your way out of it.

"Laurel is a valuable tool: critical to Trionfi's defense. She is a weapon—and I'll not see her released from here and sent off to foreign lands. But I cannot wed her in our court, with the litha pervading her mind so strongly."

Headmistress Elan pursed her lips. She was contemplating something, and I dared not use my ilex to try to press into her thoughts and see what stirred in her musings. If she sensed me, I was certain I would be sweeping ash and scrubbing waste alongside Suzette.

"Laurel needs to be matched. Quickly," she said. "Keeping her at the Accademia is proving too burdensome to the vedovas; it is disruptive to the other filia, and she is damaging our reputation."

I hung my head low, choking back tears. *Burdensome. Disruptive. Damaging.* Each word was a sword through my heart. I knew it to be true—all of it—but it caused me no less pain to hear it spoken aloud.

"There, Filia Laurel." The headmistress's hand smoothed circles on my back. "There is a solution for all of this. All will be well." Sniffling, I pulsed my fingers, forming and releasing fists. The litha began to scratch at my throat.

I was losing control.

"There, filia, there." Headmistress Elan crooned. With three pats to my back, she turned her attention to Suzette.

"Verdetto, calm her. Now."

Suzette shuffled in front of me and I felt the weight of her hands on my shoulders.

"Cherissima," she whispered. Her words turned to music and she coaxed me to be seated. Kneeling before me, she stroked my hair and murmured in my ear, and I surrendered myself to the warmth of her breath, an unbroken melody flowing like a stream of silver. My eyelids grew heavy and I let my shoulders fall forward, my forehead pressing against Suzette's. She squeezed my hands while the litha left my body.

"Hm," I heard Headmistress Elan utter. She was silent for a moment, and then she spoke, her voice strong and unwavering. "Suzette, stand."

Suzette released my hands and I tried to hold onto the sensation of her fingers locked with mine. I lifted my head and watched her fold her hands in front of her, taking her place in front of the headmistress.

"I have made my decision," Headmistress Elan said, arms crossed. "Since it seems you've done better with Laurel than any of my vedovas, Filia Suzette—against my better judgment, I will allow you to join her at the palace. You will be responsible for both of your sister-Lunare: Bethany, too. You understand the purpose of this trip, the expectation. Filia Laurel is running out of time. If you prove your worth, I may consider keeping you at the Accademia as a vedova."

I let out a loud sigh of relief. My pulse soared, and I leaned forward too far, catching myself by gripping my hands on my knees. I glanced at Suzette, my proud friend, and a sense of awe glowed in my chest. Somehow, she had done it: she had managed to carve a path out of her predicament—while at the same time helping to free me of the litha and the vendrake. I leaped forward and threw my arms around Suzette. She lifted a brow and staggered back, patting me lightly on the back.

"Filia Laurel, mind yourself!" Headmistress Elan scolded. "There will be none of this at the palace. Do you understand?"

"Yes, headmistress," Suzette said—and to my surprise, my ilex told me she meant it.

I remembered when my Mama spoke to me of marriage. I closed my eyes and focused on her gentle voice, the tenderness that embraced me when she spoke.

"My bridal gown was lighter than I had imagined," she had told me. "It was made of silk, and I wore a cloak with peonies—beautiful pink-and-white flowers, embroidered all over. It was clear I was no longer a filia; I dressed as a woman, and I would be required to carry myself as one. No longer would I wear my hair loose and free; I had the honor of wearing it in braids."

She had twirled a long lock of my hair in her hands, twining it into a braid and before releasing it, letting it fall free across my shoulder. Always a dreamer of beautiful things, Mama continued to speak in her wistful manner, elaborating on the oaths and promises that a Damica spoke to her husband. A bride called her betrothed her *ammorante*. Headmistress Elan insisted us we must call him by this name. It was a term of deep affection, one meant to stoke the flames of our heart. In all my years at home, I had never once heard my Mama call Papa by this name; she simply called him Phillip. It pleased me that she used his given name rather than calling him her *ammorante*. Phillip was simple—and Papa liked simple. The syllables of his name fit in my ear comfortably—the words warm, familiar, like the slow-burning embers of our hearth.

Ammorante rested wrong on both my ear and my tongue.

But I could not say this. I would not. I resolved to keep my thoughts, my feelings, to myself, and I would not disturb Suzette with them. It was not as though my situation were nearly as dire: I did not have a family beckoning me to return so they may use me for their own perversions, nor did I find myself attracted to women. Our trip to the palace was Suzette's chance to escape her predicament—her only chance, her last chance—and whatever my fate may be, I could not let her fall.

"We depart tomorrow afternoon," Headmistress Elan said, breaking through my thoughts. "Laurel, you are to pack your trunks. Suzette! Follow. We have much to cover."

THE POWER IN BREAD

The palace was located on an isolated stretch, not much more than a stone's throw from the capital. We took two carriages to reach it: Maialinne, Riognach, a vedova, and Headmistress Elan herself occupied the first, while I rode with Suzette, Bethany, Vedova Oriana—the Vigore who introduced me to vendrake. Though we were a blend of gifts, Bethany, Maialinne, Riognach, and I had equally traded our short, girlish gowns for skirts as thick as drapes, sitting atop hoops and petticoats that contorted us into new, unfamiliar shapes.

Suzette's vedova garments fit her flawlessly, her peony-colored gown crispy accentuating her beauty, her dark curls and pretty face. The quiet rattle of wheels on stone carried us away from the Accademia and a smile cracked on my face.

Arrivederci.

Seated beside me, Bethany leaned against the window, her cheek pressing against the glass as she stared at the world outside. Suzette and Vedova Oriana huddled together across from us, the older vedova speaking to Suzette in hushed whispers. Amid the clatter of hooves and the steady roll of wheels, I heard clips of her words.

"Vedovas get to keep some of the gold when a filia is matched. We do most of the work, so it's only fair." Suzette nodded as the vedova spoke, her eyes sharp and attentive, while I felt the carriage ride beginning to lull me to sleep.

"Vigores and Fortunas are quite popular in the court.

Landlords with large holdings enjoy having a little luck on their side. Vigores match easily with governors, as they are able to handle many of the social arrangements required by the position. Verdettos go for a high price, but the royals want them young," Vedova Oriana said, drawing out the word *young.* "They don't like the ones who can think for themselves, talk back. Aside from you, the Verdettos we have right now are *too* young, though. The headmistress won't allow it."

She continued, pointing a polished nail at Bethany and me. "Matching a Lunare pays the most, but they are a difficult sale. And—lucky you—you have two on your hands. Look for the military. Lunares pair well with generals, commanders. If you find the right match, you'll make a fortune."

"Oh, I will find a match," Suzette said. She touched the silver brooch fastened to her lapel and smiled quietly.

Vedova Oriana flashed her a wry smile in return. "I wish you luck with Filia Laurel. It's been a terrible tragedy, her failure to flourish. We all had such high hopes for her." She pursed her lips and continued. "Headmistress Elan will have no trouble with Maialinne and Riognach. They'll be seated beside her at the Damica's dais. You and your Lunares will be relegated to the kitchen to serve as ladies-in-waiting."

"What?" Suzette exclaimed. "How does Headmistress Elan expect me to match these filia when we are all stuck in the kitchen?"

"I am sure you will find a way. You have a very powerful linguina d'argent, after all," Vedova Oriana said. "Your memory, though—not so powerful. Pay attention and try to recall. We reviewed all the literature on the Lunare class last night. Remember what you learned?"

Suzette twisted her lips, her long lashes flicking upward.

"Ah," she said, after a moment.

"Staying in the dining hall for long periods of time would overwhelm your Lunares. The lights, the music, all the voices, the faces—all of them draw out the litha."

"Yes, yes. I recall now." Suzette said, waving a hand. "Where will the other vedovas be?"

Vedova Oriana cleared her throat, her hand tensing ever so slightly on her skirt. "We will be in the kitchen. Watching you. Making sure you perform your duties."

Suzette raised one of her thin, black brows. "Ah, so this is a punishment."

"That is correct," Vedova Oriana confirmed. "Headmistress Elan is determined to teach you some humility. Your command over the Lunare is impressive, but the life of a vedova is a life of service. I'm sure you understand: you cannot simply say and do whatever you wish, with your linguina d'argent."

"Yes, I understand what you are saying. I understand it very well." A mischievous smile crossed Suzette's lips. "This is a punishment for you, too. The headmistress would like nothing less than to take me as a vedova, but she has little choice, as the rest of you have failed with Filia Laurel, over and over. She wants you to suffer in my company."

Vedova Oriana wrinkled her nose and scowled. "As I said—no one likes a Verdetto who can think for herself."

A smile blossomed on my lips and I gave a silent chuckle.

The sour expression on Vedova Oriana's face deepened and she crossed her arms. "Unlike you, I did not ask to be a vedova. Most of us do not ask for this fate. It was foul luck that my husband passed." Vedova Oriana sighed. "Regardless, for the sake of Filia Laurel, I wish you luck in your endeavors—wherever they may lead you."

Our travel carriage arrived at dusk when the last pink rays of twilight sunk below the pointed rooftops of the palace. It was dark, but the palace thrived with chatter. Two bright lights guided us toward the large wooden door of a tenant-house. The headmistress met us at the door and, by lantern, ushered us up a winding set of stairs to our sleeping chambers. Our beds were spacious and private, with wisteria cuttings arranged on our nightstands and linens that still carried the scent of fresh sunlight.

With Suzette by my side, I drifted into a short sleep, dreaming of flowers and service.

In the hour before the sun crept over the horizon, Vedova Oriana roused Bethany, Suzette, and myself. With scarcely time to rub the sleep from our eyes or weave a comb through our hair, we were rushed downstairs, frantic and half-dressed, and ushered into a carriage.

Our journey across the palace grounds was pleasant but lengthy, as ours was among the many in a caravan of carriages. The palace was like the sun compared to the Accademia. We ambled across roads that reminded me of the marketplace of the Localita di Fiore. They clamored with gilded hooves and sizzled with voices and colors. Frantic, abrupt noises pierced my head, and I pushed my hands against my ears in the hope of making it stop.

"Come, cherissima." Suzette sidled up next to me and took my hand in hers. She led my fingers to my pendant and the ringing in my ears lessened. I saw Bethany's face contort into a perturbed state and I knew she found the bright lights and sounds disturbing as well. Vedova Oriana reached across to Bethany and guided her hand to her pendant as well.

"Suzette, pay attention," the vedova lectured. "The Lunare are an unpredictable class. A vedova must keep eyes on them—all of them, not just Viper."

I jerked my head back in surprise. I had never heard a vedova call me by that name; I was not even aware any of them knew it, since my sister-Damica only used it in whispers when they believed the vedovas to be out of earshot.

A thick teardrop rolled down my cheek. Clearly, they

were not. I released my pendant and found Suzette's hand, lacing my fingers through hers.

"Oh, look at what you've done!" Suzette scowled. "Shame on you, calling Laurel by that detestable name." She made a pass at her brooch and I sighed, ready for her words to overtake me. "She's no viper. You're gentle as a lamb, aren't you, cherissima?"

I did not have the heart to tell her she was wrong—so wrong—about me. I could not tell her what the litha had caused me to do, how my heart throbbed with fear, terrified it would come out again. And I would strike. Suzette. Bethany. Vedova Oriana. Anyone who came close to me.

I was no lamb; I was Viper.

We reached the inner court and Vedova Oriana led us inside through the back, moving through a narrow corridor behind the main hall. The noise from the palace was muted, more subtle, while we were cocooned within the stone corridor. In the kitchen, we were greeted by another vedova and she guided us past kitchen workers and ladies-in-waiting: a clamor of greasy pots, carrots and greens scattered on tables, and a spread of plates, forks, and spoons. The vedova stopped at a counter and cleared some space, stacking pans on plates, forks in cups.

She handed aprons to each of us and I watched Suzette's eyes narrow in defiance. Her cheek flinched and her lip pulled back, a tooth, pale like my moonstone, peeking through. Vedova Oriana joined us at the counter with a hefty sack of flour squashing her shoulder. With a grunt, she dropped it before us and took a step back. My eyes watered and I coughed as it cast a cloud of dust.

"Your task is to make piandia," she said.

"You mean our *punishment* is to make piandia,"

Suzette retorted, pulling the ribbons of her apron into an angry knot behind her back. "How far we have come to be making bread like peasants."

It was no punishment to me.

In the old tongue, piandia translated to daily bread—a simple bread made from flour, egg, yeast, and salt. My papa had taught me it was the bread of life: that which sustains us through the darkest, most harrowing hours of life. We made it weekly, and he distributed it to the poor taking up residence in the in-between spaces: abandoned structures, alleys, and bridges. I followed him curiously through these places, skipping over cracked beams of wood and broken stones. He was a kind man: generous, always, even though he had little wealth, and he had a gift for knowing where to look to find the broken, the sick, the unfortunate.

I was able, still, to keep his image in my heart—to retrieve it from a hidden pocket of my mind and shine it with the heel of my hand until it glowed in my palm. When we made piandia together, locks of my Papa's dark hair fell across his forehead, and he would wipe his hands on his apron, scooping me into his arms and dusting my cheek with flour as he pressed me against his shoulder.

I felt happiest when I stood beside him and we rolled dough in our kitchen. Between my hands it was a white, pulsing heart, and I kneaded it with care, allowing it to expand between the folds of my fingers. My lips vibrated with music as soft light spilled through the small window above our counter, casting opaline prisms across our hands, igniting pots and pans with bursts of red and gold that filled our kitchen with warmth and comfort.

Ah, this morning song was a prayer spoken between the rise of the sun and the fall of the stars. In this hour our kitchen mended the world as my Papa and I, standing side by side, pinched serpents of dough into moons.

"Blessed filia," Papa said. "Never forget the power in bread."

There is power in bread, cherissima.

I let the thought permeate my heart, sending it toward Suzette like a pretty tune, but these words did little to ease her chagrin. Her nostrils flared and she exhaled, stirring up a cloud of dust in front of us.

I moved my hand across the counter and rested it atop Suzette's. She flinched, and I saw the sheen of tears glistening in her eyes and felt her anger toward our headmistress at being brought to the domicile of the king himself, only to be locked away to toil in the kitchen. She withdrew her hand while I watched her shame turn to shadow, clinging to the spirals of her hair. My ilex told me she fretted over Maialinne and Riognach—what they would say if they were to see us in the kitchen—this bare-lipped, sleep-mottled assembly line of filia in shambles, kneading wads of dough into piandia! Were it possible for her to spread vitriol through her fingers, she would have poisoned every crescent of dough she touched.

For all of Headmistress Elan's uncouth remarks toward Suzette, it displeased me to admit that she was correct in one of her assertions: Suzette knew no humility. She and I were both descendants of a long line of Damica women, but I had been raised in modest means, whereas Suzette was thrust into a combative world of wealth and power. My ilex made me sensitive toward her plight, how she would have struggled to keep veritas in such an environment—and not simply abuse her linguina d'argent. My heart softened when I thought about her— my beautiful friend, so strong—too strong. Her heart was a fist of clenched fears and beliefs: that the strongest climbed to the top, and people must either be controlled or conquered. Humility was the cage against which she railed. As much as I cared for her, and she cared for me, she had never been taught the purpose of restraint. She did not understand the power in bread; she was blind to the value of service.

These lessons my father had bestowed upon me before I had come to the Accademia Marl. He had pledged his life to serve the Order Umbilicus, and I knew little about his order, except that he was an *aedituus*—an archivist, scholar, and scribe. His work led him to travel far past the borders of Trionfi in search of temples, treasures, and relics that had fallen from the memory of the world, items, places that were hidden in cracks. He carried parchment and pen to record his discoveries and when he collected enough, his order bound them into tomes and kept them in their library. Although Papa received a small payment for his contributions, most of his wages came from restoring relics and selling them to collectors.

He had been an aedituus since before I was born. His was a slow craft, sometimes stealing him from our home for months—and upon his return, he toiled further for many days and nights, polishing trinkets, dusting statues. Some weeks my mother turned cross toward his sluggish profession, and she performed tea readings and divinations for the local traders in exchange for a few coins. I looked in my father's eyes, and I understood that this was duty, his passion; he had sworn an oath to seek out and preserve that which was lost, forgotten.

I imagined this was why he fell deeply in love with my mother. And why he loved me—before he knew I was something to be feared.

The service that the Accademia taught was a far cry from what my Papa had taught me. To him, service was a vow one makes in his heart; service was love, pure and white, like dough. Its purpose was to feed those who hurt, but in the palace, it was a weapon—a cumbersome sack of flour to beat humility into Suzette.

I scanned the room, noting two enormous, mahogany doors at the front and back. I would have been happy, then, to pull Suzette through them and run with her until day turned to night and we stared up at the moon. To run beneath Her, free of the Accademia, its vedovas, the filia, and our headmistress.

Together Suzette and I could find our way to the mountains and live out our days in the Order Umbilicus: she and I with my Papa in the true heart of service.

But there were eyes everywhere in the palace, so many eyes, always—and Suzette and I each had been given a different fate. We would finish making piandia, and she would go forth into the dining hall, seeking to sell me.

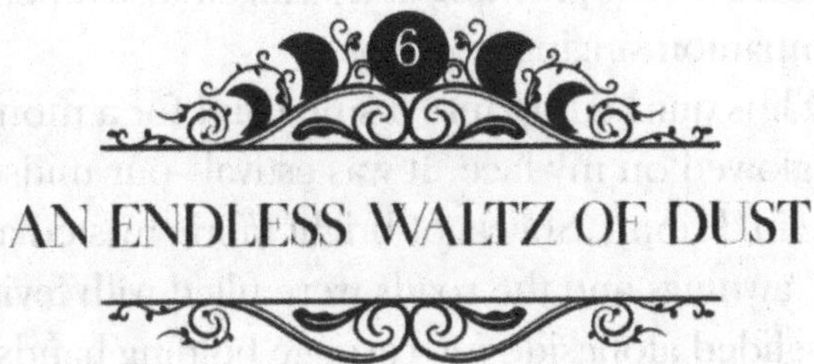

AN ENDLESS WALTZ OF DUST

I endured an entire season of vendrake and vedovas before Headmistress Elan allowed me to return to the Localita di Fiore. She hesitated, of course—who would not give pause to release one so young, with the litha already taking root in her heart? Perhaps she thought it was too cruel to keep me confined longer than a season: I had just crossed into my ninth year of life, and my mama was gone.

My stomach was in knots in the carriage, each bump we hit shaking loose a new feeling. Joy—a thin ray of sun flashing across my face. Our wheel hit a stone and I was jostled in my seat. Sorrow, worry—what would it be like to sleep in my own bed, with Mama gone and the litha threatening to envelop me? Headmistress Elan had sent me with a package of vendrake in my trunks, instructing me to give it to my father.

Would it dull my senses so that I became numb to the scent of flowers through my window; would the music from the market still reach me? So many anxious thoughts vexed me— worries over beautiful, delicate moments to be lost.

Bands of sun and shadow swept through my travel carriage while I passed under the wisterias and I drifted into a light slumber, dreaming of my home between stretches of lavender and sky. The marketplace roused me at the end of my journey. The voices of merchants and clattering carts mingled with the bleat of a trumpet. I pressed my cheek against the window. A colorful troupe of musicians swayed down the road:

a man in a calico coat plucking at a stringed instrument—his female companion singing high notes.

My lips quirked up into a smile and for a moment, happiness glowed on my face. It was estival—our midsummer observance in Trionfi. Sheets of bright fabric twisted across merchants' awnings and the roads were filled with levity; a line of dancers glided alongside my carriage holding hands, kicking up their feet while the calico musician picked up the tempo of his song. Men and women waved flowers, sashes, while the music careened to its conclusion. A roar of applause ignited when the calico man took a bow and I put my hands together quietly clapping along.

My carriage ambled through the roads while the festivities carried forth, the wheels slowing as we rounded the corner of the market. A shiver passed through me as the familiar frame of my home came into view—three arched roofs side-by-side, the one farthest from the market our own. Delight still painted my face as my driver helped me out of the carriage, and I closed my eyes as he took my hand. The sun warmed the crown of my head and I breathed in the scent of home—wood and spice, horses, and tarnished metal, all bathed in a light scent of flowers. I opened my eyes and turned to the plants that grew at the side of our home. The smile fell from my lips. Dried tangles of weeds sprouted from the ground, choking out my memories of the bright buds that normally greeted me in the summer.

"*Diosemma!*" I cried.

Mama never would have let this happen; it simply could not stand. I crouched on hands and knees and buried my fingers in the dirt, yanking at the shriveled heads of the weeds poking through the soil. My pendant tapped against my chest as I worked, the moonstone jangling as my appetite for annihilation grew. The weeds spiraled around my joy, tightening around the memories of my mama and the gardens behind our home. I grunted as a thick weed stem came free in my hand, pushing away the pervasive thoughts of my trellises and wisterias in ruin.

While I tossed clods of root and mud behind me, my carriage driver stood, arms crossed, and my ilex ignited in my chest. His thoughts appeared in mine as a pale whisper—just two words, little more than a tickle of the wind in my ear.

Lunare. Pity.

It was not only the Damica who knew of the litha.

The carriage driver lay my trunk at the foot of the door and departed with one last crooked look at me. I shook my head free of his feelings and, wiping the dirt from my hands, I moved to the door, my hand resting on the knob. My breathing quickened while I willed my fingers to do more than sit idly—but I did not want to face what lurked within: Mama's forlorn chair, an empty tea kettle. Had she been buried with her serpents, or did they reside on a sad counter beside herbs and dry cuttings. I clenched my jaw and squared my shoulders. Papa would be expecting me. I turned my thoughts away from my lonely, dark heart and summoned the image of his face. We would meet at the hearth; he would be making soup. I would be lulled by the babble of boiling water and the rhythmic *thunk* of his knife against the counter. A few short steps into my home and I would hear him hum, his lips forming words in the old tongue—and I would join in him in his song—our words harmonizing in a beautiful, bitter mourning.

I twisted the doorknob and pushed the door open.

It was worse than I feared. A delicate snow of dust floated in the sunlight, a blanket of neglect coating our table, our chairs—our hearth. Wisps fluttered around me, catching in my hair like dandelion seeds. My eyes began to water and I wrinkled my nose, pinching it just in time to stifle a sneeze.

"Laurel?"

I blinked and looked up to find my Papa. His dark eyes carried a sheen of sadness as he approached. His eyebrows folded and with my ilex I heard the words he held back from his tongue. *Are you well?*

I ran to him, embraced him in reply, pressing my cheek against his robes, the light scent of bread filling my senses.

"I missed you, Papa."

"I know, filia. I've missed you, too." His lips brushed my cheek and I returned his gesture. Papa looked tired, more fatigued than I had seen them before. Even his smile wore exhaustion.

"Since your mother died . . ." he began.

"Please." I nestled my ear against him. "Stop."

"She would have been so proud of you, Laurel—studying in the Accademia, becoming Damica . . ."

A knot formed in the back of my throat and my mouth dried. No, she would not have been proud of me. Not at all. I cleared my throat and smudged my eyes against my sleeve.

"Papa, what is the meaning of this?" I dragged my finger across a trail of dust, carving a path through it. "We must eliminate this, at once! Mama would be mortified. Come, this house is filled with shadows. We must clear all of it."

My father sighed and took me by the wrist. Sorrow brimmed at the bottom of his dark eyes. Tenderly, he turned over my hand and blew at my fingertip.

"Filia, we are all dust."

Dust.

Papa believed it was like piandia—that sorrow, brokenness could be kneaded, somehow, into nourishment. We lived, we died; we rose; we fell—each of us performing our part in an endless waltz, no different than the dancers I watched from my carriage window in the market. We were linked like the chains of Mama's bracelet, each one of us moving in unison but as separate parts—and we stirred up dust in every movement we made, every word we spoke.

Fate and chance.

Ilex and litha.

Veritas and linguina d'argent.

Dust.

I did my best to wipe Suzette's flour-dusted gown before she entered the grand hall. The dust shone on her dark curls and I threaded my fingers through her hair, pulling her spirals straight to shake it out.

Out of shadow, Vedova Oriana appeared at my side and she slapped my wrist.

"Stop that at once!" she snapped. "Suzette needs to learn humility. Do not interfere."

I unlaced my fingers from Suzette's locks and rubbed my wrist. Pinpricks of pain needled at my skin, a rose-colored mark starting to form where the vedova struck me. I clenched my throat and cradled my hand to my chest. The tears were coming. I felt them—they were coming, and I could not stop them. I blinked and they veiled my vision. It was not so much the pain that bothered me; it was the fact that she had done it. Vedova Oriana of the Vigore class had struck me. First, she called me Viper; then, the strike. The Vigore were supposed to be our guardians. Had the vedova simply grown weary of caring for me, or had she always held such disdain—and the vendrake made me numb toward it?

I looked at Suzette. She was no longer beautiful—her jaw set, her expression hardened, her eyebrows folding in ire.

"Cherissima." I brushed the back of her hand with mine and she whirled around, putting three indignant steps between us.

"Don't," she said pointedly.

I pressed my back to one of the kitchen's stone walls while the two vedovas led Suzette to a serving table lined with silver trays of piandia and an assortment of honey, ruby-colored jam, and tea leaves.

"There is a situation in the hall that has everyone terse, on edge—ignore it, Suzette. Focus on your service," Vedova Oriana said. "Serve the head table first. While you're pouring tea and handing out sweets, sweep the room for the military men. Generals first, then lieutenants, then captains. I do not know who all is here—but it is your task to find out. Leave your Lunares at the back of the room."

"Can they not stay in the kitchen?" Suzette asked, lifting her tray.

"Absolutely not!" the second vedova said. "You must have eyes on them—always."

"They will be serving, too," Vedova Oriana explained. She motioned for Bethany and me to come, and I peeled myself from the wall, taking hesitant steps to the counter.

"There, filia. Come now; don't be frightened," the second vedova said. She moved behind me and guided my hands under one of the trays. She leaned over my shoulder and brushed my hair back.

"Smarten up, filia. I hear one of the Deos Tactigit has returned," she whispered with a wink. "Don't let Bethany steal him from you."

I folded my brows, utterly confused. My cheeks flushed with embarrassment at how little I understood the court: names, titles, rumors, competition—any of its intricacies. It all felt exhausting to me.

"Smile, but don't show your teeth. Flash your leg, but make it look like a mistake. Good luck, filia; we all want to see you betrothed. Oriana more than most. She means well. Do not take her brutavis to heart."

She smoothed my hair back into place and with those words whirring in my mind, Suzette, Bethany, and I were thrust from the kitchen into the main hall—each of us with an arrangement of piandia on a silver tray. My legs buckled from the enormity of it all. Row after row of arched windows perched above me, each a different mosaic of flowers comprised of hundreds of pieces of colored glass. Rainbows of light poured across the signores and signoras seated in the hall, their gowns and tunics glowing as if they were alive—and perhaps they were. Silver buttons, garnet rings, and jewels woven into their collars caught the light, and between flickers of their estival attire—ah, I found them, at last: demon-whispers. A black ribbon of tension burrowed along the piping of a signore's coat; with a signora, it wove itself between her frilled neck piece. These shadows were not like the demon-whispers I encountered as a youth; they lingered, quiet—resting in places that were easy to overlook. But their presence tickled my ilex, and the hairs on my arms stood rigid.

Six months and he's still missing. No word on his whereabouts. What shall they do if he does not return? Who will be named? We deserve to know. The silence is dreadful. We need answers. We need the truth.

The words streamed silently between a pair of signoras as I served them piandia and tea. They spoke blithely to one another about their quarters in the palace, never uttering a word of their fears—but they eclipsed both their hearts and minds.

At the front of the hall Suzette carried her tray to a beautiful dais adorned with yellow flowers. Headmistress Elan was seated at one end with Maialinne and Riognach perched around her. At the center of the dais, two crowned figures in golden robes ignited the hall with their opulence. My king— King Armando the third, and his wife, Queen Norina. I had never laid eyes upon either of them during my lifetime and I squinted at them from the back of the hall, eager to know just what they looked like—every feature, from the tip of the nose to the color of their eyes. I set my tray down to move closer so I could commit their faces to memory.

As I approached, the energy of the hall shifted instantly. From across the room, I felt *him*. His gaze at my back, studying each of my vertebrae. I turned just enough to see him in the corner of my eye.

He was seated near the end of a table: a hardened man, lean and angry. Unlike the other signores and signoras, he did not don a festive outfit suited for estival. He wore a simple blue tunic with a crest on his left breast pocket. From afar, I could only make out white lines upon black, but as I edged closer, they took on a more complex shape. The lines coiled into a symmetrical circle, a sinuous spine with vertebrae humped along its form and specter-like ribs whisked with the fine point of a needle. One end led to a serpent's skull—its empty eye socket a vortex of darkness. The other end narrowed into a tail, which lay within the venomous jaw.

An ouroboros. I felt an odd reminiscence. I had gazed upon this form in my Papa's tomes and he told me it was a representation of the infinite—the beginning and end merging into one, life and death indistinct from one another. This particular depiction of the snake, stripped of its flesh, only skull and spine, I had never before seen.

But it was not the man's blue-hued tunic that drew the attention of most. Both of his forearms were wrapped with thick, white bandages that ran from his elbows to the backs of his hands, looping around palms. His fingers were raw and red, their skin shiny, fresh, and blistered. I pressed the toe of my slipper against the floor and twisted it in a circle, squeamishly trying to avoid my thoughts of what wounds hid beneath his bandages.

The skin of his long, angular face was like leather—each fold and wrinkle distinct. His dark hair began at the peak of his forehead, sprouting into thin, feathered locks that ended near his chin. His mustache, too, was strange and thin like thread, and his beard ended at the shoulders of his tunic. Sharp and pointed like his other features, his eyes held an amber hue.

His gaze penetrated my back, his eyebrows folding. Yearning. Desire. He sunk his teeth into his lip and I shivered while my neck flushed with discomfort. It was not a desire born from his heart; his longing came from the pit of his stomach. It was more than lust: he wanted something deeper . . . far more personal, from me. I scurried to find Suzette, but among the many faces and voices of the court, she was lost to me. I finally spotted her leaving the dais with an empty tray and I rushed toward her, threading my hand through hers.

"Laurel! What is it?" she asked, alarmed.

"Something is terribly wrong," I gasped.

"What?"

"There are words, unspoken . . ."

Suzette squeezed my hand, looking in both directions.

"Come! Now!" she commanded. She gripped my arm, leading me swiftly into the corridor between the hall and the kitchen.

"Suzette . . ."

"No, cherissima! You must stop this, now! You are jeopardizing us both." She set down her tray and reached for her brooch and I pushed her hand aside.

"Listen! Suzette, listen! You must not silence me!"

Suzette blinked once, twice, and sighed. She glanced nervously in both directions and pulled me into a quiet corner of the kitchen.

"Speak! Quickly."

"S-something terrible is happening; my ilex . . ." I buried my face in my hands, drawing a deep, uneven breath. "Six months. Missing. They are eager for answers. Starved. No one will talk about it. But the words . . . they are hanging in the shadows."

"Cherissima!"

"The man in bandages." I shivered. "He is watching me. There is something wrong with him. Something terribly wrong."

"Diosemma! Listen to me, cherissima!"

Suzette seized me by the shoulders and brought me to the floor behind a counter. Her gray eyes brimmed with panic.

"Vedova Oriana warned me about this," she said, keeping her voice low.

"What?"

"Bringing a Lunare into the high court can be risky. There have been . . . incidents in the past."

"Incidents?"

"Yes, incidents. Incidents like Damica Sofie. Are you aware of her, Laurel?"

"No," I replied.

"Well, you should be. Her husband was a captain—well-admired, wealthy. He brought her to dine with the high court one evening. She was barely seated when she killed the signore beside her," Suzette hissed.

"Killed him?"

"Yes. Picked up a dinner knife, drove it straight through his throat. They had never met before and had only exchanged a few words prior to the attack. He bid her good evening, and she drove the knife through his throat. It took her captain and two men to pry her off him."

I cringed, my stomach turning at the thought.

"Why would she do that?"

"No one knows. It was entirely unprovoked. He was well regarded in the capital and his loved ones remembered him as kind-hearted and generous. He brought food and clothing to an orphanage in the winters. After his death, a few rumors surfaced that he had a fondness for young girls, but they were unfounded."

I wrung my hands, harrowed by Suzette's story. The horror Damica Sofie must have felt—how it pressed against my ribs: beneath the layers of silk and skin, darkness staining the heart of a signore so innocuous to the eye—yet so dangerous beneath the surface.

"What happened to her?" I whispered.

"Damica Sofie? What do you think?" Suzette hissed. "She was put on trial and executed. They asked her over and over to explain herself, but no one could make sense of what she was saying."

"Maybe they did not want to understand."

"What?" Suzette tilted her head, gave me an odd look.

"It would have been easier to keep her quiet." I nodded at Suzette, confirming my words.

Suzette grasped my hand and squeezed it with such force that I cried out in pain. Her knuckles white, she drew in a deep breath and let it out slowly.

"Do you think this brings me pleasure? Parading around the court in this ugly pink dress, handing out bread and jam while trying to find you a husband? Listen to me closely, cherissima, as if your life depends on it—because it does! Before we came here, the Headmistress pulled the record of Damica Sofie's trial and made me read through the entire thing with Vedova Oriana. Every word of it! Afterward, she asked me about it—what I would have done had I been there. Now, why do you suppose she asked me that? What do you think I've been instructed to do with you, should you fall to the litha?" I heard a twitch in her voice and she quickly turned away.

I cast my gaze down. "I am sorry, cherissima. I will speak no more of this. Please, use your linguina d'argent. *Daremi pacce.*"

She brushed my cheek with her lips. "I will."

Her fingers moved to her brooch and she slid a lock of hair behind my ear and began to whisper her beautiful, silver words. I felt the tension of the high court begin to ease, the colorful light from the mosaics ascending, the weight of the stone walls lifting from my body. Words and gold melted together as if they were ingredients in a broth. But the words stopped; they changed. An ember in Suzette's mind ignited my ilex; it jumped across my thoughts like a speck of dust from a hearth, twirling playfully, flaring orange and white.

I recognized the sensation as curiosity—a dangerous speculation into matters better left alone.

Suzette lifted her hand from her brooch. "Laurel?

"Yes?"

"When you said something is wrong?"

"Mm?" My eyelids felt heavy and I wanted to extinguish Suzette's curious spark, blow it to the stone floor and let it fade to ash.

"Why did you tell me?"

I exhaled deeply and lay back on the floor, resting my head in my arms. "I trust you, cherissima. You are my only friend in this place."

"Are you sure?" Suzette asked. I picked up a quiver in her voice.

"Am I sure that you are my friend?" I sighed. "You are my best friend, Suzette."

"Oh, cherissima—you are a sweet little lamb." Suzette's cheeks flushed and she smiled wryly. "I, ah—what I meant to ask is—are you sure about what you said?"

I nodded. "Yes, Suzette. Yes. Something terrible has happened in Trionfi. Someone is missing; someone is dead. A lot of people are dead—and no one will talk about it. But the words . . . they are hanging in the shadows . . . and that man, the man with the bandages . . . there is something wrong with him. Something terribly wrong . . ." A scream began to rise in my throat. "Please, make the litha stop. Tell it to leave me alone."

"Shhh." Suzette made a pass at her brooch. "All will be well, cherissima. All will be well."

She lay a hand on me and the murmurs of the dining hall, the bread, jewels, signores, and signoras all began to whirl together. I sighed as they trickled from my limbs, escaping like a film of soap rinsed away.

But I still carried within my heart one worry.

"Terror," I whispered. "I heard it in your voice. Please tell me, cherissima, what fear plagues your heart?"

Suzette hesitated, but after a breath, she answered.

"The scribes had a special name for Damica Sofie's trial."

"What was it?" I murmured.

"They called it 'A Viper in the Court.'"

A VIPER IN THE COURT

I had finally learned the origin of my moniker. Viper. Damica Sofie suffered under the weight of this name, her life's story marred by the scales of the court, her knife like a fang. How long ago had she committed her act? Had it been twenty years, or more? Did Headmistress Elan, the vedovas, or any of my sister-filia know anything about Damica Sofie, save her name and execution? Where did she reside; how long had she been married to her captain? Did she find that night root calmed the litha, or was she like me—helpless when it rose in her chest?

What was it, truly, that caused her the kill the signore? Did bravery swell in her heart—an intrepid spirit possessing her fingers as she grabbed the knife? Or was it her fear—for the shadow demons inspired it, always in me—blind terror that willed her blade through the signore's throat? I would have liked to believe it to be both, but the truth was lost to time. I could neither ask Damica Sofie, nor feel into an unbeating heart or a deceased mind. She could not have been much older than I when she performed her feat—at least, I did not think so, as Suzette did not speak of her children—but perhaps she simply did not bring them to dinner. I knew so little about her and I resigned myself to never knowing—for who would tell me, the new viper in the court, about my predecessor?

The only thing I knew for certain was that the culprit in her death was the litha.

I saw it once—the litha. It was only once, and I never told anyone in the Damica. Not Headmistress Elan, Vedova Oriana—any of the vedovas—nor did I tell Suzette, Bethany, or my other sister-filia. The summer of my ninth year, during estival—she appeared to me.

Reunited in our entryway after my Mama's death, Papa and I embraced each other—and cocooned by the warmth of his robes, I let myself go. My pendant jangled softly, its tinny notes tinkling between my sobs. Papa held me to his chest for a long time. I know not for how long—only that he fell into grief with me; I trembled in his hold while his shoulders wracked with sobs. *Despair.* His heart nearly burst with it. He knew not what to do, nor how to speak to me. I clutched my pendant and trailed my thumb along the moonstone, willing my breathing to slow. The coolness of the stone calmed me and I breathed out, long and steady. I slid my hand into my father's and gave it a reassuring squeeze.

"Everything will be fine, Papa."

It was the only time I could recall in which I had succeeded in keeping the litha from rising—and I believed, in that moment, I was fine. We were fine. Fine, fine—like dust, like breath. All would be well.

We wiped our eyes and then we purged our home of dust, mopping, scrubbing on hands and knees until our legs ached and our knuckles matched the redness and rawness of our eyes. When we finished our work, Papa slipped a card from one of his tomes: an illustrated portrait of Mama in her bridal gown. I traced my fingers along her fragile features: she rested her head on a crimson sleeve adorned with the ornate petals of peonies. A silver serpent's head peeked from beneath the hem.

"Where did this come from?" I asked breathlessly.

"It was a wedding gift from Headmistress Elan," Papa

explained. "Some of the Damica take to the brush quite naturally—and your headmistress has them make portraits."

I had never heard of this practice, but I presumed he meant the Vigore—with their steel minds and steady hands, it seemed only right. Unlike the rigid portraits I had grown accustomed to seeing in my books in the Accademia, this one felt natural; it captured my Mama's wistful nature, as she constantly slipped in and out of daydreams.

I pressed the portrait to my heart. "I would like to keep this over the hearth, Papa, so she can smile at us, every day."

Papa smiled sadly. "Yes, Laurel. I think I would like that as well." He plucked the card from me and I helped him shuffle some of our pots and candles on the ledge above our hearth. We secured her picture against the wall and stood side-by-side, staring up at it—neither of us knowing quite what to say to one another.

"She would have wanted us to be closer," Papa said. "I know so little about you, Laurel. With my duty to the order, and you being away at the Accademia . . ."

"I wish to see it someday," I interrupted. "The Order Umbilicus, where you spend all your time. I dream of sitting among the trees, listening to falling snow, reaching for the moon and the mountains . . ." I twirled in a slow circle, lifting my arms in a pantomime.

A grin cracked across Papa's cheek, brightness returning to his cheeks. "Filia. An aedituus has duties to fulfill. We do not have time to sit idly under the trees or dance in the snow."

"Truly?" I tilted my head, creasing my brow. If I had been given the opportunity to travel as I wished, it would have been all I cared to do.

My father chuckled. "You are just like your mother—a dreamer, through and through. An aedituus's life is one of scholarly pursuits. Perhaps it is time I should show you my work."

Treasures! He was going to show me, this time! My eyes

widened and I hopped up and down in excitement. Any time he brought his relics to our home, he kept them locked in chests that he slid under his bed. He only opened them at dusk when I was tucked away in bed.

"Yes, Papa! Yes! Are you truly going to let me see?"

"It is time." He smiled sadly. "I would like us to grow closer."

Papa moved to his bedchamber and returned carrying a large wooden chest he struggled to keep upright. We lay blankets across our floors and I peeked eagerly over his shoulder while he opened the chest. He reached inside, gingerly removing a carved stone and placing it on the edge of the blanket. He continued to reach within, placing an arrangement of such relics in a neat row: pendants, blades, orbs, and coins inscribed with ancient writings I imagined were even older than the old tongue. Entranced, I lay on the floor while Papa dusted over his collection. I moved from one object to the next, draping delicate, tarnished chains across my knuckles, pressing my cheek against the smooth glass of orbs.

But it was the blades that drew me most.

One of them stretched more than half the length of my body, with a worn-out hilt and strange jewels gleaning at me. I dared not try to lift it and I shifted my attention instead to a line of shorter blades, drawing them, one by one, from leather sheaths and examining my reflection in their sheen.

In these blades my flesh shone gold or bronze, and then I unsheathed a blade with steel so pure it seemed white. Within it, I became a soft, angelic being. Pale as a gardenia, but with features even more striking. Powerful green eyes gazed back at me from a face decorated like the dead: flesh fragile like ash, and lips and nose dark as stone. I gasped at my beauty and turned the blade over to find the same reflection gazing at me from the other side. I pressed the flat end of the blade to the tip of my nose, clouding my image with a light breath.

It was me—and it was not.

It was the litha.

"Laurel!" With a swiftness I had never seen, Papa rushed to my side and ripped the blade from my hands.

I gasped. "Papa?"

"What did you see?"

He examined the blade cautiously before stuffing it into its sheath. A flash of worry crossed his eyes and creased his brow.

I flattened my palms against the blanket and breathed deeply. Anger rumbled in my gut, brewing like an ugly tea. His demands, his terse tone—and the way he had pried the blade from my very hands—it shook the litha awake within me.

I trembled before its force.

"Speak, filia!" he commanded.

I bit my lip, squeezing my skirt between my hands. "Nothing."

He eyed me suspiciously while I knelt with my head bowed.

"I'm sorry, Papa."

Hastily, he packed the blades back in the trunk, and I was left only with orbs, coins, chains, and dust.

It came to me that night.

My memory of it was hazy at best. I only recall that I rose late the next morning feeling unusual: jittery, spirited. A hum of energy pulsed through my body and my fingers and toes throbbed. I grinned at the sunlight and music spilling into my room and threw my arms wide to greet the morning. A jolt of pain passed through my arms and I gasped, paralyzed. I balled both my hands into fists and examined my forearms. Tiny red scratches appeared on the front of my wrists.

I shook my arms loosely, vowing to avoid both mop and rag for the day, and then dressed for the day hastily, tugging my sleeves over my wrists to hide the marks. I found my legs to be sore, too, as I headed down the stairs, but I did not let it spoil my mood. Perhaps Papa still had the orbs and pendants laying on blankets, and I could study their unusual inscriptions. Midway down the stairs, I paused to take a breath, waiting for the scent of bread cooking over the hearth to fill my nose, but its aroma was absent.

When I reached the entryway, I did not find Papa nor the relics. I glanced at his bedroom door—closed. Perhaps he had stayed up late working to clean the relics while I slept. I moved across the room and opened a window. Chords of estival music streamed into our home. A breeze tousled the tips of my hair as I leaned out of the sill. The market was alive, scintillating, with golden light.

Behind me, I heard Papa's door open; his footsteps muted by his robes. I smiled, closing my eyes. The sunlight kissed my eyelids.

"Papa," I said absently. "I think I should like to play the fiddle. I could play in the market, collect coins in a dish, and—"

"Laurel." His voice, short and strained, stopped me mid-fantasy. I pulled myself back from the window and turned to face him. His face was obscured by a hood and he gripped a peculiar staff in one hand: a sturdy wood with a dual-headed serpent at its top. I traced my fingernail along the windowsill, a wad of dust collecting in my finger. Something was wrong. I should have welcomed the sight of the serpent; it made my stomach fold in knots.

"I know Headmistress Elan would not approve of the fiddle, not for a Damica," I said, my voice pinched. "But it could bring us closer. I would play for you until you smiled and clapped."

Papa said nothing. He stood, shoulders back, his hand gripping the staff—unmoved. My throat tightened.

Something was terribly wrong.

"Papa?

As I neared him, Papa edged back, holding the staff in front of him. From beneath his hood, I caught a brief glimpse of his face—his brow twisted, his rich, brown eyes brimming with terror.

"Stay back," he rasped.

"Papa, what—?"

Wordlessly, my father pulled back his sleeve, holding his arm in the light of the window. The sun cut across his skin, illuminating three deep gashes traveling from his elbow to his wrist.

I gasped, both hands immediately clamping over my mouth.

"Oh, Papa!" I cried. "You're hurt!"

I rushed toward him and he blocked me with his staff.

"Back!" he hollered.

My breath caught in my throat and my legs began to shake. Slowly, I lifted my arm, turning my palm toward me. It was not only dust that clogged my fingernails. I fanned my fingers on the window. My nails were short, raw, and caked with dried blood. My mind spun in circles—sun and music and Papa and I rolling together into a wad of horror. And my heart—oh, my heart—

"It cannot be true!" I cried. "It cannot!" I wiped my fingers furiously against the folds of my skirt. "I could not have done this!"

Papa removed his hood and I screamed, falling to my knees. A crisscross of claw marks—long and pink and horrible— tore across his cheek.

"No!" I shouted, "No, no! It was not me! It was the litha! I lied, Papa—I saw it in the blade—the litha—I did not tell you, and I'm sorry!"

I buried my face in my arms and sobbed. "I'm sorry, Papa!"

"Laurel." The sun bathed Papa's injured cheek in hues of gold, and his voice felt like a warm crackle in our hearth. "It is time for you to return to the Accademia. A carriage is on its way."

"You are sending me away?" The music outside no longer shone; the notes sounded skewed and unnatural. The drums beat with anxiety, filling my chest with fear.

Papa nodded. "The blade you looked into is called a purity blade. It reflects what is in your heart—your truest, and purest, self."

"But I am not the litha!" I gasped. "I despise it! I wish it away, every night!"

"You and the litha are inseparable," my father whispered, closing his eyes. "Headmistress Elan instructed me to give you vendrake as soon as you arrived. I should have listened to her. I did not want to believe it."

"You should not have believed it, because it isn't true! I am not the litha; I can control it; it does not control me!" I cried.

"No, Laurel, you cannot," Papa said, his back bent, shoulders sagging. "When night fell, you climbed out your window and wailed at the moon. The market thought you had gone mad."

"N-no! It isn't true!"

I searched my mind frantically for any trace of truth of what my Papa had said.

A flash of silver.

Papa strained against me as he held the staff against my body.

I clawed at him. I spat at him.

He shook his staff, his two-headed serpent hovering over me.

He cried out in the old tongue.

Another flash—bindings. My wrists and ankles tied.

It was true. All of it.

The muscles in my face all pulled together and I howled. "I'm sorry, Papa! I am so sorry!" I lunged at him, longing to shake him, demand that he accept my apology. He could not send me back—he could not! Without Mama, we were all we had left!

He recoiled as I came near, thrusting his staff between us.

"Back! Filia—do not force me to bind you again."

I dropped to my knees and pressed my hands hard against my temples. I wanted to disappear, to dissolve into the cracks between our floorboards, sink into the shadow I was—and never return again.

"What is happening to me?" I choked. "Please. Help me, Papa."

My father breathed out heavily, hiding his face beneath his hood. "I will seek help for your affliction in the order," he said flatly. "I will study it, learn its origin—and seek a cure for you. But until then—your headmistress and I agree it is best for you to return to Accademia."

I shuddered, squeezing my nails into my palms. "No—please do not send me back. She will force me to drink the vendrake, and then I'll—"

"It is for the best," Papa interrupted.

I continued to protest but, in the end, it was futile. The purity blade had not lied; I had peered into it and the litha stared back. My fate belonged to the litha—and it would bat me around like a hapless ship caught in a torrent—and I, untethered from fortune, had no anchor, no means to resist.

"Is she well?"

In our quiet corner, I lay on my stomach, lost in Suzette's linguina d'argent—and I had forgotten, entirely, about Bethany. I looked up to find her standing over me, an empty tray tucked under her shoulder.

Suzette jumped. Her hand moved from her brooch to

her heart.

"*Diosemma,* you scared me!" She threw back her shoulders and exhaled sharply. "This is vedova work, Bethany. Gather more bread and take it to the dining hall."

Bethany ignored her.

"Are you feeling well, Laurel? Did you sense it, too?" Lowering herself beside me, she stroked my back in slow circles. Still hanging onto Suzette's sweet murmurs, my eyelids drooped, fluttering closed and then open again like wings.

"Sense what?" Suzette asked pointedly. "The litha?"

"The tension in the hall—everyone laughing and carrying on, pretending to enjoy themselves, while their anxiousness threatens to spill over."

"I felt it," I murmured.

"Riognach told me that it's Prince Brennan. I caught her on the way to the latrine and she confirmed it. He has been missing six months—six!—and the king and queen are beside themselves."

So, it was the prince who was missing. I had heard his name, on occasion, when I passed the courtship conscription queue—Headmistress Elan and the vedovas scheming over which of the filia would be best to put before him, when the time was right. Prince Brennan was the only son of King Armando, fated one day to rule Trionfi.

I clenched my teeth and summoned the words from the signores and the signoras of the court. *What shall they do if he does not return? Who will be named?*

"Well?" Suzette asked. "What else does Riognach know?" Her eyes carried all the features that the headmistress disliked most: pride, willfulness, defiance. And most bothersome of all—curiosity.

"Nothing," Bethany said. "I brushed her arm to find out more, but nothing stirred in her mind but fear."

Ah—yes, fear. It was abundant in the court.

Bethany continued. "Unless I were to use my ilex on

King Armando himself, I cannot discover more. And before you ask—no, Suzette. I will not be put on trial for treason."

"So that is all, is it?" Suzette frowned. Shadows of frustration began to descend from her curls, falling on her forehead. She needed this information; it was every bit as critical as when she called me to meet her in the Catene chambers. The desperation was beginning to consume her—and I needed to understand why.

I threaded my fingers through hers and pushed my ilex deep. Past her skin, through her veins. I arched my back and gasped while the sensation passed through each of my vertebrae. The hairs on my cheek, my arms, my legs stood erect and I drew in a shallow breath. I had never plunged so deep in all my days in the Accademia. Her bones sighed, heavy like the hull of an old boat; the valves of her heart pulsed and released with a moan. Her entire body ached for this.

She did not care about the prince—not truly. She needed a way to gain leverage over Headmistress Elan and the vedovas. Being from the exalted Isparza bloodline, her life as vedova would never be a life of service in the eyes of the headmistress, but a life of servitude. The vedovas would take pleasure not in her humility, but in her humiliation—watching her wake each day to don the pink gown and be tasked with setting tables and cleaning chamber pots. It was more than even she could bear, and in her heart, Suzette could not survive being broken in this manner; the shame would kill her.

My temples throbbed with pain; a squeal tore through my ear. Six months. Six months.

More words from the signores and signoras flowed through my mind. I squeezed my eyes closed and moaned. I was losing control; I felt it slipping from me, falling—falling away. The ringing in my ears intensified and I released Suzette's hand to wedge my head between my elbows.

"Cherissima?" Suzette's voice bent with concern. "What did you do?"

I pushed my elbows harder against my head. The truth was in these words—somewhere. Somehow. With my ilex, I knew it for certain.

What shall they do if he does not return?

The silence is dreadful.

We need answers. We need the truth.

My body felt warm—too warm—the heat unbearable, like the sun beating down on me. My face twisted in agony and my hands smoldered white-hot, like coals. I sat up and spread my fingers apart, fearing my body may bore a hole into the floor. Desperately, I reached for my pendant, praying for the moonstone to alleviate the burn.

Truth. Truth.

Raw fingers, blistered skin.

Fire.

"Suzette, it's the litha! It has her!" I heard Bethany cry. "You must act, now!"

Suzette lifted me and pried my arms free from my head. She gripped my shoulders and shook me. "Cherissima, come out of it! Look at me!" She reached for her brooch and I seized her wrist.

"The signore in bandages—he knows something," I rasped.

"What?"

"He knows. Cherissima . . . promise me. You'll stay away. There is something wrong with him. Some poison—some perversion. Do not speak to him. We can find another way. Promise me."

"Shh." She pulled free of my grip and her silver words came down on me, soothing my body.

I was powerless as she stroked my hair; there was nothing I could do—my ilex warned me that Suzette had made up her mind. To speak to the bandaged signore, challenge him, break him—if necessary—to gain the knowledge that would give her power.

She was like the rain, Suzette. To me, she was pleasant and well-received; people were fond of light showers—soothing, steady drumming upon the rooftop. Among the venom of the headmistress and her vedovas, though, Suzette was a torrent—whirling through alleys, rattling at shutters as if to say, "Come on, now! Open your window and just try to stop me!"

Suzette rose and studied her reflection in a cooking pot. She fluffed her hair and adjusted her bodice to accentuate her bosom.

"Bethany, stay with Laurel," she ordered.

"I thought you told me to serve more bread!" Bethany protested.

"Do as I say!"

Adjusting her brooch on her collar, she touched one finger at its center and practiced a smile. I watched her hurry out of the kitchen and exchanged an uncertain glance with Bethany.

Suzette played a dangerous game of fate and chance.

Litha or no litha, I could not let her confront the signore in bandages alone.

BLIND TO THE SHADOWS

If there was one thing I was adept at, it was shadow. I had grown familiar with it through the litha. Shadows stained the faces of my loved ones during moments of anguish; shadow-whispers haunted my sleep. And in my ninth year of life, Papa witnessed the shadows stirring in me—the litha howling in my blood as I tore at his flesh with my nails.

The blade in which the litha appeared fractured us, splitting our fate in two: Papa returning to the Order Umbilicus in the mountains while I was sent back to the Accademia.

My sister-filia plucked the memory from my mind upon my return: the crisscross of lacerations on my Papa's cheek. Even to an untrained Lunare, the story was not difficult to decipher. They called me "Viper" and cast me out of favor, sentencing me to live out my days in shadow: litha, vendrake, sleep. Litha, vendrake, sleep.

Yes, shadow I knew well.

I deceived Bethany into fetching a cup of water for me while I absconded into shadow, leaving her dumbfounded in the kitchen. I felt no remorse for my action—it was a small act of vengeance for what she had done to me in the conscription queue.

Keeping several paces behind Suzette, I lingered by the

walls in the dining hall, letting the darkness wrap me in its fingers so that I was invisible. Near the bandaged signore, I situated myself under a rafter so that it cast shadows on my face to obscure my features.

The signore sat alone at a table near the dais, a delicate white cup perched in front of him. With bandages restricting his hands, he fumbled for something within his pocket. A gust of wind swept over me, one of the kitchen servants nearly bumping into me as she passed with a tray. She stopped at the signore's table, offering to him a packet of tea leaves, but he waved her away. His attention shifted back on his pocket and he produced from it his own wad of dried leaves, dropping them into his cup.

"Filia," he snapped, calling the servant back. "Water."

Keeping her distance, the servant bowed and acknowledged his request, scurrying toward the kitchen. The signore swirled the dry leaves in his cup, contorting his face as they scurried around the bottom. He studied them closely, narrowing his gaze, and he pinched one from the cup, smoothing it flat on the table. Then, he reached for his cup and brought it down on the leaf, grinding it to powder.

It was easy to sense that his mind was poisoned, seeded with animosity. My stomach shuddered with dread and I squeezed my pendant, praying that someone would take notice of his disturbing behavior and dismiss him from the court. But the signores and signoras ignored him, keeping their attention fixed on their own drinks and conversations. The kitchen servant soon returned with the signore's water and she poured it quickly, scurrying away.

She bumped Suzette as she passed and uttered a small apology. Suzette huffed and straightened the brooch at her collar, her gait undeterred toward the signore's table.

"Cherissima, no," I whispered—but as the shadows concealed me, my plea fell into the dark. The signore paid Suzette no mind as she neared, his attention on his tea. He swirled the dark contents around and around and then lifted his cup. His lips moved slightly and two words pushed through them.

"Per vertui."

These were words of the old tongue—words that belonged to my father and his tomes and hymns. On the lips of the signore in bandages, they were a dirge.

"Per vertui?" Suzette's melodious voice cut through my thoughts. "May I inquire, to whom do you make a toast?"

"Mm." The signore stared straight ahead, stirring his tea.

Suzette squeezed her lip between her teeth; a thin band of shadow sweeping over her eyes. The litha was rising in me; it would only be a matter of time before it took me. My ilex swelled in my chest, squeezing my heart against my ribs. Pressure. Suzette, too, felt the pinch of time; with each moment that passed, she was losing more than the signore's interest; her control of her own fate was dwindling. She bit down hard on her lip, huffed, and squared her shoulders. A flare of defiance rose in her chest. She burrowed a hand deep into her curls, and I noticed the side of her little finger slide upon her brooch. Ah, cherissima. She had learned well how to disguise her gift; I envied her ability to do so.

Suzette leaned over the signore's shoulder, lightly brushing her lips to his ear.

"Shhh. Listen to me. All will be well. All will be well."

The signore closed his eyes and his bottom lip flinched. It was a slight movement, almost imperceptible to the eye. I stepped back, flattening my spine against the wall. A sensation washed over me—odd—like a humming through my skin. Hearing Suzette mouth the same soothing words she murmured to me . . . . it felt strange. Was this how her gift simply worked—or was it a ritual she had created for herself? How many hundreds of times had she uttered these words into ears—all shapes of ear, all skin tones—a myriad of faces and titles receiving her silver voice with a blush to their cheek, the flutter of an eyelid.

For a moment, a different hum vibrated through me—one of dread. What if the signore resisted her? He was in the court; surely a man of some significance, and after the trial of Damica Sofie . . . I surmised that the signores and signoras of the court kept a wary eye out for us Damica. Perhaps some of them discovered a counter to our gifts—a talisman, perhaps, similar to the ones my father carried in his chest of relics. No. I shook the thought from my head. Suzette's ability was formidable, and she could command the litha—crushing it with her velvety voice until it cowered and retreated from my body. A signore, even one of stature, would be little match for her linguina d'argent.

Suzette touched two fingers to the back of the signore's neck. "Give to me all I desire from you," she commanded. "First, your name and title."

"Vitis Grimstaad," the signore murmured. "General of the Deos Tactigit."

"General? Military?"

"Mm. I am surprised you had to ask," Grimstaad said.

"Ah, general. Our headmistress frowns upon the study of war. Tell me of the Deos Tactigit. The Damica's knowledge is sparse on such worldly matters."

"A shame your headmistress keeps you blind. You should know it." He took a bandaged hand to the breast of his tunic, placing it over his ouroboros emblem. "The Deos Tactigit are Trionfi's guard—your first, and sometimes your last, means of defense. We are the reason you have a headmistress, and are enjoying this court, having your tea and piandia. We make it so. The Deos Tactigit is life and death itself—we kill, so that you may live. Even if you are blind to our presence."

"'We,' then." Suzette brushed a lock of hair from her shoulder, her thumb subtly pressing on her brooch. "You appear to be quite alone, general."

"Yes," he replied, his voice bending with grief—and something else, something heavier. With each pulse of his heart, I felt poison—his malevolence seated in the core of his chest. It growled like a restless animal, pacing impatiently across a cage. I sensed the heat under his bandages, charred flesh hidden, a mash of musculature and veins.

Whatever was at the heart of General Grimstaad and the Deos Tactigit, I did not wish to know.

Suzette slid her hand lightly over the general's shoulder and stared deeply into his amber eyes. There was more. So much more, beneath the skin. Until she gained the knowledge she sought, she would not cease.

Headmistress Elan had been foolish to believe she could ever subjugate Suzette.

"Perhaps you would enjoy my company," she crooned.

"Mm."

He did not flinch or pull back, but there was a shift in the shadows. They no longer appeared in bands, nor did they hide between the lips of the signores and signoras in the hall. They were here—along the walls—with me. They pooled at Grimstaad's boots. A verdetto like Suzette was unfamiliar with the shift; she lacked an awareness of how death, so close to the heart, could warp the litha, stretch ribbons of shadow and fray them at the ends so that they became tender, sensitive—sharp. She gambled dangerously with duality and pushed too far with her linguina d'argent—and it snapped like a dry twig.

Please, cherissima. Move away from him.

Alas, she could not hear me or see me—for I was a shadow as well. She breathed softly, one hand on her brooch, and lifted a finger, tracing it gently down the general's chin.

"Tell me what you know of Prince Brennan's disappearance."

Grimstaad blinked once, twice, and shook free of Suzette's words. He snatched her wrist and my stomach turned in knots.

"You are a verdetto!" His face contorted with fury.

Suzette turned a panicked gaze toward our headmistress, who was enraptured in conversation and paid her no mind. I pressed my hand over both my pendant and heart. Suzette's eyes glistened with fear. She tilted her head and a wild curl escaped from behind her ear as she tried to free herself.

Stop. Please. Let her go.

Grimstaad raised one of his thread-like eyebrows. The shadows shifted again, rescinding from the walls and floors; they rose, like dust, into the rafters. Something—some distraction—assuaged the darkness within—ever so slightly.

The general yanked on Suzette's arm and she stumbled toward him. "Take a seat, verdetto. You are drawing too many eyes."

A chair groaned as Grimstaad dragged it beside him. He forced Suzette into it.

"General," she pleaded with shaky voice. "Take a moment to think about what you are doing."

"I am finished with your tongue—and your demands," Grimstaad growled. "The only reason you are not dead is because you have something I want."

"Huh." Suzette's shoulders rose and fell as she took a deep breath and let it out. The tension in her eyes melted, and she straightened her spine.

"You're a vedova?"

Suzette flashed a wry smile. "Not quite. But soon."

Grimstaad eyed her with suspicion. "An unusual thing to say. You wish for the death of your husband?"

"Oh, no! You misunderstand!" Suzette's cheeks flushed. "I am not a vedova by the usual means. I, ah . . ." Suzette bit her lip, turning her gaze upward, likely in search of words.

"You have given your headmistress trouble." Grimstaad concluded.

"Perceptive, general." Suzette leaned forward, folding

her hands together on the table. "Shall we drop the cloak of pretense? You have something I want—and I believe I have something you want."

"You do," Grimstaad said.

Blood rushed to my ears, and I could scarcely hear over the beating of my heart.

"Well?" Suzette asked finally. "What is it?""

"The filia I saw you talking with earlier." Grimstaad murmured. "Pale, slender, light hair? Not the brunette with the big nose."

A flicker of concern bent Suzette's brow. "What of her?"

"What's your price, vedova?"

The rumble of anxiety in my stomach deepened into dread, and it quickly spread through my chest. No. He could not be asking for me. This signore, with his poisoned heart and hatred in his eyes.

"General." Suzette's voice faltered, just for a moment. "Laurel is not like the other filia. She is one of our most sensitive Lunare."

"Laurel." I hated the way he said my name, as though he were studying it, tasting it on the tip of his tongue and checking for poison.

"She came to me to express her concern over you," Suzette said.

"Mm." Grimstaad frowned, glancing down at his hands. "I understand my wounds are harrowing for a filia to look upon, but they will heal."

"Her concern was not your appearance, but what you carry in your heart."

Grimstaad twitched and crossed his arms over his chest. "What did she tell you?"

"Ah, you care what she thinks!" Suzette lowered her voice and brushed her lips against his ear. "You want her. Timid, sweet Laurel. Standing by your side, twining her finger around yours. Whispering secrets to fell your foes. Spread across your bed with her moon-kissed skin. Anything you command, she is trained to obey."

Grimstaad drew a sharp breath and his nostrils flared.

My mouth folded into a grimace. How could she encourage such debauchery? It was my duty, as Damica, to submit to my husband—Headmistress Elan reminded us, constantly. We were expected to do so, our duties twofold: to use our gifts and to conceive, securing our husband's bloodlines with a son while imbuing any daughters we may produce with our gifts. This was the purpose of all Damica. But, I would never–never!–touch this signore of my own will!

Why was Suzette doing this? Dangling me before this wretched man, as if I were tied at the neck to a post? A foal to be fitted with a saddle, and shoes, and blinders—then pounced upon. This was not the Suzette I knew—the one who had held my hand through the night, the daring filia who smirked at the litha and raised her silver voice, banishing the shadows that tortured me so. My cherissima who combed her fingers through my hair as if it were gold, sweeping her hand over my eyes to coax them to rest.

Suzette propped her elbows on the table and rested her chin in her hands, watching Grimstaad as he twisted, restless in his seat. His eyes closed and he pulled a thin breath through his lips.

"It seems you and I are alike—we both have an appetite for things best left in the dark," Suzette said, tilting her head devilishly.

Grimstaad opened his eyes while he exhaled, a forceful stream of breath fluttering his bandages. Wearing confidence in her posture, Suzette fixed her gaze straight and deep into the general's light brown eyes.

"She buckled so easily under my command," Suzette said to Grimstaad. "She would be a bashful wife, dutiful—at your behest, she would turn her pretty lashes to the floor, denying her curiosity to feel into you while you satisfied your needs. Unless, of course, there was some urge in your heart you wished her to feel while she lay with you."

Grimstaad moaned at her words while heat crept up my chest, swelling on my neck. I swallowed, dry, while despair dropped in my chest, heavy as a sack. My heart stopped beating for a moment and I wrapped my arms over my chest. I felt bare, exposed—repulsed. Suzette would not betray me; she would not have me betrothed to this monster! Would she? Bile churned in my belly and I swayed back and forth, nauseous, heavy. One of its shadows reached up into my throat and I gagged, biting my lip to keep quiet.

I turned my gaze to the dais at the front of the hall— King Armando feasting in golden garments, Queen Norina engaged in deep conversation with Headmistress Elan. With her chin raised, a quiet smile rested on the headmistress's lips, while she stroked Riognach's forearm. She was foolish—all of them were foolish—to underestimate Suzette.

Was I?

So treacherous, so clever, was Suzette d'Isparza. I could not comprehend how Headmistress Elan had convinced herself that she could subjugate her, that she could keep her contained, somehow.

Even when she was at a disadvantage: she always found a way. She must have realized that with Grimstaad, she could no longer spin lies without incensing him. Her linguina d'argent had been detected—and she could not use it again.

She was leaning in the other direction of her gift: veritas.

Using truth to drive him mad.

"You want her," Suzette whispered. "*Need* her. That sweet face, it will haunt you tonight, no?"

Grimstaad's hand curled into a loose fist and I winced, imagining the pain that echoed through his damaged skin.

"Bring her to me," he growled.

A small smirk hung on one corner of Suzette's lip. "As you command."

AN ECHO OF WHAT ONCE WAS

I struggled to limp back to the kitchen without falling, or spilling the contents of my stomach on the palace floor.

The litha scraped at my ears. Suzette would not sell me. She could not do this to me! I placed my arm on a wall, letting the chill of stone bite my palm. I wanted to scream. The litha coated my arms in thick black patches, oozing droplets falling to my skirt, staining the fabric with spatters of hatred.

I lurched into the kitchen, pushing past Bethany without a word to her. She called my name at my back and I ignored her. The litha veiled my eyes, lights and trays obscured gray, aprons and gowns and flour running together in a gray sludge, like too many paints bleeding together. I pressed the heels of my hands over my eyes. Make it stop. *Daremi pacce.*

"Laurel!" Bethany seized me by the shoulders and shook me. I growled at her and shook her loose.

"Where is Suzette?" I cried.

"I don't know; I—"

"Where?" I cried, prying my hands from my face. Two kitchen servants stopped kneading their dough and looked at me, their features becoming gnarled with concern.

"You are making a scene!" Bethany hissed. "Come! Now! Before you ruin this for us both." She pulled me around a counter, and we crouched beneath a collection of trays and jams.

"It's taken you, has it? The litha?"

95

I squeezed my eyes shut and nodded.

"Here." Bethany placed a small object in my hands, and I opened my eyes to find a small twist of root.

"Vendrake. Suzette slipped some to me in case you got out of hand. Chew it."

I placed the root in my mouth and squeezed my teeth over it. Its bitter juices numbed my tongue where they touched, but the litha began to turn to vapor, and fade. I swallowed the wretched vendrake, the fibers of the root sticking between my teeth. I touched the tip of my tongue to one and it tasted of shame. Salty, brackish—like mud—and there was no remedy I could swallow to make it go away—nothing my body could absorb to numb my disappointment in myself. Why could I not be simple, like Bethany—and want nothing more than to leave the palace betrothed?

My thoughts floated away, rising like dust above me and I let out a small sigh. I imagined I was looking upon the stars and I held my breath, and made a wish. A normal life—ah, what a dream—one in which I were far from the palace, a life in which I had never known the litha.

"Ah, look—Suzette has returned." Bethany said. She sounded far away, even though she was beside me. I struggled to keep my eyelids open.

"Cherissima?" Suzette's dulcet voice swam in my head.

"She gave me the vendrake," I whispered.

Suzette folded her lips into a scowl and turned to Bethany. "You should have waited for me!"

"I couldn't—she came in here raving, and—you told me to do this!"

"Enough!" Suzette lashed at her with her tongue. My mind rolled their words together as each of them erupted into an ugly percussion of words. Suzette threw her arms wide, pushing her hands on her hips. Bethany reached for her pendant and thumbed the moonstone. A shudder passed through her and she closed her eyes, drawing in a deep breath.

"There is no reasoning with you," she said shakily. Her hair fanned behind her as she spun around, lifted a tray from the counter, folded it under her arm, and stomped back toward the dining hall.

I detested being the source of so much controversy and disagreement. Were it not for the vendrake, the unease would have been more than enough to beckon the litha to blanket me. It had almost been too much for Bethany.

However, it did not seem to faze Suzette at all. Her gray eyes flared, reflecting like a stream of water catching the sun.

"There now, cherissima. All will be well. Cast Bethany out of your mind and try to focus. Listen to my voice; we have much to review," she crooned, extending a smile and a hand to me. "The man who frightened you—the one with the bandages— he is General Vitis Grimstaad, one of Trionfi's high guard—the Deos Tactigit."

I hugged my arms to my chest and scowled. "I am aware, Suzette. I hid in the shadows and listened to you speak with him." A lock of hair fell over my eye, obscuring my view of Suzette's o-shaped mouth.

"Laurel." Suzette's voice curved with a gentle inflection, like a willow sweeping the grass.

I wrinkled my face painfully. "The things you said about me . . ."

"I am sorry," she whispered, crouching down beside me. "You must believe me when I say, I did not wish for you to hear those terrible words."

"They were vile! And they were true! How could you use your veritas like that? If that signore made a bid for me and you accepted, you know I would have no choice but to heed him."

"Look at me, cherissima." The fine hairs on my cheek tickled me as Suzette brushed away a lock of my hair, and she took my chin between her thumb and forefinger. With tenderness, she raised my head, holding it level with her gray gaze. The flare from her eyes had faded; they were a gentle rain in the spring, clear and full of promise. "I would never let him lay a finger on you."

Though the vendrake numbed my ilex, it still tingled beneath my sternum—and I wanted to believe it, but could not quite trust Suzette.

"This is not you speaking with your linguina d'argent?"

"No, cherissima. It is veritas. You are my little lamb, and I am your shepherdess. I do not care who Grimstaad is; I will protect you, cherissima." She kissed my cheek then, and smudged away a half-formed tear from beneath my eye.

"Listen, now! I think Grimstaad may have been training Prince Brennan to become a general," Suzette said. "He said the prince never drew his sword from its sheath, not once. He spent his days hunting on horseback, or he lingered in the kitchen, sampling wines and meats. It seems he is the same as my brothers: coddled, stupid. Shielded from the ways of the world. Grimstaad told me that King Armando sent him to the Accademia for a short time to study the history and tactics of war."

"The Accademia Marl?"

"Yes, our very own Accademia. But it did little to fix his coward's heart."

"What else did he say?" I asked.

Suzette huffed, blowing a sprig of dark hair from her shoulder. "That is all I know."

I sensed unease in her statement, and I squinted, studying her hardening features. Her eyes dulled like stone. Even with my ilex numbed, it was evident.

"You are hiding something from me," I said.

Suzette grew quiet, pulling in a sharp breath. "Grimstaad wants me to bring you to his private chambers. He will tell me no more unless I do so."

"No! I will not do it! How could you humor this?" I shook my head vehemently, stumbling over my words. "He will defile me—or worse! You do not know what I felt in him. That signore . . . there is something wrong with him—something deep inside, which is broken."

"Please, cherissima. You will be with me the entire time. I will keep you safe. No harm will come of it; all will be well."

"Suzette . . ."

Her mouth turned down and she reached for her brooch. "This is too important. Bigger than you or I. Do not force my hand!"

I blinked and scooted back, clanging against a set of pans.

"You would not!" I cried.

I clasped both hands to my heart, hoping she could feel my fear, but she towered over me, a fossilized stone figure—a rook, positioning herself to slide across the board.

"Please," she whispered. "We need to find out what the general knows."

"We? No, you need to find out! I want no part of this. Please, leave me be—I want to sleep and forget about this day."

"Well—you can't," Suzette said pointedly. "We have come too far and cannot back down now."

"You are too late. I cannot extract the general's secrets for you. The vendrake has numbed my ilex."

"I would never ask you to take such a risk." Suzette shook her head, taking both my hands in hers. "Injured as he is, Grimstaad is dangerous. Lethal. Deos Tactigit. But, he is enamored with you—so let us use that, yes?"

"Why?" I wrinkled my nose, my disgust rising as bile in my throat. "Why me? Why not you? I am no Isparza; my bloodline is of no significance beside yours. Your gift is so powerful; mine is chaotic, discordant . . ."

"He sees you as pure, Laurel. Like a fawn learning to walk. Innocence like yours stirs up some men's blood; they like the hunt; their arrogance will bloat up like a pig if they think they can conquer you." Suzette rolled her eyes. "Men. I find them repulsive."

I cracked a smile and my ilex buzzed with my affection for Suzette; even with my subdued sense, it was clear as a stream. I called her my sister-filia, but in my heart she was my sister; her loyalty to me was as mine was to her—a spread of peacock feathers, proud, unwavering.

I sighed, my chest falling, relief flowing through my lungs. "If this is truly what you need from me, cherissima—I will do as you ask."

Suzette pushed my hair back and kissed my forehead. "Thank you."

She called me a lamb, but she was blind to the darkness that marred the Lunare class. Perhaps it was because she could assuage my shadows and drive them away that she felt at ease holding my hand or wrapping me into an embrace—but she was exceptional, phenomenal in that regard, my cherissima. And she took it for granted. The world outside the Accademia—the merchants of the market, the signores and signoras of the court, even King Armando and Queen Norina—they were wary of the Lunare, having little defense against what it is we did.

A Lunare herself, Headmistress Elan held a firm grasp of what we were—and we were not a sweet and innocuous class. She called me a weapon. My sister-filia called me Viper. The implication was clear.

Do not get close.

My thoughts turned to Mama's portrait, hanging above our hearth. Her tender face, dreaming of fanciful worlds, that she may one day travel to, with my Papa. Even as she was Damica, for the most part, she was popular and well-liked among the marketplace—a woman who spun kindness with her serpents, one whose world was beautiful, trails of whimsy following her like a train of flowers.

When we lay in the garden, she sometimes described her marriage to Papa—pointing, with her fortune-teller's fingers, to where the Accademia's trellises would have sat, twined with wisteria and moonflowers. She filled my mind with white upon white blooms, braided with ribbons, adored with orbs.

But it was because of the Lunare that marriage ceremonies like my Mama's no longer took place.

When I turned eleven years of age at the Accademia, Headmistress Elan assembled all my sister-filia in our courtyard. I rested my head on my knee, gazing up at the trellises my Mama had described. Bare white wickering stared back down at me, no white buds, vines, nor wisteria, hanging down in clusters, casting shade. A web of wickered shadow enveloped my body like a net, and with vendrake clouding my mind, my head swam as the sun shone through in stripes.

"The peace we knew then is gone, filia," Headmistress Elan addressed us, drumming her fingers on a book resting on a stone table beside her. I blinked unevenly and tried to keep myself cross-legged, upright. I turned my attention to the headmistress's cloak. Blades of grass poked up around the hem, and I imagined this had always been so when she walked through the courtyard. I pushed the palm of my hand into the grass beside me. Had Mama done the same as I; did she picture the headmistress as dragging a trail of dirt and grass flakes behind her? I blinked again, long—the headmistress was speaking. I tilted my head, trying to pay attention to her words.

"The world has become a much more dangerous place. To be a Damica in a time like this . . ." Headmistress Elan touched her hand to her heart and breathed out. "I worry what will come of it."

My sister-Lunare fidgeted, whispers of worry passing between them. The headmistress flipped the tome open, gently turning the pages until she arrived at one with a small, painted card nestled in the spine of the book. She removed it and lay it in front of us, revealing its image: a handsome, light-haired man with a scar across his nose adorned in a military tunic, with one hand resting on the shoulder of a woman beside him. She wore a crimson robe and held a book toward the sky, a crescent crown resting atop her head. I shivered at her appearance while she stared back at me—her robes billowing in a gust of wind behind her. The headmistress studied the pair with a knifelike gaze. All my emotions rolled together; I wanted to know everything about the woman in the card, but she frightened me so—and I wished to know nothing, wishing never to gaze upon her again. The war within raged through my blood, so powerful that it erupted as a squeal in my ear. I winced, burrowing my face in my arms.

"I've heard concerns stirring among you about our neighbors in the Localita di Neve," Headmistress Elan said, while I recovered my composure. "I try to shield you from such matters, filia. But news has spread far and wide—it has permeated our walls here." I tried to keep my focus on the Headmistress's words, but my eyes drew back to the woman on the card. I had heard of no such siege and did not care about it. All I wished to know was about her. My skin felt heavy upon my veins, my blood like a congealed brew, anchored in my lungs, my stomach, my innards. The vendrake took such a toll on my body, I barely captured the nuances of anything happening.

"The city of Serenellia has fallen—hundreds of our own men, perishing with it. And one woman—Damica Cosetta— whose image lies before you." The headmistress's eye twitched, and she pulled her lips taut. "She was the first to die. They executed her at the start of the siege."

A knot worked itself into her brow and her fingers quivered as she lifted Damica Cosetta's card. "She was my sister-Lunare; we came of age just a few years apart. She wed her lieutenant in this very courtyard."

She fixed her thumb over the lieutenant's face and ripped the card evenly down the center, balling up the signore's image and dropping it into the grass.

"Savages," she said. "We live in the times of thoughtless men. They parade you around like they've won a prize, with little regard for your safety. Your identities and your gifts should always be kept secret. Trionfi has many enemies—and Damica Cosetta has paid in blood for her husband's brashness. I do not trust these signores can be clandestine, filia. Any of them. With any of you."

She turned the card over. On the back, she inscribed something.

"In honor of Damica Cosetta's life, and to ensure your safety—I am putting a stop to Damica weddings in the courtyard," she said. "You—and all filia who come after you— will marry by proxy. A madame—a woman of your ammorante's choosing—will complete our arrangements and retrieve you, and you will accompany her in stealth. Together you will travel to your new home, where you will be united with your ammorante."

She lifted Damica Cosetta's card, blew gently on the back, and tucked it back into her tome.

Suzette led me by the hand through the shadows of the dining hall and we slipped out one of the doors at the back, the sun warming my body as we moved into an open-air corridor housing a row of identical doors. Suzette moved swiftly and I struggled to keep pace with her. As we rounded a corner, one of the doors slid open and a woman in a mustard yellow scarf slipped out, disheveled, reeking of spirits and unsteady on her feet. Suzette did not give her a second glance and continued onward, but I clung to a stone pillar, waiting for her to pass. I tilted my head back and let out a long breath, willing my pulse to slow as my hands instinctively found my pendant.

Suzette looked over her shoulder and doubled back to

retrieve me. "Stay close, cherissima. And lift your head while you walk. You look as though you are in mourning," Suzette lectured.

"I do not think I can do this. Did you see her?"

"The lady of the evening?" Suzette tilted her head. "That is not our purpose here. We are Damica. Dignified. Remember this, Laurel. If the general needs to be reminded of your standing, he will have to face my tongue."

She trailed her finger across the hematite stone at the center of her brooch. "I will not leave you alone with him, not for a moment. I will not even blink."

Suzette led me to one of the palace's wooden doors and she rapped loudly, three times calling the general. I lurked behind her while she meandered by the door. No sound stirred from behind the door, no shadows whisked by the bottom of the door.

"Perhaps he does not wish to be disturbed," I said to Suzette. I took a few steps back, edging into the open-air corridor.

"Pah! There is no chance he would miss the opportunity to see you." Suzette stepped up to the door again and knocked, to no avail. "Perhaps he is resting."

I looked to my feet and a strange sensation set over me, all of a sudden—strange because it felt malevolent, but it was not the litha. It smelled of acrid smoke and tumbled over my face, clogging my senses. A breath came upon the top of my head like a bright tongue of flame.

I spun around and came face to face with Grimstaad.

His sharp features were no longer pointed and angry; like a sculpture, they had been smoothed, worked into an expression that would not cause alarm.

"Laurel Aleandri," he mouthed quietly.

He had been watching us. Stalking us like prey.

I could not shake the thought from my mind. Grimstaad lowered himself to kneel tenderly, clenching his jaw as he bent one knee. "Do not be frightened of me. I am known as General Vitis Grimstaad. I asked your vedova to bring you, so I could see you for myself, speak with you."

Grimstaad extended a bandaged hand and I glanced frantically at Suzette.

"Ah!" she cried. Her heels snapped across the floor as she came and grasped my hand. "General, she stays with me at all times. Laurel is quite sensitive; we would not want to overwhelm her."

"Mm." Grimstaad's cheek twitched and for a moment his face lost its placidity. He studied me with a spark of excitement, the muscles in his cheek, his lips straining to keep his expression together. The vendrake numbed me, but it did not numb him—the ferocity he kept caged in his heart paced back and forth, yearning to break free and leap at me.

"I am tired, cherissima," I whispered, tugging at Suzette's sleeve.

"Filia, I will not keep you from your sleep for long. You have my word." He grimaced, lifting himself upright. "Come into my chambers, both of you."

Grimstaad pushed open the door and Suzette and I followed him into his chambers. I let go of Suzette's hand and covered my mouth, taking in the enormity of the room—it was larger than our entire entryway in the market, larger, even than the Lunare's shared quarters. It was adorned not with knick-knacks and herb cuttings, nor black sheets and boards; a chandelier cast light into the space, shining upon a vanity and a writing desk. Each held two brass candlesticks for extra light at night, should Grimstaad fancy strike to peer into the mirror or pen a letter, during dark and moonless hours. A tapestry—two boats on a green lake—decorated the wall across from a four-poster bed, plump with more pillows and bedding than I had ever seen, with curtains that could be drawn for privacy. I wished such a bed existed in the Accademia to allow my struggles with the litha to be private from Bethany and the vedovas. Grimstaad crossed the room and a candle cast a dim light on his cheek; its soft light revealed a cluster of scabbed flesh beneath his beard.

I thought of tugging on Suzette and whispering of it to her, but thought better of it. The embers of curiosity would ignite in her eyes, and she would keep us longer in Grimstaad's chambers, pushing deeper into matters best left alone. Her appetite to draw more information from Grimstaad—beyond Prince Brennan—would grow larger than Grimstaad's chambers, expanding until it reached the size of the palace, and even then, it could not be contained. I did not wish to know any of it.

Grimstaad lowered himself onto his bed, sighing. He patted the spot beside him.

"Filia, please sit."

"Thank you, general, but we will remain standing." Suzette swooped behind me and threaded her arm through mine, gripping it tightly.

"You may stand. I invited Laurel to sit." Grimstaad curled his fingers around the blankets, kneading a small lump into the bed.

"Shall I remind you of our arrangement? One question for her, and then you tell me about the prince."

"I remind you, vedova, I do not need to tell you anything." Grimstaad scowled. He patted the blankets, flattening the lump. "Have her come to me. Alone."

I threw my gaze to Suzette. What does he want with me?

"Go on," Suzette said, motioning with a little wave. "I'm right here if you need me."

I took my place beside him and hung my head, focusing my gaze on my knees. He placed a hand on my thigh and I yelped.

"General," Suzette warned.

"I am not a patient man." He patted my thigh and I crossed my legs, turning away from him.

"Ahhh, filia. So proper and pure." He adjusted his weight and edged away from me. "I will not order you to open yourself until we are wed."

"I have not accepted your bid for her," Suzette interjected.

"Silence, vedova!" Grimstaad barked.

He brushed my hair behind my ear and I tensed at his touch, shrinking my neck into my shoulders. Suzette raised her hand to her brooch and began to object, but Grimstaad spoke over her.

"Laurel, what I seek now is your gift." He stroked my cheek with the back of his fingers and I cringed, taking rapid and uneven breaths.

"I was not always a general. Before I was Deos Tactigit— long before, when I was less than even a captain in the high guard—I was merely an enforcer. A patrolman in the low guard—a simple man. A virtuous man," he said. "I need to hear it from you. Feel within, and tell me I am that man."

Suzette raised an eyebrow and she pressed her lip between her teeth. "Go ahead, Laurel."

Lowering my head, I picked up my pendant and pressed the moonstone to the center of my forehead. Lightly, I rocked myself back and forth, trying to shake both the stupor of the vendrake and the sharp exchange between Grimstaad and my cherissima from my mind. I ran my fingers over my scalp and pushed my palms hard against my temples, focusing on the sensation of Grimstaad's finger on my ear—listening. His pulse was hollow, haunted—a chasm of stillness. I pushed with more might and the void within became clearer, like the moon on a clear night.

Once he may have been the patrolman he described, but I could find nothing of it in his heart—only an echo of what had once been. The vendrake numbed my ilex so that confessions and truths came through clouded like the tea itself—but it did not shroud my gift in its entirety. If there were truly any remnants of the patrolman in General Grimstaad's heart, I would have been able to lift it—even just a corner.

My chest tightened as I tried one more time: reaching to Grimstaad's hairline, fixing the pad of my thumb at the top of his forehead. I drew it down, down—past his eyebrow and the thin skin of his eyelid, following the curve of his cheek. I stopped at the corner of his lips and brushed my thumb across them tenderly, his breath warming my hand as it passed.

I drew nothing from him. His heart was as barren as the eye of the serpent he wore on his breast.

"Signore," I whispered. "Forgive me. I cannot find that which you seek."

General Grimstaad's controlled expression cracked, a shadow of surprise crawling across his face. His lips pulled back, his teeth flashing in the candlelight, his worry-lines transforming into creases of deep despair. Before I grasped what was brewing within, he lunged for me. I screamed and tried to leap from the bed, but he seized me by the shoulders and shook my body violently, desperately.

"Do it again! Look harder! Search deeper!"

My neck strained back and forth, clumps of hair tumbling over my eyes, and the heat from Grimstaad's flesh seared through my skull, boiling my thoughts. Choking on their pungent taste, I cried, "There is nothing, general! Nothing! Your heart is but a shadow of what it once was!"

"Let her go!" Suzette reached for his arm and Grimstaad turned and swung it hard, knocking her to the floor. I screamed, clamping my hands over my mouth.

Slowly, Suzette came to her feet, a smear of blood staining the corner of her lips. Her gray eyes darkened with defiance and she cast an obstinate grin at Grimstaad, wiping the blood on her sleeve.

"Laurel is right about you," she spat, her voice bending, struggling under the weight of her venom. "You are a hideous monster."

Grimstaad released me and roared, thrashing as he leaped from the bed. He reached to his belt and unsheathed a knife. Flickers of low flame reflected from its mirrored blade as he cushioned its handle in his palm, holding its point to Suzette.

"Stop! Please!" I cried. The general ignored me, his scowl twisting into a grin while he backed Suzette against the tapestry with the boats.

"Hideous, hm?" He broke into a rueful laugh. The tip of his blade met Suzette under her chin, and he lifted her head so that she gazed straight into his eyes.

With the turn of his wrist, he pressed his blade deep into Suzette's flesh, splitting her skin from chin to cheekbone.

I thought I screamed, but I am not certain. From that moment forward, my life was no longer my own; I belonged to the litha. The demon-whispers were demon-shrieks, and they careened through my blood stronger than vendrake. I saw myself stand; I was aware that I was the one swinging my legs over the edge of Grimstaad's bed—but it was not me. My feet landed on the floor and my body shifted into an upright position. Litha. I spent so many nights cowering beneath the rafters, wedging my head between my elbows. I squeezed my pendant and prayed, took bitter sips of vendrake and allowed the sparkle to fade from my eyes. I did anything, everything to keep it from swallowing me, forcing me to holler and wail until my throat gave out, to thrash and claw and bite at my own Papa—who had shown nothing but love for his broken daughter.

I was tired of fighting—so tired, bone tired—and I let go.

My arm slid across the vanity beside Grimstaad's bed; and I felt a chill on my fingers as they circled the base of a brass candlestick. A breath passed through my lips and the flame dissolved into smoke. One foot in front of the other, small even steps brought me behind Grimstaad. My arm curved back and then lurched forward, the brass candlestick connecting with the back of Grimstaad's skull.

And then I was holding her. Combing her hair, pressing her bloodied cheek to my gown. My arm slid up behind her shoulders. My cherissima. She had sung to me, soothed me in my darkest hours—believing that she could temper the litha, scrub it from me like a stain. Oh, on those beautiful nights, we had both fallen to the linguina d'argent—believing that the litha was something that could be driven away.

I had never understood myself or the litha, and I never made an attempt to do so. I always trusted that others knew more, studied more, lived longer, that they had a firmer grasp on what it was and what should be done about it—how best to care for me. Had I made the effort myself, would I have recognized this as a lie I told myself, both to make my life easier as well as theirs?

If I had glanced up, even once, while holding Suzette's hand in the Catene chambers, would I have recognized that the demon-whispers still perched in the rafters, that they were as enchanted as I by her nocturne, waltzing in the darkness to her voice?

Through my body, now, the litha sang to Suzette—crooning while she wept, her blood drying, sticking against my skin. It was not a silver song, a melodious tune for a sweet lamb: the litha sang through blood and brass.

It followed us both in demon-whispers while we limped out of Grimstaad's chambers.

A UNION OF MONSTERS

For weeks after we returned from the palace, Suzette could not speak. The official story at the Accademia was that she slipped in the kitchen while holding her knife; only Headmistress Elan and I had full knowledge of the events that unfolded.

Under the litha's control, I had walked Suzette back through the palace's corridors, and I kept to the shadows as well as I could. The litha seemed more at ease in the darkness; and it helped me to carry Suzette. When we reached the kitchen, Bethany was at the threshold. She turned pale, dropped her tray, and ran to fetch Vedova Oriana in an instant. I cradled Suzette in a corner; we sat upon sacks of flour, dust stirring up around us, sticking like soot to the smears of blood on our gowns and our skin–and we waited.

Headmistress Elan herself swept into the kitchen to collect us, Vedova Oriana following close behind. Together they pried Suzette from me, and I felt the litha escaping through my fingertips as I relinquished Suzette to their care. Vedova Oriana hurried Bethany and myself into a carriage, our caper to the palace finished. Our carriage clattered, shook the three of us about. Across from me Bethany, ashen and shivering, clutched her pendant while Vedova Oriana sat stoic beside her. I stretched my body across the empty space Suzette should have occupied, resting my head in my arms. The litha had faded, entirely from my body—and I buried my face in the plush seating of the carriage, the cushion catching my tears while I drifted into a soft, red sleep.

I waited, at night, in the Catene chambers, but Suzette did not come.

In the morning, I dressed again in my girlish gown, free of the scent of iron and flour, and I found my place in the queue for breakfast with my sister-filia. In our single-file line we walked toward the dining hall, and I peeked over my shoulder, several times, in an attempt to spot Suzette's tangles of wild hair, but she was absent from the queue.

I found her in the dining hall, dressed in a fresh pale-pink gown, setting tables with the other vedovas. I nearly fell to my knees when I gazed upon her: she looked nothing like before. Long, white bandages covered her from chin to cheek, circling her head like streamers. Her dark curls had been crushed against her head, one eye hidden in its entirety by bandages.

The litha bubbled in my mouth, dark and warm, and I tasted the flash of silver from the previous night, the blood.

"Suzette."

A dull gray eye shifted in my direction before darting away. I broke free from the line and ran toward Suzette, but she turned her back as I approached, moving hurriedly into a corridor.

Give it time. My Papa would have advised me that time heals wounds, but the cut that Suzette bore would not heal. Grimstaad looked her in the eyes while he dragged his blade across her face. He moved his blade with deftness, confidence.

Suzette said nothing and withdrew to her chambers as often as was allowed. Her eyes no longer flared with curiosity and she sat hunched, her shoulders drooped like a wilted flower. She played a dangerous game, and lost terribly—the bandages and what lay beneath, a reminder of her failure—on display for others. This was true humiliation, and for all our time together in the Accademia—I found myself absent of any skill to bring solace to her heart.

I had no choice but to return to the vendrake to temper the litha. The acrid taste on my tongue and swallowing it had, somehow, become more unbearable than it had been before Suzette had come into my life. My heart went numb, my tongue became useless and limp, and I faded into silence. Days, first, and then weeks, passed in a blur.

Worse, still, was the day Headmistress Elan called both Suzette and I to the Lunare's room in the learning hall. She rested her hands on the lectern at the front of the room and Suzette sat at the lecture table alone, head bowed, her bandages obscuring her profile. She reminded me of the rose at my bedside after Mama's passing: silent, withering from within—one deft stroke of steel having separated it from the other blooms on the bush.

"Sit, Laurel. It is time we discuss your future," Headmistress Elan said. She clasped her hands, impatience sparkling on her jeweled fingers while I situated myself beside Suzette. I peeked at my cherissima, trying to catch her eye, but Suzette stared blankly at the table, unmoved.

Headmistress Elan cleared her throat. "I have kept you filia shielded from the realities of unrest, war, famine, terror. Outside these walls, these run rampant in our world, but as you have been here, my sole focus has been training you in your gift."

She crossed the room as she spoke, circling behind me. She slid one hand on my shoulders and the other on Suzette's.

"Filia—ah, my filia. This is the last time I shall address you as such. Today, you are no longer filia. Vedova Suzette. Damica Laurel." She squeezed each of our shoulders and released us. Her crimson coat swept back in front of us, and she clasped her hands once more.

"Trionfi has been at unease for some time now. We have an opposing force that has been growing in size—and it has infiltrated our borders. If given the chance, these criminals, these . . . *banale*, they would see to it that we are all executed. You and I. The vedovas. Every filia in the Accademia, as well as King Armando, Queen Norina and the entire high court. All of us, swept up in fire, hanging in chains, or beheaded."

A harrowed look crossed Headmistress Elan's face; each word she spoke rang true in my heart. My pulse quickened in my neck, and I touched my tongue to the top of my mouth; it felt dry, cracked. I reached for Suzette to take her hand, but she pulled away.

The headmistress continued. "Prince Brennan's disappearance has Trionfi on edge. Damica Laurel, I am told both you and Bethany sensed the tension in the dining hall. You were more sensitive to it than Bethany; your ilex is much more powerful. The prince vanishing as he did . . . it is much worse than you know. Without an heir to the throne, we are on the cusp of lawlessness. It is crucial that Brennan be found. Soon. It could be explained away at the beginning, but after six months of secrecy, with no sign of the prince . . . the signores and signoras of the court have their eyes on the throne. They are beginning to treat each other with suspicion, looking at each other, and at King Armando and Queen Norina's backs, for the best place to stick a knife."

She unclasped her hands, moving with purpose back to the lectern at the front of the room. My ilex rattled beneath my sternum, shaking my ribs. The hairs on my arms stood upright, as if some demon had blown with night-breath upon my skin. I hugged my chest, stroking my arms to keep warm.

But my ilex told me something was wrong—something beyond the headmistress's disturbing tale of restless eyes and dark temptations. It was something else entirely, and I writhed in my seat, trying to shake the feeling loose.

From beneath the lectern, Headmistress Elan retrieved

a book. It was not one from our library, made of leather and embossed with a simple design in the corners. Her book appeared to be of much greater importance; silver stems swirled around the cover, burgeoning with textured blooms. At its center, a milk-white stone matched the one that rested at my heart. I touched my pendant while Headmistress Elan lay the book in front of Suzette and myself, lightly flipping through the pages. Names lettered at the top, and boxes decorated in ornate swirls fluttered past us while the headmistress worked her fingers through the book. Every few pages, an illustrated card wedged in the spine stalled her search—fresh, eager faces smiling back at me, each adorned in different styles of crimson that my Mama wore in the card hanging above our hearth.

Headmistress Elan's fingers stopped at a page with my name at the top, written with bold, ornate loops. Beneath it, my birthdate rested in a box, my mother and father's names penned below it. The ink had started to fade, turn brown. Two fresh, black sentences appeared in the box below. My chest constricted at each intersection of the pen-on-parchment.

General Vitis Grimstaad, husband. Marriage by proxy to Madame Isolde Exley.

Today's date glared at me beneath Grimstaad's name.

No. My whole body began to convulse; my pendant jangled against my breast. I could not slow the terror-pangs coursing through me; they forced themselves through my bones, my back, each spasm lurching me forward. I grasped Suzette's arm and she did not pull back. She drew heavy, labored breaths through her bandages.

My nails bit into Suzette's forearm and I squeezed my eyes shut. So that was what Headmistress Elan meant, calling me Damica Laurel. My bride-price had been met, and she sold me.

"Damica Laurel, calm yourself. I have done what is best for you—and best for Trionfi. As you are going to be close to Grimstaad, you will learn all of this soon." She swept behind me and squeezed my shoulders with such force that I cried out.

"Do not repeat what I am about to say to anybody else. Trust no one. We do not want to end up with our heads on pikes. If any of this leaks outside this room, there will be rioting, anarchy—and everyone in the Accademia will be dead."

She released me and I sighed, slumping onto the table. Headmistress Elan clamped her hand around the back of Suzette's neck.

"As for you," she said. "You are included in this because I know you would coerce it out of Laurel, regardless. If I hear that you've spoken so much as one word of this, I will make you wish the general finished what he started with you."

Suzette let out a muffled cry and I winced, clenching my jaw. I shifted my gaze, peering outside at the mountains.

"General Grimstaad is one of the Deos Tactigit—Trionfi's venerable high guard, our elite warriors, our defenders. The official word is that the Deos Tactigit is engaged in war against those who seek to destroy us. Grimstaad was injured in battle and sent back to the Localita di Fiore to recover from his wounds."

Headmistress Elan wrung her hands, twirling her rings around her fingers. "The reality is far different. The Deos Tactigit is no more. We are exceedingly fortunate that Grimstaad survived. Among the generals, he is the hunter—the one known for tracking down *banale*, bringing them to justice. He will heal from his wounds and be sent back to battle. Only, he will have one of Trionfi's best tools at his disposal, to hunt those hounds and slaughter them."

The headmistress patted me on the back, a sense of hope, pride flowing from her palm to my body. "Who needs to interrogate prisoners when you can just rip information from their souls?"

I gasped, lurching forward. It was as though she had punched out my heart. How had she known? Thin shadows crept up my arms, living—swarming, exhaling their cold breath on my skin. I had always carried the ability to claw deep into memories, bore down into souls. The litha told me when I was a child, and I kept it a secret, a knot tied deep in my body for no one to unfurl. For my first years in the Accademia, I thought I may be the only one who carried such a ravenous venom within, until Headmistress Elan plucked the portrait of the late Damica Cosetta from her book.

We were the same—the litha twined around our spirits like a vine, rooting itself deep. If we pressed too deep with our ilex, or searched too frantically, recklessly—we would pass the litha to others.

Once, my mama had shed tears for what I was. Did she see this twisted version of me in her tea leaves? Had she been taught that some of the Lunare could inflict the litha upon others?

Suzette protested against her bandages and Headmistress Elan threw her arms to the side, exasperated. "Suzette, I told you what she was when you started playing your little games, did I not? I warned you about Laurel. The damage she is capable of inflicting. Forming a deep bond with a Lunare ends in a chasm of heartache—especially with this one."

I withdrew my hand from Suzette and lay my head in my arms, sinking into the table. Even if she denied it, I knew it to be true. I bore the weight of responsibility for Suzette's heartache; I held blame for her disfigurement. It was not she who wielded the true power in our union; like a lamb lost in a meadow, I had baited her. She came to me because of my struggle against the litha—and it had fooled her into thinking she was in control, with her linguina d'argent.

My thoughts whirled back to the day in the palace: Grimstaad's amber eyes boring into my back, his hand on my thigh, his blade against Suzette's chin . . .

I squeezed my lip between my teeth until I tasted blood.

If I had not told her what my ilex revealed about Grimstaad's connection to Brennan, she never would have spoken to the general. None of this would have happened if I simply refused to accompany her to his chambers. It was my fault.

Were it not for my presence, my cherissima would still walk through life with dignity: her chin held high, shoulders pushed back, flashing a sly grin from beneath her wild curls.

I wished I had never met Suzette d'Isparza. Never once had she suspected she had fallen to me—and while I had protested her actions, I had, selfishly, remained by her side. I let her fall, spiraling blindly into peril and madness with me.

I understood why Headmistress Elan deemed it fitting to sell me to Grimstaad. We were a union of monsters.

"There, there." Headmistress Elan smoothed my back. "All of this ugliness will soon be behind us. General Grimstaad has taken up residence at the Tenuta d'Exley at the southern end of Trionfi. It is best for him to be away from the palace—the pressures, the urgency to return to the battlefield. They will not allow him to heal. Madame Exley is a skilled healer—a curandria. She teaches the medics, on occasion, in the back wing of the Accademia. Her teas are potent and she mixes some of the most popular salves in Trionfi. Grimstaad will heal quickly under her care. You will be departing with her today, traveling with her to your new home and husband."

I wrenched away from Headmistress Elan, folding my hand into a fist. "No!" I cried, pushing my chair back. "I will not do it. You cannot force me to wed that monster!"

Headmistress Elan pushed a smile on her lips, running her hand through my hair.

"There, Damica Laurel. Calm yourself—unless you wish to be calmed."

It was not an idle threat. I dug my nails into the flesh of my palm and remained silent.

"Better." The headmistress pushed my chair back into place. "I told you when you first arrived at the Accademia: a Damica must do what she is instructed, even if it brings her pain. I understand your concern: General Grimstaad is a hard man; his heart is like stone . . . but he has a fondness for you, Laurel. His eyes soften when he speaks of you."

There was an uncomfortable bend to her words, one which sent my ilex into a frenzy. I could not pinpoint the cause, but some whisper of deceit perched in the shadow of her lips. I had grown sensitive to such a ruse, growing up amid echoes of "Viper," dark whispers concealed in the mouths of my sister-filia when they spoke of me. Though she meant for her words to soothe me, Headmistress Elan's words were nothing like Suzette's. They seemed contrived, practiced, as if she were delivering a eulogy at a rival's funeral. She brushed my hair from my forehead and began separating it at my scalp.

"When you arrive at the Tenuta d'Exley, your duty as wife is to settle Grimstaad's heart. He needs your soft touch, your pureness. His heart bears the scars of war and he mourns his fallen. Call him ammorante. Open your heart to him, even when he is foul tempered. You may bear the marks of his cruelty for some time, but you will be drinking vendrake for the litha—and it will help. I've put in word with Madame Exley to brew it strong."

I shivered at her words and she touched my cheek. A teardrop splashed on the table; I had not realized I was crying.

"There, Laurel." Headmistress Elan continued to work her hands through my hair, weaving strands together in a braid, giving it a firm tug as she moved down my scalp. "His fists will relent when you conceive—and it is your duty to do so. Do not resist him. Place a small piece of vendrake under your tongue, if you must. Grimstaad's mind needs to be clear when he returns to battle; he cannot be preoccupied with winning your affection. We will lose this war if you spurn him. Remind him of his virility and give him peace, knowledge that his bloodline will not end."

My throat swelled and I wheezed, trying to pull a breath through my teeth. I could not do it—any of it. It was too heavy of a burden to bear on my shoulders—and it felt wrong, so wrong in my chest. Even though I was a monster just the same as Grimstaad, I could never surrender my body to one who felt no remorse for what he had done to Suzette. A signore who had seen me and decided I was his to use—my ilex, my body. I could not give myself to one who would strike me on a whim and expect me to call him my ammorante. I imagined his hand on my shoulder, like Damica Cosetta's general had placed his onto hers, in their marriage portrait. In my mind, Grimstaad would be marching me into some dungeon while I was bloated with child, positioning me in front of criminals of war. At his command I would burrow into them, full force, shredding their minds to ribbons while I bore their screams and curses. It would be worst for those who tried to resist.

The thought made me want to wretch.

Headmistress Elan finished braiding my hair and she patted my back. "Rise, now. We must get you ready."

The litha howled in my chest, demon-whispers pounding in my head. *Do it. Do it to her!* The flesh at her throat danced in the light, like a wrinkle of lace, beneath the clasp of her coat.

Make her suffer!

I clasped both hands over my ears.

"Bid farewell to Suzette."

"No!" I pulled my lips into a snarl, jumping to my feet. "I won't do it! I won't!"

"Calm yourself, Laurel. You will only be apart for a short time. When you conceive, I will send Suzette to tend to you, as you will no longer be able to use the vendrake."

The scenario cut through my mind. Grimstaad, scanning Suzette's lip and cheek, his lips creeping into a satisfied grin. Shivers ran up and down my skin, and I struggled to keep my legs from shaking. A growl rose first in my throat, passing through my teeth and I could taste it—the bitterness, my desire for her blood.

"I should surrender to it, let it make me a monster," I rasped. I extended my arm forward, pointing squarely at Headmistress Elan's heart. "You are a monster, as well."

Headmistress Elan glowered. The features of her face contorted into something ugly, sinister—savage. "Suzette, restrain her."

Wordlessly, Suzette stirred. She reached forward and grasped both my wrists forcefully. I let out a sharp cry and wrestled to regain control of my arms, but she did not let go. Headmistress Elan leaned in close to me, the cloying scent of flowers filling my nose.

"There, Laurel. All will be well."

She pried my jaw open and slipped something in my mouth.

Bitterness blossomed on my tongue and I gagged on the putrid taste of vendrake as my senses dulled.

It had been foolish to fight. Fortune had never favored me; I could not defy my fate. Eyelids heavy, my chin sank to my chest, and I soon pressed my cheek to the cold wooden surface of the table.

∞

I came to in darkness: my sheets familiar over my body: soft and black, the fabric tumbling into my vision while my mind whirled into painful consciousness. I touched my tongue to the remnants of vendrake in my mouth. The juices had melted away, leaving only a small, hardened husk behind. I sat up and my blood pounded against my head. The vendrake took no mercy on my body, and I questioned whether Headmistress Elan coated it in something more potent. I pushed my palms against my eyes and squeezed gently to ease the throb restricting my thoughts. My sleeves fell down my arms and my heart jumped; they were longer, smoother than those of my gown. I cracked my eyes open and discovered I was no longer in the dress I had been wearing while I was talking to Suzette. During my sleep, I had been fitted into a red robe, ablaze like rubies against my black bedding. A pattern of peonies crawled up my arms—just like in my Mama's marriage portrait hanging above our hearth. I brought my knees to my chest; my body was wrapped in a white gown which tied at the waist.

I smoothed my hands over my clothing. Who had undressed me during my sleep and slipped me into a travel gown—had it been Suzette or Headmistress Elan herself? Or perhaps I was passed from one vedova to another, each of them pulling my arm through one sleeve of my marriage coat. My braid fell over my shoulder and I yanked it loose, raking my fingers through the tight criss-cross of hair on my scalp. I was still fluffing my hair when my chamber door cracked open. I bit my lip, forcing my breath to stand still.

They had come for me.

"Laurel?" Bethany peeked her head through the doorway, her pendant dangling below her chin. "Quickly! Rise! We must go."

I relaxed my shoulders, tension rolling out of me. "*Diosemma*, Bethany, you frightened me half to death!"

She sat on her bed beside me and hunched forward, exhaling, closing her eyes. "Suzette sent me to find you. So, you are aware, she is even more capricious than usual. She is so difficult, Laurel—I wish Headmistress Elan would assign me to a different vedova, one who did not give such unreasonable tasks."

I tilted my head, pressing my hands to my eyes again to numb the ache. "What did she say to you?"

Bethany glanced in both directions over her shoulder and leaned in close. "We must leave. Now."

I blinked at her. "Are you mad?"

"You, calling me mad. Now I have heard it all." Bethany snorted. "I was passing by the learning hall when

Suzette grabbed me, all of a sudden. She started muttering something through her bandages."

"What did she say?"

Bethany thumbed her pendant uncomfortably. "I haven't a clue. I had to use my ilex to understand her."

"Bethany, *what did she say?*"

She glanced over her shoulder again and leaned in close. "Everything. Grimstaad. Your marriage . . . Madame Exley."

She reached for my forearm, grazing my flesh with her fingertips, and I pulled back, arching my spine.

"Calm yourself, Laurel! I am not going to hurt you," Bethany said. "Suzette told me to use my ilex on you, since I have seen Madame Exley. She made me watch her from a window overlooking the Accademia's atrium. If I share her with you, you will see her face and we can know her location."

My brow folded in bewilderment. "You can do that?"

"You *can't?*" Her lips parted in surprise. We stared at each other for a moment in uncomfortable silence. "Never mind what we can and cannot do. Please, take my hand. You need to see who is coming for you."

I threaded my fingers through hers and a flash of red emerged in my mind—a haze, at the beginning, like a sheer curtain obscuring sunlight. Two pulsing blue eyes emerged from the shapeless form, which soon grew a slightly pointed nose, small lips. Madame Exley unfolded in my mind like a portrait, layer upon layer revealing warm brown hair, a body closer to mine in its shape than Suzette's, a peony tucked within a thin nest of braids. A few wrinkles of age tugged at her eyes and the sides of her mouth. She was stoic, humorless in my vision, her expression unchanging: the pulse of her eyes ebbing and flowing as she stared, straight and unblinking, into nothing. My stomach lurched with unease, queasiness bubbling up my throat. She was a night-demon come to life, one who had stepped beyond the realm of shadow. Surrounding her, I could just make out the shapes and colors of four gray-blue tunics, similar to Grimstaad's in color. Enforcers. Madame Exley had not come to collect me alone. Should I resist or try to run, I would be easily restrained, outrun, or caught.

I pulled my hand free from Bethany. "I am beginning to feel ill."

"My apologies, Laurel—it is an effect of my ilex. I am still working on it." Bethany said. "Hold your pendant and say something to calm yourself. It will help."

I did as she instructed, mouthing the words of the old tongue: *daremi pacce.* A panicked thought flashed through my mind.

"Does my Papa know she is taking me?"

Bethany scrunched her face, blinked. "What?"

"Exley. Grimstaad. My father does not know."

"He did not meet with the headmistress and sign for you?" Bethany asked.

I shook my head, no. Bethany's countenance changed suddenly, her spine straightening, confusion hardening into disapproval. She lifted a pair of slippers at the foot of my bed and tossed them at me. "We must go. Now. Quickly, Laurel!"

She yanked me from my bed while I was still working to wedge my shoes over my heels. Together, we clamored out of my chambers, down the stairs, spilling into the hallway that led to the courtyard.

"There is a passage in the back to the main corridor. We will take it and turn toward the southern wing—the medics are studying outside of the Accademia today," Bethany said.

"Bethany, how do you know this?" My words were choppy, abrupt, and I gasped for breath between each.

"My ilex. I was told it pairs well with navigation. Maps."

It struck me how little she and I knew about one another and our gifts. Though we shared the same bedchambers for years and sat in the same lectures, I had not known any pairing of the ilex besides my own. I shook my head to free it further from my vendrake daze, pumping my legs to keep up with Bethany. We passed through corridors that appeared identical—stone wall after long stone wall. Bethany ignored some passageways and took us through others. I admired her gift: her sense of direction rang clear in the halls. I envisioned it on the seas, steering fishing boats clear of storms, or in the mountains—perhaps saving the lives of a lost aedituus like my father. Hers was a steadfast gift, bringing livelihood and reunion to the people of Trionfi.

Meanwhile, mine was anchored to the litha, and it called for the headmistress's blood. It was no wonder she kept me slumbering and sedated, whereupon I had little sense of what occurred around me.

I stopped for a moment, planting my hand against the wall, struggling for breath.

"Faster, Laurel," Bethany panted, turning toward me. "We're almost there."

It happened before I could reach out to warn her. Bethany turned and collided with a young signore—a percussion of books falling to the floor, pages beating the stones like a flurry of wings.

"Ah!" A male voice bellowed with surprise. I clamped my hands over my mouth while Bethany straightened herself, dusting off her skirt.

"I am deeply sorry, signore," she muttered. She bowed politely and extended her hand in apology. The signore's brow furrowed, but he accepted her hand. While they shook, I smiled at them and knelt to collect his books.

"Allow me to help," Bethany offered, and I heard her voice bend with falseness. With the books stacked once again in his arms, Bethany brushed past him, murmuring another apology. When he was gone, Bethany narrowed her eyes. She pulled me around a corner and clamped her hands on my shoulders.

"The door at the end of this corridor leads to the

courtyard," Bethany said. "You must pass the fountain. Make your way all the way to the back of the gardens. From there, climb the trellis—all the way up—and lower yourself to the other side of the wall. Slip into the woodland. Stay out of sight. There is a trail that leads east. It will bring you to a town called Reveille. Are you listening, Laurel?"

I blinked, my cheeks wet. "I cannot go without Suzette."

"She will be fine. When you reach safety, you will write to her, yes?"

I nodded my head weakly. She threaded her fingers through mine and they vibrated slowly, striking chords of lament when they brushed against my skin. At the end of the corridor, a small, wooden door awaited us. Her palms felt heavy, sorrowful in my hold.

"All I have ever tried to be is loyal, obedient—just like Headmistress Elan wanted. I've always done what she and the vedovas have asked. Even Suzette." Her eyes glistened with tears.

"Bethany," I whispered.

"I worked my entire life to be dutiful so that they would select me for courtship. I wanted so badly to go to the palace, meet a signore and be swept up into the life of a signora of the high court. And then, the day before we are supposed to go, you showed up. You—Viper, the unwieldy one—you came into the conscription queue, threatening to take away everything I worked for. Something inside of me broke. I saw my dream beginning to vanish . . . I tried to keep my feelings inside, but I failed."

The litha had taken her. It must have caused her such shame, sorrow, regret—and fear. It could come for any of us, even a Lunare such as Bethany, who had succeeded in containing it.

I leaned in close to Bethany, squeezing her hand. Her lip jutted and her voice broke. "I was furious when I was sent home from the palace because of you and Suzette. I did everything that was asked of me, but you two ruined it for me, with your recklessness." Her hands shook and she balled one into a fist and reached to her pendant with the other.

The sting of tears pricked my eyes. I had not considered how my actions had hurt Bethany and taken her away from her dream.

"I am sorry," I whispered.

She heaved a sigh, grew quiet and moved to the door at the end of the hall, throwing it open with a groan. The light of the early afternoon spilled into the hallway; birds chattered outside, calling me forward.

I flashed Bethany a thin smile. "Thank you for guiding me, despite . . . everything." The smile dropped from my face and I brushed past her, moving toward the light.

"Wait," Bethany called. I turned while she tucked her chin into the crook of her elbow, a strand of hair falling over her eye. Blotches of pink and red spread across her usually colorless skin, her cheeks flushed. Teardrops clung to the corners of her eyes and she blinked, her long lashes brushing her skin like the sweep of a drape.

"I trusted them, Laurel. Headmistress Elan, the vedovas—all of them. They broke all the rules, arranging your marriage in secret. Everything they said—everything we have ever been taught . . . was it truly a lie?" Clutching her pendant, Bethany touched her hand to her heart. "I am Lunare, too. It could have been me, sold and then sent away, with no one to question what was happening. And I would have obliged; I would have done whatever the headmistress had asked of me. Infuriating as I find her, Suzette was brash enough to challenge it and concoct this mad, half-cooked plan for you . . ."

"She would have done the same for you," I said.

Bethany tightened her grip on her pendant, pressing her thumb hard against the moonstone. "I always believed Suzette to be an opportunist: doing what she must to save her own skin, using who she will to carry out her schemes. But conniving as she is, she . . . fought this iniquity. For you. For all of us."

Bethany sniffled, wiping her eyes on her sleeve. A bitter expression, almost a half-smile, folded her cheek and she walked to me, lifting my arms. She turned my palms upward and placed a small coin purse in them.

"I took this from the signore I bumped into. I wish I could say Suzette told me to do it, but . . . it was my own ruse. Look, I am becoming more like her! Won't she be proud?" She let out a peal of sarcastic laughter and folded my fingers around the pouch. "If you hurry, you may be able to reach Reveille before nightfall and hire a carriage. Do not tell me where you go from there."

I threw my arms around Bethany—my adversary turned ally in these strange times. Her arms tightened around my back and I pressed my lips to her cheek.

"*Arrivederci*, sister-Bethany."

She clasped my hands tightly. "Be quick, sister-Laurel."

I pulled away from her and she thrust me into the garden. As it shuddered closed, the small wooden door clipped the hem of my coat.

PART TWO

They all saw me as a weapon to be leveraged—a means to gain that which their hearts desired.

THE OTHER SIDE OF THE WALL

It was all backward, turned on its head, and I did not know how to make sense of it all. The midday sun pierced my eyes, and I cupped my hand over my forehead to shield them. The babbling of a tiered fountain drew my attention. The courtyard was absent of people; my only company was a scattering of birds chattering in shrill, staccato notes amid the grass. Inviting me into the courtyard was a carpet of pink and white flowers—row upon row of flowers stretching before me with leaves pruned and colorful heads pointed skyward. Beyond them, twists of wisteria crisscrossed the far wall of the courtyard, their knots and blooms so thick that I could hardly see the white of the stones behind them.

I remained pressed against the Accademia's door, the chill of it all creeping up the small of my back. In the Damica's courtyard, the walls sparkled in the sunlight, but here in this obscure corner of the Accademia, the courtyard was a cold, looming behemoth, washed in shadows. I thought of my own garden at home. When I sat with my mama, I never felt cold, even when the night wind turned bitter. Mama and I drank tea and huddled together in blankets, gazing at the sky.

I wished Mama were still alive and I could speak to her about all that had transpired: Grimstaad, with his eager hand on my leg, desperation burning in his amber eyes while he demanded I find the long-lost heart of the patrolman he once was. I shivered, thinking of the hatred and vindication carved into the creases of his face while he mutilated Suzette, in both flesh and spirit. And Bethany, ah—my sister-Lunare who had been so callous toward me in the courtship queue, now aiding me in my escape. The Accademia had swallowed all of us in its shadow—Suzette, Bethany, even Riognach and Maialinne, as well as Headmistress Elan, Vedova Oriana. All of them, entombed in its cold stomach.

Only I had found my way out.

I rubbed my arms for warmth. The sleeves of my coat reminded me that I had been marked as Madame Exley's ward. Soon to be Grimstaad's.

In these shadows I would find no peace. I took a breath, filling my nose with the scent of beautiful flowers while I tucked the coin purse beneath the folds of my skirt, hiding it from sight. I tied the drawstring at my waist and steadied my countenance.

I must go.

I moved to the back wall of the courtyard and ran my palm along the thick vein of a vine twisting upward on the old, time-thick walls. I wedged the toe of my slippers into a knot of roots and hoisted myself up, using the trellis it snaked around as a foothold. My dress caught on a vine and I snared the fabric while yanking it free. Each step, I drove my foot into a piece of lattice to steady myself. As I climbed, dried pieces of vine continued to nip at my skirt and sleeves. I kept my head low as I ascended, careful not to peer into the sun. Frightened of losing my footing, I held on so tightly my knuckles ached, the muscles in my arm burning as I pushed my body upward.

The wall was thick at the top, much wider than I had imagined. I breathed a sigh of relief, hoisting myself on top of it; given the difficulty of my ascent, I doubted I possessed the strength to hang free on the edge and move myself about. I bent to my hands and knees on the ledge, crouching low. The afternoon breeze tangled my loose hair, and I swept it from my eyes.

The silhouette of the mountains stretched before me—snow-capped, cutting into the cloudless blue sky. From my view, they looked as though they sprouted from within the forest, rising from a carpet of trees so vast that I saw neither their beginning nor their end. I turned my head and took one last look at the Accademia. Though the sun rested high over the world, its light was blocked by a tower.

My hair whipped at my cheek as I shifted my gaze to the ground. On this side of the wall, there were no vines; it was simply a straight drop into a bed of tall grasses and stones. I shook my hair out of my face, taking note of a tree a short distance from me with a crooked trunk leaning perilously against the wall. One arm, one knee at a time, I crawled toward it while the wind tugged at my coat. My forearms and knees screamed each time they met the pavement, and I could already imagine purple and blue bruises forming on my skin. I had to reach Reveille and depart before nightfall. I could not stay on the wall, paralyzed with fear or pain.

I edged myself closer to the tree until I could stretch one arm, reaching for a branch. Its leaves tickled my fingertips in greeting. Extending my leg, I placed my foot on the edge of a branch that appeared hefty enough to hold my weight. Blood pounding in my ears, I hoisted my body onto it and squeezed my eyes shut. In my mind, I heard it snap under me, but when I opened my eyes, the wood cradled me. I wrapped my arms and legs around the branch and moved myself toward the tree's trunk. Twigs rubbed against me, leaves rustling my hair. Soon, I was able to hug the trunk of the tree. Holding my breath, I lowered myself, branch by branch, until my feet hovered close to the ground.

I hung for a moment and then dropped the final distance, landing hard and unsteady. Pain passed through my knees and I clutched my hands into fists, throwing my hair back. A tightness seized my lungs, constricting my chest as though it were bound by stays. I huffed out a breath, unfurling the fingers from my hand. It struck me, then, that I had been holding my breath for some time.

I shook the tension loose from my body and peered ahead. A trail unfurled before me—a stone-and-gravel tongue that tapered into the dense woodland. Branches stretched like arms on both sides of the road, a banner of golden leaves wafting overhead, rustling like the drapes of estival as they floated high above the market. Small glimmers of sunlight punctured the dense tarp and I took a step forward, small rocks crunching beneath my slipper. I took a step off the path and the heel of my shoe sunk into the ground. I slid my foot out and crouched down to retrieve it, wincing at the cold as a clod of mud stuck to the bottom of my foot. I wiped both my shoe and foot on the grass and looked back at the Accademia. A quick glance back revealed nothing but the wall.

The Accaedmia Marl was gone—out of my life.

I pulled my coat around my chest, turning toward the woodland.

From my childhood, I had grown familiar with the scent of tea—the dried leaves my Mama purchased from the market to perform her tasseomancy. The trees surrounding me carried their own scent, green, water-rich—teeming with life. I smiled as I walked under each ray of light that broke through the awning of leaves. It felt nice to breathe the earthy scent of the woods. In the sunlight, thinly woven webs glistened between their branches like celestial looms. I walked in a state of peace, my feet swaying happily to the rustling of the trees and the crunch of gravel under my heels.

After some time, I came across an enormous, hollowed trunk with flat mushrooms climbing up the side like stairs. I paused and leaned my back against the bark, sliding my toes from my slippers and stretching them across the grass to relieve their ache. I closed my eyes and heard the babble of a stream. Spreading my toes, I smiled and imagined the cool rush of water running over them. Tucking my shoes under my arm, I followed the murmur of the water, and I was soon rewarded with the sight of water rushing over stones and sticks—a small brook, narrow enough that I was confident I could step from one side to the other without trouble.

I crouched at the edge and gazed at my reflection. I was a wraith—my hair sprouting in wild clusters from my scalp, my skin as pale as moonstone against the grass. My coat was tangled around my arms, hanging crooked on my body, with tufts of frayed silk and raised threads poking from every direction. I averted my eyes from my wild appearance, cupping my hands and dipping them in the stream. The cool water splashed against my lips, soothing my tongue and throat. A slight hint of moss lingered in my mouth—odd and unpleasant, but much preferable to the taste of vendrake.

As I lowered my hands back into the water, the ground rumbled and I startled back, my reflection breaking apart. I wiped my hands on my gown and clutched my pendant. That sound! It was one I knew: carriage-wheels, ambling leisurely along the trail.

I bit my lip, scolding myself. I was a fool to stay close to the trail in my bright coat where I may be spotted. So close to the Accademia, this road was surely trafficked by travelers, both on foot and in carriages. I reluctantly slipped back into my shoes, resolving to walk parallel to the trail where I would be obscured by the trees. I glanced up to the treetops; the sun peeked through in spots, shining from center-sky. I had never made this journey, but I felt confident about my progress. If I kept moving, I could reach Reveille by mid-afternoon, perhaps evening.

Away from the road, the unpaved woodland peaked with hills and dipped into treacherous valleys. The grass consumed the heels of my slippers with almost every step forward. While the muscles in my calves protested, I leaned down frequently to pull my delicate shoes free from the hostile terrain. Sweat pooled at the back of my neck and I panted, my mouth parched. I cast my gaze to the canopy of branches overhead. The sun perched in the sky much lower than it had before. Time was slipping by. I clutched my pendant and forced my legs forward, pumping my arms, quickening my pace. My muscles screamed, but I forced myself through the trees. I placed my palm on a mossy trunk, looking in all directions to orient myself. The road had long since vanished. Golden trees and patches of green-and-brown grass sprawled before me, extending infinitely in every direction, indistinguishable from one another.

Above me, the sun dipped lower and my heart drummed against my ribs. The last rays threatened to wither. *How could this be?* I had ventured no more than a stone's throw from the trail, yet time and location slipped easily from my grasp—the road, Reveille, and the Accademia Marl all rolled into forest, never to be seen again.

I forged blindly into the dying light, twigs snapping under my feet as I ran. The forest grew dim, and new, ravenous sounds began to fill my ears—rustling bushes and the buzz of crickets that awakened shadows lying dormant in the grass.

And, litha.

It emerged from between blades of grass, its shadows were different from the demon-whispers that perched in the rafters of my bedchamber. These were heavy and wet—formless—and they moved slowly, lurching forward, carrying the scent of moss and primal secrets. Demons, old and heavy, carrying a primal history. They did not whisper or scratch in my ear; their shrieks ripped through the night. My legs trembled and I covered my ears, pushing away their distressing cries. I forced my mind to summon Suzette in their stead—her warm hand closed around mine, her silver, soothing voice in my ear.

In the darkness, her words turned to sobs.

I realized the sobs were my own.

With shaky fingers, I found my pendant and squeezed it until my palm hurt. The shadows surrounded me. They caressed my skin; they wriggled between my lips and teeth, tasting of iron, anguish, and blood.

I fell to my knees, clawing at my arms to drive them away.

And then one fell from the trees, different from the others—spiraling light and quick, like a feather. A wisp of breath tickled my earlobe, a voice deep and frigid—murmuring.

"They are looking for you."

VOICES THROUGH THE SILENCE

"Who is there?" I whispered shakily, stretching my arm up to my ear. I expected the tickle of feathers on the back of my hand, but it was only my hair that swept my knuckles. The night crickets stirred, trilling between the roots of trees, clicking by my ankles, buzzing, from afar, in the darkness. Their music was relentless in my ears, and the forest shadows ambled around me, crying into the night. With no legs, no shape, they shuffled past, raising the hairs on my arms as they brushed my skin. Their shrill cries paralyzed my heart and my teeth chattered, another night-rattle in the cacophony of darkness.

"What are they?" I asked. "These shadows, they are different from the ones I know."

And then, like a feather, a spectral voice blew into my ear: *"Be still."*

I stretched my arms before me and fanned my fingers. I could see little beyond the distance of my hands. The scent of wood and dirt filled my nose. Around me, in all directions, crickets buzzed, insects lighting up the grasses with bright, iridescent eyes.

I looked up into the trees above me. The moon—waning and white—waved at me between the branches. She revealed herself differently in the wild: solitary, bright, with clusters of stars all around Her; a beacon of stillness and guidance for those, like myself, who had lost their way. I had not seen Her in this state since I was a child—before the Accademia kept me from Her—and I had forgotten how She appeared in the sky.

For a moment, the forest's heavy scent faded and the aroma of tea leaves and lavender filled my nose. She was taking me, my moon—leading me gently away, plucking me from woodland and shadow. I closed my eyes and inhaled the familiar scents of my childhood, allowing her to guide me—take me there—to the gardens of my youth. In my mind, my mother stretched out beside me in the grass, her hands soft in the pale moonlight, her serpents sliding down her wrist while she pointed to the night sky.

Her fortune crossed my mind.

My gift pairs well with death.

Leaves rustled above me; grasses rattled below. The lavender and tea faded with the moon as a cluster of clouds swallowed Her. The forest pulled me back into its black mouth—the shapeless shadows wandering, screaming into the depths of trees far beyond me. My breath shuddered on my lips. The shadows moved past me, melting into the darkness ahead. I felt a distinct buzz in my ribs as they passed; it was not malevolence they held but sorrow—their wanderings, aimless.

"They are the dead!" I whispered. The sensation settled into my bones, its familiarity impressed upon me, like a seal in hot wax.

"Departed," the voice from before breathed. *"Death comes in many forms."*

I rubbed my arms, stroking the chill from my skin. "And you?" I asked.

"Go, now." The voice ebbed in and out of my ear. *"They are looking for you."*

"Who is looking for me?" I rasped. "Speak!"

"Go."

The word was a needle in my eardrum, splitting my thoughts in half. Should I trust the voice? Was it a shadow looking to lure me into the darkness, and consume me?

I heard a thud and then another. Footsteps coming

from behind me.

I could no longer contemplate the voice. I clutched my pendant and sprang into a sprint. Branches snarled at me as I ran into the thick darkness; twigs whipped my face. I turned, choking on fear, listening to see whether I had lost the footsteps. Something tugged on my heel and instantly, my body lurched forward. I plummeted to the ground, landing hard upon sharp roots and stones. A knife of pain sliced across my forearm. I touched my fingertips to my skin and they came away wet.

The footsteps. They had not ceased, but drew closer. A flickering light hovered above me, waning in and out of view. My elbow throbbed, as it approached. The silhouette of a man appeared, and it became clear he was holding a hooded lantern. My pulse quickened and I squeezed my pendant, praying that it would move past me.

Please, please. Do not find me.

A curse rang out through the night, and the hooded lantern dropped.

Behind him, another lantern flickered and a second man came into view. "What happened, Enzo?"

"I burned myself," the one named Enzo said, shaking his hand.

The first man snorted. "Yea, sounds like something you'd do."

"Shove off, Luca; you're one to talk." Enzo leaned down and picked up his lantern. He gave it a quick brush and checked the flame. Miraculously, the flame flickered weakly. A dying ember had survived the fall.

"This is your fault, you know."

"Mine?" Luca cried.

"Aye. You made us late to the Accademia Marl. You just couldn't hold it in, could you?"

"When you've gotta go, you've gotta go. It's a long way back to Exley."

"You took forever," Enzo said. "I waited out there by the bushes for at least an hour."

"It wasn't that long."

"Aye, it was." Enzo let out a growl. "If it wasn't for you, we would have arrived before the Damica got away. And we wouldn't be out here, in the middle of the night, chasing crickets and ghosts."

"You think she's dead?"

"Dead as Brennan. Dead as we're going to be, if we don't find her."

Luca choked. "Shut it, man! You're not supposed to say that."

"What? That Brennan is dead? Everyone knows it. Or, they should."

"There's no body."

"Yet." Enzo mumbled. "Just hasn't turned up yet. Probably burned him up, like Grimstaad."

A short distance from me, something stirred.

"Hoi!" Luca held an arm up, and both men fell silent. "Did ya hear that?"

They moved closer to me, and I held my breath. In the light of their lanterns, I caught a flicker of their blue tunics, the same hue as Grimstaad's. A scream began to rise in my chest, but I forced it to stay in my throat.

"Just a squirrel or rabbit," Luca sighed, kicking at the grass. "We should've followed the others to Reveille. Probably where she's headed."

Enzo snorted. "You ask me, a little nugget like that got snatched by the first brigand that caught sight of her."

"No way." Luca shook his head. "These Damica, they're dangerous."

"She looked like a waif, from that portrait Exley showed us," Enzo scoffed.

"They all look like dolls in those paintings. Like you might break them. But they say this one, she can snap your mind like a twig."

"Aye?" Enzo turned. "And Grimstaad took her as a bride? Is he mad?"

"I think you've got it backward." Luca said. "It's the Damica they say is mad. She's a Lunare. You know what that is? Means she's out of her mind. That's why they sent so many of us to go get her. In case she . . . snapped."

Damica Cosetta's portrait card flashed through my mind—her flowing robes and serene expression. And, Headmistress Elan dipping her quill to mark her death on the back.

The litha was rising.

I held my breath to keep it within me, but the litha shook my skull, dizzying me. It stung in the wound on my arm, the blood wet, warm, and black. I reached for my pendant, my fingertips brushed the edge, and it tinkled lightly.

Both men traded looks. "What was that?"

Please don't find me. Please don't find me. I squeezed my eyes shut and forced my body to stay in place, still and cold as a corpse. The litha rushed through my ribs, filling the spaces in between, squeezing against my heart.

"Another squirrel."

"Nuh-uh, squirrels don't jingle." Grass crunched under a boot-footsteps, coming closer, closer . . .

Please don't find me. Please don't find me.

The owner of the footsteps—Enzo—crouched and held his lantern to my face, squinting at first, and then shaking his head.

"I'll be damned," he whispered. He rose to one knee and turned toward his companion. "Hoi, come here!" He waved his hand furiously, while my heart jumped to my throat. I tried to breathe, tried to move, but my arms and legs refused to cooperate. I was a fallen statue, rigid and frightened, in the night.

A second lantern flickered and another pair of eyes

studied me. I shielded my face from the light and the lantern lowered, its owner—Luca—holding it so close that I felt its warmth on my cheek. I shivered, cradling my pendant.

"Please," I whispered. "Leave me be."

The men traded looks again.

"Damica Laurel?" Enzo asked.

I turned away, clenching my jaw. Luca slid past his companion and placed a hand on my shoulder. I flinched, the litha surging to the spot on my skin that held his touch. I gritted my teeth, forcing myself not to scream.

"Relax," Luca coaxed my chin toward him and stared deep into my eyes. "My partner and I, we're enforcers, sent here to find you. Help you."

"We're fooling ourselves," Enzo scoffed. "It's not her. What are the chances we'd stumble upon her, way out in the middle of nowhere?"

Luca lifted his lantern; the flare of his light blinded me. "Looks like her," Luca said. "She's wearing the same red coat."

"It's just a coat, and it's red. Doesn't mean it's her," Enzo countered. "Look, we're not going to get anywhere wasting our time on this filia."

Luca's fingers clumsily brushed my pendant's chain, and I yanked my pendant out of his grasp.

"Take your hands off of me!"

Luca recoiled, and he turned to Enzo.

"Whoa, what are you doing?" Enzo asked.

"It's *her*," Luca said, adamantly.

"Let me see that." Enzo crouched in front of me and pried my fingers open, taking the pendant in his hand. He turned it over, examining it under the light of his lantern. His eyes widened and he cursed under his breath.

"It is her," he whispered, breathless. Luca edged closer, and he held my pendant to the light. The moonstone blazed.

"I told you!" Luca stamped his foot, his lantern swaying. "Come on, let's get her up, get back to the Accademia and be done with this nightmare."

"Please, no!" I gazed into Enzo's eyes, clutching my pendant to my heart. "You cannot return me to that monster . . ."

Luca and Enzo exchanged looks. The litha pressed into my chest, and I struggled to breathe, choking on shadow.

"Well." Enzo shrugged. "What should we do?

"Huh?"

"Grimstaad. Should we take her back? Maybe we should just let this one go . . . She's so young. Still a filia. Hate to think of what he's going to do to her."

"It's not our job to sort that out," Luca snapped. "She's Damica. Dangerous. Let's just pick her up, tie her hands if she puts up a fight, and . . ."

The litha surged in my chest. It was like the drumming of hooves against my ribs. My face contorted into a snarl, and my jaw shifted. I screamed into the night. In the dim light of the lantern, Luca's features contorted in terror, his lips pulled back, teeth clenched tight. Enzo pushed past him and forced a muddy palm over my mouth.

"Easy, filia! Quiet! Stay calm; we're not going to hurt you."

I screamed between his fingers, dirt and tinder catching on my lips. The air mingled with the litha's warm throb in my throat. Shadows spilled into my mouth, pulsing on my tongue with their familiar bitter taste.

It was only when I heard Enzo cry out that I realized I had bitten him.

He pulled back his arm and swore at me. Before I realized what was happening, his fist cracked against my cheek and eye.

Pain. My world erupted into pain. The night sky flashed white, hundreds of stars winking at me, cutting at my face with sharp corners. I blinked the stars away and darkness spilled into the corners of my eyes, the world threatening to fade beneath me. Through the piercing ring in my ears, I heard the enforcers speak.

"Hoi! What happened?" Luca called.

Enzo cursed. "She bit me! Hard! Look, my finger's bleeding!"

"I told you, she's dangerous!"

"Aye, you think?" Enzo shuddered, holding his hand to the lantern light. "Think she got me to the bone."

"Let me see." Luca lifted the lantern and held it closer. While Enzo turned his hand, I touched my tongue to my lip, the taste of iron mingled with mud. Luca uttered a quiet curse. "It's bad. Wrap that up tight and keep pressure on it; let's get the Damica and—"

"Wait, wait—"

"Huh?"

"Don't touch her," Enzo growled.

"Come on, let's just bring her back to town, get her back to Grimstaad," Luca said, shifting his weight anxiously.

"I don't think we should do that," Enzo whispered.

"Huh?"

"I don't think we should bring her back to him."

Luca narrowed his eyes. "What do you mean?"

"He's our general, aye? A whole lot rests on his shoulders, and he's already hurt. How long do you think it's going to be before she bites him—or worse? One wrong word, or sideways look—that's all it would take. One day, we'll find him curled up on the floor like a baby, babbling to himself."

The two men fell silent, turning their gazes to me. Crickets punctuated the night, and after a moment, Luca spoke.

"No one knows she's out here, except us. These woods are dangerous at night."

"Full of *banale*."

"Maybe we just bring back the body. Say we tried everything we could."

My face throbbed with a dizzying pain, and I bit my lip

to stave off the darkness.

"*Filia.*"

I blinked rapidly and turned my head. That voice! It was the spirit from before! His voice rang in my ears. I planted my elbows into the earth and propped myself up.

"*Stay with me, filia. Do exactly as I say.*"

I squeezed my eyes shut, tears spilling down my cheek. Pain streaked down my cheek as the salt grazed my skin.

Luca crouched beside me, lifted my chin. His breath passed over my neck and for just a moment, a flicker of light flashed through his eyes. He tugged at my collar, exposing the chain upon my bare skin. I heard the delicate fabric rip, and a gust of night air chilled my shoulder. Careful to avoid my touch, Luca tore my pendant from my neck.

"What are you doing?"

He turned to Enzo. "All we need is the necklace."

"Huh?"

"What do you think Grimstaad's going to do, if he hears we brought back a body full of stab wounds? He's going to think we killed her, is what. What do you think will happen next?"

Both men grew quiet, their words hanging in the night.

Luca held up my pendant, jingling it. "All we do is, we bring this back to Exley, tell her we found this."

"Aye." Sighing, Enzo shook his head. "Lugging her body all the way back to town would be a pain, anyway."

I dug my fingers in the folds of my dress. They were going to do it. They were going to kill me! I folded my arms over my chest, shivering.

"*Reach for the blade at his belt. Now.*" The spirit's voice reverberated in my ears. "*Quick. While they are distracted.*"

My heart beat hard against my ribs. The litha tingled in my fingertips—faint as it was. I imagined it passing through my veins, surging in my hand. I twirled my finger in a circle. In my mind I pictured my fear shattering and the litha pulsing.

There was no more time to think or fear. The litha flowed through me and I lunged forward, yanking the knife free from Luca's belt. I swung it wildly in an arc, slicing the bridge of Luca's nose. He stared at me, bewildered for a moment, his mouth agape. Then cursing, he pressed both palms to his face. They came away smeared with a crooked line of blood. A knot formed deep in his brow, and his lips came together, pulling back into a snarl. He squeezed his hand into a fist and I could do nothing but watch him pull his arm back to strike me down.

"Kick him! Now!"

I pressed the soles of my feet to Luca's breastbone, bent my knees, and pushed hard against him. He sprawled backward into the darkness. The light of his lantern flashed across his blade, pressed firmly in my hand.

"Run, filia!"

I rolled to my knees and using a trunk to guide me, pulled myself to my feet. The muscles in my calves tightened and I stretched my arms blindly, preparing to leap into the darkness and sprint. Behind me, one of the men shouted and cursed. Before I could move, a hand clamped around my waist. I cried out, quickly spun around, and was met by Enzo's harrowed face.

Arms trembling, I swung the knife and sliced Enzo's flesh. He howled. A spatter of blood trickled down my wrist and I twisted free from him. Remorse swelled in my throat, bitter and acrid—it was worse than vendrake and did not fade. Without looking back at Enzo, I dropped Luca's blade and ran blindly into the darkness, bumping into trees and roots. Thick, ragged chunks of bark scraped against my exposed flesh, while twigs pecked at my face like birds. The back of my gown flapped like a tongue against my legs, punctuating my ragged, desperate breaths.

The voice buzzed in my ear.

"Follow."

A SNAP IN THE DARK

Litha, enforcers, Grimstaad. Litha, enforcers, Grimstaad. The thoughts reeled in my head, repeating in short, chaotic bursts, countering the rhythm of my feet on the grass. Twigs cracked, snapped, and scratched at my face. My eyes welled with tears; they burned my face as they streaked down my cheeks. As I ran, I realized I lost my shoes and I winced, my feet aching with each strike against the ground. My heels screamed as shards of wood and stone embedded themselves into my skin.

Litha, enforcers, Grimstaad.

Litha.

I had cursed it, spurned it as the incessant source of all my misfortune and pain in the Accademia, but it had saved me from Enzo and Luca. It urged me to bite, to kick, and for my legs to run.

I thrust these thoughts aside and pushed my legs forward as hard and as fast as I could. Behind me, the light of a lantern winked at me through the trees.

"Filia, stop!"

The voice! It burst through my mind like fire.

I grasped at my head, but the sensation grew louder, sharper in my mind, piercing the backs of my eyes. I reached for my pendant and grabbed nothing.

Nothing! There was nothing I could do to stop it.

Pain. So much pain–and pressure, built in my forehead.

Not shadow, not litha—a crescendo of light and pain. Footfalls pounded behind me. Against my will, I dropped to my knees, choking on a lock of hair as I fell.

"Listen!"

I pulled the hair out of my mouth and sputtered. *Daremi pacce.* I whispered the words in my mind. *Daremi pacce. Daremi pacce.* I hugged my arms to my chest while a shudder rolled through me. The fire in my mind quelled to a low ache while I rubbed at my arms, letting shivers pass through me. I swallowed, took a deep breath, and counted a beat. I forced my chest to hold it until it burned in my lungs. My head continued to throb, low and dull, but in the silence—I heard something. The voice told me to listen, and it was dim, but amid the drumming of feet, I heard it.

The rush of a stream.

I lunged in its direction, my heart jumping to my throat when a flicker of light appeared behind me. The scent of blood caught in my nose. Luca. Enzo. I did not know which one, but they were near. I pushed myself to a sprint, weaving through ghoulish trees and black ferns. I stumbled over my feet as the relentless terrain gave way and the ground became smooth and pleasant beneath me.

I slowed to a walk: cautious, confused. Calves aching, lungs on fire, I panted, drawing in much-needed air. The chill ached as it hit the roof of my mouth, and it grated like sand as it slid down my throat. I turned my gaze skyward. The moon hung high above me, clear and white, trees no longer shrouding the sky.

Daremi pacce. I whispered. *Please.*

I closed my eyes and moved forward, inviting Her light to wash over me. In my haste, I collided with something.

Someone.

Startled, my eyes shot open and I looked up at the figure before me: a loose, black hood shrouding the features of his face. His clothes were washed in moonlight, and though I could not discern their color, they were plain—absent of the serpent that Grimstaad, Enzo, and Luca all wore.

He was clearly not an enforcer. *But what?*

My gaze shifted to his tensed arm, holding tight to a blade. Wordlessly, he raised it in my direction, my heart stopped and I screamed, stumbling backward.

"Don't—" the figure cried.

A snap rang through the night. Something whirred and tightened around my ankle. Before I could shake loose, it bit into my skin and yanked the ground from beneath me. I screamed, my garments twisting around my body as I tumbled across dirt and grass. A lock of my hair, thick with mud and sweat, wrapped around my face. In a desperate attempt to steady myself, I thrust my palms against the grass, burrowing my fingers into the dirt—but it was not enough to keep me grounded. A burst of cold wind hit my legs and I went up—up— my skirt bunching at my hips as I waved my arms at the emptiness around me.

"Would you look at that?"

I batted my hair from my face and caught sight of a pair of leather boots. The voice belonged to one of the enforcers.

"Luca! Come here! We caught a lucky break!"

"What?"

A second pair of boots crunched as he drew near. My ankle seared with pain as I twisted in the breeze. A tear rolled from my cheek and fell from my chin, lost to the darkness below.

"Cut her down."

A swipe of steel cut through the air. It whistled beside my ear and I plummeted to the ground. I gritted my teeth upon impact with the grass. Aching, my ankle pulsed, throbbing with sharp pain.

Luca hovered above me, a smear of blood glittering across his nose. Enzo, flashing a cruel smile, drew a small blade.

"I say we slit her throat, watch her bleed out—for what she did to us."

I lay in dull, throbbing pain, blades of grass abrading against the wounded flesh of my ankle. A shudder rolled through me, deepening the ache. Another shiver—different—passed through my body. My fingertips tingled, pinpricks of nervous energy jittering through my hands.

Could I use my ilex to hurt them?

I had never tried it before, and the thought of failure terrified me . . . almost as much as the thought of succeeding. I curled my fingers into a fist and squeezed tight. *Should I?* The question echoed in my mind. I shivered harder, unable to keep my body still. Anticipation and fear flowed through me equally. The litha sounded in my ear, a small trickle of shadow scratching at me. *Do it. Do it to him, now!*

"Filia!"

The voice from before screeched through my ears. My head pounded, pressure growing behind my eyes. From the trees, I heard a shrill whistle—somewhat like a bird, but not a song that I had ever heard before. The leaves rustled and then stood still. A thunk—like the sound of a cleaver through a thick cut of meat—caught my attention. Luca shuddered and took a step forward—and I howled. A silver blade, glistening with blood, protruded at an odd angle between his chin and throat.

"What the—!" Enzo cried.

Another wet thunk, and Enzo crumbled to his knees. A mist wet my cheek, and I pressed my palm to it, recognizing the sticky warmth as blood. A long blade erupted through Enzo's chest and I screamed, and screamed, until I was out of breath.

For a moment, I felt as though I had come out of my body, the scene unfolded before me surreal—as if the litha had enveloped me in its black shroud. Shadows, like slivers of wood, burrowing between my body and soul, until they had come loose, separate from one another.

I blinked and stuck my fingers into the grass to try to

ground myself. Behind Enzo, I spied the silhouette of his killer—a swordsman, long, lean, and hooded. The swordsman planted his boot on Enzo's thigh and pushed against the enforcer's body to pull his blade free. In my mind's eye, his movements seemed mournful, but his blade did not waver as he lifted it and whipped it across Enzo's shoulders. A thick, crimson ribbon of blood spread across the grass. Beside me, Luca choked, blood spilling across his chin and throat. His fingers twitched as he reached and grasped in my direction. The swordsman planted a boot beside him and drove his blade through the wayward hand. Luca uttered a bubbling cry and lifted his gaze to his assailant. His eyes grew wide, and he swore, sputtered.

"Cor . . . cor . . . an."

The swordsman's blade glowed in the moonlight. Beside me, Luca wheezed—his breaths growing slower and more labored until they ceased. I screamed and turned my head, squeezing my eyes shut. I heard the swordsman's footfalls between the terrified throbs of my heart.

Silence. I waited for more, my breaths shallow and labored. Waited for the cut of steel across my throat, waited to feel the heat of my blood as it poured over my chest—waited to feel the flapping of skin at my neck as I tried to draw a breath, waited to hear the gurgling of my own death-throes.

I waited—

And waited—

But no blade met my throat. I opened my eyes. The swordsman was gone.

Trembling, I walked my fingers down my leg and found it slick with blood. My hands found the source of my pain—a knotted length of rope cinching my ankle. I wedged my fingers beneath it and bit my lip. My flesh was torn, flaking, tender to the touch. With care, I loosened the rope, passing it over my heel, and I heaved it into the grass.

Luca's hand, twisted like a claw, still reached for me. I

rolled onto my back and cast my gaze to the sky. The moon, shrouded by thick clouds, no longer bathed me in its light. No voices pierced my mind, and the litha had sunk back into the trees.

I was alone in the night.

I remained cold and quiet as the corpses beside me, unsure of what to do—or even what I could do. I could not close my eyes to sleep; fear and pain collided, turning in reels in my mind, trembling in my nerves.

I lay motionless on the grass for a long while.

Although covered with bruises and scrapes, my ankle throbbing—the steady sting reminded me I had survived, and the enforcers had not. Was it the litha or was it the swordsman who had saved me? Was it fate or was it chance that given me life?

Or was it the voice in my ear, which led me to the stream and urged me to this clearing?

"Spirit," I whispered aloud. I arched my back and listened deeply into the night, but it was only my breath that replied.

The clouds lazed over the moon like a slow-moving net, dragging the hours of the night onward. How different She looked—my moon—from this side of the Accademia. From here, She controlled Her light, choosing when and how She danced with the clouds, and to whom She winked coquettishly through black branches. Tonight, She had chosen to reveal Her full light to me, bathing my small, broken body with hope, in a field of darkness.

I was alive. Alive—though what it meant, I was not sure.

I wondered if Suzette was looking at my moon tonight—gazing at Her from up high, through a stone window. *Oh, cherissima.* My stomach lurched with the guilt of leaving her behind, without so much as a goodbye. Without so much as an apology.

I'm sorry, cherissima. I am sorry for it all.

I choked back tears, no longer caring about the aches and cuts across my body. The swell of darkness in my heart sickened me with guilt. My tears felt black, hopeless, hot on my cheek, the salt mingling with my blood, stinging my skin. Shadows began to slither in the grass. Litha. They spread over my legs, shrouding me in terror. I breathed in short, staggered gasps and reached for my pendant—remembering it was gone.

"Spirit," I gasped. "Help me. Please."

The woodland responded with a loud crack in the trees a short distance from me.

"Who is there?"

A wave of black leaves shook frantically; the branches groaned. Another crack rang in my ears—beside me, this time. I pulled my arms to my chest.

"*Daremi pacce!*" I cried. "Please!"

A shadow scratched like a sharp needle inside my ear, then a whisper, like dust, tumbled a dried-out sentence in my mind:

"*Twist the ropes, make gallows for the Serpentine.*"

What did it mean?

"Please—stop!" I pressed my hands over my ears, burying my face between my knees. I squeezed my temples until they ached, but I could not keep the words from pervading my ears.

"*Twist the ropes, make gallows for the Serpentine.*"

The sorrow—the malice this phrase held—I could not bear.

I forced my palms against the ground and rose to my knees. Tenderly, I shifted my weight onto my ankle and let out a yelp, pain cutting through all my senses.

The shadows swirled around my feet, pulsing back and forth, back and forth, in an endless circle. They knew they had me—they were trying to tell me something, and I did not want to hear it. There was nothing I could do to stop them. I could not move; I could not escape them. They could prey on me as they pleased, nibbling at my ears until there was nothing left of me but bone and dust.

"Stop! Please! Stop!"

"Twist the ropes, make gallows for the Serpentine. Grimstaad. Grimstaad."

I heard a shuffle in the trees, and the swordsman's silhouette reemerged.

Grimstaad?

I cursed at my foolishness. Of course it was him—Grimstaad! The skill, the brutality with which he cut down the enforcers—he showed no mercy! After striking him in the palace and absconding from our marriage arrangements, I was sure he would show none for me. I tried to breathe, but my chest tightened with each attempt. I could only draw a trickle of air through my throat.

Within a few short steps, Grimstaad's shadow spread over me like a shroud. I crossed my arms over my face and screamed out the last of my breath, my mouth growing cold from the night air. The corners of my vision dimmed. Between the shadows of the swordsman's hood and my waning consciousness, I could not make out his features—and I was glad for that small kindness.

Grimstaad crouched beside me, and I felt his hands at my shoulders. I forced a jagged breath down my throat.

"Stay back!" I rasped, pushing his arms away from me.

"Get a hold of yourself!" Grimstaad gripped my shoulders and shook me, but I did not stop. I could not stop. The litha surged through my throat, and the shadow's horrible rhyme spilled from my lips.

"Twist the ropes, make gallows for the Serpentine!"

Grimstaad's eyes grew wide. "What?" he hissed.

I squeezed my eyes closed and threw my head back,

casting my gaze to the sky. The clouds had shifted, the rounded edge of the moon peeking through.

"Grimstaad," I moaned.

"Grimstaad?" The figure's voice bent with bewilderment. "What's a matter with you, filia?"

I blinked and gazed into the swordsman's colorless eyes. He did not sound like Grimstaad; his words were curved, fluid. They did not hold the sharpness, nor the cruelty, of Grimstaad's pointed tongue. The clouds gave way to the moonlight and my eyes adjusted to the light. I glanced to my side and screamed. Enzo's decapitated head rested just a hair's length from my body, his vacant eyes gazing into nothingness.

Shivering, I recalled his final words.

"Cor . . . co . . . ran," I whispered. "Corcoran."

The swordsman's eyes flickered with recognition. He released me and drew back, deftly returning to his feet. His blade came free from its hilt.

"Corcoran!" I shrieked his name into the sky. "Corcoran!"

It was my last memory of the night.

THE SWORDSMAN CORCORAN

I awoke with a sharp, throbbing pain in my skull, and an ache worse than that of any vendrake-induced stupor from which I had ever woken. My head pulsed with pain, and I pushed my palms against my eyes. They came back freckled with flecks of iron-scented dirt. The inside of my mouth, nose, and throat felt dry, splintered. The discomfort was accompanied by a growl in my stomach. My last meal had been a few meager bites of apple, and some spoons of oats while I was still in the Accademia.

The mid-morning sun squatted on the branches of the tallest trees. The air was crisp; the last of the morning dew sparkled on blades of grass. A slight chill brought bumps across my skin, and I raised my arms to my chest. Pushing back a sleeve to my elbow, I expected to see the red sleeves of my coat, but it was gone. Gone, too, was the top half of my gown. The fabric I wore in its place was coarse to the touch and my skin itched against it. I sat up and examined my new garments. I was enveloped in a too-large blouse that appeared to have once been an even-toned ivory hue, but it was stained with earth and soot.

My ears picked up a quiet lapping of waves; I turned my head and found that I was resting beside a small stream. I recalled hearing it while Luca and Enzo chased me into the night. Water. Ah—what a luxury. My body yearned for it to provide relief to my dry mouth and aching head. I wanted to wash away the blood and filth blanketing my body.

Strips of red silk from my coat circled my ankle and foot, with small, masterful knots holding them firmly in place. I was not alone. Somebody had taken the time and care to mend me. Corcoran, I assumed. Was he still with me, or had he gone?

Crawling to the edge of the stream, I puckered my lips and drank deep. Ah—reprieve. It flowed like an icy balm on my throat, quelling the hoarseness in my throat. While I drank, my hair fell into the water and I allowed my forehead to sink below the surface—the blood, dirt and the harrowing memories of the night before washing off my skin. I surfaced for a breath and gazed into the water. A reflection that I did not recognize as my own stared back at me: I was like a drowned wraith—my face a patchwork of bluish bruises and small scratches accentuated by clumps of matted hair. I pushed back the sleeves of the blouse and plunged my hands into the stream to rid myself of my wild reflection.

With my thirst and aches somewhat soothed, I found myself able to hold thoughts in my head beyond pain. My mind reeled around my fear, memories rushing through: the weight of the blade in my hand, the smear of blood across Luca's nose. His wet cough as he lay dying, his rigid fingers pointed at me. The whip of a blade. Enzo's freshly severed head thudding to the ground. The scent of blood, fear, and death.

Ilex.

Litha.

That horrible voice in my ears, the pulse in my fingertips urging me: *Do it. Do it.* I could have done it. I was certain of it. I could have caught him by the wrist and shred his mind.

It would have been like peeling an orange, plucking each tiny white strand from the pulp. But, something had stopped me. The spirit, the voice—at first, yes. But then . . .

The swordsman. Corcoran.

My stomach churned with dread. Had he meant to kill me, only to change his mind? I held my breath and listened for his footsteps, but the forest was placid, the lapping of water and the occasional call of a bird.

I crawled alongside the banks of the stream, taking small breaks to sip water and trickle it over my wounds. I had only gone a short distance when I noticed a pair of boots sitting in the sunlight—old and tired, with their tongues hanging out. I heard a snap in the trees. The leaves behind me thrashed as the hooded swordsman emerged.

Even from a distance, I was struck by his eyes. Bright blue, tinted gray like steel—they were a blend of beauty and pain, like a snow globe shaken up and left to settle. My cheeks grew warm, and I found myself wondering: *Was it his pain that made him beautiful, or was his pain more pronounced because of his beauty?*

He pushed his hood back and shook his hair. Like a forest fawn, a cascade of straw-colored locks fell to his shoulders, decorated with fragments of leaves and grass. Corcoran raked his fingers through his hair, little golden strands at his forehead catching the light.

His face flecked with dirt, Corcoran stood tall—much taller than I—his form slender. He smiled at me, his lips pulling at his cheek. The sun bathed the side of his face in its light, reflecting the golden hue of his beard beneath the dirt. Beneath his hood he wore no shirt; his chest was bare. I tried to look away, but I caught my gaze pulling toward his form. His belt, pressed tight against his skin, the contours of his abdomen . . .

The blush returned to my cheek. I had never been drawn to a man's body; it was improper for me to do so. I bit my lip and tried to force myself to look away.

"Ah, you woke up, did you?"

I gasped—half in despair at the brusqueness of his words and half-entranced by the pleasant strangeness of his voice. It was soothing to my ears, but not the same as Suzette. His voice sent a flutter through my gut. I wished to watch his lips and teeth form the shape of more words. My mind tripped over a tangle of thoughts.

"Thank you," I choked.

He glanced at me oddly, tilting his head to the side. "For what?"

"For my life," I said softly. "For saving me from those men."

He scoffed. "I didn't do it for you."

"What?"

"I said, I didn't do it for you. You brought enforcers into my camp. I had to get rid of them. Simple as that."

I felt heat rush back into my cheeks and I turned away. "Sorry."

"Ack, filia, don't do that," Corcoran said.

My face grew hotter. "Sorry."

"Hopeless," he said, breathing the words a sigh. He approached me with a proud gait: a stride that reminded me of the signores of the high court—but it was clear he was anything but a signore.

I covered my face, peeking through the cracks of my finger to meet his bright blue gaze. His cheek pinched in a cynical half-smirk.

"So, what kind of trouble are you in?"

I closed my fingers like shutters and shook my head. "I cannot say."

"Those enforcers were trying to kill you. They wanted to cut you down, like their lives depended on it," Corcoran said. "Seems a bit extreme, for a tiny thing like you."

I shifted uncomfortably, crossing my arms over my chest.

"So," he continued. "Why don't you tell me? What are you doing out in the woods, being chased by enforcers?"

I glared at him. "I have done nothing wrong, if that is what you are insinuating. Those men were brutes; I was lost, and they . . ." I choked on my words, biting my lip to keep my tears behind my eyes.

"Easy. Take it easy," Corcoran said. "I know their kind."

I buried my face in my hands. "They do not know I am here! They know nothing of what happened—nothing of my fate! I would have died and they would have never known! They wouldn't have known to ask Suz—" I choked on a sob and Corcoran stiffened.

"Ack, don't do that," he said, lowering himself beside me. "Why don't you slow down and start from the beginning?"

I quieted myself, pressing my teeth together firmly. I thought of my cherissima, the way that she would raise her chin in defiance, holding her secrets close to her chest. Spinning her words while she stroked her brooch, shifting herself into a position of power. I lacked the power behind my words, but for a moment I pretended I held some wisp of it in my throat. I imagined that some part of Suzette had remained with me, even though she was gone. I tossed my hair over my shoulder, lifted my chin, and said to Corcoran:

"I do not know you. And, you know nothing about me."

He sneered. "I know one thing about you."

He reached into a small satchel on his belt and pulled out my pendant. My eyes widened and before I could stop myself, a gasp pulled through my lips. My pendant! Oh! It had not been swallowed by the woodland or pocketed by the enforcers. Corcoran had found it; it was safe.

"It's yours, isn't it?"

I hardened the muscles in my face. Suzette would not trust him, and I decided I had no reason to, either.

"No," I said, "What is it?"

"Fascinating," Corcoran said, dangling the pendant so that the moonstone piece twirled mid-air, clinking softly.

"It certainly is," I said.

"I meant you, *Damica*." He stressed the word.

"Fascinating that you think I'd fall for that rubbish. You know, for someone who doesn't trust people, you're not very good at this."

My heart jumped. "Good at *what?*" I demanded.

"Keeping secrets. You're a terrible liar." He enveloped the pendant in his palm, forming a fist around it. "I found it on the enforcer calling for your head. Explains a lot."

"Yes, this pendant is mine," I whispered. Shame hung on my lip as I spoke the words. I needed not say more.

He set his jaw and did not reply. The thin air dancing around us, tickling the ends of his hair so that they brushed beautifully against his throat. I studied the folds and contours of his neck, the patch under his jaw where his beard gave way to his sun-deepened skin. His folded hood casting shadows across his skin. The apple in his throat moved and he extended a hand to me.

"Show me your ankle," he said. "It looked real bad last night."

"What?"

His blue eyes shifted to my leg, and he beckoned me with fingers. "Come on, Damica. Daylight's wasting."

I shuffled forward and timidly slid my ankle toward him. Without warning, he lifted the hem of my skirt and wrapped his fingers around my calf.

"Ah!"

Corcoran scoffed, his blue eyes sweeping to my ankle, and then back to my face. "Easy, Damica. I'm not going to hurt you. Can you walk on it?"

"A little."

"Show me."

Before I could grasp what was happening, he took my hand in his. My cheeks burned at his touch. I had never felt a hand as hardened as his before. My sister-Damica, my headmistress, and the vedovas all had skin like silk, and my Papa's hands were frail and soft as well, like the dough we kneaded together.

Shakily, I gripped his hand, bending on one knee to lift myself.

"Has anyone ever told you, you're . . . odd?" Corcoran asked.

Planting my toes into the grass, I shifted my leg, leaning tenderly on my ankle. I tried to put weight on it, and it responded with a sharp jab.

"A bit like a foal." He nodded, approving of his word. "New to the world. Unsteady on your feet."

"What?" Without thinking, I shifted the entirety of my weight onto my leg. I cried out, folding into the grass.

Corcoran chuckled, his teeth flashing. My cheeks burned bright with a blend of embarrassment and pain. And suddenly his laughter ceased.

He was staring at me again, this man. Staring, with a blend of amusement, concern, and . . . something else. *What is it?* I pushed my fingertips against my palm, pulsing them open and closed, open and closed.

What is he feeling? I called upon my ilex. My eyelids fluttered closed, and I fell deep into myself, trying to hold the touch impression Corcoran had left in my hand when he took it.

Fear.

Because I was Damica.

He was both afraid for me—and afraid *of* me.

My heart dropped, heavy in my chest—each throb, a painful stab reminding me of the terror and heartache I was capable of inflicting upon others, whether or not I intended to do so. I opened my eyes and found Corcoran gazing past me, his eyes and the sky reflections of one another. I caught a glimpse of his tongue as he rolled his lip between his teeth, deep in thought.

Beautiful.

He was so, so beautiful—and I was afraid, too. Afraid of

him. Afraid *for* him.

"All right, Damica. Let's do this," Corcoran muttered, giving a slight shrug. He wrapped one arm around my waist and I shrieked, pulling back in protest.

"Take your hands off me!" I cried.

"Whoa, whoa! Easy!" Corcoran pulled back and held his hands, palms forward, toward me. "Stay calm. I'm not going to hurt you!"

"Do not touch me!"

Corcoran scowled, shaking his head. "Don't you think I'd have taken my fill of you by now, if I wanted you like that?"

I felt my eyes widen, a crest of horror rushing over me. I had not thought of this. *Had he?* I rolled the thought over in my mind. From the time I called his name, all the way until the morning, I had no recollection of what transpired. Had he . . .? *Had he?* I crossed my arms over my shirt and shuddered.

No. Not my shirt. *His* shirt. A pit formed in my stomach and shivered—shaking so hard that I could not stop myself.

"How do I know you have not already done so?"

Corcoran raised a brow in surprise. "Are you serious?"

I pressed my lip between my teeth and punctured the skin. Tasting my blood, I balled my hands into fists.

"Easy, Damica." Corcoran's lip twitched and he cocked his head to the side. "You'd know if I'd done *that* to you."

I blinked, confused. "What?"

A smile cracked on Corcoran's cheek and he laughed gently. "Oh, that's cute. You really are like a little foal. Clueless. Naive. Let me go ahead and educate you. Even if I were that kind of man—which I'm not—you're not one I'd take my chances with. Seeing as you're Damica, I'm likely to get hung, just keeping your company. And if I don't? Well, I hear your kind in particular has a knack for terrorizing your victims."

A ray of anger broke through my embarrassment and shame, like sunlight piercing the clouds.

"Well," I huffed. "You killed two men in front of me. Two *enforcers.* What does that make you?"

"Dangerous." Corcoran smiled. He swept his arm to his side dramatically. "Why don't you get on back to your headmistress, little foal."

Foal. Lamb. Viper. Which one was I? Or as a Damica— was I all of them?

We stared, again, at one another, saying nothing. His eyes changed as we watched each other, cracking, like ice, his feelings shifting, flowing into something less sharp. Quieter, softer, they picked up the light more naturally.

He understood—I could never return.

Corcoran extended his arm to me, opening his palm to reveal my pendant.

"Here," he whispered. "I fixed it for you."

In the fray of the night, the stone had been smudged and the silver had lost its sparkle. I rubbed it against my shirt and held it to the sunlight and let it twirl, slowly, between my fingers. The fragile silver chain had snapped when it was yanked from my neck, but it had been repaired with a fine braid of red silk.

"Had to use your coat," Corcoran said. "You shouldn't be wearing that thing out in these parts, anyway. Red makes you easy to spot, and with silk like that . . ." He whistled. "Anyway. Hope your necklace is all right."

"Thank you," I whispered.

He shrugged and shuffled past me. Even without my ilex, it was easy to hear in the curve of his words that he felt bashful. Corcoran turned away from me and untied the hood that rested on his shoulders. I was surprised to find that it was not a proper hood; he had simply folded and knotted a piece of cloth.

Corcoran plodded toward a tree, collecting a small array of items resting beside it—a cooking pan, a deck of cards, a small box—and he placed them in the center of the cloth. He bent down to lift the bundle, his golden hair shifting over one shoulder. A black marking peeked from the back of his neck, and I squinted at it. Before I could discern what it was, Corcoran stood upright, a delicate wave of hair obscuring it. He collected his sword and situated it at his hip.

"Come on," he coaxed. "You need to get up on my back." He shifted his travel satchel, sword and pan clanking against his side while he adjusted. Bending to one knee, he exposed his back to me.

Pretty. His back was so pretty, smooth, and strong. He was so beautiful—and to be pressed against him, like a flower between the pages of a book . . .

Ah! Such thoughts! My skin grew red-hot and I did my best to snuff them out; I need not give him a chance to question my hesitation. Hastily, I slid my arms around Corcoran's shoulders. He pushed my skirt up past my knees and I gasped as he gripped my legs, hoisting me up. *He's holding me. The beautiful man is holding me. He is carrying me!* My breathing turned rapid, my face burning brighter. I wanted to shrink from my embarrassment and disappear.

"Damica?" Corcoran's curved words broke through my thoughts. "You're choking me."

"Ah!" I squeezed my eyes shut, loosening my grip. Forcing my thoughts to turn elsewhere, I whispered, "Where are you taking me?"

"Away," he said.

"That is no answer!"

"Away from the *enforcers*, then," he replied. "Nothing good's going to come from keeping company with their corpses."

He carried me until evening through the woodland, my body rattling with each of his footfalls, his face and mine both enduring the scrape of branches and trees that beat against us as the brush thickened. The sky grew dark, and I raised my head to the sky and I saw Her—ahh! The precious white curve of the moon, little more than a fingernail in the sky. I closed my eyes and bathed in Her tranquility. In these lawless lands she watched us—seated in Her throne of night, wearing a veil of clouds. My mind wandered back to Corcoran's beauty. Under the moonlight, I was compelled to act upon my thoughts. An impulse seized me, beckoning me to draw my lips across the lobe of Corcoran's ear and envelope it gently, taking it between my teeth. I had never desired a man before; I had never even been so near to one. His hair carried with it the scent of freedom, an intrepid blend of mud and sunshine.

No! This is foolish!

I bowed my head, pressing my cheek against Corcoran's shoulder. My ilex shuddered in my chest—and I felt it. An unwelcome name.

Grimstaad.

My ilex spoke it in my heart. Was I its source, or was it Corcoran, or the forest itself? I was unclear about what it meant. Was it a warning that Grimstaad was hunting me? Or was it Corcoran who was being hunted by Grimstaad? I tried to use my ilex to peek into Corcoran's heart again, but with the ache in my skull and my weary limbs, I could explore nothing more than the surface of his skin.

BOUND BY HONOR

As daylight faded, I had expected we would stop to rest, but Corcoran and I pressed forward. At the deepest point of the night, my arms grew weary, and the shadow whispers returned to my ears—hollow voices, forceful and fragile at the same time.

"Twist the ropes, make gallows for the Serpentine."

The words picked at the insides of my ears—echoing until I was near mad. I longed to plug my ears, digging my nails in as far as they would go, but upon Corcoran's back, I could do nothing of the kind. I tightened my arms around Corcoran and moaned, low and light. He did not pause or respond, and my troubled ears found no relief.

From above me, a branch rustled.

"Who is there?" I whispered into the night. My head felt heavy, my pulse weak. When I looked up, I was greeted by a black beak and feathers and a pair of talons clutching the branch above me.

"Filia."

That voice! I knew that voice!

"Oh, gentle night-spirit! You have returned to me!" My lips turned up into a smile. Above me, a bird shifted its wings, adjusting its grip on the branch. It was then I noted its enormity: jet-black wings, face, and eyes ominous against the blackened forest. So, it was a bird—a blackbird who had appeared before me and warned me of the enforcers.

I felt Corcoran's pace slowing, coming nearly to a halt.

"Damica," he uttered.

"Yes?"

"Who are you talking to?"

"I, ah—" I stammered. I licked my lips and swallowed. *Tell him. Tell him.* The thought throbbed in my forehead, but I stayed still, frozen with embarrassment. I looked at the moon, but She did nothing more than wink back at me through a cloud veil. *I'm sorry. I can't.*

How could I explain to him? The demon-whispers—the litha. I loosened my hold on Corcoran's neck, my lips touching the bristles of his cheek. The wild, woodland scent of his skin sent a shiver through me. Beneath his skin, a ripple of emotion flashed through him.

Unease. He did not quite understand what I was, and I frightened him.

His feet further slowed, and we stopped suddenly, slinging his satchel into the grass. "We'll rest here for a while."

He crouched and my toes touched the grass; reluctantly, I released him. Above me, I thought I heard the blackbird beat its wings, but when I looked up, the trees were empty. Corcoran lay his belongings in the grass and arranged a collection of twigs and leaves in front of me. Rummaging through his artifacts, he selected a small, metal box and removed a square-shaped stone from it.

"What is that?" I asked.

"A tinderbox."

Corcoran struck his knife across the stone, sending a shower of sparks to the bottom of the box. I watched, wondrously. He blew lightly on the box; a flame hissed to life.

"You're a Lunare," he said.

"I beg your pardon?"

"There's different kinds of you."

I pressed my thumbs into my temples and bit my lip, hard. How much did he know about the Damica? The enforcers seemed to have an understanding of us, but Luca and Enzo's knowledge seemed based in rumors, whereas Corcoran's appeared to be rooted in something more solid.

"We each have a gift that is unique to our class," I replied. "My mama could read tea leaves."

Corcoran touched the tinderbox to a branch and used it to light the pile of sticks and leaves before us. Soon, I found myself enveloped in warmth while he sat across from me, bathed in an orange glow.

"Seems like you can do a lot more than read leaves."

"It is not I who can tell fortunes. It's my mother who wields that gift."

"A Fortuna, aye. And you're a Lunare."

I buried a toe into the grass. We sat facing one another, and I burned with embarrassment while he sized me up. His blue gaze washed over the crown of my head, pausing briefly at my chest, which bore my pendant, before tracing over the rest of my body.

"They say you're mad, you know."

"Yes, that is what they say. I am what I am. I cannot change. I reach into the heart of each person I meet and I hear their thoughts and intentions. I have done this since I was a child. It is all I know, all I do, all I am. My gift, my curse."

His cheek twitched at my words and he said nothing. Instead, he turned his attention to his belongings, pulling from them a small, bundled cloth. He untied it and revealed a collection of dried fruits and seeds. My stomach growled and I clutched my midsection.

"Here. Eat." He offered the bag to me.

"Thank you." I extended a quiet hand and picked a few berries and seeds. "'Corcoran,' is it?"

His eyes flashed with alarm. Within his irises, a war raged between steel and cerulean. His jaw tightened. The muscles in his lips stretched into a frown and I sensed a shadow passing through him.

He does not like my knowing his name.

I lowered my gaze, a thick silence hanging between us. The fire crackled and I swallowed hard, clearing a knot from my throat.

"I—ah, heard the enforcers speak your name, before," I said, my voice pinched. I breathed in deeply, my chest feeling constricted. "I truly am grateful to you and, ah—I hope you will forgive the intrusion. Your heart says that you do not care for your name, and do not wish me to speak it."

Corcoran tilted his head and cast me an uncanny glance. "Damica—"

"Laurel," I interrupted. Raising my chin, I held my gaze steady. "My name is Laurel." I wiped my hand and held it to him, waiting for him to take it, but he did not. Corcoran twirled a lock of his flaxen hair around his finger, pulling his lips taut and staring beyond me into the trees.

"It's *your* name I don't care for," he muttered. "Don't care much for your company, either."

A bolt of pain flashed through my chest, and I blinked, tears sticking to my lashes. "It is as I said, Corcoran—I cannot change what I am."

"That's enough," he said coldly. "Your 'gift,' as you call it. That's why those enforcers were hunting you, isn't it? Don't think I don't know it. Keep it to yourself; you're in enough trouble already. Shouldn't be asking for more."

I stifled the shudder that rolled through my body, clamping my teeth to keep the litha from rising. Corcoran turned his attention away from me, poking at the fire with a small twig. *Oh, Corcoran.*

My mind drifted back to the tinderbox Corcoran used to spark the flames. It reminded me of one of my Papa's treasures, and my heart lurched—lonesome. I was alone, painfully alone. *Always alone.* My heart cried out for my papa. Would I find him in the mountains? Or would I find my death in these woods?

"Damica," Corcoran called to me. "What's the matter?"

I lifted my head, watching the moon and the darkness move across his face, shadows of concern alternating with wariness.

"You seem to be quite adept at finding your way," I whispered, trying to hold my feelings steady. "My gift . . . it tells me that you are a man of honor. You saved me from the enforcers. Carried me. Fed me."

"Honor?" Corcoran snorted. "What do you think you know about honor, Damica?"

I blinked at his question. My mind cycled through the faces of my sister-Damica: Bethany, Maialinne, Riognach. Vedova Oriana. Headmistress Elan. Their emotions vibrated on the same thread as Corcoran's: this strange concoction of concern and annoyance flowing through them at any given time. *Burdensome.* That is how they felt about me.

My mind added Suzette to the kaleidoscope of images moving through my head on repeat: my cherissima, with her twinkling eyes and confident smile.

Oh, Suzette. Tears spilled from my eyes and I wiped my face with the back of my sleeve. In the Damica, I found no honor, but in this swordsman—I did.

"I am heading to Reveille," I said. "Will you take me there?"

Corcoran blinked. "You want to go *where*?"

"Reveille."

He scoffed, his hair whipping across his cheek, from side to side. "I'll take you as far as Sarte. Then we go our separate ways."

"Where is Sarte?" I asked, panic rising in my throat. "How far is it from Reveille?"

"Doesn't matter, Damica. Reveille is crawling with enforcers. I won't take you there."

I bit my lip in dismay, watching the embers flare. I remembered the coin purse Bethany had given me.

"I can pay," I said quietly. "You are banale, are you not? You would take me for some coins."

"Banale," he snorted, crossing his arms over his chest. His blue eyes shifted—steel and skylight flashing. My heart fluttered. *Pain.* Somehow, I had caused him pain. It was nothing new; I was always one to cause pain, whether I meant to inflict it or not.

"I am sorry," I whispered. "I thought . . ."

The corner of his lip twitched as he rose. He shook his head, a strand of his pale hair catching a ray of moonlight.

"I'm no thief, Damica," Corcoran snapped.

A sting of embarrassment cut me like a twig whipping across my face. I furled my lips and plucked at a stray thread on my skirt. How presumptuous it was for me to assume I knew anything about this man.

"Are you, too, an enforcer?" I asked Corcoran.

"Ha!" He tossed his hair over his shoulder, his outcry shaking the peace of the night. I touched my finger to my lip. He turned his attention away from me and I let my coin purse be.

"You were heading the wrong way, you know," he muttered.

"What?"

"You said you're heading to Reveille?"

"Yes."

". . . You were heading the wrong way."

"How?" I threw my arms up in anguish, my cheeks burning crimson. "I followed the road! I walked right beside it, the whole time!"

Corcoran tapped a fingertip on his temple, "Remember this, Damica. You either walk *on* the road, or you come to an understanding that you're charting your own path. Once we get to Sarte, think about getting yourself a guide so you don't get lost again. You may not get so lucky next time."

His advice rang true, but it brought me no comfort. If I

were able to find a driver or a guide in Sarte to take me, by carriage or by foot, to Reveille—or even to the Order Umbilicus—how could I trust that I would arrive safely?

How could I be certain that a stranger would not discover my pendant while I slept and have me killed—or defile me at night and then tell the world I had dreamed it up in my madness? I shivered at the thought. I brought my knees to my chest and tucked my head between them. Still trembling, I slid my fingers back to my coin purse and untied it from my gown. I took a long, deep breath to steady myself.

Tell him. Tell him.

Yes, I needed to tell him the truth.

"Corcoran?"

"Oi?"

"I do not simply need to travel to Reveille. I need to reach the Order Umbilicus."

"Then I wish you luck, Damica," he said, flippantly. "It's all the way up in the mountains. It'll take you weeks by foot if you stay off the roads. Maybe more."

"I wish for you to take me." I lifted the coin purse, digging my nails into its grooves and folds. Giving it a firm shake, and tossed it to him.

He caught it and rolled it over in his palm with a frown. "No." He tossed the coin purse back to me. "It's too much trouble."

I wrinkled the pouch in my hand. "I do not understand. With your knowledge of the woodland, and your skills with a sword . . ."

"The problem isn't me, or the woods, or my blade. It's *you*," he said, his tongue curving sharply. "*You're* too much trouble. I already told you, if I'm spotted walking around with a Damica? What do you think is going to happen? Especially seeing as you're being hunted down by enforcers."

I grew silent, pressing my cheek into my knee. I let my tears roll freely across my skin, wishing they would smudge my features and somehow make me vanish.

"Ack, don't do that." Corcoran sighed heavily. "Why don't you just tell me, what in the world is your problem, anyway? The enforcers are hunting you because you want to go to . . . the Order Umbilicus? That doesn't make a lick of sense."

"My father is there," I told him. "He will know what to do. How to help me, how to keep me safe from *that monster.*"

Corcoran eyed me warily. "Safe from *what,* exactly?"

"Vitis Grimstaad." I shuddered, the embers from the campfire no longer keeping me warm. For a moment Corcoran's breath stopped. His shoulders tensed, his jaw stiffening.

Tell him. Tell him.

He needed to know what we were up against. I pressed my forehead to my knees. "He is the one hunting me."

GRIMSTAAD'S BRIDE

"Grimstaad?" A deep knot formed between Corcoran's eyes. "How could he be hunting you? He's dead."

"Dead? No, Corcoran—this horrible man is very much alive."

A spark of skepticism flickered through Corcoran's blue eyes. "We just talked about how you're a Lunare. When I was carrying you, you were whispering some nonsense."

My lip quivered. "What are you saying?"

"Well." He shrugged. "Maybe you just imagined Grimstaad. Maybe you saw someone you thought was him, or maybe you heard someone say his name . . ."

"No, Corcoran!" I shook my head vehemently. "He was real, and he's alive—I am certain of this. He is a tall man with dark hair, a widow's peak. Slender, dressed in blue. His arms—" A shiver ran through me, the litha rising in my chest.

"Yeah, that sounds like him," Corcoran said flatly. "But there's a lot of men who look like that; it doesn't mean anything."

I twisted my fingers through the tips of my hair. "I only saw him for a moment. Both his arms were bandaged to the elbows. And, and—" I curled my body into a ball and fell to my side, clutching at my forearms. "It burns! Ah—Corcoran!" The white-hot heat seared through my flesh. My breath sputtered as I choked on the sour scent of smoke and shadow. "Burned alive," I muttered, resting my cheek on the cool grass. I stretched my body on the earth, allowing the chill of the ground to permeate my muscle and bone. I turned onto my back and looked to the moon. Under Her cold eye, the litha began to dissipate, shadowy wisps of smoke sinking into the ground.

"Easy, Damica. Easy," Corcoran whispered.

"You must believe me," I panted, clutching my pendant to my heart. My teeth began to chatter, and my words came out in bursts. "Grimstaad . . . is very much alive."

I felt Corcoran slide his hands behind my shoulders and knees, and he lifted me from the earth. The color had drained from his cheeks. A shadow of terror passed through his blue eyes.

"Easy," he said softly. "I believe you."

"Corcoran," I whispered. Damp with cold sweat, my shirt clung to my back. My hair stuck to my neck. "He said something in the court. In the old tongue. *Per vertui.* He raised his cup and said it—*per vertui.* For honor."

Corcoran tensed, and draped across his arms, I felt the rapid rise and fall of his chest. He adjusted, shifting me against his body, and brought his boot down on the embers of the fire, stamping at the ashes as though he were trying to snuff my words. He scraped his heel against a rock to clean his boots. Soot clung to the hem of his trousers, and I remembered my Papa's words.

We are all dust.

"Aye, honor," he muttered. It was easy to hear the upset in his voice—his throat pinched, his words sharper—curved like a crescent moon.

"Grimstaad." He muttered a curse under his breath, one hand curling into a white-knuckled fist. He crouched down and snapped his tinder box shut. "You say he's hunting you? Why?"

Oh, no. He was starting to ask questions. Not about Grimstaad, not about me. Questions about *my relationship* to Grimstaad.

What should I do?

If I answered him truthfully, he might leave me in the woods with my twisted ankle, unable to walk on my own. Or maybe he would conclude that the enforcers had made the right decision in wanting to kill me. I rubbed the tips of my fingers together, feeling into Corcoran. *There.* My ilex fluttered in my chest. There was something there. Some connection to Grimstaad. A relationship that vexed him—a shadow that lived in the creases of his neck and hid in the folds of his hair.

I thought about my cherissima again—her strength, the steadiness of her words, even when she was in peril. Though I did not possess her confidence, nor her linguina d'argent—I did possess at least one thing that might help me.

Corcoran's feelings. The shadow I lifted from his skin. His fear, his contempt, toward Vitis Grimstaad. I licked my lips, my mouth hollow, dry.

"Why are *you* so concerned about Vitis Grimstaad?"

"Who in Trionfi *isn't* concerned with him? He commands the enforcers in most of the towns outside Cortellion. You just brought two of them into my camp."

"Sorry," I uttered.

"Ack, Damica! Don't do that. What's done is done. Two enforcers is nothing to me. You need to know what Grimstaad does . . ." Corcoran heaved a sigh. "His handiwork is all over these parts. You don't have to look far to see it."

I cast my gaze to the trees above. I could just make out the blackbird's silhouette illuminated by the moon. I wanted to ask why he was there, and what Corcoran had meant about Grimstaad's handiwork, but I found my mind growing weary— too tired to properly form the thoughts.

Corcoran's boots thumped in the grass and he bent to one knee before me, extending his hand. "We should keep moving, Damica. I think I can get you to Sarte by morning if we keep going. If you think you're feeling better."

"Yes, thank you." I nodded. "I feel much better."

Corcoran lay me gently in the grass and began to gather his belongings. I was awestruck, again, by his beauty, the contrast of it all: his measured steps, the wild shake of his hair. The firmness of his back, the compassion in his voice.

Per vertui. For honor. I turned the words over in my mind.

He helped me onto his back and I clung to him. Wearily, I lay my cheek on his shoulder, a veil of moisture between my skin and his. I listened to his breath, his pulse, his feet.

Safe. With Corcoran, I was safe. In my thoughts, I ascended—floating over the alabaster walls of the Accademia, soaring over the road to the marketplace. I imagined myself spreading my arms wide and floating like a sheet, the sun warming my back—breezing past the colorful mix of tarps and wares, until I arrived home: where I entered the kitchen as a beam of light, reflecting from pot to pan.

Safe.

I faded in and out of brief snaps of near-sleep while Corcoran carried me through the night. His footsteps were short, hurried. The steady drum of his pulse and his feet alternated—*thump-thump, clomp, clomp, thump-thump, clomp-clomp.* I felt the strain in his body—the ache of his arms, the muscles in his legs struggling to continue under the weight of my body while a lack of sleep bit at us both. But morning did arrive, and I blinked at the trees at dawn, draped in a soft, golden sunlight.

"Damica?" The rumble of Corcoran's throat buzzed through my forearms.

"Yes?"

"We're just outside Sarte."

I breathed out quietly. I wished it were not so. Against

Corcoran's flesh, I was able to rest my body, without worry of the treachery of the forest or the malice of the enforcers.

Corcoran hardened his voice. "I'm going to put you down, and you're going to see if you can walk."

He crouched and I released my hold on him, my eyes drawn once more to the black markings at the base of his neck. I wished to sweep my hand across his hair to study them, but my toes touched the earth. I knew I must let go.

I shifted my weight onto my ankle and cringed, expecting to feel a jolt of pain. To my surprise, the pain was only a small twinge, and I found that my leg could hold me. Extending my arms wide to keep my balance, I took a tentative step, and then another. I stumbled and lurched, but was glad to find myself mobile again. Corcoran squinted at me, his lips pursed as he studied my movements. After I had taken a few successful, steady steps, he crossed his arms and nodded.

"This is where we part ways."

Sadness gnawed at my heart as Corcoran turned from me, adjusting his belongings on his back. I would never see him again, never again be pressed against the safety of his back. I wanted to stay with him. I bit my lip and blinked, the salt of fresh tears stinging the corners of my eyes.

"Thank you," I called after him. "Truly, you are a man of honor."

Corcoran turned suddenly. "You can't hide, you know," he said. "You've heard what they say about Grimstaad, right? He always gets his man. Or in your case: his *bride*. Once he's set his sights on you, he won't stop coming."

His words floated across my ear and for a moment, my breath stopped. I was shocked. My vision blurred. Panic stirred in my pulse, filling the space between my heartbeats. I shook my head, folding my lips into an uncanny shape.

"How did you know?"

"Figured it out while we were walking," Corcoran said. His eyes flickered up and down, studying the tears smudged beneath my eyes. He flashed me a rueful smile. "Sorry to hear it, Damica. Didn't think you were half bad. A shame what's going to happen, once he catches up to you."

"What do you mean?"

"You don't know?" he asked, alarmed. "Grimstaad's as bad as they come. He's not going to take kindly to his wife running off on him. It's better for you to die out in these woods than it is for you to live to see his face again."

I leaned forward and tucked my head between my knees. The shadow whispers were back, biting at my ears like scissors, my lobes bleeding shame. I plugged my ears, willing the whispers away.

"I didn't have a choice."

"Huh?"

"I said." I righted myself, raising my voice. *"I did not have a choice!* My headmistress signed the parchment and did not tell me! She just sent that horrible woman to retrieve me, with four enforcers to take me if I resisted. That's why I'm trying to reach my father—he doesn't know what's happened! He still thinks I'm at the Accademia!"

Corcoran blinked, dumbfounded. I yearned to tell him of Grimstaad's poisoned heart, how he had cornered Suzette and ruined her flawless face—that he had taken more than her beauty; he had taken her spirit. But I could not form the words.

"Damica," he whispered, his voice softer than I had ever heard. "It isn't a real marriage."

"What are you talking about? It's in the headmistress's records, sitting right there on the shelves in the Accademia!" I swept my arm through the air, motioning toward the trees.

"Huh. That's interesting." Corcoran crossed his arms. "What do you think they're trying to hide?"

"What?"

"You said it yourself. Your father doesn't know, you didn't have a choice, and it seems like they were trying to get you away, fast. Why the secrets?"

I pressed my lips together and shook my head. I was in enough peril as is; how could I divulge what Headmistress Elan had told me about Grimstaad? The urgency in finding Prince Brennan, how Trionfi teetered on lawlessness . . . and my role, at the center of it all. The headmistress's warning in the Accademia cut through my mind.

"Trust no one. We do not want to end up with our heads on pikes. If any of this leaks outside this room, there will be rioting, anarchy—and everyone in the Accademia will be dead."

But to remain silent would mark me as a liar—one who withheld secrets, the same as they did. And Corcoran had proven himself to be more than just a swordsman. He was smart. Smarter than he wished me to know. My ilex rumbled in my chest. *He hides it behind his rawness, his beauty.*

I strained myself to think. How would Suzette handle this? When Grimstaad caught her in a lie, and she could no longer influence him with her linguina d'argent, my cherissima had found a way to keep control . . . through veritas. She had leaned into the other part of her gift; she had told the truth.

The truth she wanted him to hear.

"They wish me to conceive quickly, so that Grimstaad can return to his battle with the banale with a clear head," I said. "They told me he will be more focused, knowing he will have an heir."

Corcoran rolled his eyes. "Doesn't surprise me. Hope you make it to your father before Grimstaad gets to you. Last thing this world needs is another one of him to worry over."

I breathed a sigh of relief. *It had worked!* Somehow, I had successfully pulled it off, and Suzette's tactic had drawn the focus away from myself. The part of the truth I did not want him to hear . . . about using me as a weapon.

"A battle with the banale. Is that what they're calling it?" Corcoran scoffed. "You know, Damica, what you said earlier, about me being banale . . ."

I plucked at the hem of my sleeve. "I really am sorry I called you that," I said.

"Ack, well." He shrugged. "You're not completely wrong about that. When I was a youth, I used to be a runner for a group of brigands. Just outside the town where I grew up. It was good money. Easy money. Or it was . . . until a job went wrong. Horribly wrong, and I ended up pleading for my life in front of a judge. He gave me a choice: join the army, or serve my time in jail."

I leaned toward him, curious. "Which did you choose?"

Corcoran cracked a small smile. "You're missing the point. What I'm trying to tell you is, *I had a choice.* They let me pick my own fate. It wasn't handed down to me like an old blouse."

I blinked and wiped my face, smearing away my tears and shadows alike. "You chose for yourself. How? Your entire fate rested on one choice. How did you choose? And how did you know it was right?"

He flashed a wry grin. "Keep heading straight and you'll hit the road to Sarte. Keep it in your sight, and for the love of all good things: try not to get lost. Good luck to you."

"Wait, Corcoran!"

"Get out of here, Damica. Shoo! Begone! Or however I get rid of you."

I closed my eyes and clenched my fists, my cheeks flushed with indignation. How could he leave me like this, with his half-finished story, and not a care in the world? I breathed in cold air, but my skin prickled with anger. And—against my Papa's teachings, against all my training in the Accademia—I allowed myself to feel. To *truly* feel, in all its fullness.

"Hoi!" I shouted. "Come back here! You cannot say that and then turn your back on me!"

But Corcoran had already disappeared into the trees.

I stumbled after him into the thick of the forest, abandoning the instructions he had given me. My ankle wobbled and I leaned on the trunks of trees, praying that my foot would not catch on root or vine and render me unable to walk once again. I stamped and stumbled and pressed on, guided by the burning need to speak my mind to this . . . *banale*, before the chance was lost forever. As I quickened my gait, I heard the branches ahead of me rustle, twigs bending and leaves rattling.

"Hoi! Stop!" I lurched onward and was soon halted by a cluster of trees spaced too near one another to pass through. Just ahead of me, I saw the shadow of a man, a flash of boots and clothing. I squeezed my body between the trunks, gasping as I struggled to pass through.

"Corcoran! *Stop!*" I charged forward and the figure came into full view.

It was not Corcoran.

It was not living.

Dangling just above the grass, with slender boots pointed toward the brush, a figure grinned at me horribly. The wind caught its trousers and blouse, turning it like a sun catcher. It disturbed the leaves as it slowly swayed back and forth. A burst of light brightened its cracked teeth, and below its half-opened jaw, a frayed, blackened rope decorated its throat. I squeezed my eyes shut, pressing my hands over my ears. I did not wish to hear it. I had already heard its voice. I knew the words it would speak.

Twist the ropes, make gallows for the Serpentine.

I fell to my knees, wailing, screaming over and over until my throat grew hoarse and my screams turned to retching. The meager contents of my stomach threatened to spill from my throat, but I could not remove my hands from my ears. A hand suddenly clamped over my mouth, and I shrieked. Another seized me at the waist. I thrashed wildly to break free.

"Easy, Damica! Stop screaming!"

I breathed in the scent of my assailant. Earth, steel, and sunshine. Corcoran. My terrors began to disperse and my body was wracked with sobs. Corcoran removed his hand from my mouth and I whipped around to face him—his lips a finger's width from mine. Our noses brushed. The deep lines on his forehead stretched thin and shallow spurts of his breath fanned against my cheek.

His features contorted into a snarl and he whipped his blade from its sheath.

I whimpered, shielding my face with my forearms. He swung past me, his blade cutting above the hapless corpse hanging from the tree. With a brittle snap, the rope gave way and the hanged man's bones crumbled into the grass.

Corcoran dropped to one knee and bowed his head, whispering a prayer. He touched his fingers to his lips and touched them to the skull.

"Corcoran," I said. "This is what you meant, about Grimstaad's handiwork."

He said nothing, his attention fixed on the corpse. In silence, he placed his hand on its chest. One by one, he worked his fingers through the buttons of its blouse.

"You should not have left me!" I cried. I balled my hands into fists, my face dripping with tears and mucus. "I thought you were a man of honor! You know I will never make it to the Order! If Grimstaad is the monster you say he is, and that I know him to be . . . and this—" I pointed to the corpse— "this is what he does? I'll never even make it to Sarte! Someone will spot me on the road, and then . . ."

I could not finish the thought. Sighing, Corcoran removed the blouse from the corpse and threaded one arm through its sleeve.

"I know. I'm sorry. I was trying to be nice to you, as best as I could. But I can't help you. No one can. You're as good as dead."

His words sent quivers through my breast. My chest heaved and my arms shook—whether with fear or with fury, I could not discern. My cheeks glowed red, my feelings dripping from my chin, salt mingling with grass and dust.

"You said I had a choice!" I cried.

Corcoran pushed his other arm through the dead one's sleeve, shaking off a fine gray dust. "You do. Die lost in these woods, or die as Grimstaad's bride."

I drew in a breath, a chokehold of fury and fear igniting in my chest. I raised my chin and glared at Corcoran.

I unclenched my jaw and opened my mouth, but words did not fall from my lips.

No. The litha had taken me.

The muscles of my arm ignited and I raised my hand, striking it against Corcoran's cheek.

NOTHING LEFT TO REMEMBER

Corcoran's eyes grew wide. The tip of his lip twitched and his breath stood still. I fanned my fingers, gazing in horror at my hand. Pinpricks of pain ebbed and flowed in my palm, pulsing with the quickness of my heart. I gasped and closed my fist, my fingernails biting into my palm.

Why had the litha caused me to do such a thing? To incense a swordsman who had killed two men without hesitation only two nights ago? Was it trying to kill me? The strike of my palm against his cheek tingled in my fingertips. My chest ached with each breath I took. I erupted into a coughing fit, wheezing as I reached for my pendant to calm myself. My arms quivered and I failed to grasp the moonstone. Instead, I dropped my head and vomited into the grass.

I turned my head skyward and spotted a black beak and talons perching on the branches above me.

Spirit!

"Filia."

I flexed my fingers, the sensation of the strike humming in my palm. *What do I do now?*

"Speak your heart."

I forced myself to breathe, pressing my tongue against my teeth. What was in my heart was the litha. Terrible things transpired when I surrendered myself to it. The blackbird beat its wings.

"Speak the truth."

Ah, veritas—like Suzette. My nostrils flared as I drew in a breath. Litha. It needed to be different; this time, I needed to be one with it, whole. That was what the blackbird was trying to tell me. In the woodland, it perched above me in support. I could do this. I could be in control of my body, my words. I wrung the fabric of my gown and I raised my eyes to Corcoran.

"You say you were banale when you were young?" I spat, a froth of saliva dribbling down my chin. "Then, you are banale now. I stumbled into your camp by chance, and my fate is in your hands! We are walking among the dead now. We have been, for days—have we now? I pleaded with you for my life. You tended my wounds, fed me—and now leave me to be hunted by Grimstaad, or swallowed by the trees, like his dead. Banale!"

I coughed and heaved to expel the remainder of the contents of my stomach. Something deep within me convulsed—choking, gasping for life like the corpse lying before me. A fire bore through my gut, eviscerating both bile and fear.

"If I had your choice, then I would choose honor!" I snarled. "I will sooner die—by my own hand, if I must—than to be returned to Grimstaad! Do you understand?"

Corcoran raised his hand and patted his check—once, twice—where I struck him. I lurched toward him unevenly, my ankle bandage trailing behind me. He twisted the toe of his boot against the grass. He shook his head, strands of his blond hair sticking to his cheek. "All right, Damica. I'll take you to the Order."

I furled my brow, tilting my head to one side. Had I heard him correctly? Clutching my pendant, I looked up at the blackbird. It perched stoic, stalwart, in the branches, unmoved.

I blinked at Corcoran. "You will?"

"Aye. I like your spirit." He patted his cheek, a smile cutting across it. "Besides, anyone who hates Grimstaad that much has earned my respect."

A small smile crossed my lips in return. I had forgotten

what it meant to smile, how bright it felt to hold a small glint of happiness on my lips.

"Give me your gold. Hand it over." Corcoran extended his hand, snapping his fingertips against his palm in impatience. I reached for the pouch and extended it to him. He snatched it from my hand and stuffed it into his pocket.

"Now. We have a problem, Damica."

"What is it?"

"Your blow to the face won't do anything but piss off an enforcer. Won't even do that for a banale. Best not to strike one, if that's how you're going to go about it."

The small smile that brought me such warmth fell quickly from my lips.

"What are you insinuating? A moment ago, you lauded me for striking you!"

"I praised your willingness, Damica—not your strength. You hit Grimstaad like that, he might cut off your hand."

I crossed my arms over my chest. The enforcers' laughter, suddenly, cut through my courage; the pain from Enzo's strike pulsed on my cheek. The hairs on my neck stood on edge. I swallowed hard, my chest tight, each of my breaths becoming shorter, desperate.

Weakness. My entire existence had been spent in weakness. I was born a Lunare, helpless against my fate. I raised my chin, aligning my gaze squarely to meet the blue of Corcoran's eyes.

"You live by the blade, yes?" I asked. "Teach me to wield one as you do."

Corcoran raised an eyebrow, a grin turning up the corner of his mouth.

"Laurel, is it? Your name?"

"Yes," I replied. "I am called Laurel Aleandri."

He wrinkled his nose. "Damica. Laurel. Aleandri." He chewed on my name like a hardened piece of bread. "Can I just call you 'Lor?'" He did not wait for my answer. "All right. First lesson, Lor. Never give all your money to anyone." He rifled through his pocket and shuffled my coin purse between his hands, tossing the pouch back to me, where it jangled, lighter, in my hands.

"Half at the start, half at the finish. That's how it works. You got it?"

My cheeks flushed and I folded my hands into my skirts, shrouding my coin purse and my embarrassment. "Thank you."

"Second lesson," Corcoran continued.

"Yes?"

"The roads, Lor. We stay away from them. You have a good chance of being seen if you don't want to be found. Have some sense and avoid them. Sometimes we might need to cross a river, and we'll need to wait until . . ." He paused, drumming his fingers on his leg. "On second thought, our best bet is to stay away from the rivers if we can. I don't want to be fishing your body out of the banks."

I began to open my mouth to protest, and he waved his hand at me.

"Third lesson. Come here." He knelt beside the corpse and motioned for me to come. I limped to him and leaned on his shoulder, staring at the skeletal remains.

"This was someone's son, someone's father maybe, or a brother." Corcoran placed his hand at the base of the corpse's neck and raised its chest, propping it against a tree. He gazed at me, his eyes hardened like winter. "He's nobody now. Grimstaad got him, and there's nothing left to remember him by. If he gets you, Lor, there will be nothing left of you, either. You get me?"

I felt a sob rise in my throat, and I clamped my hand over my mouth, forcing myself to swallow it. I nodded in acknowledgment.

Corcoran gave a quick nod in return. "Don't let him get you."

He lay the corpse on the grass and reached for his boots, twining his fingers around the laces and pulling at them. Gripping the heel of his left boot, he gave it a swift tug. It came free from his foot with a sigh. Corcoran tossed it in my direction and it thudded in the grass before me.

"Put it on," he said.

I lifted the boot, turning it over in my hands. It was crafted from leather, though from its appearance, it would be difficult to discern. The heel was nearly worn through, and a coarse, sticky tar plugged a mottling of small holes. The top of the toe was the color of rust—a sharp contrast to the tallow color of the rest of it. My stomach churned at the thought of what may have caused this peculiar stain. I lifted the boot, stretching its sides to fit over my swollen ankle.

"Quickly, Lor." The other boot hit the grass. "The mountains are cold. Can't go in your bare feet."

I slid his shoes onto my feet. They still carried his warmth, though they were much too large for me, and I struggled to gain my balance as I walked.

"What about you?"

Corcoran pressed his lips together and motioned to the corpse stretched before us. "The dead don't need boots anymore."

During the days that followed, our trek through the woodland grew more treacherous. Corcoran drew his blade to cut through savage vines gnarled around tightly clustered trees like fat-bodied serpents. He stopped in the afternoon to rest, his cheeks flushed red, and hair slick with perspiration. Wiping his brow, he sank to the ground, patting the patch of grass beside him. I groaned as I lowered myself to sit, my calves sore from all our walking.

"Next lesson, Lor," he said. He reached for a small

sheath on his belt, removing from it a blade that fit easily in his hands. He flipped it between his fingers with grace and held the hilt to me.

I took the blade from him, shuddering as the wooden hilt pressed against my skin. My ilex buzzed and I recognized it as the blade I stole from Luca. My breathing turned shallow and jagged as the memory of my attack cut through my mind. The litha tugged at my throat, and I felt a scream rising. I cupped my free hand around my pendant and held it.

"No matter what," Corcoran said. "Never leave your blade behind. Especially with your enemy. You need it more than he does."

He rose, forcing me to walk ahead of him and slash through the vines. The trees hissed at me, their jagged branches pulling loose threads from my blouse as I passed. Corcoran meandered at my back, foraging roots and berries from the ground. Even with the afternoon air crisp, sweat pooled at the back of my neck, and my blouse was soon soaked. I repeated the brutal cutting and breathing until night fell, at which time I was rewarded with a meager handful of berries.

Corcoran insisted we sleep pressed to each other so we did not grow cold like corpses in the trees around us. Though my Papa and headmistress would have deemed it reprehensible, I agreed to it. I dared not wander and meet any more of Grimstaad's victims whispering verses to me through their vacant skulls.

Though he never spoke a word to me, I felt, beneath Corcoran's flesh, that he was bashful, sensitive—believing his closeness might be unwelcome, that he may hurt me, tarnishing my reputation by lying beside me.

But I felt no such concern. I lay awake deep into the night, watching wisps of clouds billow over the moon. I glanced up at his face, his lips soft in the moonlight, his hair colorless, delicate. I listened to his steady, shallow breathing until I fell into a fragile sleep. With Corcoran, I was safe.

Safe for one more night.

ROLAND, ROWLEY, GROWLEY

In the woods, I dreamed differently than I did in the Accademia. In my slumber I twirled like a feather into other worlds and memories. While I slept beside Corcoran, I drifted over a field in my sleep, a stretch of flat ground with patches of trampled grass. The earth under my feet was pockmarked with holes where hundreds of boot prints had stamped into the mud.

Dozens of men—each wearing the same matching garments—populated the field. Their tents populated the field in every direction. Some were missing buttons on their tunics or boots from their feet. The scent of sweat and char invaded my senses. As I floated over them, I saw a group of men roll a pair of dice, a spread of cards laid face down beside them. Behind them, a hazy red sky as the sun began to bow behind mountains, giving way to the night. Amid the twilight, their uniforms appeared to once have been the color blue, but had faded as a result of both time and terrain. Glassy-eyed, they looked through me. Lodged within the spread of men, I spotted a pair pressed back-to-back against one another, stretching their legs in the mud.

"Rowley!"

Corcoran! I jumped suddenly, his familiar voice tickling my ear—but it was odd. His words flowed much more quickly, more fluidly than I was accustomed to hearing, his accent heavier, more pronounced. I hovered closer to him and his blue eyes stared through me, past me. They were absent of the hardness, and steel I had grown accustomed to seeing; here, they glowed with eagerness—an irreverent love of adventure captured in his irises like a spark of lightning.

"Are you awake, Rowley?"

The man pressed to his back stayed still as a statue. The head of an enormous hammer, more than half my height, rested on the ground beside him. I could not imagine anyone strong enough to raise it. I studied the man, his jet-colored hair reaching past his thick-set shoulders. His tunic did little to hide the sinew of his chest. Corcoran's form appeared exceptionally lithe compared to his counterpart. The enormous man rested his arms, face-up, on his stocky legs, and I noticed the musculature of his right arm was much thicker than his left. He raised his chin slightly and grunted.

"I told you not to call me that. Here, it's 'Roland.'"

"Roland, Rowley, Growley." Corcoran chuckled to himself, twirling his sword idly. "Suppose it's 'Growley,' today. You're in a foul mood, aren't you?"

I expected the remark to stir Roland, but he did not so much as flinch at it. How this man could sit motionless both bewildered and impressed me; I would have desired his mastery of stillness in the Accademia.

"I do not know what you find so amusing," Roland said, his voice flat. "There is not much for us to smile about." He looked through me with deep brown eyes, a shade nearly matching the color of his hair.

"Have it your way, *Roland.*" Corcoran rolled his eyes. "It's your fault we're out here. Could have knocked back a few and played cards til our lanterns died. But no; you decided to be merciful. Try and be good. Fair. *Honorable.*"

Roland bristled. "There is nothing honorable about what you wanted to do."

"Look around you, you dumb sod," Corcoran swept his arm across the horizon. "This is a *battlefield.* We kill people here—before they can kill us. We do it enough times, we get promoted. Maybe get to sleep in proper beds instead of sleeping in shifts out here in this cesspool."

"That's why you have us sleeping in shifts?" Roland asked, his even-toned stoicism bending into an exclamation. "You told me it was so we could hear the meal cart passing!"

Corcoran grinned wide, his smile spreading across his face. He drove the tip of his blade into the mud and laughed. "You thick bastard. You'd believe the moon rose up out of your ass if I didn't tell you different."

Roland bristled, his eyes filling with disappointment. Raising an enormous arm, he rubbed his eyes, watching the final rays of twilight wither away, shrinking into the night.

"I didn't need to kill," he said, finally. "The one you wanted dead was a youth. He was pleading for his life. Begged on his hands and knees for me to spare him."

Corcoran snorted. "You believed him, did you? All that sniveling for his life? You're as thick as they come, Rowley. Believe me, he'll be back any minute with his friends to slit our throats."

"I told you not to call me that," Roland groaned.

"Right. It's 'Growley.'"

Corcoran grinned and jabbed him with an elbow. Roland remained stoic, motionless.

"There is some good in this world," he said. "Some lives worth sparing."

"Ack, will you give it a rest? You keep saying that, and it's driving me mad. When are you going to get it through your skull that it's not the way of the world?" He sunk his sword deeper into the earth. "Best for you to come to your senses, give it up already. The more harmless they look, the more dangerous they are."

"You are too hardened from your days as a brigand. Try to let it go. Start fresh. Find some honor in what we do." Roland shifted his weight, closing his eyes. "Get some sleep, brother."

Corcoran pulled his blade out of the mud and shook his head. "Not a chance."

I blinked and the men were gone, the dream having faded. I found myself back in the forest, lying beneath a gentle awning of branches, surrounded by the scent of pine. I turned to my side and found that Corcoran was no longer with me. At some point, he had awoken and situated his back against a tree. Propped upright against its trunk, he slept with his head bowed, his sword across his lap.

I looked up to the boughs above me. A gathering of birds, as if on a clothesline, perched in formation. They reminded me of my days in the Accademia when we were made to assemble before my headmistress and the vedovas so they could inspect us. I scanned the trees for the blackbird, but it was impossible to pluck him out from all the birds' silhouettes.

Had it brought the dream to me—or had it simply brought more birds to haunt me, new demons to whisper in my ear?

FALLING TOO DEEP

More and more, I dreamed of Roland—inseparable from Corcoran during the stretch of their youth. Days spent in sunshine and fields—Corcoran, grinning and pulling a slice of apple from his pocket, offering it to a horse. Some nights, I watched him blow into a horse's muzzle while Roland lurked behind him, scared of the creature, in spite of his own girth.

I grew braver, more curious, and began taking quick brushes against Corcoran to burrow deeper into his emotions— my arm bumping his now and again while we cut through the dense brush. The feelings that flowed through my ilex were pleasant, warm. As I held them within, they revealed that they were more than feelings; they were memories. In the beginning, they came to me veiled, showing up as blurred lights and colors. While we traveled through the woodland, I practiced holding them in my mind, attempting to polish them into something more tangible. I made a pass at my moonstone and let each memory reel slowly through my thoughts, turning it over and over. When I needed more clarity, I took another light brush against Corcoran.

I worried that he may grow suspicious, but he did not know how, exactly, my ilex worked. I continued to secretly enjoy his remembrances while he remained ignorant, spending his days hacking through the thick forest foliage. Most of his memories were about Roland. *Rowley.* In the battlefield dream, Rowley had called Corcoran his brother. I was unclear as to whether he meant it as a term of endearment or if they were siblings by blood. In the memories I pulled, Rowley was a youth, chasing Corcoran through a field of wheat while the two boys dueled with sticks. The sky above was placid and blue, the sun shining warmly upon the boys' game.

I tried to curb my sordid curiosity, but I ached to uncover more. I wished to know what Corcoran held deeper, more sacred in his heart so that I may study it, draping it across the floorboards in my mind—the way my Papa had done with his artifacts. But I continued to only sweep Corcoran's skin lightly, restraining myself. I was afraid of what I might do, if I were to fall too deep into him, use my ilex to tunnel beneath his nerves and veins, reaching deep into his heart and mind.

Days passed slowly in the forest. My hours were consumed by cutting through brush, my arms becoming so sore that I could scarcely move them when I stopped. My hair clung to my skin and I fanned it to cool my neck. For days, I believed this torture would never cease, but in time my efforts were rewarded by the end of the thicket. We emerged into a pleasant space, a place in which the trees gave way to a blanket of green and yellow grasses. Rocks, coated in moss, jutted out of the earth.

I glanced back at Corcoran. He examined the grass for a moment, then plucked a beautifully shaped leaf from it. Lightly, he tucked it behind his ear. Wordlessly, he extended a hand to me. The lovely scent of the sunshine and freedom filled my senses and I accepted his gesture, brushing my fingers against his. With his other hand, he slipped the hilt of a blade into my palm and closed my fingers around it, holding my fist in his.

My heart jumped, and the restraint I had placed on my ilex unraveled like a spool of thread knocked from a table, rolling too quickly across the ground for me to catch it and wind it back without tangling the string or bunching it into knots.

Fondness. Tenderness.
Attraction.

I faltered, stumbling on the uneven ground. My pulse quickened. A surge of giddiness fluttered beneath my sternum. *Had I felt it right? Did he truly desire me?*

"Lor, listen closely," he said, ignoring my misstep. The whisper of attraction I had felt floated away. It was gone so quickly that I questioned whether it had been real or if I had misconstrued some other feeling, perhaps a distant memory my ilex had picked up.

"There's a stream near us. Your next lesson is to lead us to it. I want you to mark your path back to this spot." He guided my hand to the base of a tree, using it to carve an X across the bark. Corcoran's hand came free from my wrist, but he clutched it again abruptly. I felt into his skin, hoping to find the ripple of attraction I had sensed before, but he was focused—firm and authoritative.

"Lor?"

"Yes?" I gasped.

". . . Don't mark them all. It'll lead the enforcers straight to us."

He taught me to score thin marks across the bottoms of the trees as we moved—bold enough so that they were visible to my eye while remaining abstract, following no distinct pattern so they would not appear to be conspicuous to one passing by. I had believed we would arrive at a small brook, but the stream we found was much larger than I had expected, a body of water that separated us from an outcropping of rock and trees on the other side. Pebbles and minnows gathered at the rocks at the shore. Staring into its depths, I felt small; there was no way of knowing how deep the waters ran.

A smile bloomed across Corcoran's cheeks at the sight of the water. He removed the sword from his back and placed it on the grass, and then his satchel. His shirt soon followed, which he draped across a branch before lowering himself to the banks. I turned away when he reached for his trousers, trying to hide the heat on my face.

Corcoran laughed, a hearty ring rippling across the placid waters. When I peeked back at him, his boots lay unlaced on their sides, his trousers pushed up to his knees. He dipped his legs into the water. As he looked down at his feet, his long hair shifted from his back to his shoulder. Two black, curved lines peeked coquettishly from the base of his neck and I traced the lines with my eyes, trying to guess at the image.

"Hoi! Come on, Lor!" Corcoran cried.

I blinked, clearing my mind of the marking on his neck. Shuffling to the edge of the water, I removed my boots while he waded deeper into the stream. I gathered my skirt in my hands and dipped one tentative foot into the water. The chill bit my toes and I yelped, pulling my leg back.

"Ack, Lor." Corcoran chuckled. "Such a Damica."

He rested his shoulders in the water and kicked his legs, floating farther down the stream from me. Since the time we had first crossed paths, his body was in constant movement. He was always flipping a blade, making idle marks in the dirt, fidgeting with sticks, or simply stretching his limbs. Motion was a necessity for him, as natural as the flow of the stream. His movement reminded me of my sister-Damica, Riognach. Inasmuch as she was not my friend, nor I hers, I admired her gift as a Vigore. She was always the lead when the filia learned to dance, her footing flawless while the rest of my sister-Lunare stumbled along. I remembered how Corcoran twirled his blade in the field of men while pressed back-to-back with Roland. A thought sheared through my mind. He was also swift to avoid the truth, so eager to swirl around it, like the minnows at my feet scattering when I dipped my toe in the water.

"Corcoran," I cried, cupping my hands around my mouth to call for him. "Why will you not tell me you were a soldier?"

Corcoran whirled around; his eyes narrowed with

caution. *Mistrust.* He was like one of the horses from his dreams with Roland—a creature unsure of whether it could trust the fruit sitting in the palm stretched before him.

"How did you . . ." he mouthed.

The words tumbled from me without fully thinking them through. "I dreamed about you in the fields. With all those other men in gray tunics."

Corcoran uttered a curse and began to wade back toward me. "I'll tell you something, Lunare," he said. "That gift of yours. It scares the hell out of me."

Bowing my head, I watched the water lap up against the shore. The minnows scattered in all directions.

"Then you should have told me when I asked," I said. "You should tell the truth."

"The truth?" Corcoran shook his hair, squeezing the water from his trousers. He took a seat beside me, stretching his legs on the bank. "You think because I didn't tell you, you had the right to siphon it out of me?"

I had not thought about it before, and I stumbled over an apology.

"Stop, Damica. Just . . . stop." Corcoran scowled. "It's called boundaries, Lor. Consent. Privacy. Are any of these familiar to you?"

Shame crept up my cheeks, pressure welling behind my eyes. I blinked away a mist of tears. "We're taught obedience. Loyalty," I repeated my training from the Accademia. I had heard the phrases so often they rolled off my tongue easily. "Allegiance to her headmistress, through courtship, marriage, motherhood—always."

"Huh! Is that what they tell you?" Corcoran snorted. "A lot of good that seems to have done for you."

"I'm sorry," I whispered.

Corcoran was quiet for a moment and then stood. "We're told to kill you," he muttered.

"What?"

"Soldiers. If we find one of you, our orders are to kill you on sight. If you find a Lunare, snap her neck. No questions. No hesitation. Those are our orders."

I felt my chest grow tight, and I grabbed a handful of grass. "So, you have killed my sister-Lunare?"

"Me?" Corcoran scrunched his face. "No. Never came up for me. But I'm telling you, that's what soldiers do."

I thought back to my time in the Accademia, Damica Cosetta's image in Headmistress Elan's hands. Holding the memory in my mind, I could feel new emotions whirling around it: disappointment, careful and measured, hiding in the headmistress's throat. Fury, threatening to seep through her meticulously practiced countenance.

"Why us?" I asked. "What did we ever do to you?"

"Lor, don't be naive!" Corcoran explained, plucking his shirt from the branch on which it hung. "You're terrifying. They don't even let your kind marry outside of Trionfi anymore. They used to, until someone figured out they can use you to interrogate prisoners of war. Did you know, one of your kind once shook out the identity of a king posing as a wounded soldier?"

I blinked, my lips parting. I could feel, now, the pulse in Headmistress Elan's thumb as she held it against Damica Cosetta's commander. She wanted to crush him. She wanted him to bleed, to suffer for bringing her friend into his war.

"Even the most unwilling men will fall to your kind," Corcoran continued. *"Present company included."*

"I'm sorry," I whispered, shame creeping up my cheeks. "I didn't mean to invade your private thoughts."

For a moment, I felt the hot, acrid taste of shame on my tongue. I moved to the edge of the banks, cupping my hands and allowing a cool stream of water to flow over them. I brought it to my lips and drank deep.

I vowed, to myself, then, that I would not speak of Roland.

"Your days as a soldier . . . I discovered them by mistake," I blurted. "You must believe me. You were sleeping and your days on the battlefield came to me in a dream."

Corcoran shifted his weight uncomfortably.

"I am still learning how to control my gift," I explained, wiping my mouth. "I have tried, and tried, and tried, to keep it repressed until it is time for it to be called upon. I have been practicing control for years. And . . . failing."

"Holding it in, trying to control it." He breathed in and released a long breath. "Lor, I'm not so sure that's a good idea."

I looked up at him, crossing my arms over my chest. There was no satisfying this man. "Why would you say such a thing. A moment ago, you told me that I needed to practice boundaries."

"Two different things, Lor."

My fingers wandered up to grip my pendant, resting it on my breastbone. Corcoran took a seat beside me and reached for my hand, unfurling my fingers. My heart lit up, but I pushed the sensation deep into my chest.

"I've known you for about a week now. And every time you feel something unpleasant, or you have something on your mind that you don't want to say—you go straight to that necklace."

"It keeps me calm," I explained. "Keeps me from losing control."

". . . that's the problem."

I tensed my brow. "What?"

"Every time you try to say something important—about Grimstaad, the enforcers, finding your Damica friend—you break down into tears. You crack. Come apart. Scream. You get paralyzed by fear. You've got to learn how to talk, without siphoning secrets out of people . . . and without holding your power in. You're letting it eat you from the inside."

I moved my lips, unsure of what to say to him in

response. His words were awful—for all his brusqueness, they were the worst I had heard leave his lips. I twisted away from him and bent my knees to my chest, sinking into the grass. The pain of humiliation was one I knew well from my days in the Accademia—but to hear this. It was new and carried with it a special sting, like a forked blade.

"Ack, there you go again, falling apart." Corcoran sighed. "You've got a lot of anger hiding in you. Too much. More than that necklace can hold. I bet it's killing you, trying to keep it all inside."

I sniffled, a tear rolling down my cheek. "I'm not sure what else to do," I whispered.

"Well, you slapped me before. It was a good start—first helpful thing I've seen you do on your own." Corcoran extended a hand and I took it. A gentle, sympathetic smile shone in his eyes. "You know soldiers—they carry a lot of anger, too. I can show you what we do about it. Got a feeling you'd have a knack for it."

JUST BEYOND REACH

We walked along the banks of the river, following the minnows and the stones beneath the surface of the water. The farther we went, the narrower the river became, until we could move from one side to the other with a small hop. Corcoran stepped from one side to the other, inviting me to follow. From the other side, we followed the stream again until it widened back into a river, its placid waters quickening into a roar. Corcoran beckoned, and we left it behind, then. On this side of the banks, the trees were thinner and large outcroppings of rock jutted from the earth. We walked toward one and Corcoran flipped a wave of his golden hair over his shoulder. He cupped a hand around his ear and listened intently.

He climbed to the top of a cliff, helping me to ascend. Together, we walked along the rocks until the sun moved from midday to late afternoon. He paused often to listen, and it soon became clear what he was listening for: the loud hiss of water rushing over one of the ledges. He guided me across a rocky precipice and pointed down to a smaller one with a waterfall shouting over the edge.

"It's small, but it'll work for what we need it for," Corcoran said. "I want you to climb down with me and we'll walk to it. I'll help you. You'll be safe; don't you worry."

He maneuvered himself down the ledge and lifted his arms to me. I lay on my belly and crawled to the edge, swinging one foot over, and then the other. I found my footing beneath the overhang and Corcoran hugged my waist. I did not flinch or pull away—nor did I reach for my pendant, which swung wildly as he helped me steady myself beside him.

"This way," he called out. The steady rush of water around us nearly drowned his voice. He took my hand and with a cool mist spraying our bodies, he led me into a cavern behind the water.

"Now, Lor, do what I do!" He perched forward, stuck out his chest, and cried out, "Yeooooooo!" He turned to me, grinning. "Your turn!"

I clamped my hands over my mouth, my cheeks hot. "Corcoran!" I protested. "I don't think I can do this!"

"Sure you can! You've just got to let yourself go, Lor! You want to see it again?" He bellowed once more into the rushing water. "Come on, now!"

I shuffled forward and taking a deep breath, I called out, *"Ah!"* My cry was swallowed whole by the water.

"Ack, is that the best you can do?" Corcoran scoffed. "Come on; no one can hear you here! Scream, Damica! Scream like you mean it!"

The drumming of the water, the pressure, and the scream—it was too much. I buried my face in my arms, wishing I could vanish. "I—I can't."

"You need to let it all out. Can't keep it inside you—don't you see? It's tearing you up; it's killing you!" The water sprayed over his face, his shirt, his hair—and I felt sorry for him, as I'd felt for Suzette, for taking on such a hapless one as myself.

"I feel foolish," I said. "I don't think this is going to help."

"How about this, Lor? Why don't we stop the screaming, and you just tell me about your life?"

My tongue felt as though it were stuck in my mouth. I inhaled and smoothed a hand over my skirt. "I will try," I uttered.

I closed my eyes and let the rush of water pound against my ears. My eyelids fluttered closed and instinctively, my fingers crawled up my chest, searching for my moonstone. Corcoran caught me by my wrist, blocking my fingers from finding it.

"Stop," he said. "I want to hear what you have to say without that damned necklace."

My breath stopped in my throat. I struggled to keep my hold on my ilex while his fingers pressed against my skin. My heart desired him—every part of him in that moment—but I could not let him know. I would not let him know. He would think me childish—my feelings fickle, foolish. I folded my lip between my teeth. The shadows of the cavern began to emerge between the rocks.

Litha. Sliding serpents at my feet, then wrapped around my ankles, sliding up my calves—

"Twist the ropes, make gallows for the Serpentine."

I tore away from Corcoran and screamed into the falls. I screamed, and I screamed, and I did not stop, even when my lungs threatened to burst, even when my throat swelled and clamped shut. The raw, painful rattling continued to push through, and I fell to my hands and knees. Corcoran's arms circled me.

"Whoa—whoa! Easy, Lor—easy!" He pulled me back and panting, I looked to the ground. No rhyme. No shadows. No litha.

"They're gone!" I cried. Something about the scream had driven them away. It was not a shriek of terror, like all my screams before. This was one of . . . release.

Still not quite believing the litha to be gone, I scanned the cavern for shadows.

None.

"Lor, I don't know what in the world you're talking about, but that scream was a holy show!" He cursed under his breath. "How do you feel?"

My thoughts swam in my head. None of them made sense.

"I—" I rasped. "I don't know."

Corcoran said something in response, but I did not hear him. Breathlessly, I pulled free from him and crawled to the edge of the rocks. I pushed my face past the curtain of falling water and let out another cry. All the words, all the feelings, they spewed from me as if I were vomiting poison.

"I did not ask to be Damica!" I cried. "No one seems to care! They act as if I chose this for myself! Why would I choose a life of such misery?"

I sat back and let the water drum on my words.

"Keep going, Lor," Corcoran called from behind me.

"They locked me in a room with no light! They forced me to drink that awful tea!"

"Tea?"

"Vendrake! Terrible, bitter, cloudy tea." I knotted my fingers through my wet hair and brushed it over my shoulders.

"What, vendrake?" Corcoran exclaimed. "Really?"

"Yes, Corcoran—vendrake!"

His voice flared with alarm. "Lor, ya know what they use that for?"

"Subduing us!"

"No," Corcoran said. "They give it to the battle-wounded, if they have to take off an arm or a leg. It just . . . numbs you out, makes you into a ghost of what you were."

Ghosts. Spirits. Blades.

Litha.

I let out a scream, pulling at my hair.

"I saw her—in that blade."

"Huh?"

"The litha—I saw her."

"Lor, what are you talking about?"

"She's the madness in me. She was there—on the other side of the blade—and I . . . I couldn't reach her." I shuddered, a ripple of anger passing through my bones.

"My father ripped the blade away, and she came for me that night! Everything poured out of me—I held it in for so long, and it all came out at once! Every feeling I ever had came rushing to the surface—*all of them*! And . . . it frightened everyone. It appalled them! My sister-Damica cast me out; they called my Viper—whispered about me, mercilessly, with that horrid name!"

"Viper?" I heard curiosity—interest—in Corcoran's voice. "I like that name. It suits you."

"*I hate it!*" I cried, beating my hands against the rock. "*I hate that name! Hate it!*"

"Easy, Lor. Sorry."

I clutched my hair in my hands and my scalp screamed with pain. I folded to my hands and knees. We sat, saying nothing, the rush of the falls punctuating our silence.

"I didn't mean to hurt him," I whispered. "You have to know that."

"Huh?"

"My Papa. That's who I hurt when I . . . lost control of myself. When the litha took me. He sent me back to my headmistress and went back to his brethren in the mountains."

"His brethren? At the Order Umbilicus?" Corcoran asked.

"Yes," I breathed, my voice barely audible amid the falls.

Corcoran startled, shifting his weight. "Why didn't you tell me that? I thought he was just a visitor passing through."

"A visitor? No. He is one of the oldest, and most treasured, of the aeditii."

"The *what?*"

"Aeditii. They are the archivists who preserve hallowed artifacts . . ." I shook my head, uninterested in my explanation. "I need to see my father, Corcoran. He's the only one who can help me now. If I tell him about Grimstaad, I am certain he will march over to Headmistress Elan and demand she reverse the marriage. Or maybe the Order can reverse it . . ."

Corcoran chuckled, then, chewing on private thoughts. My hand hummed with desire; I wished to slide against his skin and find the source of his amusement, but I remembered his sentiments toward my ilex—my apology, and the promise I made to myself to respect his wishes. I surrendered my hand to the falls and let the water wash my curiosity away.

"You wouldn't have to reverse your marriage," Corcoran said. "The Order—it's outside Trionfi's borders. You aren't subject to the same rules and the laws there—your marriage to Grimstaad wouldn't hold. If you make it, you'll be free. On parchment, at least."

I twisted toward Corcoran, slinging my wet hair onto my back. "Is this true? How can you be so sure?"

"Oh, I'm sure," he said, standing. "Time to go, Lor. Let's get a move on. We've got to be prepared for a trip up into the mountains. You feeling any better, letting all of that anger out?"

"Yes," I said, breathing a sigh. "Much better."

"It's good to feel your anger—not to ball it all up and keep it all inside. Feeling it helps. More than you might know."

Feeling. Honest, raw emotions. Feeling them deeply, wholly, in their purest form. I had always been frightened to do so, taught that it was wrong. My ilex felt like a beautiful dance, swirling through my body, buzzing like a fiddle inside my chest—and with it came praise. But with it, too, came the litha— which had brought nothing but humiliation, pain, and misery.

But ahh—to feel deeply . . . to let it all go . . .

It had been different. Frightening—and freeing. I reached for my pendant, tracing the chain. The litha pulsed on my fingertips.

Do it. Do it.

I shivered and gritted my teeth. Yes. This time I would listen. I would let it run free, and I would not try to stop it. I would heed its call without regret. I set my jaw, resolute.

"Corcoran?"

"Aye?"

"I have something to do before we go."

"What's that?"

I removed my pendant from my neck and heaved it into the falls.

Corcoran raised his fist overhead and cried, strong and deep, into the cavern. "Yeoo!"

VIPER, RABBIT, BLADE

My act of bravery was also an act of foolishness, and I soon came to learn that the two were intertwined, like the elegant silver strands of my chain tied with the unsightly red threads from my coat. I admonished my foolhardiness in the days that followed. Without the moonstone, I was defenseless, alone against the litha—and I had only just begun to understand it. Once Corcoran and I had left the falls, there was nothing I could do, nothing to protect me from it, were it to return.

We moved far, far past the sanctuary of our river and the clear terrain disappeared behind us—an unfriendly woodland, more thick leaves and branches, stretched endlessly ahead. Time passed slowly; I slashed, and slashed—my arms burning with the repetition of each motion. And there was always more ahead—more leaves, more branches, more vines. Over the next few days I followed Corcoran, I started to feel unwell. My appetite vanished and I struggled to keep up with Corcoran's long strides. The days grew cold, and the wetness of the brush bit into my skin while I cut it apart, my fingertips growing numb first, and then my entire hand. Day after day, I struggled to force my blade through the foliage. Corcoran worked ahead of me, slicing evenly through it, singing as he worked.

His melody sent a flicker of sadness across my heart. The words of his song were foreign to me, curved and pinched—some of it nonsensical. But when he sang, I missed my papa. I wished it were my father's hymns filling my ears instead, the rich timbre of his voice flowing through my veins—grounding me, keeping me safe and warm. Sometimes I let my lips vibrate with their memory, and my ilex responded, fluttering under my sternum. I could almost hear the crackle of the hearth in my home. The scent of the woodland greens momentarily faded and my nose filled with the aroma of piandia browning in the hearth. Blood rushed back into my fingertips, sending shivers and pinpricks through my hands while I held the warmth of my Papa's eyes in my mind.

I dreamed fevered dreams—dreams which led me back into the battlefields in Corcoran's dreams. I walked among flat, trampled land, a scattering of weary soldiers and cards scarring the landscape. I woke from these dreams, sticky with perspiration and dew, only to slip into them again. Day and night, I wandered the battlefield aimlessly. I searched for Corcoran's blue eyes, but the muddied landscape and sprawl of gray tunics offered me no solace.

I was in constant flux between worlds—woodland, battlefield, home. The words and melodies from Corcoran's song blended with those of my father's hymns. After a time, I could no longer distinguish them from one another. Soon after, my worlds mixed together and I found myself joining in battle, fighting beside dirt-streaked faces. My opponents donned the garments of enforcers, and I froze when two faces emerged among the many I did not know: Enzo. Luca.

I pulled my blade, but Enzo caught my arm before I could strike him. Luca forced me to the ground, ripping my weapon from my hand. I thrashed and bit, but I could do nothing to escape: I choked on Luca's laughter as he tightened his hands around my neck.

I awoke, damp from dew and perspiration. After this dream, I avoided sleep as much as possible and shuffled through the forest with my blade always in hand. I lost my hold on which world I was in, and I would have become entirely untethered were it not for Corcoran's blond hair swaying at his back, acting as my compass. My legs grew weary, heavy as the sky itself. I might have continued like this endlessly in this manner had my body endured. At some point, I stopped and rested my head against an old tree, allowing my eyes to close for a moment. When I opened them, I found myself back on the battlefield. I shrieked in apprehension of seeing Luca and Enzo, pawing at my eyes to force myself awake, to no avail. A war-drum rolled. My nerves jittered in my body, my heart pounding fast and hard.

They are coming. Oh, diosemma. *They're coming.*

The fighting broke out, soldiers swarming from all directions toward each other. The mud ran red. I gripped my blade and crouched low to the ground, shielding my face to avoid the spatter.

They're coming. It was only a matter of time. Seconds, minutes, before Luca and Enzo found me. I pressed my hands over my ears. I could not think. I could not breathe.

"Lor!" I opened my eyes to Corcoran's bright blue eyes. They were narrow, pinched by a worry-crease in his forehead. He shook me violently and I blinked rapidly. "Lor! Come out of it!"

"Hi." I flashed him a smile and looked past him to the sky. I was back in the woods. The warmth of his breath tickled my throat and chin. My heart surged. *To have him so close . . .*

"You've grown weak, Lor. Too weak to press on. We need to stop," he said. "Find another clearing, somewhere quiet where no one will be looking. We can't make it up in the mountains, not with what we've got."

My stomach lurched. So, this was it. We had hit an impasse; we could go no further. My papa's face flashed through my mind—the movements of his lips as they moved with the words from his tomes. My heart fell, and I choked back a sob.

"Don't leave me . . . please." I whispered. "I should like

to stay a moment longer, and gaze upon you . . ."

He drew his blade and studied it, moving it at different angles. He uttered a curse under his breath and turned to me. His intention had become clear. He would rid himself of me, slicing a quick, sturdy "U" across my throat. I would fall to my knees, the burden of my hunger given to the land, the roots feeding on blood and secrets. The trees would feast upon my sorrow as I stared up at Corcoran, his name, never to fall from my lips again.

"*Arrivederci*," I whispered. I raised my head and steadied myself, preparing for the ill-fated bite of steel. But it did not come. He tucked his blade back into its sheath.

"Lor." I closed my eyes and shivered at the sound of my name. His hands slid under my knees, and I felt myself being lifted.

"You've gotten thin. Too thin, too fast."

I pressed my forehead against Corcoran's chest. "You are not going to kill me?"

"Kill you?" Corcoran's voice sounded with alarm. "No, Lor. I'm not going to kill you. We need to feed you. Get you more to eat than berries and roots. Find something warmer for you to wear. All you've got is that red coat."

I shifted in Corcoran's arms, nuzzling my cheek against the warmth of his body. It glowed in my heart. But he could not carry me forever, all the way to the Order. I hated that I was a burden. That was all I had ever been, to nearly everyone whose path I had crossed. My sister Damica saw me as one, as did the vedovas, and Headmistress Elan. Even my own father had seen me as such, shipping me to the Accademia because he could not handle the litha.

My litha. It was mine. My ilex, my litha: my gift, my curse. My fault Suzette had been disfigured. My marriage to Grimstaad; my desire to find my way to my father.

The journey through the woodland: it was mine. All of it was mine.

I had asked Corcoran to teach me, not to do for me . . . not to carry me.

"Put me down," I demanded. I pulled my cheek away from his comforting warmth and shifted in Corcoran's arms. "I want to walk."

"Lor, no. You don't know what you're saying."

"*Put me down*," I growled. "You said it yourself: I should have a choice. And I choose to walk."

Corcoran nodded, hesitation hanging between us before he set my feet gently in the grass. "This is a bad idea. Your mind isn't all there, and—"

"I won't be your burden," I interrupted. "You have taught me a lot, but I need to learn to stand on my own."

I steadied myself on the ground, struggling to keep my legs from buckling. Corcoran reached for me and I snarled, waving him away.

"*Lor*," he scolded.

"No! Leave me be. Tell me what we must do to reach the mountains."

Corcoran scowled, wrinkles of disapproval forming on his beautiful face. He kicked at the grass.

"We need to make sure you don't die."

I walked with him until the sun fell in the sky. When night arrived, with it came a bitter chill that penetrated me to the bone. My teeth chattered while Corcoran gathered a small pile of leaves. He struck his tinderbox, and while it flared, he spoke.

"You need to get some meat in you to keep from getting too thin. And you need something warm. Means we need to hunt," he said. "This thicket, it's a good place for rabbits. We're after the meat and the fur."

He showed me how to drag my blade with quickness

and precision between two stones, and it ripped my flesh twice before I was able to follow his movements without damaging my fingers.

I took solace in the repetitive *shk-shk-shk* of my blade meeting stone. Corcoran left me to this activity while he sharpened his own blade. I begin to hum to myself, filling my mind with the warm and familiar. I wondered where Suzette may be, if she was recovering, finding some new way to adjust to her circumstances in the Accademia. Staring into the fire, I envisioned the sparkle of her eyes, her silver brooch perched on her collar.

I did not allow myself to think about Grimstaad's blade, or the scar across my cherissima's face.

"Lor." Corcoran snapped me from my thoughts and pulled my hand from the sharpening stone. "Let's see it."

He bent my index finger and guided it along the edge of my blade. I flinched, crying out as my blood stained the steel red. Corcoran nodded in approval while I wrapped my hand into a fist, cradling it against my chest.

"I had always believed hunters used arrows," I said.

"There's no quivers out here."

"Can we not find someone to trade with?" I shivered.

Corcoran flashed me a sideways glance. "There's no one to trade with but enforcers or banale."

I felt foolish for my questions, and even more at his brusque answers. My lip quivered. The blade trembled between my fingers. A thick teardrop clung to my lashes, and I squinted to keep it from falling. I raised my chin, lifted my arm, and flung my blade at a tree. The handle bounced off the trunk and landed in the grass.

"Are you sure you're well enough to do this?" Corcoran tossed his pale hair over his shoulder and moved toward the tree. He lifted my blade from the ground and handed it to me. "Maybe we shouldn't have been so quick to throw your necklace into the falls."

I bowed my head and sheepishly took my blade. "I am having trouble, Corcoran."

"This cold, it's not helping things." A sigh escaped his body as a thin, cold wisp of breath. "Let's get the snares set as quickly as we can."

My ilex bucked against my ribs. For some reason, Corcoran felt uncomfortable with snares, and my fingertips pulsed, urging me to find out why. I had told him, though, that I would respect his privacy, so I could only speculate as to the source of his discomfort. Perhaps it had something to do with my getting caught and injuring my ankle.

"Lor." Corcoran snapped me back to attention. "If we catch any rabbits, you're going to have to kill them. Skin them. Cut them up to eat."

I buried my fingers in the soil, curling them through dried grass and broken leaves. "What?" I shivered. I tried to imagine my blade cutting across one's throat—the life draining from their eyes. My knife tearing away at their skin, making jagged cuts across their flesh . . . *Like Suzette.* My stomach knotted at the thought.

"No! I don't think I can do it!" I cried.

Corcoran scoffed. "Lor, it's a damn rabbit. You catch it, you kill it, we eat it and keep its fur. Simple as that."

"It isn't just a rabbit! It's—it's—" I fumbled through my feelings, failing to find the words to capture them. It was not the rabbit that was the problem; it was me. And I did not know how to explain that to Corcoran. Everywhere I went, the innocent were maimed, marred—suffered. Papa. Suzette. It was only a matter of time before I killed someone. And Grimstaad would see to it that I would—in the belly of some dank dungeon or prison, while I harvested secrets and plans from their minds.

I crossed my arms and glared at Corcoran from the other side of our fire. He scowled, swore under his breath, and paced away from me, wrapping his arms around his chest.

Maybe there were no rabbits, and all my fretting was for

naught. In all our time traversing the woodland, I had never seen one. I pressed my palms into the mud and listened deep into the earth for any light footfalls, but I heard nothing more than my own shallow breaths. Away from Corcoran, I rested my back against the trunk of a tree pockmarked with holes and twisted knots in its bark. Swallowed by brush, the ferns and autumn foliage tickled my skin. I allowed my mind to sink to its roots. I breathed in and tasted my solitude. It felt cool and pleasant on my tongue, like the first bite of a chilled fruit. Still seated, I leaned the crown of my head against the vines, and I was met with a stirring—a rumble that differed from the timbre of Corcoran's voice. I allowed the vibration to travel through the back of my head. I listened—closely and intently—to the swirl of my own blood babbling in my ears—and then the flicker of a heartbeat, quick and frenetic.

Thump-thump-thump-thump.

My eyes darted open.

It was not mine.

In the brush, an iridescent glimmer caught my eye. I rose and grabbed my blade, squeezing the hilt in my palm. A clandestine black eye met mine: two long, delicate ears and a soft nose emerging from the brush, sniffing the ground. I gazed at the thick-bodied creature as it stumbled forward—unaware of the fate that awaited it.

The rabbit's eye flickered open and its lips pulled back, a terrible shriek escaping its small body. I pressed my hands over my ears and shuddered. The screams were childlike and full of sorrow, and they reminded me of the lonely stirrings of my own childhood—the time I entered the Damica with plump cherub cheeks and frightened eyes.

"Lor!" Corcoran's voice rang through the night, his boots crunching the dead grasses and leaves as he rushed to me. I dropped my blade and fell to my knees.

"I can't do it," I gasped.

The salt of tears stung the corners of my eyes and I

clenched my throat to contain them. I licked my lips, realizing I had been holding my breath, and I exhaled into the sky, a shallow breath departing quickly from my lips. Corcoran's features softened and he knelt before me. The tips of his hair brushed my neck.

"I was wrong," I said. "I can't do it. I can't stand on my own. It's too much. My mind is not strong enough. I—I can't do it. I failed you, and I'm sorry."

"Lor."

Gently, Corcoran pressed his lips against my forehead. They were cold to the touch. I closed my eyes and savored the flutter of his breath against my skin.

My heart stirred in the frigid night, coming alive in this thicket where autumn shivered and leaves fell to the ground. Any remaining control I had over my ilex snapped like a twig. My ilex hummed through my entire body.

A terrible discovery cut through my mind, and I gaped at Corcoran, horrified.

WILDERNESS OF THE UNKNOWN

A whirl of terrible, intrusive thoughts spiraled through me. They did not show up as a haze of colors, nor a timid bud of feelings that I must coax into bloom. They were not dreams like the stampede of soldiers flooding the fields with blood.

Just a rush of words, like my screams at the falls.

Corcoran was a soldier. But no more.

A traitor of Trionfi. He absconded.

The enforcers are looking for him.

He is wanted for treason.

Grimstaad is looking for him.

Grimstaad.

My stomach lurched, and though it was empty, the burn of bile seared through my throat. Grimstaad was seeking him, like he was after me. *Why?* The question flared on my fingertips. Why? I could, of course, find out. It would be effortless for me to reach for Corcoran and stroke the pads of my fingers across his arm to get my answers. But I had made him a promise.

A promise I had broken.

It was an accident; but, nevertheless, I had peered into a piece of him that he did not want me to know. He had betrayed Trionfi, but I had betrayed him by taking this knowledge from him. Was there a way to give it back? If I still had my pendant, I would have tried pressing my thumb into the moonstone to smudge the knowledge away. I did not know if such a feat was possible. I had never tried it, and my mind reeled with panic, searching for some solution. Any solution. Anything to erase this harrowing secret my ilex had lifted from his heart.

If Corcoran had wanted me to know of his past, he would have told me. My ilex frightened him; it had terrified Luca and Enzo enough to try to kill me—and it caused me fright, as well. I had lost control for but a moment and Corcoran's darkness had flowed into me. It had come so easily, so naturally. Deep within, my ilex hummed, glowing with the knowledge. There was no ridding myself of it; Corcoran's secret was mine to carry, from now until the time of my death.

The words whirled around me, expanding in my mind. *Traitor. Treason.* And, from the repetition of them in my mind—a feeling surfaced.

Shame.

Whether it was mine or his, I could not tell. It tangled up into a knot—one that formed between my eyes and spread, a dull ache across my forehead. He was fated to be a soldier and I was fated to become Grimstaad's wife. Perhaps we both carried the shame between us: each of us running from our fate—breaking free from a prescribed role, running toward chance in the dark wilderness of the unknown.

I raised my eyes to the moon, clenching my teeth to keep them from chattering. She shone white and proud—a fingernail away from Her full phase among the stars.

"*Sweet goddess, hear me please,*" I whispered to Her. I had never prayed to Her, not in this manner. Although we had been separated in the Accademia, and I was never taught to study Her, I had always sensed her presence, that She watched me, guided my ilex. Whether it was the forest, my ilex, my litha, or something else entirely—I did not know what inspired me to speak to her, but nothing was clear or known. Everything hung in fevered, black uncertainty.

"Take my shame, so that I may no longer suffer. Let me forget these words, and end my misery." Her light spread across my face and I lay on my back—my head, and torso like ice—and I closed my eyes: starving, delirious, with his secrets vexing me.

"Lor!" Corcoran cursed and I felt his arms circle me. I had forgotten he was beside me . . . forgotten about his presence altogether. I opened my eyes and gazed longingly at the moon.

"Take this curse from me, please. I cannot endure it any longer," I implored Her. Her gentle light enveloped me and my ilex buzzed beneath my breastbone. Corcoran swore, and I felt my body being lifted from the ground.

"I don't care if you want to walk on your own. You're not even going make it to the foot of the mountains like this." He spun me around and the moon fell from my reach. "Don't you go talking to the sky. Don't need you dying on me tonight."

For a time after he lifted me, I waned in and out of consciousness, pain clawing constantly at my gut. I was uncertain how many days or nights I slept, or for how long. Shadows enveloped me—but they were not litha.

The scent of charred meats and smoke flooded my senses. My head heavy, belly screaming, I struggled to roll from my back onto my knees. My stomach turned with a strange mix of hunger and repulsion. Briefly, I surveyed my surroundings. It seemed Corcoran had brought me to a cavern: a dark, private nook in the rocks, sheltering me from the dampness of dew and the winds of night. Without further thought, I crawled toward the sunlight spilling into the darkness. Smoke from a nearby fire stung my eyes as I crossed through the cavern's exit, light blinding me as I emerged.

Two thick skewers of meat rested on the embers of a campfire. With no hesitation, I pulled one out, sinking my teeth into charred flesh. I retched at the gamey flavor, but continued to rip the meat from the skewer. The animal's juices and blood ran down my chin. I could hardly find time to chew the meat before swallowing and tearing away my next bite. I was not human as I devoured it; I cared not for what it was, nor for its taste—only that the persistent gnaw in my stomach cease.

When my hunger was—at last—satiated, there was nothing left of the creature except its bones. I lay in the grass, my abdomen aching. The act of consuming had taken all my energy.

Corcoran emerged in the corner of my eye, and I watched him take a seat beside the fire, two rabbits in his arms. He twisted a blade between the fur and meat of a rabbit, his fingers weaving deftly between knife, meat, and muscle. The scent of blood flooded my senses and I retched. If Corcoran noticed, he paid it no mind.

"You get enough to eat?" he asked. He fed the fire and the flames beside him began to lap over a pair of pink flanks on sticks. I stared into the light, entranced by the pop of oils falling into embers, the flame and sizzling flare that followed. Corcoran lowered his knife and blew on his blood-stained fingertips. I imagined they had grown cold quickly.

I held my stomach and tried not to expel its contents. The heaviness in my stomach, the scent of blood, and the life I had consumed mingled together, and I pressed my palm over my nose and mouth. My gut churned, nausea swaying me back and forth, back and forth . . .

If I vomited, I hoped I could somehow purge myself of Corcraon's secrets in the act.

Should I tell him I broke my promise, how I had fallen too deep into his heart when he kissed me? I could tell him it was a mistake. He must understand that I was nowhere near skilled enough to use my ilex . . . especially without my pendant to keep myself calm, stable. I tried to form the words, but my lips hesitated, my tongue refusing to move.

Corcoran's focus shifted from my gaze to a small, lifeless rabbit beside me, and then back to me. "The sooner we reach the mountains, the better. Put this debacle behind us. Find your father, start a new life."

I stared past him, looking skyward. My ilex buzzed in my chest, rattling my ribs with more force than I was accustomed to feeling. There was a reason it wanted me to have Corcoran's secrets. Corcoran's words flowed through me—a slow, horrifying realization beginning to climb through my bones.

Start a new life.

He was not talking about my life; he was talking about *his. He* was wanted for treason.

His statement at the falls echoed in my mind. *"The Order—it's outside Trionfi's borders. You aren't subject to the same rules and the laws there,"* he had said. *"If you make it, you'll be free."*

Free.

"On parchment, at least."

The words crashed together, each one a whip across my face. My gut clenched; my stomach twisted in knots.

It was not I for whom he was seeking asylum. He wanted it for *himself.*

I was nothing to him beyond a treasure: a lucky card he could thumb in his pocket, keep hidden away until it was time to draw his hand—and he could swap for his freedom.

That's why he's so adamant about keeping me alive. From the moment he discovered I was Damica, he planned to use me, somehow, to win his freedom, whether it was by holding me ransom, selling me off to the highest bidder, using my ilex to his advantage, or simply using my connections to Papa and the Order to seek amnesty.

I had trusted him, but he was no better than Headmistress Elan.

No better than Grimstaad.

They all saw me as a weapon to be leveraged: a means to gain that which their hearts desired.

THE BLACKBIRD

I waited until night, when Corcoran came into the cavern and lay on the ground to rest. Waited until he had shut his eyes completely. Watched his chest rise and fall steadily, his breathing slow and relaxed. Waited, still—until I was certain he was asleep, before I left.

I could stay with him no longer, continuing my journey to the mountains alone.

Always alone.

My chest ached as though it had been split open, my heart pale and lifeless inside. I had learned a little of how to navigate the terrain, and it was better than having no knowledge at all. Somehow, I would make it. I had to; there was no better option than to *try*. My stomach full, and my ankle on the mend, I could find my own way.

Or die trying.

The trees welcomed me with their branches outstretched, offering me refuge from my feelings. Corcoran. *Liar. Traitor. Treason.* Ah—it was cruel, so cruel of him. To keep this from me, then keep me by his side—feed me, carry me, tend to me, only to sell me for his own freedom. The betrayal tasted bitter on my tongue—worse than vendrake, and its flavor did not fade.

I put one foot in front of the other, my moon's large, pale eye waning underneath a canopy of black leaves. Twigs snapped under my boots as I stumbled on my tender ankle, fragmented pieces of wood jumping to bite at my calves. I trusted him . . . and I had believed he cared for me. I had felt it.

Did he?

Or was the flicker of desire I felt stir in him nothing more than his own greed? A selfish desire to be free of the law—and free of me? A man, free to live out his days with the sun at his back, doing as he pleased. The thought made my stomach churn, and it turned over and over until a swell of bile bubbled in the back of my throat.

Perhaps the problem was that I cared for him.

Because who could truly care for one so dark as myself? My ilex was a treasure to be sold, or traded for some greater purpose—some ambition that was more important than love, belonging, or trust. I did not even understand my own ilex. How deep could I reach, truly? How much pain could I inflict upon others—by mistake, or otherwise?

Suzette.

She had loved me—truly, purely. Even in our brief time, my cherissima had put aside her own ambitions to care for me, sing to me with her lilting voice—and in the end, she chanced her own safety to aid in my escape.

And I had hurt her.

Would I have hurt Corcoran in the same way, had we carried on? My gift paired well with death; was my presence not an omen of pain? I had already hurt Corcoran by pulling his secrets from his heart—and I knew not the extent of that damage. Had I created a crack in his mind, or was it just my promise, broken, that would create a fissure in his heart?

It did not matter. Our journey together was ill-fated from the start, both of us running from pasts that haunted us, refusing to leave us alone. All along, he had planned to barter me, leverage my ilex for his own gain . . .

No more. I would think about this no more. I never wanted to see him again.

I pushed through the brush until the moon's pallid light

was fully extinguished by the treetops. Darkness. I had grown accustomed to living in shadow—invisible, except when needed. I limped and stumbled among the trees until I was surrounded, wholly, by darkness, the silhouettes of trunks disappearing in front of me. I pushed deeper into the darkness, my feet determined to take me far, far away from all who would hurt me. I stretched my arms in front of me to navigate by touch. The ache of my heart spilled into my chest, and my eyes burned—salty, full of tears.

As I meandered through the thicket, the trees opened again, frail moonlight washing over me. My shadow stretched and warped over dried branches and patches of browning grasses. A tendril of darkness sprouted up from the base of a tree, and it scuttled up the bark. *Litha.* A shadow circled once, twice, around a low branch, and then it spoke, its voice ragged, hollow—like a stiff pine needle in my ear.

"Twist the ropes, make gallows for the Serpentine."

I plugged my ears and lowered my head to my knees. *Do not listen. Do not listen.* The ugly rhyme repeated in my mind, and I clenched my teeth. The litha was rising inside me. Wild, boundless panic surged through my veins. My hands curled through my skirt and squeezed, and I shouted.

"Why won't you leave me alone?"

"Twist the ropes, make gallows for the Serpentine."

The words echoed in my mind in reply. I threaded my hands through my hair, kicking at the grass, spitting at the trees. The voice continued to chant from afar and I grabbed a handful of leaves, hurling them in its direction.

"What do you want with me?"

Their rhyme repeated in my head. I pulled at my hair and shrieked, a fistful of strands coming free in both hands. Trembling, I squeezed my lip between my teeth.

Why? *Why* were these horrible, hollowed-out men speaking to me?

My sister-Lunare. Bethany. Even Headmistress Elan

herself! None of them had suffered such terror! No. Their gifts were always calm, quiet, and contained—manifesting in a silent touch, a furtive word whispered into an ear. Mine was unbridled—dangerous and unhinged—always a breath or two away from clawing apart everything that came close.

I turned and ran in the direction opposite the shadows, the night air burning in my lungs. The toe of my boot caught on the ground, and I jerked violently. I felt myself falling—falling into the ground. Pain throbbed through the whole of me.

I had neither the desire, nor the strength, to rise.

Two knots of pain pulsed in my chest as I coughed, struggling to breathe. The branches above me swayed in my ears, offering me a brief rustle of sympathy. I stared up into the blank slate of black and a flicker of movement caught in the corner of my eye—the scratch of talons and bending of a branch just above me.

The blackbird.

"Filia."

I blinked, and when I closed my eyes, I saw a silhouette, a beam of moonlight glistening on a lock of dark hair.

Rowley?

He had only appeared in dreams, with his dark hair and somber eyes; I had never seen him beyond. *How could he be here?* My mind flooded with images of the battlefield I had seen in Corcoran's dreams.

The blackbird beat its powerful wings. *"I told him not to call me that."*

"It is you!" I cried, climbing to my feet. "Spirit! You are Roland!"

A rustling in the distance pulled my attention—a presence that lingered near me. I whirled around and looked up to the branches, but I caught no black beak or feathers peeking from the leaves.

I held the buzz of the blackbird's voice in my mind, focusing on it, sharpening it as though it were a blade between rocks. The voice became a murmur fading in and out of my ear—throaty, with a low timbre. I squeezed my eyes closed as tightly as I could to focus. When I opened them, a pale light glittered before me, a faint path stretching forward. I pressed my palm to the trunk of a tree and listened, hearing little more than my own breaths and the buzz of crickets underground.

I looked up and Roland—truly, Roland—stood before me. I was familiar with his enormous physique from afar, but I had never been close enough to study his features. His eyes were small and intense, brown, and they carried a sadness that was both unnatural and beautiful—like a trickle of rain holding onto the point of a thorn. His hair, pin straight, fell past his shoulders. In the darkness, it would be easy to envision it as feathers. Roland carried his enormous hammer with him; the arm with which he held it was noticeably thicker than the other. *Why has he not appeared to me before, as a man?*

The reason struck me suddenly, knocking the breath out of my lungs.

"Roland, you are deceased."

"Departed," Roland whispered. *"Death comes in many forms."*

I shivered at his words. I remembered them from before—the night that Luca and Enzo chased me. So much had happened since I left the Accademia, and I found myself skimming through all of it in reverse: Corcoran and the falls, the spray of water on my face. The swim in the stream. Corcoran carrying me on his back. The death of the enforcers, the chase through the woods . . .

I thought back to the Accademia, Suzette and I, huddled together in the Catene chambers, her whispering to me, soothing me.

Catene. The ones who could control life and death. Was this what Roland was?

I had believed that it was only women who possessed the gifts of the Damica. Yet, I had never met a Catene in all my years in the Accademia—nor had any of my sister-Lunare, nor anyone else I knew. I held the memory of the Catene chamber's single bed, its frame against my legs as I sat at the edge, blanketed in Suzette's embrace. One bed, one nightstand, one alone. One. Had there only been one Catene, in all the time of the Accademia—and was I in its presence? *Was it Roland?*

If this was so—was Roland like me? Was he like Bethany? We each had the ilex; we could feel deeply into others, but my gift and Bethany's differed, regardless. While I was a destroyer of secrets and minds, she helped others to navigate; she could guide the lost, find the missing.

Perhaps this is Roland's gift, as well.

"It was no accident, was it? You guided me, the night of the enforcers . . . You led me to him, to Corcoran."

"Yes."

"I saw you with him in the fields," I said. "He is your brother."

"Yes. Foster brother."

I turned away to hide my anger, but it shook in my voice. "You shouldn't have led me to him. It was reckless."

"Reckless for who?"

"All of us. I . . . lost control of my ilex. Pulled secrets from his heart when I promised I would leave him be."

Roland swept his thumb across my cheek, rubbing away an invisible tear. His mouth pulled into a tight, grievous smile. *"He has always had a thirst for recklessness."*

My chin dropped. "My gift, my ilex—it has caused us nothing but pain. I learned he wishes to ransom me."

"Ransom you?" Roland took a step forward, his enormous shadow bathing me in darkness. "My brother is many things, but a tradesman he is not."

"You do not understand!" I huffed at Roland. "He was going to hurt me—or I was going to hurt him. Or we were going to hurt each other. No matter what, it would end in tragedy—

and it would be my fault. My fault, for being Damica. My fault, for being a Lunare and carrying the ilex . . ." A lump swelled in my throat.

"Perhaps you have grown accustomed to being alone. Your gift has brought out the ugliness in all that you've met— and all who you'll meet. So, you keep to yourself. Isolated. Maybe you even find it comforting. Familiar."

Like shadows. The thought cut across my mind, and I pressed my lips together. Roland bent to one knee and met me at eye level.

"Filia, do you know why I chose to appear as a blackbird?"

Was it not evident? From his features, it was easy to see why one would think of Roland as a blackbird. His nose ran the length of his face, and protruded into a fine point at its end. His mouth was carved into a perpetual frown, even when he smiled.

"It was what I was called when I served in Trionfi's army," he said. *"No matter where I went, death would soon follow. They began to think of me as an omen of death."*

I raised an eyebrow, his words settling in my mind. Blackbird. An omen of death. A Catene.

"It is rather unfair," I said.

"Sooner or later . . . you must accept what you are."

"What I am?" I scoffed. "I am fated to die. All paths lead to my demise. Shall I return home and be given to Grimstaad? Or shall I die out here, in the cold?"

"You've sensed it, haven't you? That you have always been this way?" Roland asked. *"I have always been this way. My father was a blacksmith. I grew up in the darkness of the forge, and I lived in my father's shadow. I am Blackbird. Everywhere I went, soot, darkness, and death seemed to follow."*

Roland's words rolled through my mind. He was called Blackbird. A name he had come to accept, and embrace, even in death.

"Take out your blade and have a look. See who you

are.”

Reluctantly, I pulled it from my belt and peered into it. My breath fogged on the blade and I pulled it away from my lips. The moon reflected my own eye—sharp, black, wild, ravenous. Not a Damica. *Something else.* Something that had existed long before the Damica.

I did not belong in the Accademia, nor did I belong to Headmistress Elan, nor to Grimstaad, nor to Madame Exley. Neither my ilex nor litha could not be trained to follow the traditions of the Damica. The litha refused to be quelled. My ilex was nothing like my Mama's gift—her suerradio, which could be shaped and groomed . . . and it was neither fate nor chance that had led me to Corcoran. It was Roland the Blackbird—the Catene, the omen of death.

"They called me Viper," I admitted.

"You deny this name?" Roland asked.

I closed my eyes and shivered. "Yes. It is a shameful name. For all the terrible things I have done—and will do. It is a name that has followed me since I was a child. I couldn't control my litha and I hurt my father deeply."

"Shameful or not, you cannot deny the deeds you have done. You can only choose what they mean, how they shape you, and who you will become because of them. What future you will choose."

"For all the terrible things I have done—I can, and will, do more. It is only a matter of time before I kill someone."

"Then make sure the right ones die." His gaze swept over my face and, gently, he placed a heavy hand on my brow. *"Close your eyes."* His glove shaded my view; the forest faded into darkness.

"Which will you choose? To be Viper—or to die in the shadows?"

The weight of his hand lifted and when I opened my eyes, I found myself back in the forest. *Viper. Shadows.* I was uncertain of which one belonged with me. I stayed still for a long time, listening to my own blood rushing in my ears. A cricket eventually emerged from the ground to rub its legs together in song, and the brush stirred with unease. The song halted abruptly.

And then, I heard it. Not a caw nor a hymn, but something else entirely. At the edge of the trees—the patter of small feet. A furred ear appeared in the brush. I pressed my lips together and silenced my breath. A proud, brown-coated creature emerged, sniffing at the grass. His ear bent in my direction, and he turned his head.

The ground shifted beneath the rabbit and a crack rang out through the night—a snare. The rabbit jumped, but it was too late. A stiff coil of rope tightened around his leg, and he flailed, helplessly pawing at the ground. His dewy black eye shifted to meet my gaze and his body stiffened, his joints and muscles locked in fear.

The moon—a full, white pearl—smiled upon me.

Lamb. Foal. Rabbit. Damica. I was nothing like them. I had to accept what I was: soft, beautiful, meek, and waiting to be devoured—by shadows, enforcers, hanged men, my headmistress, Corcoran, or Grimstaad.

I had to accept what I was.

I was different from Suzette—different from Bethany, even different from my Mama herself—with her silks, smiles, and fortunes.

I was a Lunare.

No, different than a Lunare. More than just a Lunare.

I yanked my blade from my skirt and sliced through the rabbit's flesh, knowing from the warm, wet liquid running through my hands that I had taken its life.

I am Viper.

PART THREE

Survival was not love. That much was clear. The two grew from two different roots—survival, a weed growing from the ash—love, a flower tended to in a garden.

TO FEEL EVERYTHING

Freefall.

There was no better way to describe my feelings. The rabbit's blood wet my fingers, warm and lovely for a moment—and then it turned bitter, burning cold. My flesh, my heart—waxing and waning. Hot and cold. Hot and cold.

Was that not the entire state of my being? Embers—flickers of life, alighting my heart. My Papa's warm eyes, the bread in the hearth. Suzette's soothing nocturnal lullaby, blanketing me in sleep.

Each of them marred. By claw, by blade. By self-deception. Because I denied the face I had seen in the blade.

Viper.

A name that was mine, a name that I embraced. A name that writhed in my hands, like the creature I held.

My mind drifted to Corcoran. He was, in many ways, the mirror opposite of Grimstaad—each of them half rejecting me. Like so many others, Grimstaad accepted my ilex, but spurned the litha. Corcoran eyed my ilex with suspicion, praising the litha instead.

Why can't anyone simply love me for all I am?

I moaned in frustration, twisting the rabbit's neck. With a pop, the animal fell limp in my hands. It was a silly question—a frivolous one. Headmistress Elan would have deemed it childish; even Suzette would have huffed at such foolishness.

241

Survival was not love. That much was clear. The two grew from two different roots—survival, a weed growing from the ash—love, a flower tended to in a garden. Of all his lessons on surviving in the wild, this was the one that Corcoran never spoke—but I had learned it, regardless. I was not sure I believed Roland's assertion that Corcoran would not try to sell me. It did not matter. I had made my choice: I was Viper . . . and because of my gift, I would always be alone. I did not need Corcoran's boyish grins, pretty body, nor his tenderness with me. He did not love me, anyway. He loved what I could *do*; he loved what I could *buy*. But he did not love me.

How could anyone love a viper?

They could not—and he did not.

My feelings bunched together like a tangled wad: discordant, mismatched threads rolled together. They did not make sense, and I did not know how to untangle such a mess.

Hot and cold. Hot and cold. My desire for Corcoran blossomed under the moon—a dark, frightening yearning—and within it, my wretched heartache.

He was a liar; he meant me no good.

Ahh—and yet . . .

The rabbit gave a final twitch in my hands before the last warm ember of its life fluttered away.

Cold.

I was fooling myself. There was only one thing a viper could do: steal others' warmth, rip free that which they held most dear from their hearts. *And take their blood.*

My feet moved of their own accord, steering me back to the cavern where Corcoran slept. Taking quick, shallow breaths, I tucked the rabbit under my arm. With my back pressed against the wall, I waited—listening. Did he stir, or did he still sleep soundly? I counted my breaths one by one, shivering beneath a tree—*on, deu*. The churning in my gut caused acids to shoot up my throat—an acrid, burning flavor blanketing the back of my mouth. Were the moon veiled, perhaps my heart would have been quelled with my counting. But with Her wide eye shining upon me and the scent of my kill fresh . . . I was *ravenous.*

"Sweet goddess," I whispered. "It was in your light that tonight I saw my reflection. Bless my endeavor, to take Corcoran's life, claim it as my own." I breathed out slowly, tightening my grip around the hilt of my blade. I rubbed it with my thumb, focusing my words into my weapon. A cricket chirped somewhere, buried between roots and soil. I breathed in and tasted wind on my tongue. The fire pit perched on the ledge of the outcropping was quiet, but it smelled of ash and blood. A shiver ran through me and I rolled my shoulders, moving the knife behind my back. A caw cut through the night, the blackbird beating its wings.

Ah, Blackbird. My omen of death.

Placing my hand tenderly on the rabbit, I stroked its fur and laid it beside the fire pit. White-knuckled, twisting my skirts between fingers, I slipped into the cavern. And there I saw him—Corcoran. Lying flat on his back, his sword resting beside him. Just as I had left him. The tension he carried in his body was at ease, and, studying him, my resolve wavered. A knot formed in my stomach, and I nudged the sword from his reach with the side of my foot.

I breathed in slowly, then out again. The blade felt heavy in my hand. I studied Corcoran's body, slowing my breaths to match the rhythm of his sleep. I licked my lips and squeezed the hilt of my knife. Outside, the blackbird flapped its wings frantically, scraping its talons.

Perhaps I should turn back?

No! I lectured myself. Corcoran betrayed Trionfi. *And he betrayed me! Better for him to die.*

I tossed my skirt across Corcoran's legs and straddled him. Sweat from my palm made my blade feel unsteady, and I planted one hand firmly on the ground beside Corcoran. He drew in a sharp breath, a deep crease forming on his forehead.

He blinked—once, twice—shaking the stupor of sleep. Slowly he opened his eyes—slender blue cracks caught in the twilight between a dream and waking.

"Lor?"

"Corcoran," I whispered. My voice shook, and I nearly did not recognize it. I swallowed and steadied the blade.

Corcoran shifted beneath me, and he threaded his fingers through my hair, brushing a lock behind my shoulder. "What's the matter? You have a bad dream?" He flashed me one of his beautiful smiles.

A pang in my stomach rose, a wave of anger and bile. I swallowed and steadied the blade, sliding it to his throat.

"Shut your mouth," I hissed. "I am finished with your words."

With small, quick flickers of his pupils, Corcoran followed my movements. His irises expanded and retracted, adjusting to light, darkness, and blade.

"Easy, Lor," he said. "It's me. Take a deep breath and put down the knife."

"Do not tell me what to do!" My lips trembled as the words pushed through them; my veins coursed with desire to puncture his flesh—my pulse rising while the ebb and flow of life and death coursed through my bones.

"Easy," he repeated. He blinked the last of his sleep away and murmured, his voice soft and smooth. "I . . . think I understand. Come to me, darling. There's no need for the blade."

My brow tensed, and I tilted my head. "What?" A whip of anger caused me to flinch. "How could you insinuate . . ."

He chuckled quietly. "Well, your cheeks are bright red."

My eyes widened in horror and my fingers shot up to my cheek before I could stop them.

"They do that every time I touch you. The way you hold onto me, your sighs when I carry you on my back, and—

you give me these looks, sometimes. You bat those long lashes and . . ."

"Stop it!" I cried.

Hot and cold. Hot and cold. My cheeks burned, my desire to strike him cutting across my mind like a flash of blinding light. As quickly as it came, the feeling passed, falling back into the steel before ebbing into my body. I sucked a breath of cold air between my teeth to calm my mind.

"I am not here to seduce you!" I pressed the tip of the blade against his throat. "I am here to kill you."

"You're safe, Lor . . ." Corcoran slid an arm around my waist.

I cried out and nicked his neck. "Do not touch me!"

"Whoa, whoa—easy! Easy!" Corcoran released me. "Lor, I don't know what I said to make you so upset, but I didn't mean to hurt you. I hope you know that."

"It is not what you *said*, Corcoran," I whispered, cold, furious air buzzing between my teeth. "It is what you *do*."

He pinched his brow and gazed deep into my eyes, his— clear and blue. "What did I do?"

"You are a *liar*. You are no soldier." I twisted my lips. "You are a deserter—and they want you for treason."

Corcoran's chest rose, and then it fell with a sigh. "So, you know."

"Of course I know!" A fat bead of sweat rolled down my cheek, matting the hairs on my face. As it passed my lip, I touched my tongue to it, tasting the salt, imagining it to be his blood. "When were you planning to sell me and buy your way to freedom? Were you going to hand me off to the next pair of enforcers we came across—or wait until we found someone with more clout? Or did you plan to wait until we reached the Order so you could barter with my father?"

Corcoran blinked. "Lor, what are you talking about? I'm not going to sell you!"

"Liar!" I forced his chin up with the blade. He did not

flinch, or cower in fear as I would have. A corner of his lip peeled back—a scowl wrinkling his handsome face.

"So, this is what it's come to, Damica? Well, I'll have you know something, before you stick that knife in my throat," he sneered. "You're a liar, too. You told me you'd leave me be, stop prying into my mind. And here we are."

My mouth fell open and I snarled at him. "It is not as if I did this on purpose!"

"Whatever you say, Damica. You broke your word," he said, his voice bending with scorn. "But you don't see me running a blade through you, or snapping that fragile little neck of yours."

I cringed at the way he underscored the word. Damica. My expression soured and I wedged the tip of the blade a little deeper into his throat. "You are in no position to lecture me, let alone snap my neck."

I adjusted the blade in my hand. "You think you are the only one who is dangerous?"

"Oh, I think you're plenty dangerous." He shook his head, a wisp of his flaxen hair sticking to his cheek. "Enforcers chasing you, Grimstaad wanting you. Seems like everyone's trying to get their hands on you. Haven't you learned yet, Damica? You have a strength or a talent or a power that makes you special and people find out about it? Everyone's going to try and use you."

I gritted my teeth. "You think I am weak! Like a rabbit. A beautiful, frail creature to be trapped, slain, *consumed.*"

"Aye, Lor, I do. Your gift as a Lunare? It's as powerful as they come. You don't deserve what's coming to you! And I can't stop it." Corcoran's brow tensed. "Vitis Grimstaad? With all the fear *he's* brought into Trionfi, with his hunts and his hangings? He shouldn't be anywhere near you! Using your gift to win his wars, using your body to give him children! And you can't seem to make up your mind about what you want, or even who you are! You keep leaning into it . . . . and then hiding from it again. Over and over and over. You want to stand on your own—but you won't do what you have to, to survive. Won't kill a rabbit. You want to lie next to me and have me carry you and be close—and then you use your gift on me without my knowledge, and stick a knife to my throat! And I shouldn't be trying to protect you. This whole thing is just . . . banjaxed, Lor! You know what that means? It's utter madness, thinking I might be able to save you! *You* won't save you!"

"I am sorry." I withdrew the tip of his blade from his skin, dancing it across his neck. "I am trying, Corcoran. You must believe me. While you slept, I left the cavern, and the moon—I smiled at Her, and She smiled back at me."

"You went out *tonight?*"

"Yes. I killed a rabbit. Tore its flesh with this very blade. I saw the blackbird—"

"Blackbird?" Corcoran closed his eyes and inhaled deeply. "Lor, I have no idea what any of this means. Talking to the moon, killing a rabbit, seeing a *blackbird?*" His voice pinched at the word. "What are you trying to tell me?"

"I am learning." I pressed my nose to his cheek so the bristles on his face tickled it, my lips a hair's breadth from his. "And I discovered I am more than just a Lunare. I am Viper."

Shivering, I lifted the blade from his throat and pressed my fingertips into his wound. I turned my hand over and studied Corcoran's blood, warm and wet on my fingers. Corcoran shuddered, his lips parting slightly, teeth clenched. He swore under his breath. My heart bucked against my ribs. I licked my lips and tasted the salt of my skin.

Viper. It felt right. It *was* right.

But it was not his blood, nor his life, that I wanted.

His gaze shifted from my eyes to my lips, and I caught a slight quiver in his cheek. He wished to kiss me. My lips hummed with desire. He bit his lip and frowned, the apple of his throat bobbing. I abandoned the blade and pressed my lips against his, the tart taste of dried fruit mingling with the chill of his flesh. Corcoran flinched beneath me, drawing in a sharp breath. His lips did not move with mine. Mortified, I prepared to break our bond and retreat—but then I felt his lips push back sweetly, softly against mine. His fingers moved to the nape of my neck and he drew me to him, his kiss deepening in fervor. My blood surged—a strange, uneven braid of hunger, yearning, and power twisting in my chest.

Corcoran broke the seal between our lips. "You sure you didn't come to seduce me?"

"I—think I want to," I whispered. "But I am frightened."

"You're safe with me. Lor, we can take it slow—we can just kiss, if you like." He threaded his fingers through mine. "I really wasn't going to sell you, you know. I've got this brother—"

"Rowley."

Corcoran squeezed his eyes shut and opened them wide. Tension formed a crease in his brow and he uttered a curse of disbelief. "Aye, Rowley. Suppose you'd like to tell me how you know about him sometime."

"Sorry," I whispered. Heat crept up to my cheeks, a chord of shame passing through me.

"Ack, well—" Corcoran set his jaw. "Rowley. When he was alive, he was always trying to get me to be a protector, make better choices. Use my blade to try and do some good, instead of killing people blindly because that's what I was ordered to do. Killing people who don't deserve it. Rowley wanted me to do right by others." He grunted, shifted his hips, and wedged his knee between my legs. "I shouldn't touch you. You might still decide to go back. If things get worse, and you're starving and half frozen to death, serving Grimstaad as his bride—in a nice, warm bed—might start looking a lot more appealing—"

"Stop." I clamped a hand over Corcoran's mouth. He protested, his voice muffled against my palm, and I applied more pressure. "I belong to myself," I said firmly. "Are we clear? I choose this. I want you."

Corcoran nodded.

"Good." I removed my hand. Corcoran's fingers trailed down my throat, pausing at the hem of my shirt. I shivered at his breath upon my neck. And I felt it in him—a tremor in his heart.

"Wait," I whispered.

"What is it?" he asked, his blue eyes heavy with concern.

"You're frightened, too. I feel it." My pulse raced, my mouth dry. "I want to tell you something first."

Corcoran raised a suspicious eyebrow. I guided his hand to my cheek, feeling as though it may burn through him.

"I truly am sorry," I whispered. "Without my pendant, I do not know how to control my gift. It slips out of my grasp so easily, and I am trying. I was doing so well to hold it in—until you kissed me."

"When did I kiss you?" he exclaimed.

His words bit at me, sharper than the wind. *He does not remember.* My lips hummed—the taste of sweet, bitter fruit choking me.

"It does not matter."

I blinked to hold back tears. Corcoran's hand slid from my cheek and he drew his thumb beneath my eye. "Aye, it does, Lor. If we're going to do this, then we can't have secrets." He swore under his breath, "Me—not understanding your gift, what you know, what you think you know—it almost got me killed tonight. If I lie with you—what's going to happen? What kinds of secrets will you pull from me?"

"I do not know," I whispered. "I have spent most of my life locked within the Accademia, with my gift numbed by vendrake. But under the moon, I feel . . . what I feel. My dreams have grown more intense. I will always try to respect your private thoughts, but . . . you must be patient with me."

Corcoran pulled me into a kiss, the pin-pricks of his beard brushing my cheek. His skin was marked with the scent of freedom, horses, and wind etched into his spirit.

"No more secrets. I'll tell you everything, Lor," he said, flushed. "But you've got to give me time."

I cast my gaze to his trousers. My heart pounded against my ribs, my breaths shallow and staggered. "I want to know you. I want to feel everything."

"I want it, too. But—I'm telling you, Lor, you won't find happiness in me," Corcoran whispered. "Just a lot of suffering and death."

"Viper." I was Viper. My life would be full of suffering and pain and death—but like Roland the Blackbird, I could not deny this about myself any longer.

"I do not need you to protect me from this," I said, and before he could protest, I pressed my lips hard against his, quieting words. Corcoran's face contorted. Wide-eyed, a muffled cry stopped in his throat and his objections ceased. His tongue pushed through my lips and I uttered a small cry. I tasted within him his hunger, his desire, like a clear stream.

My hand slid over my collarbone and I worked to undo the top button of my blouse. Corcoran's fingers worked quickly to meet mine, unhooking each button with ease, while I stumbled. He slid his fingers down my breastbone and stopped at my heart.

"Viper," he uttered. "I feel it in you, that name . . ." He tapped my skin gently. "When you strike, you go straight for the heart."

My heart pounded beneath his coarse touch. My ilex hummed under my breast, and I could take no more. I wanted this. I needed this. I wanted *him*.

"Please," I whispered, closing my eyes. "No more words."

The moon had called to me to him with Her light, and I would howl in reply.

HIS DANCE OF DEATH

Though I was no longer a stranger to the moon and Her pull, I was new to love. Love, that hallowed space in between all things, the gulch between life and death, the sky where both moon and sun meet.

I felt strange when I awoke—my body tender, skin chilled—my red coat draped as a blanket over my chest and torso. Corcoran was not beside me, but his boots lay faithfully at the entryway of the cavern. I pulled my coat around my shoulders, breathing in the scent of grass and firewood—one I had become familiar with during our travels and found comfort in. I set my coat aside, gathered my garments and began to dress. A twinge passed through my lower body as I dressed myself, my face flushing while I closed my blouse and slipped my skirt over my legs. A shy smile pulled at my lips. I was no longer a maiden. The thought should have brought me shame— my Papa would be mortified; my headmistress would have me cast to the streets, or worse. I halted my thoughts before my mind turned to Grimstaad, and the torture he may inflict upon me should he ever know. *Should he ever find me.*

I propped my boots beside Corcoran's and emerged from the cavern to greet the day. Sunlight pulsed behind my eyes and I cupped my hand over my forehead. I was unclear about how much time had passed, how long I had slept. The wood from our fire pit smoldered, flickering from the ashes. The scent of meat filled my senses, calling attention to the gnawing in my stomach. Corcoran had found my rabbit and left it warming. *For me.* My heart surged and I sat cross legged by the fire pit, removing a flank of meat from the embers.

I knew I was tempting fate. I, a Lunare, not a Fortuna—daring to cross the threshold between danger and . . . I did not know what. But I had chosen to do it, and Corcoran had accepted, receiving me with warm lips and skin, neither of us quite knew how long we would remain safe—or alive.

But I did not care. It had been *my* choice. *Mine.* All that mattered was what I felt in my heart. I looked to the sky; even with the moon gone, the embers of love still glowed in the sun. I dusted the ash from my meat and ate quickly.

A short distance away, I heard the rustling of leaves, the snapping of branches. I walked through the trees, cool blades of grass catching between my toes, twigs tugging at my skirt. I found him in a clearing by the stream, his sword gripped in both hands. I watched, silently, as he twirled his blade. Deftly he spun: his golden hair woven with rays of sunlight and strokes of the ink on the back of his neck peeking at me. Branches bent and knelt before him, a flurry of leaves spiraling to his feet as he swung his blade in an arc.

My breath caught in my throat. His dance of death was beautiful.

I stepped forward to take a closer look and my heel crunched over a fallen branch. Corcoran whipped around, startled. Eyes more gray than blue, he was focused, holding his blade at the ready. I did not flinch or cower before his sword; I was no longer fearful of his sword. Corcoran's gaze combed over my features and his brow softened. The muscles in his arms relented, his pose wavering.

A smile spread across his lips, and his grip on his weapon loosened. "Got to get used to having a partner again."

Partner.

A smile bloomed on my cheeks. Not a Damica. Not a filia. Not his ward, his rabbit. Something to be protected, shielded.

A partner.

"This is foolish. Ill-fated. And you know it."

Corcoran grinned, his teeth flashing. "Aye." With a measured sweep of his arm, a branch sighed, falling at his feet.

"You know who I am. *What* I am. And what is going to happen to us if we're found."

"Aye," Corcoran said. "That's why I'm out here. Practicing."

"You do not have any regrets?"

He approached me slowly, a smile spreading across his lips. His blade landed carelessly in the grass with a soft thunk, and he drew his arms around my waist. I pressed my lips against his with force.

"Lor," Corcoran muttered, pulling away.

Terror seized my heart. Had he changed his mind about us? Had he come to his senses and realized how much danger we both faced?

Trembling, I whispered, "What is it?"

"I told you last night, there's a lot we don't know about each other—a lot we should." Corcoran turned away from me and my heart fell. He looked at the ground uncomfortably, and I imagined if he still had his blade in hand, he would have twisted its tip into the earth.

"Laurel," he muttered at the grass. "Lor. Damica. Lunare. Viper. I know every one of your names. But I haven't told you mine."

A crease formed in my brow. What was he talking about? I knew his name: Corcoran. The enforcers called him by it. I had felt his heart reverberate when I first spoke it to him—a conflict brewing within about whether he wanted to share it. Why would he say such a thing?

It dawned on me, then—he must have felt freer around me, more relaxed, and he was circling back to his boyish ways. I rolled my eyes, the knot in my brow deepening, my cheeks again glowing hot, but with ire, rather than passion. "I do not understand your humor. If this is some kind of joke . . ."

"It's not—"

"Then know that I do not appreciate games. 'Corcoran' is what the enforcers called you! It's what I have called you, every day since—"

"Bryce," he said simply. "Corcoran is my family name."

"*What?*"

"Alastair Bryce Corcoran. But—ah, Bryce."

I blinked, my mouth falling open. *Bryce?* How common of a name he had! How strange it felt to sit on my lips. Bright and clean like a garment in the sun, it did not suit his furs and steel.

"Corcoran, I—"

He pressed a finger to my lips. "No more 'Corcoran.' Call me Bryce."

I shook my head, incredulous. I did not know what to say.

"Bryce," I repeated tentatively. "Are you certain you can see me as your partner?"

"Aye, Lor." He nodded, swiftly and affirmatively.

"Roland was your partner."

He let out a small chuckle. "You're a lot better looking than Roland."

"I do not wish to be your partner only in the sense of the flesh."

Bryce wrinkled his nose. "What would make you think that? I didn't take my *brother* to bed."

"No, you misunderstand. I mean that I wish to be like Roland. Your equal." I crossed my arms over my chest.

"Aye? You think I don't see you that way?"

"No."

"Huh." The smile trickled down Bryce's chin, fading into the grass. He set his jaw. "You know what it means to bed me, Damica? You've been promised to Grimstaad. If they find out, they'll blame you, you know. Hang you, if you're lucky. You made a mockery of them. Thinking for yourself, choosing for yourself. I wouldn't have let you do that if I didn't think you could be a partner."

"Roland could fight," I murmured, lowering my gaze to my boots. "I have only seen him in visions, but—he was a terrifying man to encounter."

"Oh—he was," Bryce confirmed. "Strong as a bull. Stubborn as one, too. You did not want to be on the wrong side of his hammer."

"I cannot fight," I sighed.

"We'll be looking to change that."

"Even if we do, I have no other skills that could be of use—hunting, navigating . . ."

"Listen, Lor. I was raised on a farm. Spent my whole childhood working the fields, running around in the woods any chance I could get." Bryce cupped my chin in his hand and raised my head from its bowed position. "What I'm teaching you? It took time—and a lot of mistakes—for me to learn. You killed a rabbit. That's progress. You can learn enough to survive long enough for us to get through the mountains. That's all you need to learn from me. I need something else from you."

"What is it?" I asked.

He took a deep breath and held it in his chest for a long time before releasing it. "I need you to learn to use your gift in a way that helps us survive."

My ilex, helping us survive? No. That was not my gift. Mine paired with death. It was more Bethany's talent, with her ability to navigate.

"I heard that Lunare know how to sense an ambush, before anyone knows it's coming."

I hung my head. "I don't think I can do that."

"That needs to change, *Viper*," Bryce said. "I'll teach you how to use a blade, but your gift is a weapon. It's much more powerful than my sword, or even anything Roland could do."

I was not certain of this, but I remained silent while Bryce took another long, staggered breath and let it go.

"I need you to work on honing your ability. Bring that to our partnership and we'll call it equal."

"I will do my best," I whispered.

I touched my lips together. They still tingled from touching his. Corcoran—no, Bryce—had always spoken the truth with his body. I had come to understand this through my travels with him. While he dodged or dismissed my questions, he always paused with me to check my gait, adjust my grip, or hold me upright. If such gifts could be held by men—if he could be Damica—Bryce would be a Vigore: a tiger's eye, perhaps, not resting on his finger, but sitting at the front of his neck, drawing attention to his pretty face.

I thought about the marking on the back of his neck, the black spines. Turning the image over in my mind, I concluded it to be a blade. My arms circled Bryce's back and I sank my fingertips into the nape of his neck. I felt the discomfort in his body with frightening clarity—the muscles in my fingers twitched as his pulse began to rise.

"What are you doing?"

"You carry a symbol here," I said.

"Aye. You curious about it? It's not something I'm proud of." Bryce gathered his hair in hand, his muscles tight, hesitant to pull his hair aside to reveal it. "It's . . ."

"Wait," I said, pausing his hand. "Perhaps I can use this to practice. See if I can summon the image in my mind."

"Aye, we can do that." Bryce breathed a long sigh. His discomfort showed up as a tremor in his skin. "Take your time with this one."

His shame was clear as the sky. He did not possess all the words he wished to speak to me, but I felt the emotions— regret, stuck to his ribs, swelling in his chest. Dishonor, clamping his throat closed.

I removed my fingers from his neck and kissed him. "I will be careful with your heart."

He pressed his mouth atop mine and my back thumped against the trunk of a great oak. Together, we sank beneath a canopy of leaves.

SHAME CUT IN SPINES

Watching his breaths rise and fall in fluid, perfect movement, I found myself slipping—falling, somewhere, between love and death. Bryce was tangled up, somehow, in Trionfi's wars, and Headmistress Elan had warned me that all such men bring ill fate to the Damica. Her own sister-Lunare, Damica Cosetta had died serving one. Under the moon, the headmistress's lecture held little space in my heart. Damica Cosetta's fate and mine were separate, distinct—because I had chosen to be Viper. I was free to make my own decisions and define my own fate. While I watched Bryce, I relished the gentleness of his breath, the softness of his sleep. I had been raised by my mother amid flowers and silk, and like her, I was fated to fall in love with beautiful things.

And with Bryce, there was no lack of beauty.

We settled into a cadence. In the evenings, I foraged for roots and seeds, gathering them in my skirt, while Bryce checked and set traps. He was disciplined, this soldier of mine, this farmer's son, my *ammorante*.

The word no longer felt wrong on my tongue. Though I questioned the term in the Accademia time and again, its meaning blossomed like a rose when I was with Bryce. *Ammorante.* He was the man to whom I shared my body and spirit. They were mine to give, to do with as I pleased, for as little or as long as I wished—and each night the moon smiled upon our union, urging me to share both wisdom and fervor.

He woke before me in the mornings, rising with the sun to check traps, prepare the meat, and skin furs, laying them in the sun to dry. I watched for his shadow in the cavern's walls, smiling to myself as he worked. Though he washed his hands and blades in a stream, he carried the scent of the wild when he greeted me. I was always eager to receive him. Breathless between kisses, I lay on my back, warm atop a growing collection of furs we had spent first days, then weeks stitching together. I pressed my cheek against Bryce's neck and listened to his pulse in his throat. I followed the frantic, staccato throb, cooling it into a lullaby, dark and lovely. My blood rushed to my ears and I could hear nothing past it.

The fire crackled just outside our cavern, the scent of meat wafting from our fire pit. With the urges of our flesh fulfilled, we filled our bellies and walked, hand-in-hand, to the stream to wash. My thighs still tingling, I hummed softly to myself and sat at its edge, combing my fingers through my hair, separating it into three pieces. My thoughts wandered as I twisted my locks together.

Each night I spent in the cavern, my dreams grew stronger, my visions clearer. But they were not as before, whereupon I dreamed of Bryce and his boyhood, and his days on the battlefield. Now Papa and the mountains called to me. When I focused, my papa's hymns buzzed in my ears, mingling with the chatter of the birds, and I caught the scent of piandia. I held my breath to keep it with me. My heart warmed at the memory of our hearth, a smile pulling at the corners of my lips. In my mind, my papa's strong, steady hands greeted me—each kneading a ball of dough into piandia.

I wondered, what would Papa say when he saw my hair in braids? He would know that I was no longer the filia he had left in the Accademia. I had become something else: someone unrecognizable to all who had known me before. Would he be surprised that I had run, that I had defied the wishes of Headmistress Elan and refused to fulfill my role in Trionfi's war? I vowed to make my father understand: I did not belong in the alabaster walls of the Accademia. They blinded me, choked me with shadow at night. I pulled my braid tightly and wrung the thought from my mind. And what of Bryce, who I called ammorante?

I am happy when I am with him. That is all that should matter.

Bryce trained me constantly, without relent. He took great care to avoid direct blows to my body, though his caution did little to prevent my palms from chafing, my skin red and raw from gripping the hilt of my blade. But after witnessing his dance of death, I begged him to teach me to wield his sword.

He was adamant that I could not use it to fell a man. "Not before he gets the jump on you, Lor."

Seeing my face fall, he tried to appease me, but I struggled with tactics that required much more girth than my own. I could not catch his arm as he had shown me, nor could I use my elbows to throw him to the ground. It was with great reluctance that I exchanged his sword for the smaller blade in my belt: the only tool I seemed to be able to wield with any skill. He gave me his own knife and taught me to spin on the ball of my foot, one blade in each hand—my braid slicing the sky like a ribbon while I struck, one fang at a time.

One afternoon, he lifted my braid and let it slither in his hands, each peak and valley alive with movement.

"I like this, Lor. It's smart. Keeps your eyes clear." His voice was scratchy but gentle, like the coarseness of his hands.

My lips met his earlobe and Bryce flashed me a crooked grin. "I used to wear my hair like that in battle, you know."

I smiled at him wistfully. "If we were to wed, it would be how I would wear my hair."

"Oh?"

I flashed my teeth and let out a peal of laughter, burying my hands in his flaxen locks. "I hardly see marriage and warfare as one and the same, but I would like to see your hair braided."

"Happy to do it, but then you would see my tattoo. Have you figured out what it is yet?"

"No." I shook my head, folding my fingernails into my palm to hide my embarrassment. "No, Bryce. I have not."

"I'm distracting you." He twisted his lips and freed his hair from my hands. "Nothing's changed, Lor. We're still in the woods, struggling to survive."

"Everything has changed."

He shook his head. "No. Grimstaad's still looking for you, and I need you to be able to sense if he—or anyone else—is coming up on us. Don't get your head in the clouds. Focus."

In truth, I hated the thought. I did not want to unearth any more ugly truths, nor to hear any more voices from the trees, nor whispers crawling along the earth, tickling the fine hairs of my ears until I screamed. I only wished to gaze upon my ammorante's flesh, to lose myself in his pulse and hear the thick, beautiful words that echoed in our cavern when I received him. But much as I railed against shattering our picturesque romance, I had promised him my ilex as part of our union—and I had to keep my word.

Mid-afternoon, we checked traps for rabbits and I helped Bryce tear threads from my coat so that we may use them to sew. Bryce had shown me how to make a rudimentary stitch and we sat side by side each day, trying to create our makeshift garments from the animals' hides. My thread work was childlike at best. I recalled Riognach and her extravagant embroidery work. As wretched as her mouth may have been, she was skilled with a needle and thread. Most of my sister-Vigore class were; it was as if they could see spools of thread already woven into their final form before they were even placed on the loom.

A thick silence blanketed Bryce and me together, weighing on us like the furs we would wear on our shoulders and backs. I raised an eyebrow at Bryce as he worked his needle through his furs, hoping he would hum or whistle as he had done many times while performing this perfunctory task, but he remained quiet. It did not seem right for me to sing one of my papa's hymns and add to the weight of the fur, and I certainly would not utter the horrid words from the lips of the hanged ones, as they were the only thing worse than silence itself.

In silence it was, then, for me to practice with my ilex. Could I use it to see the image on my ammorante's neck? Perhaps. Bryce's past was a trail spattered with pain, blood . . .

Death.

I rolled my sewing needle between my fingers and lifted the furs that were draped across my lap. I held them to my nose and breathed in the stench of death. The sting of hot tears blinded me and I retched, gagging on the putrid odor.

Bryce looked up from his work. "Everything all right?"

I wiped my eyes dry with my sleeve. "I am practicing. Trying to explore my ilex."

His brow quirked. "Just be careful. Don't make yourself sick with it."

I could not explain to him that I must. My gift was one of darkness, and I was unsure of how deep it went, what I was capable of seeing and knowing, through scent. I closed my eyes and focused on the serrated edges I had seen on the back of his neck. My vision blazed white and the lines revealed themselves to be skeletal spines. I pinched my sewing needle between my thumb and forefinger. More. I needed to see more. I needed to *feel* it. A knot formed in my stomach and a wave of bile rose to my throat. I knew what I must do. In my mind I traced the spines, meandering down one, pausing at its tip. Keeping the image in my mind, I plunged my sewing needle into my fingertip and flinched; a droplet of blood welling on my skin. I massaged it with my thumb, spreading it across my skin. Focusing on the sting throbbing on my flesh, I allowed my eyelids to flutter closed and when they opened, I was no longer in the calm, green woodland with my ammorante.

I was enveloped in a plume of rolling smoke. Gagging, I tried to take a breath of the thick air around me. My lungs rejected it and I erupted into a fit of coughs, dropping to my knees. The smoke hit my face and I dropped to my knees, my eyes and nose running, tears and mucus streaking down my chin. Embers flaked above me, twirling like snow, flecks landing on my arms, biting my skin. I crawled blindly forward on hands and knees, my chest tightening around my lungs. The pressure squeezed my ribs and I could push forward no more. The heat climbed around me and I lay motionless: dying.

Too much, I thought. *I cannot stay in this dream any longer.*

"You must."

Blackbird!

A pair of soot-stand hands grasped my forearms and dragged me. Raked across dirt and soot, splintered pieces of wood caught my torso and legs. He continued to pull me while I coughed and lay limp, until a burst of clean air hit my face. My lungs ignited with new life.

Thank you, I whispered in my mind. Sputtering, I wiped my face clear of ash and mucus and tears and shakily climbed to my knees. I expected to see Roland's towering form above me, but I was alone in this dreamscape; he no longer guided me.

I shook my braid to rid it of debris and regretted the action: my head throbbed and the world slid sideways, heaving me back into the dirt. After a series of long, painful breaths, I rose and surveyed my surroundings. *Chaos.* I pressed both hands over my mouth. *War.*

The ones before me were not soldiers. They were farmers; they were every day, peaceful people—families. The men were like the merchants in the marketplace near my home, selling crisp, red apples, perhaps fish, or other wares. The women were like the dancers who joined hands at estival and sang.

But here, they were fighting soldiers. They were bleeding; they were dying.

A farm hand raised a sickle high above his head to catch the sword of a soldier. A woman, with a long braid like my own, thrust a pitchfork like a trident, attempting to keep a trio of men away. Others ran, tripping over the bodies of soldiers and farmers alike.

Beside me, a barn—the structure from which I had been dragged—roared with flames, its wood fracturing like bones as it crumbled upon itself. From the far side, I heard a distinct set of shouts.

A curse.

A thud.

A growl.

Pain, rage.

This is what I am here to witness.

Bryce. I knew it: instinctively.

I rounded the smoldering remains and found him locked in battle with an opponent. Their garments were streaked with mud and soot, the identifying features stained beyond recognition, but they appeared to be the same hue of red, with gold piping at their sleeves. Bryce's eyes were neither steel nor the color of the sky. In fire light, they were the first touch of winter on the petals of a hyacinth, a frost of a fragile blue-and-white hue. His opponent's eyes flashed green in the light; within them, a controlled anger like a shrill cry of a blade before it cuts through flesh. I felt the cruelty in those eyes. He was a reaper of men.

The man raised his fist and cracked it against Bryce's jaw. Bryce growled, shaking his head, baring his teeth. His opponent's lips curved into a smile—both ugly and delighted—

and he lifted his chin, auburn strands of hair, pulled loose from what was once a meticulously pinned bun, sticking to his cheeks.

"Come on, pretty boy," he rasped, rolling his shoulders.

Bryce pulled back his arm and yelled, swinging at the green-eyed man. With a quick swerve to the side, the man seized Bryce by the arm. He shifted his footing and effortlessly threw Bryce to the ground. I cringed and squeezed my skirt between my hands. In the folds of the fabric, I saw shadows forming beneath my fingers—darkness staining my gown, spreading up my torso, reaching for my heart. I despised this man with his cunning green eyes and arrogant chin. I bit my lip, tightening my hold on my skirt until my knuckles turned white.

Bryce heaved on hands and knees, and the green-eyed man sent a pointed boot to his ribs.

"Is that all the fight you've got left?" he sneered, spitting.

Bryce lay on his side, curled into himself. He coughed, a thin line of blood spilling from his lips. His gaze darted to the barn, and we saw it at the same time: lying flat, abandoned under a pile of burned-out boards: a shovel. Bryce wheezed. He shuddered and arched his back, rising to his knees as the green-eyed man's boots, poised and ready, waited to strike. Bryce slammed his fist into the dirt and roared—a pained creature agonizing in its last moments of life—then launched into a roll and freed the shovel from the debris.

The stench of charring flesh filling the air as metal collided with his opponent's face. The man let out a scream, almost inhuman, and Bryce flipped the shovel and caught the man's throat with the edge. His face flushed with fever, Bryce thrust the shovel through the man's neck, over and over. The blunt thud of metal against bone clamored in my ears.

It was horrible. Too terrible to watch. The most brutal act I had ever witnessed, and my stomach turned in knots. Bryce . . . beautiful, Bryce, with his boyish smile. How could this same man be my ammorante?

"*Dareme pacce, dareme pacce!*" I cried. Tears streamed down my cheeks. I choked on shadows; I choked on sobs. With each terrible, rhythmic thud, I cringed. Sickened, my legs collapsed beneath me and I sank to my knees. I tucked my body into itself and pressed my forehead against the earth. *How could it be him? How could it be my Bryce?*

The hacking ceased, finally, and it was a long time before I mustered the courage to move. Hands pressed to my ears, I lifted my gaze. Bryce stood with his back to me. Gazing far into the fields, he lost himself in their vastness. A group close to him, farmers and soldiers alike, lowered their weapons and formed a loose circle around him. Their lips buzzed with my ammorante's name.

They spoke his name in fright; they spoke it in admiration. Bryce lifted his opponent's head high, a clump of auburn hair was tangled around his fingers.

And there I saw it. The marking on the back of the man's neck: a skeletal snake consuming its own tail. An ouroboros—the same one that Grimstaad wore on his tunic.

I cried out and fell forward—dizzy, numb, overwhelmed. A plush blanket of grass spread before me. I was back in the woodland, with my needle and pelt in hand.

"Bryce! Oh, ammorante, what did you do?" I cried. Tears streamed down my face, and I could not shake the pit in my stomach, the wretchedness of it all.

"Lor?" I lifted my chin and Bryce came running toward me, dropping his needle and furs. He pulled me to his chest, and I wept and shivered against him.

"What happened?" he asked, gently stroking my back. "Did you see something?"

"You." My voice broke with fear. "The fire. The green-eyed man . . . the shovel." My chest tightened, and my breathing grew sharp, shallow. A marked breath of silence passed between us, the blue of his eyes ebbing and flowing with terror.

A pang of nausea struck my gut. This vision was not accidental, something I pulled out of a passing memory, a fleeting dream.

It had *purpose*.

I had wanted to leave, but Roland coaxed me to stay. *Why?* What was so important about such a senseless act of violence? Why was I made to witness such a wretched, vile scene? The answer cut across my mind like a knife.

Because I asked my ilex a question—and it gave me the answer.

I felt as though the earth had opened up and swallowed me in its darkness. It could not be true. It could not.

Oh, ammorante. Oh, no. No.

I had asked about the marking on Bryce's neck. The one he was not proud of. Fingers trembling, I wove my hand through his golden hair, sweeping it from the nape of his neck.

Grimstaad's ouroboros grinned back at me.

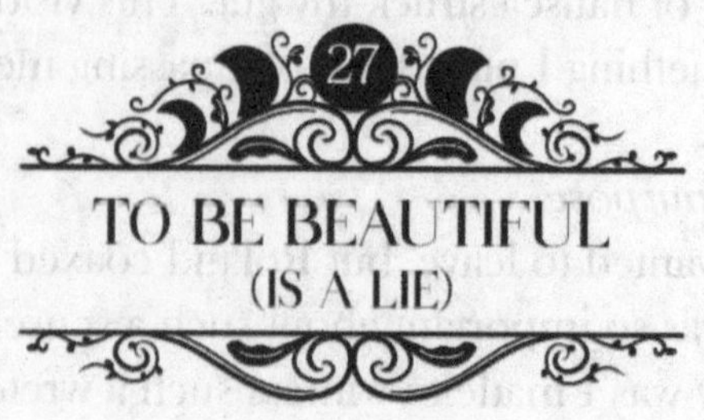

TO BE BEAUTIFUL
(IS A LIE)

"You," I rasped. "Grimstaad. You are just like him . . ."

"No, Lor—I'm not."

I traced the ouroboros on the back of his neck; my breath was shaky, so close to his skin that the hairs on his neck rose. I rested my index finger on the serpent's eye. A burst of heat roared back at me. In my mind, the flesh of my fingertips curled into blackened sheets. I pulled my hand away.

Bryce swept his hair back over the marking and turned to face me. "I don't know what you saw, Lor—"

"Felt, Bryce. It's what I *felt!* When you killed that man . . . was it really you?"

Bryce cocked his head, his brow pinched in pain. "Aye, Lor, it was." Even in the daylight, his blue eyes appeared to darken—flecks of despair blooming within his irises.

I wedged my face between my forearms. "It was appalling," I murmured. "The most depraved, brutal act I have ever witnessed . . ."

"I know," he whispered. "I'm sorry."

A shudder rolled through me and my thoughts drifted to the high court—to Grimstaad, seated alone, the proud jaw-and-spine protruding from his tunic. That symbol had a name.

"Deos Tactigit," I whispered. "Trionfi's guard. Life and death itself—you kill, so that we may live out our days in peace."

"Aye," Corcoran said. "That's what they say. And that's what I am. Or . . . was."

A traitor of Trionfi.
He is wanted for treason.
Grimstaad is looking for him.
Grimstaad.

In an instant, they made sense: the words that rushed me when I lost control of my ilex and pulled them from Bryce's heart.

"You killed your own," I said.

Bryce bit his lip. "Aye. There were nine generals of the Deos Tactigit. The court believed we were touched by the gods. Each of us had defied fate. We cheated death many times over. The ouroboros was a symbol of that for us: life and death, fearlessness. It was supposed to be a symbol of virility, pride, greatness . . . all that rubbish."

Bryce shifted his weight. "There was a town called Pouelle. Nothing special, just a few farmhouses, a barn, and a lot of fields. Pouelle was my first big assignment where I was in the lead. My rite of passage as Deos Tactigit." He chuckled to himself. "Made a holy show of myself. I couldn't do it, Lor. I choked. I failed spectacularly."

Bryce studied my expression, twisted with confusion, pain. I wanted to ask more about Pouelle; I wished to know more about his task—but I also did not wish to know, at the same time. The pain he felt would become mine to hold.

"I killed the Deos Tactigit, Lor." His blue eyes fluttered closed. "Every last general. Or so I thought."

Oh, ammorante, no. No, no, no. My mind hovered somewhere between the earth and sky, and I drifted over the clouds, back to Cortellion, to the high court. Grimstaad, seated in solitude, raised a bandaged arm, lifting his teacup to a table of departed souls.

Shame. Such shame.

"I did not know Deos Tactigit because of my vision," I said thinly. "It's because I heard Suzette—"

My throat clamped closed. The sound of her name

struck me like a blade between my shoulders. *My cherissima*. I fanned my hand over my heart, choking back tears. I'd never spoken of her to Bryce, and I regretted her name slipping from my mouth.

"Who's Suzette?" Bryce asked. "Another Damica?"

I nodded and swallowed the pain in my throat. "She was my only friend in the Accademia."

Bryce's brow softened. "Lor . . ."

"Are we all destined to hurt one another? Is that how this goes? You, with the Deos Tactigit. Suzette looked after me when no one else would come near me. And I led her to her fate . . . it is my fault . . ." Before I could stop myself, a tear splashed down my cheek.

"Don't," Bryce said, shaking his head. "You can't do that to yourself. We all have our own paths to walk, our own destinies to find."

"But that is the problem!" I cried. "Grimstaad . . . that monster. He altered her path, forever."

"Grimstaad?"

"Yes!"

Bryce cocked his head, wary. "What'd he do to your friend?"

"He discovered she is a Verdetto—"

"Verdetto?" he recoiled. "A soothsayer?"

"Yes."

His features tightened in disapproval. I felt his suspicions bubble up beneath his flesh. My face contorted against my will, and I curled my fingers into the grass, yanking a clump of blades from the earth.

"Why do you hate us so much?" I cried. Tears streamed down my cheeks, falling from my chin.

"Huh?"

"You and Grimstaad, both of you. Why do you hate the Damica? You know nothing of Suzette. She cared for me, Bryce . . . when the world was cold and ugly, and there was no one who would give me a second glance." I scraped my foot against the ground, an angry sob rising from out of my chest. "She calmed the demon-whispers; she made all the darkness and ugliness fade."

"That Damica, Suzette . . . she made it all look beautiful?"

I nodded. My hands began to quiver and my heart dropped to the pit of my stomach. "Yes. I'd give anything to feel that peace, once more. I wish she could take it all away. You . . . and that shovel."

"You can't trust her," Bryce said softly. "Lies are beautiful. The truth is ugly."

My arms slid down my face and I hid from him, shielding myself from the ugliness of it all. Suzette . . . cherissima. Grimstaad and the Deos Tactigit. Bryce and the green-eyed man and . . . the shovel.

"Lor?" Bryce whispered. "*Most* people hate the Damica. Because we can't trust you. You, with your pretty dresses and ruffles and ribbons in your hair, your eyes like jewels. You're beautiful and hallowed and meant to be worshiped; that's why they lock you away from the world. And when you finally do emerge, we never know how you're going to use your gifts on us, what you're going to do to bend us . . . break us."

My cheeks wet, I peered at him through a curtain of my hair. "I'm sorry."

"No more apologies." Bryce took my hand and squeezed it gently. "You're more than Damica. More than beauty, more than your gift. You're Viper."

Viper. Yes, I was Viper. I laced my fingers through his and squeezed his hand. His touch gave me strength; it reminded me of who I was.

"There's nothing beautiful about what you saw in your vision, Lor, and I'm not like your Damica friend; I can't make it better for you. Can't tell you that it wasn't me who did that, or that what happened before, or after, was any better," Bryce whispered, his voice barely a breath. He inhaled sharply, and I sensed the hesitation in his words. "But, what if we talk about all the ugliness together? You tell me what you saw in your vision. I'm right here with you."

I squeezed his hand harder and looked up at him, my vision blurred by tears. I wet my lips and swallowed. "I saw Pouelle. The fire. Plumes of black smoke. People . . . regular people . . . at war with soldiers. And—that man with the green eyes."

"Sloane," Bryce whispered. His body began to shake, and he uttered a curse. "Once, we were brothers-in-arms. He was a fellow general."

"You must have truly hated him to have killed him like that," I said.

"Aye," Bryce replied quietly. A sadness lingered in the cracks under his eyes. He was weary, ashamed—not my lover, nor a man of battle and blood.

He was one of the shadows.

"Sloane wasn't an enforcer—that was more Grimstaad's domain. Enforcers carry out their work closer to Cortellion. Sloane and I were vanguard. We worked the borders, keeping the enemy out. I ran the northern border with Sloane; he was training me."

I waited for him to say more, but Bryce closed his eyes. When he opened them again, they were the color of steel. He clenched his jaw. "They deserved to die. All of them—the whole lot."

His body began to shake and I put my arms around him. Throughout our entire journey, his confidence, his quick-witted smile and easeful heart had carried us past enforcers and hanged men alike, and far beyond the threat of starvation or exposure. I had never felt more frightened, holding him with his shoulders wracking, his punctured breaths hot against my sternum.

"Shh," I murmured shakily. "I am here with you."

"Sloane had a family, you know," he said, trembling. "It terrifies me, Lor. He had a wife—lots of children. Never knew anything about the kids, but I saw her once—the wife. He brought her to dine with the court. She was blindfolded the entire time. Seated beside him, still as a statue. Didn't eat. Never spoke a word. Just sat there like she wasn't even real: head bowed, hands in her lap. Don't even know her name. Wasn't even sure she had eyes. All I knew about her is that she was a Damica. A Lunare. They asked him to bring her so I could start thinking about a wife of my own."

I stroked his hair until the rapid throb in his neck slowed. A shiver passed through him. His flesh was panicked and hot, a blade of steel left too long in the sun. "They want that for you with Grimstaad, but what's more disturbing than that? It could have been *me*, Lor. Meeting you in the court, taking you as a bride. You, sitting next to me like . . . that."

"But it isn't." I kissed the top of his head and pressed my cheek to the crown of his head. "That is not who you are, either."

He sighed, closing his eyes and sinking into me. "I told you before, General Vitis Grimstaad is as bad as they come, but Sloane was worse. 'Sloane the Annihilator,' they called him. He'd been around forever. Almost as long as Grimstaad. Most of us don't live to see old age, especially the vanguard, doing what we did. Defending the borderlands, going there to die. It was cold. Empty. Snowed so heavy, sometimes you couldn't tell the ground from the sky. People were ravenous, went a bit mad. That old dog, he had all kinds of tricks up his sleeve—there's a reason he survived as long as he did. Sloane loved it all, had an appetite for blood. And out there—he could let it run free."

"Like Grimstaad?"

"When he was training me, back in Cortellion, he . . ." Bryce's throat tightened, and he set his jaw. His blue gaze darted away from me. A wild, agonized sob ripped through him, and I squeezed my teeth on my tongue, stifling a scream. "Dirty old man. He knew what he was doing. Probably did it lots of times before. I . . . fought back. But he had help. They all knew, and they all laughed. Mercilessly about how a pretty boy like me was just asking for it."

I thought back to what Corcoran had said to me. *All beauty dies, sooner or later. The world isn't made for beautiful things.*

And Bryce was beautiful.

Bryce gnashed his teeth, his heart pounding through his words. "I dragged him through the flames and killed him with that shovel!"

His rage was bewildering and powerful, and I forced myself not to take it into my body. I touched my hand to his cheek and his flesh trembled.

"Strung him up to rot." The words became a whisper on his lips.

"Shh," I whispered. "Ammorante. I am with you."

His eyes were still wild, but his breathing began to slow.

As I lulled him to peace, I thought about shadows. Demon-whispers. I had always believed them to be the burden of a Lunare—and no one else. But my ammorante had wandered through dozens of fields with boots stained with blood. He had lived horrors that I could only dream about.

The decapitated head of General Sloane—eyes white, jaw slack—flashed through my mind.

Sloane and Corcoran.

Corcoran and Grimstaad.

Deos Tactigit.

They all had the ouroboros in common.

The beautiful serpent—the seam from which they had been bound together, and the seam from which they had come apart.

WEAKNESS AND EXPOSURE

Bryce had killed eight generals of the Deos Tactigit. Inasmuch as it meant certain death for him—for what act is more treasonous than killing your own brothers-in-arms—I understood, wholly, why he did it.

It was the litha.

It had come to him not through the moon or shadow, but by fire.

I wondered, had I been trained as a filia with blades, if Headmistress Elan might have met the same fate as Sloane. I was as they said—a lamb, a rabbit, a foal—new with my gift, unsteady on my legs, and she had promised my Papa she would protect me, keep me safe. She vowed to take me under her damask cloak and teach me, but instead, she locked me away and fed me vendrake until I lost all my senses and went mad from seeing shadows, everywhere I went.

Ah—the vendrake. This was reserved for the Vigore class, yet I was the exception. It had never occurred to me before that Vigore trained with their bodies—and the vendrake made them weak. Should one of them become incensed with the headmistress, they would not have the strength to inflict harm unto her.

Throughout my entire stay in the Accademia, I had thought myself weak, pale, fragile—like my Mama; like the flower at my bedside when she passed.

But they gave me vendrake.

Me—a Lunare, given vendrake. I had been strong, and *she made me weak.*

Because I am Viper.

The name became common; it rumbled more and more through Bryce's teeth, more than "Lor." Since his story about Sloane, the beatings, a broken trust among brothers— Bryce trained me harder, more vigorously with the blades. And I loved him harder. We no longer kept our romance confined to the cavern in the mornings. I loved him at night, in the open, under a blanket of moonlight.

But no amount of strength, no amount of love, could change the fact that Bryce—despite his best efforts—had not killed *all* of the Deos Tactigit.

Grimstaad survived the fire.

I asked him about it one night while we huddled by the embers, chewing meat and bone.

"Grimstaad's injuries," I asked. "You are the cause of them?"

"Aye. I am." Bryce nodded. The fire crackled and with a hard swallow, he said, "I owe you the full story. What happened to the generals."

I leaned into him, pressing my cheek against his shoulder.

"Sloane and I were sent to Pouelle. To kill the farmers. All of them. Their wives, their children. Everyone. My orders were to raze the place, turn it to ash. It was supposed to mark the start of my career as a general, to put me on the map as more than just a pretty face.

"Trionfi—it was counting on me to make an example of Pouelle. Each year, the farms owed a portion of their harvest to Cortellion. A few years back, they came up short. The court pardoned them. Last year, they did it again. I was supposed to punish them, show the strength of Trionfi, make it known that the kingdom wouldn't stand for this. And—I failed. Couldn't do it."

Bryce shivered and I slid my hand into his. He steeled his jaw and stared into the embers, slipping from this world into one from his memories. I watched the ashes flare with him, but I did not allow myself to fall. I built, in my mind, a wall of shadow: an ink-like waterfall with black spatters like ink, to snuff the smoldering.

The litha had gripped my ammorante, but I held him with me.

"Why?" I asked. "You said you could not do it. You couldn't burn Pouelle. Why?"

"My family," Bryce whispered. "We were farmers, too. From a town, just like Pouelle."

I leaned my head against his shoulder, feeling his pulse throb against my temple. "You are a good man; you are not like the other generals—nothing like Grimstaad."

"Aye, Grimstaad," Bryce said. "We need to keep moving. If he survived Pouelle, his injuries probably slowed him down a bit. But he won't stop coming. He'll never stop— not until you're in his bed, and I've been drawn and quartered."

I squeezed his hand, wishing I had Suzette's impressive ability to spread her serenity and reassurance. But even if I could, I knew now that any reassurance or peace I could offer was a lie.

And so, our blissful days in the cavern came to a close.

We finished sewing our garments. Although crudely stitched, they did keep the bite of the wind from penetrating our bones. Bryce packed his travel satchel with dried meats, fruits, nuts, and roots, and I used what remained of my peony coat to create my own satchel to carry over my shoulder.

Bryce set a rigorous pace toward the mountains, and though my legs ached to the bone, I did not dare slow us. Anywhere we moved, Roland followed—a single blackbird, perched on a tree, hopping branch to branch. I tried to show Bryce one morning; I lifted my finger and pointed to a branch, but my ammorante bent his brow and stopped, kneeling before me. He touched his knuckles to my forehead, and I tapped my boot, impatiently.

"Ammorante, we are losing the day! I am not ill. It is my gift."

He withdrew his hand and smiled sadly. "I believe you, Viper, but part of me wishes I didn't. I'd give anything to see my brother again. And I can't see what you see."

I stayed my foot and threaded my hands behind my back, feeling foolish, regretful. It was not difficult, even without his touch, to feel the lament in his heart.

"I am sorry."

"Don't be." Half his lip turned upward while the other half remained at rest. "Your gift. It's getting stronger. *You're* getting stronger."

The sun fell; the moon rose—and then the reverse—for days. We walked, the black mountains continuing to grow in size. We avoided the river, the great source of life that Bryce had taught me to use as my guide were I forlorn in the woodland. When my feet grew too swollen to move on, I practiced my ilex by listening to the trees by laying my head against their trunks. I heard whispers through their roots, sweet, heavy like my cherissima's soothing words. I stopped cutting the trees, as Bryce had instructed me at the start of our journey, instead, stroking them with kindness, and they shared their low, peaceful murmurs with me.

Bryce and I slept in shifts and moved before dawn, hiking long, frigid miles parallel to the mountainside. Near the base of the mountains, the wind turned frigid, biting, and I covered my head with my furs while Bryce slept.

One night, while drifting in the twilight between sleep and the waking world, I heard a voice. Throaty, with a low timbre. It faded in and out of my ear. I struggled to focus on the melody as it drifted by.

It sounded like a war hymn.

I pressed my palm to the trunk of a tree and listened, hearing little more than my own breaths. A bird cawed in the tree above me and I turned my gaze, spying its blackened wings beating furiously.

"Roland!"

The blackbird spread wide and beat furiously against its body; the branch beneath shook as it thrust itself toward the sky and vanished into the treetops, cawing. Bryce snapped to attention at my cry, but I ran ahead of him without turning back. I stumbled over roots and vines. Long, pointed branches thrashed my cheeks and tugged at my hair.

"Roland, please, wait!" My breaths grew heavier, more ragged, as I moved, my chest aching from the chill in the air. I rested my palms on my knees, and coughed, letting my head hang.

My ears picked up the skittish rise and fall of boots approaching. More than one pair. It could not be Bryce. The footfalls circled me, and my ears picked up a strange, foreboding sound, like a tightening grip.

Enforcers?

I whipped my hair back and pulled my blade free. What were they doing so close to us? Had they spotted me? Bryce? Or had they, somehow, spotted Roland? I blinked and shook the thought from my mind. What foolishness. Even Bryce could not see Roland, let alone an enforcer.

I pushed my thumb to my wrist; my pulse boomed. Panic. I was panicking.

Litha. Shadows. I glanced around my feet, but they failed to appear.

No. This danger—it did not feel like the shadows. They

manifested when I suppressed my inner thoughts and feelings. This danger was something else: something far more severe. The strange, throaty voice warped into waves that crashed within my ears and made them itch like insect bites. I buried my fingers within, convinced I would find them warm with blood.

But I did not.

What *was* I hearing?

I unplugged my ears and knelt at the roots of a tree, spreading my fingers wide. *Please*, I sent my thoughts into the earth. *Share your wisdom. Tell me, what is this ominous voice?*

In my mind, I saw a silhouette slip behind a tree and I turned still as stone. My Papa appeared in my thoughts—his heart cracked in two in the days of estival following my Mama's death. I imagined the hymns of mourning he must have sung at Mama's funeral, the incense he would have burned to honor her spirit—memories I, locked away in my quarters, would never know. I knew not what had become of my Mama's jade bracelets. Fate and chance. The two serpents woven together for all time.

My thoughts shifted, pausing at the image of the ouroboros I spied on Bryce's neck—the deep, empty eye, its bony jaw, and exposed fangs.

Another shadow passed behind me—shorter, and stockier than the first. My heart clenched shut, my ribs constricted by dread, and I began to shiver. I forced myself to swallow. *Four.* I counted four shadows in my mind—meandering in the trees, slowly circling—a pack of wolves, closing in on their prey.

I pulled my hands free from the tree's roots. My head felt heavy; nausea flooded my gut. Bile rose in my throat.

An ambush.

I was sensing an ambush.

I covered my eyes, taking a disoriented step back. An arm circled my neck, seizing me by the throat.

"Got you!"

My revelation had come too late.

I twisted around to break free, but my efforts were for naught. In the scuffle, the enforcer knocked my blade free and it tumbled across the grass. Facing him, I peered into the dark, dreadful eyes of an enforcer in an ice-blue tunic, a satisfied smile forming into a cruel curve on his face. He snaked his arm tighter around my neck, folding my throat inside his elbow.

"Easy, now." His breath was hot and rancid on my face. I clawed at his forearm. He tightened his grip, pinching my breath in my throat. "Easy," he repeated. "Go down easy."

I thrust the sole of my boot at his groin, but the toe, instead, collided with his shin before slipping free. But it was enough. His hold loosened and my lungs filled with breath.

"Bryce!" I shrieked.

The enforcer recovered quickly; his arm cinched my neck and I found myself gasping for breath. I pushed my fingers beneath his elbow, but it was for naught. Two more men came into my view—a burly man with hair and a beard a shade darker than Bryce's, and another with a sharp-cornered hat resting on his bare scalp. The bearded man studied my features, narrowing his eyes.

"It's her," he said shortly.

The man in the hat crossed his arms sweeping his gaze across my body. He scrutinized my face, my hair, my attire, wrinkling his nose. "Nah. I don't see it."

The bearded man ran a dirty finger down my cheek and I cringed. "Smooth as silk, this one. Never spent a day under the sun working like the rest of us. Have a feel."

The one with the hat uncrossed his arms and approached me. Roughly, he clasped both my hands, pressing them between his thick palms. "I'll be damned. Soft as butter."

"More like cream."

"Hoi!" My captor squeezed my throat and I sputtered. "Keep your hands off her. She belongs to the general."

The man in the hat reluctantly let my hands go free. "You really think it's her? The Damica? Aren't they supposed to be wearing some necklace or something?"

"I don't know about a necklace," the bearded man said. "All I know is the general said we should look around these parts. Nothing out here but a bunch of dying trees, if you ask me. But you know he gets his . . . hunches."

"Funny how he's never wrong about these things. Scares the piss out of me, if you want to know."

"That's what makes him *the general*." The bearded man shrugged. "What do you think we should do with the old man, since we found the Damica?"

The man in the hat grunted and spit on the ground. "Don't know. Don't care."

The world was spinning beneath me, my lungs set aflame. I wedged my fingers between my captor's arm and my throat, but it was not enough to grab a breath. Exasperated, I took one final swing at the enforcer's legs, but he sidestepped me easily. The other two enforcers laughed.

My eyes felt dry as sand and I choked on what air was left in my throat.

"Hoi," the man in the hat said. "Don't put her down too quick. Did you hear what she said when you grabbed her?"

"Bryce?" I felt my captor breathe my ammorante's name.

"She's with someone. Do you think it's . . . *him*?"

"*Corcoran*? The traitor?" My captor scoffed. "Don't be a fool. There's hundreds of men with that name. And didn't they say she's a touch mad? Who knows what she meant?"

I struggled furiously against him, but each movement cost a breath—and I soon had none to spare. As I held on to the last threads of my vision, I heard a hollow whistle, and a solid thunk. A flash of pale hair and furs swept past the enforcer. A blade cut the air like a ribbon.

The laughter turned to screams. Footfalls. More shouts

erupted around me as my captor's arm fell loose. I dropped to my knees, clutching at my neck. I coughed and sputtered, each breath acrid and fiery as I took it. I wiped tears and mucus from my face as my vision returned. A thick, crimson patch welled on the tunic of the enforcer who had been holding me. His eyes widened as he watched the trail of blood run down his side and drip into the grass. The enforcer turned ashen and fell to his knees and Bryce ended his life with a quick stroke.

More shouts. The second enforcer drew his sword and Bryce twirled his blade, a kaleidoscope of light and blood dancing on its edge while he cut the enforcer's throat. He panted at the exertion, letting out a steamy wisp of breath. How he moved so quickly, and quietly, I could not understand. Something heavy, like a satchel, dropped beside me, and I turned to look. My stomach heaved, tossing upon my organs like a wayward ship. Resting beside me was the head of the bearded enforcer, sitting on its side, blood pooling under its ear. His jaw hung slack and he stared at me, his flaxen hair bright red. The cruelty had fled from his eyes—instead they were dreadful, white, empty.

I shook my head to clear myself of nausea and dizziness. Nothing that unfolded before me seemed to be true and I wondered if I had fallen between worlds, into the rust-scented battlegrounds of my dreams. I blinked and scanned the horizon for Roland, but the skies remained empty and cold.

Breathe. Breathe. Don't look. Breathe.

I rose to my knees and turned away from the severed head. The corpse of my captor was sprawled in the brush, his blade still resting in its hilt. I saw a flash in the corner of my eye and I turned quickly.

My blade! It glinted beside the dead man's head, and I snatched it up quickly, ignoring the body, the smell, the stickiness of his hair as my hand brushed past.

Don't look. Don't look.

I turned to find my ammorante's pale hair catching the

wind, his fur cloak billowing from his shoulders as he charged at the enforcer in the hat.

Bryce was soft in the soft morning light; a mist of blood shimmered across the bridge of his nose like a gentle morning rain. His eyes brewed with hatred, though every motion of his body was even and controlled. I touched my blade to my lip, half-expecting to taste blood. My heart fluttered, enraptured by both fear and awe at his flawless movements and the quickness with which he killed.

His blade locked with the last enforcer, and it was only then I saw the stain of blood at Bryce's shoulder.

"Corcoran," the enforcer grunted. "General Alistair Corcoran. Bryce. Pretty one, puppy-dog. Such a sight to see, come down from your high horse."

The enforcer balled his fist and drove it into Bryce's bloodied shoulder. My ammorante's face contorted in agony, his blade faltering.

"General Grimstaad had you pegged since day one. 'Once a thief, always a thief,' he used to say about you." Bryce grunted and pushed against the enforcer. The enforcer lurched back, Bryce's blade scraping against his.

"I'm no thief," Bryce spat between clenched teeth.

"But you are." The enforcer's blade steadied. "Grimstaad saw it before the rest of us. But now you've put it on full display. The whole of Trionfi sees it. Your greed knows no bounds. Your jealousy. You, the young blood in the court, surrounded by generals with scuffs and scrapes on their armor, ten times the men as you. You wanted their respect, but they had none to give to a boy sitting among men. So, you took their lives."

"No," Bryce whispered. "That's not true!"

I felt the energy in his grip shift. Shame, like a bludgeon, crushed his ribs to his heart, and blood. Disgrace bloomed beneath his sternum.

"Stop!" I hissed at the enforcer, my braid whipping

across my back. The enforcer's gaze drifted toward me and his lip turned up in disgust.

"Swine," he said to Bryce. "You even took my general's bride."

The sickness in my gut moved to my heart, stirring into fire and shadow. I felt my teeth grind and my lips curl into a snarl.

Litha.

"Taking what isn't yours. Always wanting more. Thievery. It's your weakness, Corcoran. Your downfall."

I wrapped my palm around the hilt of my blade, the fervor of steel consuming me. The muscles in my arm tightened. My lips pulled back into a snarl, my skin trembling as I thought of his brethren, Luca and Enzo, forcing me to the ground.

Thievery. Trying to take that which did not belong to them.

My vision flashed red, the burn in my lungs moving to my heart.

Weakness.

I would show this man what weakness was. I lunged forward and drove my blade into the enforcer's side.

His scream was tremendous. His leg faltered and Bryce turned his blade. In one quick arc, the enforcer's body crumbled, falling forward onto Bryce. The weight and the suddenness knocked him to the ground.

"Ammorante!" I cried dropping to my knees beside him. His breathing ragged, he swore under his breath.

"Viper."

I closed my eyes, pushing my horror down, down into my throat like a wad of cotton. I met Bryce's gaze; his eyes carried a torrent of anger and shame. He was a wounded soul, no different than a rabbit after stepping into a snare. I could sense in him the pride that the enforcer accused him of carrying. He flipped his wrist and flicked the blood from his sword, the muscles in his forearm flexing in time with his blade's glimmer. He inspected the blade with a routine glance and sheathed it without a second look.

"This attack," he asked. "You sensed it?"

"Yes, yes!" I pressed my lips together; fresh tears rolled down my face. My teeth came down on my lip, my heart fraught with guilt. "But I was too late. It is my fault. All of it."

"No." Relief flooded his eyes—and something else. Concern for me . . . and, respect. He clung to his side and struggled to his feet. "You did good, Viper. You did good."

He moved toward me. His legs trembled, his knees bending under each press of his boot. He lurched forward in pain and I caught him, heavy on my shoulder.

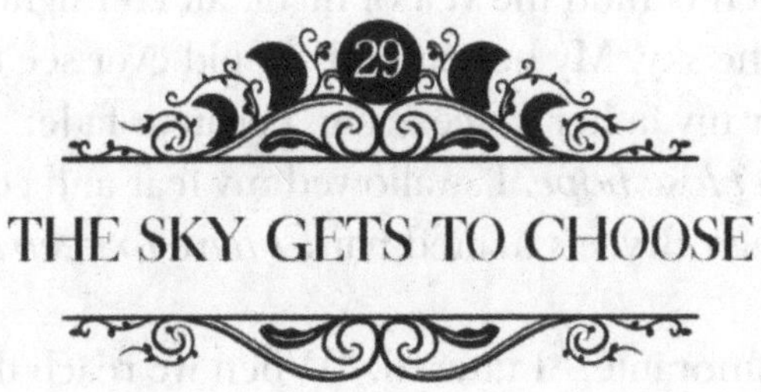

THE SKY GETS TO CHOOSE

I did not know how to tell him it was more than just the attack I sensed. It was Roland. He was trying to tell me something by leading me, headlong, to the enforcers. But I did not know what, and I did not know why.

And at the moment, it was not important.

I lay my ammorante in the grass, his skin damp, pale. He shivered and I held him tight, wishing in that moment I were a Vigore and could do something—anything—to stop his bleeding.

"Viper." His teeth chattered while beads of sweat collected on his brow. "We need to bury the bodies."

"We must stop the bleeding, ammorante."

Bryce grunted in reluctant agreement. "I need you to find your needle and thread. Sew it shut."

I removed my furs and placed them on top of him before retrieving my sewing instruments from my satchel. Bryce lay still as my needle pierced his flesh. With shaky fingers, I looped the thread around and around through his wound, hoping my childish knots could somehow keep him together.

Night fell early and brought with it little warmth or light. We ate dried meat and berries from our pockets while the wind howled at us, biting our skin and feeding from our flesh. I stayed close to Bryce. His gaze darted from me to his blade, constantly. He thrashed and stirred: hot, then frigid, then hot again—unable to sleep. I looked to the moon and She was absent, hidden behind the veil of night: all Her light was cloaked by the sky. My hope that I should ever see the gates of the Order or my father's face again, began to fade.

Don't lose hope. I swallowed my fear and combed my fingers through Bryce's matted hair. *I have to keep his spirits up.*

"Ammorante," I uttered. "When we reach the Order, I think I shall wear orange blossoms on my gowns. And perhaps a rose behind my ear."

I watched a smile peek from the corner of his lip. He sighed, struggling to keep his teeth from shaking. "That sounds nice, Lor."

"And what of your attire? Will you keep your beard?"

His nose wrinkled. "I hadn't thought much of it."

"You must be groomed!" I huffed. "I shall not have you meet Papa without a proper trim! And your boots must be washed. You will need his blessing to court me."

Bryce snickered and arched his brow. "You can't be serious."

"I am most serious!" I scoffed. "The fields may be your home, but you will be crossing the threshold into mine. And you must be presentable!"

Bryce shook his head, wisps of his blond hair catching on his lip. "None of this matters, Lor. We're never going to make it to the Order."

I bit my lip and turned away to mask my tears.

"No," I argued. "We will make it."

"He's right about me, you know." Bryce whispered.

"Who?"

"Grimstaad."

Beneath the heat of his skin, I felt a surge of shame—the same as when he was locked in combat. I sucked a cold ribbon of breath between my teeth and tried to hold the feeling in my heart. I wanted to turn it over and study it—unburden my ammorante from trying to speak and explain his pain. My fingers crawled to my wrist, and I recognized the feeling as one that I had felt in my mama when she had first led me to the Damica. The day Headmistress Elan named me a Lunare.

Not just shame.

Shame—and desire. A longing for me to be something that I was not—that which I would never be.

The realization stuck me far worse than a blow to the face.

"You are ashamed of me?" I cried.

"Huh?"

"You wish none of it had ever happened, that you had never carried me on your back, or kissed me, or—"

"Lor!" Bryce grasped me weakly by the wrist and I swatted him away. I could not keep my tears contained behind my eyes. They spilled onto my cheeks, splashing onto my shirt as I tried to wrench myself away.

"Shame!" was all I could eke out.

"Lor, stop!" Bryce hissed. "What did I tell you—about assuming things without asking? I'm not ashamed of you!"

I blinked, feeling my brow crease. I crossed both arms over my chest. "Explain yourself!"

"Give me a minute, would you?" He pressed his palm against his temple and turned away from me. I heard him sigh deeply. "Grimstaad—and that enforcer—they were right. I was greedy. Wanted too much. I would've killed anyone to become Deos Tactigit, to be treated with dignity."

My chest expanded as I drew in a breath and I touched my breastbone, saddened for him. "What do you regret, then?"

His eyes grew wide, larger and bluer than I had ever seen them; they were like the stars themselves. A staggered breath left his lips. "Becoming Deos Tactigit—it cost me my brother. I'll never forgive myself for it. If I could take it all back . . ."

He shuddered. I put my arms on his chest.

"I shouldn't have done it," he whispered. "Killed all the

other generals. There's no saving me. No future for us—as partners, or anything else. Nothing but sky, and mountains—blood, and blade . . ."

I shook my head in disbelief. "How could you say such a thing after all we have been through?" I choked.

"Because it's true."

"And you believe you can tell people's fortunes? Only my mama could do such a thing—read one's fate in the leaves. It is not up to you who may live, who will die."

"But it is." Bryce stifled a laugh. "That's all the Deos Tactigit do: choose who lives and who dies."

"Bryce." I pursed my lips. "You are not Deos Tactigit, not anymore."

He sighed. "I suppose you're right. I've no say over your fate or mine. This time, the sky gets to choose—who lives, who dies." His words drifted away, mid-sentence, as he settled into a shallow slumber.

Fate and chance. It always came back to fate and chance.

For a long time, I rested my hands against my ammorante in an attempt to slow his bleeding. I looked up to the sky—no stars punctuated the flawless blackness, no moon sat cradled in the branches sitting above. I pushed a wisp of breath from my lips, offering myself as the moon on this still night. My thoughts and feelings twirled into darkness.

Damica. Deos Tactigit.

Litha. Lunare.

Trees. Nooses.

Moon. Sky. Mountains.

Fire. Farmers. Fields.

Rabbit. Ouroboros. Blackbird.

Life. Death.

Roland. The common thread between them all.

Roland. Rowley.

He had been trying to tell me something. Show me something.

When the first rays of dawn bled through the sky, I adjusted Bryce's furs to cover his shoulder, kissed his pallid cheek, and set off into the trees. His blood stained my hands from my tending to his wound, but it did not matter. I needed to find what Roland was trying to show me—why he had led me into the ambush.

As I walked through the woods, the morning sun flashed through the branches and I thought of the time I was a child. The days that Mama and I had walked through the market, past carriages and under lattice archways and I'd released her hand to skip ahead, my head turned upward. The sun, blinking through the trellises, spoke to me in a language of light and pulse that I yearned to understand.

I turned my head upward toward the sun and treetops and discovered I was not alone. Hidden within the browning leaves around me, each tree held, on its highest branches, forked feet.

Messengers of the sun, perhaps? I thought I should try to speak back. My lips parted and I whispered unto it a prayer, in my mind.

Blackbird. I beseech you: come forth. Sun, reveal him to me!

The branches stirred with a symphony of caws. Eyes, beaded and black, bore into me. Above me a branch bent and a flock spiraled into the air, their wings spread wide. Black-and-brown feathers painted the sky before vanishing behind the treetops.

Resistance.

They were resisting me. I raised my arms overhead, slow drips of my ammorante's blood trickling down my wrists. "Blackbird, come forth," I said aloud. "Sun, reveal him to me!"

Caws rose behind me, the wild beating of wings rising to a crescendo in the stillness of the woods. I extended my arms to my side and twirled as frenetic cries from sharp beaks caught like shadows in the folds of my skirt. The world spun with me, droplets of my ammorante's blood misting the tip of my braid.

"Show yourself!" My voice shook the birds from a tree above. "Omen of death, appear before me!"

Roland did not come—and an idea began to take shape in my mind, as to why not. I was a Lunare, and the moon was my goddess. I belonged to the night; beneath the sun, my ilex was unwelcome. But I did not have the time to wait. I needed Roland.

"Blackbird," I cried louder. "Come forth!"

As quickly as the cacophony began, the birds' calls stopped, the flap of wings to follow. Dozens of obsidian eyes— heavy, black, hushed—blended back into the trees, watching.

"Blackbird!" I called. But the woods, again, were still and silent. I closed my eyes to feel into my ilex. When I blinked, I was greeted by a single, jagged branch hanging above me like a claw. I expected to see Roland perched on its edge, but the branch was empty, lonely. My eyes folded closed and I breathed in, searching for any wisp, any trace of death.

The scent of freshly baked piandia flooded my nose.

Piandia? A knot formed between my brow, and I parted my lips, sampling the air with the tip of my tongue. I licked my lips to hold its taste in my mouth: soft, porous bread warming me within. A smile pulled at my lips and I closed my eyes. I caught a flash of my papa's hands—strong, steady, kneading a ball of dough. The scent of bread rose from our hearth. I placed my hands over my eyes. My ammorante's blood stuck between my eyelashes, but I did not pull me from my vision.

I needed this. I focused on feeling warmth inside, soul-rich in this barren land. I concentrated on the piandia, and the memory of Papa's and my kitchen rooted in my mind—the hearth smoldering. Soft sunlight poured through our windows, blanketing the cupboards, sparkling along the side of a pan. My father appeared with his silver hair and aedituus robes, hunched over the countertop with his back facing me.

"Papa," I whispered. He turned and I lost myself in the familiar folds of his aged face. His eyes creased, smiling, and he opened his mouth to greet me.

A low moan snapped me out of my memory. I blinked, shaking my mind free of the kitchen and the hearth.

"Ammorante?"

A jagged branch waved back at me and I rubbed my eyes with my sleeve, clearing them of both blood and bread. The moans continued, low and painful.

"Bryce?" I shuffled toward the cries, my fingers finding the hilt of my blade. I moved slowly, weaving between the trees like a thread and needle. I followed the voice, taking a few steps at a time before plastering my back to a trunk. At the third tree, my gaze fell to my boot. Beside it, wetting fallen leaves and grasses, a streak of blood painted the ground, as though something had been dragged. I followed the blood trail a short distance into a thick patch of foliage.

It was there I found him. Pale, weak, and white—the color all but gone from his flesh.

"Papa!"

Was it a dream? I watched the apple of his throat bob up and down and he blinked, holding a lantern to my face as if to study if it were the dream. I rushed toward him, embracing him with such fervor that I thought my heart may burst. We did not speak; he held me in silence, his breathing choked and ragged.

I wept against his shoulder, and his fingers reached for something intangible, his lips murmuring a few words in the old tongue.

"Laurel." He breathed my name, raising his chin to meet my gaze. His lips folded into a worrisome frown, and he turned his head, gazing over my shoulder.

Papa wheezed, his eyes fluttering closed. I ripped my blade from my skirt and slashed at the ferns and bushes shrouding his body. I tore at the greenery, tearing apart twigs and fronds, tossing them aside carelessly. Beneath them, I found my father's body. He was clad in his robes, a large, damp stain spread above his left knee. *Blood.* The hue was much darker than that of the blood from my ammorante's wound.

How long has he been out here?

Trembling, I pulled back the edge of his robe. The image cut into my mind, searing a permanent torture upon me. His leg was cut straight through, the bone visible beneath a flap of flesh. It was putrid; the worst scent I had ever smelled, by far. I retched, covering my nose and mouth to keep from vomiting.

Papa coughed and his fingers brushed my side.

"Run, Laurel," he rasped. "Run. They . . . are looking for you."

"Who, Papa? The enforcers?"

"Yes . . ."

I squeezed my hands into fists and screamed, striking the grass. I had sensed them. I knew they were coming. And I was too late.

"They are gone, Papa." I unfurled my fingers and squeezed his hands in mine. "Do you hear me? Dead. We are safe now. We're safe . . . please. Stay with me."

Papa coughed, struggling to breathe. He was close to death—and I did not know what to do.

Fate and chance. Fate and chance.

By fate, I was a Lunare, caught in the daylight. By chance, I had managed to decipher Roland's message, regardless. His omen of death—it led me to my papa.

But it was not for me to decide if Papa lived or died.

Bryce. I needed Bryce.

By fate, he was Deos Tactigit. Though he was not Damica—and certainly not a Fortuna—he had taken up fate and chance as a general, choosing which men should live, and which should perish. I needed his strength, his guidance.

I squeezed my Papa's hand firmly. "I will return shortly."

As I wove through the trees, my heart thundered with each step. Tears stung the corners of my eyes, and they mingled with blood, running hot and free down my cheeks.

SECRETS OF THE HEART

Bryce was already sitting upright, inspecting his arm, when I reached him, the color still drawn from his face. Our furs, slick with his blood, lay beside him.

"Bryce!" My calves burning, I fell to my elbows and knees beside him, gasping for breath. "I need you. Please. Come, now."

"Viper—where'd you get off to? Are you all right?"

"No," I panted. "I am not all right. I found him . . ."

"Found who?"

"My father."

Bryce cocked his head, confused. "Your father? From the Order?"

"Yes! It is him! It was my ilex. It led me to him. Listen! The enforcers—they had him and were looking for me!"

"What?"

"My papa. He's hurt," I said. "I need you. Please. Can you stand?"

Bryce prodded his arm and winced. "Aye, I think I'm past the worst of it."

I laced my fingers through his and tugged on him. "Then we must go! Now!"

"Lor—!"

"I am sorry, but there is no time!" I cried.

Bryce blinked and the muscles in his jaw pulled taut. "You're sure about all this?"

"Yes! Papa told me himself—they were coming for *me*!"

"They knew you were heading to the Order."

"How?"

"I don't know. Did you tell anyone?"

"No!" I shook my head vehemently. "My sister-Lunare, Bethany, told me to keep my plans a secret after I reached Reveille! She did not want anyone pulling my location from her heart!" A harrowing thought blanketed me like a sheet of ice. "Her gift paired well with maps! Navigation! Do you think Grimstaad tried to use her to hunt me? Do you think he *hurt* her?"

"Maybe. Anything's possible. Grimstaad always gets his man—by any means necessary," Bryce muttered.

"*Diosemma* . . . no." My whole body began to quiver. *Bethany.* Another one I'd hurt. One more felled by my darkness.

Bryce shook his head. "Viper, there's no time to worry over your friend. There's nothing you can do for her." He bent his knees, placing his palm flat on the earth. His teeth flashed with pain as he struggled to rise. "Help me up. Let's go get your father."

Trembling, I extended my arm to him. The shaking began to slow as soon as he clasped it. We had found my papa. We could do something for him. I tried to clear Bethany from my mind.

Unsteady as I was, I led Bryce past the bodies of the enforcers and into the sun, and we hurried past the hundreds of black, glittering eyes watching us from the trees. I let go of Bryce's hand as soon as we reached the brush, and I rushed to my father's side. His coloring seemed to worsen in the short time I was gone, his skin ashen, pulse weak. I knelt beside him and touched his face. "Papa, can you hear me?"

He groaned in reply; his eyelids fluttered, but remained closed.

"Papa, it's me. Your Laurel."

He whispered something, but his words were lost on me.

"Let me see him," Bryce said. He crouched beside my Papa and pulled back the corner of his robe.

"Bryce, no! His leg, it's—"

"Ack, Lor." He grimaced, turning away. He swore and spit into the grass. "The wound is old, and starting to rot."

"Rot?" I blinked, tears falling from my eyes.

Bryce pursed his lips. "Listen to me. I've seen lots of men who've taken a blow like his. Not much to be done."

"What?" My hands hurt, and I realized I had curled them into fists, my nails digging into my palm. "You must do something, Bryce! He's my *father*!"

His eyes, blue as the sky, shifted away from me. "I'm sorry, Lor. Most we can do is get him out of this filth, make him comfortable. Help me."

Together Bryce and I pulled Papa—each of us taking one arm and dragging him in short, staggered bursts—until he was free from the brush. His leg bent at an angle that made my stomach feel ill as we moved him to a large trunk with evenly spread roots on which to rest.

"Does he have any effects?" Bryce asked.

"What?"

"What does he normally travel with? Clothing, food, anything?"

"I don't know. I've never traveled with him, and he was dying when I came upon him."

"Go back to the spot where you found him and have a look around."

Bryce knelt beside Papa and pulled a flask from his belt. Papa moaned softly as the water splashed on his lips.

I crawled on hands and knees through the brush, pressing myself on my belly through tangles of the brush and leaves. Patting at the ground blindly, I found nothing but damp leaves and soil. I shifted direction, crawling backward while the thicket of brush and branch whirled around me, tugging at my garments, closing in on me like shadows. My chest felt tight; the air damp and hot, too thick for me to swallow and push into my lungs. It was a tomb. The earth breathed with moist anticipation, waiting to devour me. I hurried my legs backward, eager to break out from its mouth. A shout cut through the air, and I froze. *Papa.* I was almost free, the sun warming my ankle as I pushed myself backward.

My papa's voice shook the earth as I emerged, and as quickly as my legs could carry me, I staggered in its direction.

"Get back!"

Bryce stood above my papa, his palms extended outward. Lying recumbent, Papa gripped his staff with both hands, holding it between himself and Bryce. He shook it and I recognized the two silver serpents entwined around the top; they grinned at me. Painful, familiar memories from my childhood rose to the top of my mind. Papa, holding the staff above me while I clawed at him under the litha's hold.

"Easy, easy," Bryce coaxed.

Papa turned his head, catching sight of me, and I caught a spark of horror in his dark eyes.

"Laurel, run! *Run!*" He twisted at the waist and drew his staff to his chest. Swinging with both arms, the serpents cracked against Bryce's knee.

Bryce swore loudly and stumbled, gritting his teeth. "You better watch yourself, old man, before I . . ."

"Bryce!" I scowled at him.

His neck craned toward me and he cursed, clutching his knee. "Sorry, Lor. Give me a minute . . ."

"*Lor?*" Papa frowned. He clutched his staff, preparing to take another swing. "Laurel, do you know this man?"

"Yes, Papa!" I cried. I rushed toward my father and wrapped my hands around the staff. "Please put that down. He is with me. I brought him here to help."

Reluctantly, Papa loosened his hold on the staff,

allowing me to ease it out of his hands. I lay it beside him and he pulled me close, resting the point of his chin on the crown of my head.

"Stay away from her," he growled at Bryce.

"Papa," I started.

"No!" Papa interrupted. "This man is banale, Laurel. *Worse* than banale."

"I know what he is!" I wriggled free from my father's hold.

"He is General Alistair Bryce Corcoran of the Deos Tactigit." Papa's voice was stern; it shook with finality. "You could not possibly understand the atrocities this man committed. You are but a child, and I have shielded you from the wickedness of the world . . ."

"I am no child!"

I felt it then: the litha, rising in my chest. It poured from my heart like a river, roaring through my limbs, and on impulse, I grasped my Papa's hand and forced it upon my braid, trailing it across the uneven ridges and valleys. Papa's face contorted, his brows folding, lips pulling into a shape I did not recognize, that which I had never seen on any person. *Failure. Anger. Disappointment. Fear.* They all circled in him and he set his jaw, pushing me aside. He shifted his weight to his hip and picked up his staff. Grunting, he rose to one knee to face Bryce, his wounded leg dragging.

"You defiled my daughter!" he shouted.

"Easy! Easy!" Bryce cried, his hands outstretched, fingers fanned wide. "You're going to lose your leg trying to do that!"

"My leg is the least of your concerns! She is my daughter! And she is *Damica!*"

I growled. "No, Papa! I am not!"

"Cease, Laurel!" Papa shifted his full weight onto his staff. "You know not of what you speak!"

I scurried to my feet and stepped in front of my Papa. I

rested my hands on my hips and raised my chin to meet his gaze.

"I am not Damica. I am a *Lunare*, and . . . something else," I said, my voice low, filled with conviction. "I see into the hearts and minds. I know what lies beneath the flesh."

"Your gift has always brought about madness," Papa said quietly. "You should not be using it to look into these matters! They are not for filia like you. And this man—" Papa pointed his finger at Bryce.

"He is my *ammorante*!" I cried.

Papa closed his eyes, his palm curved over the top of his staff. His fingers curled into the wood and metal. "General Alistair Bryce Corcoran, ninth general of the Deos Tactigit. Vanguard of the East. The Firestarter—turning everyone around him to soot and ash. You think you are *in love with him*?"

Pain. Disappointment. Failure. I focused on the image of the ouroboros on Bryce's back, and sank, with shame, into its eye, becoming a ribbon of shadow, a slip of a being—so silent, so dark—that nothing but the night could understand.

"You are enamored with your own madness!" Papa cried. "It is the same as it was when you were a child! When you knelt with me in our parlor and helped me archive the relics from my travels. You were always drawn to the worst of them: the chains worn by warlords, the orbs used by priestesses to select blood sacrifices. And the blades." He hardened his expression. "I'll never forget the look on your face when you gazed into one."

The litha. I remembered it well. Never before had I seen a more alluring sight. I was in awe of her darkness—the markings of death she wore so unafraid.

"I cannot change what I am." I squeezed my hands so tightly, I felt as though my palms may bleed.

"No—you cannot!" Papa shouted, his ashen cheeks flush with passion. "You are inflicted with madness, violence! You will always need someone to care for you, someone to guide you and keep you from harming yourself or others. I thought your headmistress would be able to teach you to harness your gift—but here you are, in full lunacy!"

Bryce took a step forward, moving behind me. "It's your fault, you know." He scowled. "You abandoned her."

Papa thrust his staff into the ground, taking a heavy lurch toward Bryce. "This is a family matter—and you are not family. Begone! Leave us!"

Bryce scoffed. "Not a chance, old man. You're going to hear what I have to say, whether you like it or not. You're the one who dumped her in a prison for filia, foisted her off on a headmistress. You know what they were planning for her?"

"I am not interested in your thoughts, *traitor*," Papa said.

"A marriage to Grimstaad," Bryce hissed, ignoring him. "General Vitis Grimstaad, the Noosemaster!" Bryce threw his arms wide. "You think I'm bad? Look around you! Happy to give you a tour of his handiwork in these parts!"

"Bryce, stop!" I whirled around, pressing my hand against his chest.

"No, Lor. He's out here calling me names, treating you like a child, refusing to 'fess up to his part in all this."

"'Fess up?" Papa shouted. "What do you think I am doing in these woods? I received a desperate letter from a vedova named Suzette d'Isparza."

"Suzette?" I clamped my hand over my mouth. Oh, cherissima. She *had* been watching over me; she made sure Papa had received word of my fate.

Papa glared at Bryce. "I was coming to retrieve my daughter!"

"Oh? You expect me to believe that?"

"I do not care what you believe," Papa heaved. "I *never* agreed to any marriage arrangements. And I certainly will not be approving of one to you. Begone!"

Bryce leaned forward and I felt his breath on my

shoulder. I pressed my other hand against his chest.

"You're going to die out here, old man, and you're going to take her with you," he said, his voice measured, flat, controlled.

"He is telling the truth, Papa." The corners of my eyes burned with salt. "I left the Accademia to seek your help. Bryce—he saved my life; he helped me to survive long enough to see you again. I am being hunted by Vitis Grimstaad—he is coming for me!"

"Yes, Laurel," Papa whispered. "His men found me on my way to you, and they did this to me." Papa motioned toward his leg, hanging limp at his side.

I smoothed Bryce's hair from his shoulder and pulled back the corner of his fur cloak. "He is hurt, too."

His wound had begun to bleed again; the stitching was a mess of thread and skin. His lip twitched, and he clenched his teeth to mask the pain.

"Now is not the time for us to argue," I continued. "We must come together and help each other, so that we may reach the Order."

Papa's features softened and he nodded reluctantly. Bryce remained tense, his posture straight as the steel of his blade.

"We will be safe in the Order—all of us. We will be beyond the grasp of Trionfi—my marriage to Grimstaad will mean nothing. Bryce will go before the council; he will be given his pardon, and—"

"His *pardon*?" Papa's expression twisted in disbelief. "Laurel, there will be no pardon for this man! What he has done is an act of war. Harboring him in the Order would be giving asylum to a war criminal!"

"For killing the generals? They are men of war—fated to die in battle!"

"No, Laurel! As abhorrent of an act as that is, the Order might have sanctioned this, given their history of violence."

My eyes narrowed. "I do not understand."

Papa turned to Bryce and sneered. "You did not tell her, did you?"

Bryce's shoulders slumped; a frozen, sweat-soaked lock of his hair fell over my brow.

"Don't," he whispered. "Please. She doesn't know yet."

"Know what?" I demanded. My heart thudded against my ribs, my lungs two tight fists.

Bryce turned his attention to me, his eyes wide and blue. "I swear, Lor—I was going to tell you. When the time was right."

"Tell me *what?*"

Papa leaned forward heavily, worry-lines deeply etched around his frown. His hand came off his staff and he held it up, shakily pointing a finger directly at Bryce.

"Laurel, this man you say is your ammorante? He killed the crown prince, Brennan."

31
AN INCENDIARY SPIRAL
(MOTH AND FLAME)

Even in sunlight, with no glowing eye to guide my path, I had believed I could do it. Weak as it was, my ilex still held power; it led me to discover my father, hidden deep in the brush, before he expired. I had convinced myself my gift had grown with me in strength and that I could summon it with confidence—unsheathing blades of truths about the land I walked, the ones I loved. I thought I could hold these truths, with their sharpened edges—let them shriek—but I wished they had remained concealed, tucked away like a scabbard at my side.

Lies are beautiful. The truth is ugly.

I shook my head in disbelief. I did not need to do as I did as a filia and run my fingers along Bryce's skin to know my father's words rang true. No, they were poison enough in my heart. Bryce killed the crown prince. *He killed him; he killed him—Prince Brennan—he killed him.*

My stomach lurched; I bit my lip. I wanted to scream. Suzette had risked meeting with Grimstaad; she risked *me* for the opportunity to speak to him—and she had suffered terribly in her attempt to learn the crown prince's fate. And I had been traveling with the very one who had *killed him?*

Litha.

I balled my hands into fists, blinking away the sting of tears. *I should just let it take me.*

I could not escape my fate. I was Viper; I was Lunare.

Fatally attracted to blood and blade—like a moth flying coquettishly above a flickering candle, fluttering its fragile wings until they erupted into flame and it fell, an incendiary spiral flaring as its body was consumed by fire.

My ears burned and I pressed my hands over them, plugging them with a terrible, cotton-like silence. The ground beneath me trembled and fractured in two, a swell of shadow spewing from the crack, bubbling over my boots.

"Laurel!" My father's call passed through my ears, muted. I ignored it, watching the shadows belch from the land's ancient, fractured core and climb my ankles and calves.

"Lor!"

I bristled. My heart rippled with waves of sorrow, regret, anger—somewhere in there, an attraction to Bryce refused to be stifled. I did not understand why. *Why?* He was a brute, a murderer—*banale*! How could my heart *ever* resonate with a man with such blood on his hands?

I twirled around and shouted, "Banale! Do not speak to me! Do not come near me!"

"Wait—"

Wiping away a blur of tears, I escaped into the trees, pushing branches from my face, no longer caring if they scraped my skin.

The woodland welcomed me with tree branches outstretched, offering me refuge from my father, Bryce, the ugly truth, and my own feelings of overwhelm. I ran, then stopped, exhausted—and I rested for a long while. I lay numb against a tree until the sun's light was fully extinguished by the branches above—and though part of me yearned to turn back, my body refused to move. It seemed determined to keep me rooted where I was until my fondness for Bryce faded.

As night began to fall, I was able, finally, to pry myself

up. I looked skyward toward the moon, a tiny crescent winking underneath a canopy of black leaves. My stomach twisted with hunger, the cold night air burning my lungs. I limped and stumbled among the trees until I was surrounded, wholly, by darkness, the silhouettes of trunks disappearing in front of me.

I stretched my arms in front of me to navigate by touch, but I stumbled over a cluster of roots and fell in the grass. What little breath I had was knocked out of me, each of my lungs pulsing with pain as I struggled to recover. The pain merged into one large, pulsing ache in my heart that spread through my veins, infecting my limbs with heaviness. I wished the ground would rise and swallow me and snuff out my life quickly.

But still I lived on.

The branches above me swayed in my ears, offering me consolation for my sorrowful state. I stared up into the blank slate of black and I unsheathed my blade, holding the steel to my chin. I pressed it against my lips, the memory of the tart flavor of Bryce's kisses mixing with metal. Cold and fragile, a fresh tear rolled down my cheek. As I lay there, each of my fingers and toes turned numb, lament blossoming in my chest. My body tingled with pinpricks of shame.

Bryce killed Prince Brennan—and *I had missed it.* The entire time I was close to him, I never once sensed this secret he had been keeping from me. The entire purpose of my ilex was to extract such secrets from men, and his greatest one had bypassed me.

Perhaps it was because I had promised him I would not reach too deep into his heart. The thought brought me a tepid feeling of solace. But perhaps it was because my ilex truly was weak, or unpracticed, at the least—I had little control over it. It was a viable explanation, as I had no control over the litha, either. Or perhaps it was because I was simply foolish, naive— and I had allowed my feelings for Bryce to cloud my ilex.

Maybe all of it was true. Or perhaps none of it. Lying in the dark, it was fruitless to try to guess.

My mind flooded with images of the battlefield I had seen in Bryce's dreams. The pounding of the drums, the stench of mud and sweat. Bryce's eyes, full of life. His companion, Roland. His brother, the blackbird, the omen of death—the soldier with dark hair and somber eyes.

"Lor?"

Bryce! I muttered a curse under my breath before I clamped my hand over my lips. *He came for me!* My cheeks flushed, and my pulse quickened in my throat. I lifted myself and pressed my back to the trunk of a nearby tree. Holding my breath, I whispered in my mind, *Please do not find me. Please do not find me.*

"Lor? Where are you? You shouldn't be out here alone." Bryce's boots crunched the dry leaves behind me and I squirmed. The tree's bark dug into my back. My lungs burned with want of breath, my heart tangled in my throat. I licked my lips and squeezed my eyes firmly shut. *Please do not find me. Please.*

"Lor!" I heard Bryce draw in a breath and release it into the night. He swore loudly, slamming his fist against the tree upon which I rested. The trunk vibrated at my back, my skin pulsing with quivers of guilt. I imagined the scowl on his face, a splitting pain shooting through his knuckles.

"I'm sorry. I didn't mean for you to find out this way," he said. "Wherever you are—come back. Please. I'll tell you everything."

He was silent for a moment. My name pierced the night three more times before Bryce heaved a tremendous sigh. I heard the rustling of fabric, his footsteps shuffling in defeat away from my tree.

I let my breath flow freely and a small, painful laugh flowed from my lips. It quickly erupted into a coughing fit. Banjaxed. That was the word he had used. This whole situation, a snarled-up thread—like the seam that was holding his shoulder together. I huddled at the base of the tree, clasping my arms around my knees to rock myself to keep warm, but my body shivered, cold and clammy, my fingers stiff.

The moon pierced the woodland and blanketed me in Her soft glow. My lips were too frigid to offer Her exaltation. The tips of my ears stung as the night air chilled me raw. My lips trembled and I wished to weep, but I did not, knowing I would only grow colder from my tears. I turned my head to the side and a short distance from me, I spotted a creature with soft, winter fur curled up in the grass, at ease.

A shudder ran through me. My nostrils flared, my breaths quick bursts, like the sputters of a dying flame. I drew my fingers across my throat, the weight of my pendant absent.

Roland's words rolled through my mind. He was called Blackbird. A name he resented in life, but had come to accept upon his passing.

"Sooner or later . . . you must accept what you are."

I was Viper . . . or so I thought. I had believed I was beginning to understand my gift, but my ilex—it had failed me!

In my mind, Suzette's beautiful dark curls—soft waves of comfort—flowed past me, mingling with her silvery voice. My heart surged with grief; I missed her so. I never should have left the Accademia; I should have stayed at her side and held her hand through her darkness. She was, truly, watching over me, in a way that neither Bryce nor my father had the capability to do. If I confided to Suzette the burdens of my heart, she would listen. Lacing her fingers through mine, she would squeeze my hand, and the liquidity of her voice would bathe me in comfort. I would no longer have to feel or dream anything but pleasant thoughts. No more fire, no more night sky. I could turn my back on the moon and Suzette would become my moon, my star, my goddess.

The thought brought a smile to my lips, and I fell into a tepid sleep—slumbering like a corpse, with my hands crossed over my chest to keep warm. When the sun rose, my blood half-awakened, running through my fingertips like broken shards of glass. I scanned the horizon. Yellowing leaves and soft grasses surrounded me. An idyllic image like the pastel paintings in the halls of the Accademia—a beautiful contrast to the treachery of night and cold and wind. An incessant pain gnawed through me, and I found that I had little strength to lift myself.

In the morning light, my dreams of returning to Suzette melted away. I was not strong enough, nor prepared, to make a journey back to the Accademia on my own. And Grimstaad still hunted me. I had little choice but to return to my Papa and to Bryce, with their ugly truths and animosity toward one another, and let them care for me. With my blade tucked firmly against me, I peeled myself from the ground.

I allowed my mind to wander as I shambled through the trees. The sun beat down on the crown of my head, mocking me. Like the hanged men in the trees, I was suspended somewhere between the sun and the moon, uncertain of which world I belonged to. Each time I blinked, I was pulled from one to the next, with no tether to tell me which was real and which was a dream. I could only follow the scent of meat, simmering, to guide me.

I soon found Bryce seated by a thick tree, mending his wounded shoulder.

"You're safe."

"Yes," I said flatly.

He smiled, his eyes suddenly soft, with a compassion rivaling my father's. "I found your father's effects. The enforcers took his travel trunk. It was full of parchment, herbs, and . . . I don't know what those other things were. Doubt they knew much what to do with it." Bryce said, with thread between his teeth. "He's a smart man, your father. Kept a thread and needle in there."

I cringed while he continued to pierce his flesh, drawing the needle all the way through and dragging the thread behind it.

"You don't need to look at me like that. Can't feel a thing. Promise." Bryce doubled the needle through the thread and bit the end free. "A few of those herbs your father has, they numb pain."

"Some people deserve to feel pain," I whispered, clutching my hands to my heart.

"Aye. Sometimes. But not this time." Bryce swept his hair over his shoulder, the tooth of his ouroboros peeking through to greet me.

"Your father's sleeping, Lor. I'm making a rabbit stew. He might not want to eat when he wakes, but you need to tell him to. It's a long way through the mountains."

"My Papa is *here*?"

"Aye, Lor. You think I took his things and left him, like a *banale*?"

There it was. Banale. I had treated him like one. But wasn't he one? Yes. Neither of us could deny that. But he was also . . . something else.

"Banale." I shifted my weight, swallowing a lump of shame in the back of my throat. "I am sorry I called you that."

Bryce pressed his lips into a wry smile. "It's all right, Lor. That pain, I probably deserve."

We worked side by side, Bryce and I, to stir the meat while the water boiled in small pots that Bryce had found in my Papa's travel trunk. I raised an eyebrow at Bryce as he stoked the fire, hoping he would speak, but he remained quiet. The stillness blanketed us, weighing us down like snow on the already-heavy furs we wore on our shoulders and backs— Bryce's still stained with his blood.

It occurred to me, then, that I hated silence. It was in silence I unearthed fear; I heard voices and whispers crawling along the earth, itching along the fine hairs of my ears, until I screamed.

The pot hissed, the flames spat, and Bryce reached forward—I thought to stir the stew, but instead he rested his hand upon my shoulder. I inhaled deeply, the scent of blood, embers, dirt, and fur expanding in my chest. I breathed out and brushed Bryce's hand away. I picked up the pot from the fire, careful not to spill the bubbling liquid.

"I'll go see my papa."

Bryce sighed lightly. "He's—ah, by one of the larger trees." He motioned to his left, looking oddly at his hand, as though it bled.

I turned quickly away from him and headed toward my father.

Papa was in a light sleep when I found him, his torso and legs covered with his aedituus robes. While his body was at peace, the folds of his face twisted and contorted, casting strange shadows across his cheek. He was caught somewhere between a nightmare and sleep, falling—like I had done so often—between worlds. I lowered myself beside him and set down the stew gently, careful to keep it from spilling. I threaded my hand through his, lifting it to touch my cheek. Papa stirred in his disturbed state but did not wake.

Pain. I could feel it clearly. He was in great pain, agony. It vibrated through his fingers, passing to me, and I caught it in my palm, wishing I could extinguish it like a flame. But I was merely Lunare—incapable of such feats. A Verdetto, perhaps, like Suzette, could quell his pain, but I was only suited to feel his anguish.

I pressed my lips to his cheek and his eyes fluttered open, his gaze wandering, lost among the trees until it finally found me.

"Laurel!"

"Yes, Papa, I am here."

A tear glistened on his cheek. "Oh, my sweet Laurel. You are safe."

I touched my finger to his face, brushing the tear away. His pain still stung my hand. "I wish it were true, Papa. But none of us are safe."

"No, we are not." Papa winced, propping himself upright. "And in my haste, I said such thoughtless words. I drove you away; I put you in danger. Oh, Laurel, can you forgive me?"

I shook my head. "Papa. There is nothing for you to be sorry for." I bit my lip and turned away, forcing back tears.

"Laurel . . ."

"You were right; I was a fool to think I was anything but a child, to believe I was in love." I grabbed the pot of stew and brought it to Papa's chin. "Eat."

"Laurel . . ."

"You must eat, Papa, and regain your strength!"

Papa heaved a sigh and pushed the pot away. He placed his hand on top of mine. "I am sorry that man lied to you. It brings me grief that he broke your heart in two. Know that I am here with you—to comfort you through your pain. Together, we will make this right."

I lowered my head. "Yes, Papa. I regret the time Bryce and I spent together, under the veil of night . . . I feel like a fool."

Papa pursed his lips. "There is a tea you will need to drink."

I shook my head vehemently. "Tea? No, Papa, no more teas! I cannot stomach another sip of night-root, or vendrake."

"Vendrake! Laurel, what do you speak of?"

"It is what they fed me at the Accademia . . . to keep the litha from overtaking me."

Papa set his jaw, his fingers curling into the grass, scraping two distinct claw marks into the dirt. "It seems Headmistress Elan taught you nothing about your gift, except how to subdue it."

Nothing. Nothing! The words rang in my ears. In all my lessons—painful, excruciating, and exacting lessons in courtship—Headmistress Elan had taught me nothing.

"I cannot control either ilex nor litha. My litha brings me nothing but pain. Whispers—death. And as for my ilex— I did not even know that Bryce had killed Prince Brennan! After all our time together . . ."

"It is not your fault," Papa murmured. He took a breath and released it, calming his countenance. "Long ago—before the Accademia—the Lunare would have a feast each year. They would gather for a night hunt, and the next day cook what they had slain. It was in preparation for their scrying ritual. Laurel, the Lunare were powerful oracles—priestesses of the night. They spent years studying and honing their powers before attempting this ritual. You are but a fledgling in your gifts."

He leaned back, weary. "What General Corcoran said about me: it is not true. I never abandoned you. After your mother passed, I kept you in the Accademia so that you may be around other Lunare, so that you may have friends. Headmistress Elan assured me she would teach you about your gift and that I would have full authority over your marriage plans. I never would have agreed to a union with General Vitis Grimstaad, not in a hundred lifetimes."

I put my arms around Papa, burying my head in his chest. "My ilex is worthless, Papa. After all my years in the Accademia, I do not know how to wield it."

A well of anger built in my chest and I realized I was squeezing my hand into a fist.

"Cease, Laurel," Papa cautioned. "Anger will do nothing but awaken bloodlust within you. As I have been back at the Order, I have been studying the Lunare.

"General Corcoran has a very troubling past," Papa said. "I am surprised you were able to discern as much of it as you were. It must have been agonizing to you, and I will never forgive myself for not being there to shield you from this. But

Laurel. You did not fail. It is simply not possible to seek answers to questions that we do not know we should be asking."

I blinked, my brow creasing. "I do not understand."

"Did you know that General Corcoran cannot read?"

"What?"

"He studied the recipes in my trunk for a long time, tracing the words with his fingers, before handing the parchment to me. I read them aloud and instructed him to make the salve for his shoulder."

"No!"

"Yes, Laurel. He is wholly illiterate. And you did not know, did you?"

"No." I shook my head. "I did not."

Papa smiled gently, pulling me into his chest. "We cannot find answers to questions we do not ask. Do you understand?"

"Yes, Papa."

"You are not broken. You did not fail. When we return to the Order, I will teach you about your gift. But we must eat and rest. Please. Go. I will heal better alone. And you will rest better. I want you to regain your strength."

I nodded. "I will return to you soon."

"Bring my recipes to me when you return, and I will make the tea." Papa smiled, his eyelids heavy, already drooping. "Rest well, my child."

FETTERED BY THE SAME
CHAINS

For several days I sipped on a thin, milk-white tea from a root called channa. It was odd, but not entirely unpleasant. Bryce's shoulder healed steadily with his stitchwork; he still could not yet use his arm to lift himself, but his wound no longer bled; a rosy tone returned to the surrounding flesh. Meanwhile, Papa's leg continued to deteriorate; it began to swell and darken in color. A strange, black line began to spread like a crack in his skin.

When he grew too weak to pray, I stayed by his side and held his hand, brushing my fingers through his silver strands of hair while humming hymns to him. Bryce dared not disturb our ritual, choosing to sit by the fire, stoking the flames. Sometimes he wandered into the brush to hunt. One night, I awoke to discover the first snow of the season had fallen. It rested upon my hair like a crown, dusting my lashes as I stroked Papa's cheek to wake him. But he would not open his eyes—and Bryce was nowhere to be found. I folded my arms over Papa's chest and sobbed, sinking into the rise and fall of his chest. I begged the moon to save him, but She was not even a half-eye, and unable to extend anything but her sympathies for my grieving.

Bryce arrived in the early hours before dawn, bringing my Papa's bag of ointments and flasks, then he gathered kindling to start a fire. While I placed the sticks and stuffed moss and grass at their base, my thoughts flashed iron. I started the fire and my nose filled with the scent of ore and blood. The flames warmed my hands and my thoughts turned to golden hues and blood. I felt far from the moon and Her call. Frightened and frayed, I clung to the warmth. I stirred the embers of the fire and they spat at me.

I threaded my hand through his and touched his face. "Papa, can you hear me?"

He groaned in reply, his eyelids fluttering.

"Papa, it's me. Your Laurel."

"The channa," he uttered. I did not have the heart to tell him that I had stopped drinking it days ago, that the root had run out while he slept.

He whispered something, but his words were lost on me.

"Lor," Bryce murmured. Pain, sympathy rested in his gaze—a flash of iron hiding behind his softness and sorrow. He was harboring something terrible. I felt his words sticking at the top of his mouth. I wrapped my arms around Papa in an attempt to shield him, keep him safe.

"Do not speak to me," I spat. Bryce ignored me and spoke softly, his voice barely audible.

"Listen to me, Lor." He stumbled over his words. "I've seen lots of men who take a blow like this. He should be getting better by now. I don't know how much longer he's going to last, but—I don't think he's going to survive."

A fat tear dropped onto my cheek. "N-no!" I pushed my body between him and Papa. "I cannot lose him."

"He needs a real doctor. Someone at the Order, if we can get him there."

"How?" I asked. "Neither you nor I can lift him."

"I'm going to need you to help me take off his cloak," Bryce said. He groaned, lowering himself besides my Papa. "We need to roll him over, get him on top of it. I can drag him once it's light out." He glanced at me mournfully.

"Why are you helping me?" I asked. "There is nothing

in it for you."

"I did what I had to do, with the prince." Bryce's shoulders fell. "I accept the consequences. I'm sorry, Lor. I really am."

Whether my father lived or died, it should not have mattered to him. He had no future in the Order, no hope of pardon for killing Prince Brennan. I licked my lips and let the light snow fall upon me like dust.

We are all dust, child.

Ah, how I remembered well my Papa's words from my youth. We were all destined to die: princes, kings, soldiers, brothers, Damica, aedituus.

My heart softened, watching Bryce with my papa. His efforts to save him were agonizing and valiant all at once.

"After what you did for my father, I . . . will choose to trust you. That you had reasons for what you did to Prince Brennan. And that you will tell me. But, I . . . cannot speak to you of those, right now."

Bryce nodded. "You need to be with your father."

I squeezed Papa's hand, mimicking Suzette when she had tried to bring me great comfort and peace, knowing I was surrounded by darkness and shadow.

It was an arduous, terrible task, dragging my father. We moved him in shifts, Bryce and I, our movements slower than a snail. We gained barely any ground between our camp and the mountains. When night fell, I tumbled into the cold earth, my hands raw, spine bent and aching. Bryce examined Papa's leg one final time in the firelight and swore. Gritting his teeth, he dug through my father's flasks, spread an ointment over his hand and rubbed it into my Papa's wound. Papa moaned, clenching his teeth, he writhed in agony, his skin set ablaze. When Bryce finished, he held a small flask to my Papa's lips, coaxing him to drink.

"Vendrake," he explained. "You use it out in the field for this kind of thing. Numbs the body—and the spirit."

My heart beat against my ribs like a captured rabbit. *Vendrake!* I wrinkled my nose, the bitter taste manifesting on my tongue. My poor Papa—to be drinking such wretched tea! But I was glad to see Papa's face release its pain; I watched it melt like a shadow into the earth. The thump of my heart slowed; my pulse and my breath returning to a steady state.

In the quiet pocket of peace that followed, I cast a sideways glance to Bryce. I had been true to my word and had not used my ilex to feel into him and to press into his mind— and my mind reeled with so many questions.

"Bryce," I murmured.

He twisted around to face me. "Aye?"

"How did they know it was you?"

"What?"

"You, who killed Prince Brennan."

"I'll show you, Viper."

He reached his hand deep into his tunic, and when it surfaced again, it was as if he had pulled the sun itself from his chest. In his hands was a sleek, metallic object: a sculpture, perhaps, or an instrument. It was both gold and crimson—a long, bright flash of metal pulled to a point, round and hollow in the center. The instrument had a grip made of ivory, which fit snugly in his hand, and a thin piece of metal rounded between the body of the instrument and its grip, a finger-rest.

In the Damica, I had watched—longingly, with envy—as Riognach and the other Vigore engaged in music-study, their fingers moving deftly over the keys of long, silver flutes. I ached to feel my hands glide over the contours of an instrument, to strum harp or violin and recreate the sweet, beautiful notes that had enchanted my ears.

"What is this instrument?"

Bryce's brow furled in confusion.

"I am eager to hear it."

Bryce narrowed his eyes and his expression became sharp. Slowly he turned the object over in his hands, tugged at it, and it clicked open. His voice lowered to a rumble.

"This isn't an instrument. The only music it plays is death."

I watched him wedge a finger into the opening, the golden vines of ivy around the barrel winking at me as he adjusted the inside of the object. I reached for the instrument, but Bryce jerked it away from me.

"Careful," he warned. "This is a very dangerous weapon. There are only nine of them."

"Nine?" I asked. I bit my lip. Nine. "Nine generals."

"Aye, that's right. Nine in the Deos Tactigit. Nine pistols."

He removed a small piece of metal, the shape of a thimble but a quarter of the size, and placed it into a small groove in front of the instrument's hammer.

"Two of us were sent to raze Pouelle, burn it to the ground: General Voralla, the eldest of the Deos Tactigit, and myself. They sent Prince Brennan with us and he was loathsome. Spoiled, obnoxious youth. Wouldn't stop talking, asking me to look at his sword, asking me what it's like to kill."

Bryce sighed. "I don't know why they chose to send him along with us to Pouelle. We just get handed the orders and we go—that's how it goes. Best I can tell, they sent the prince because it was easy, a place for him to get his sword wet, learn about war without being in any real danger."

"And you killed him."

"Aye. Moment he stepped off his horse, he whipped out his sword, cut two farmers down. Loved it. Laughed about it. And I . . ." Bryce's voice trailed off.

"You could not stand by and watch."

"No. I couldn't. The likes of him, taking up the throne . . . No, Lor. I gave up being Deos Tactigit that day.

Loaded up my pistol, shot him in the eye. Turned right around, killed Voralla, too."

His body began to tremble and I folded my arms around him.

"Bryce . . ."

"I'm sorry I didn't tell you. The whole day, it was like a dream . . . I was there, but I wasn't. And it never ended."

He adjusted the weapon and placed it in my hands. The steel was cold and the chill burned into my skin. I felt power and terror, a blend of fear and elation, coursing through my veins.

"I want you to have this to remember me by," he said.

His eyes grew wide; they were like the stars themselves. A staggered breath left his lips. Litha. It was litha. I was certain of it. He and I were one—fettered by the same chains, railing against the same system. A kingdom that praised us, exalted us, worshiped us—but kept us as its prisoners at the same time. I understood it. I was familiar with the pain, inside and out; it had become a part of my very makeup.

"After I killed Prince Brennan and Voralla, I sat by the well and stripped off my armor. Piece by piece, I threw everything down, listened to it rattle and sink to the bottom. Gauntlets, grieves, cuirass, tasset. All of it. When I was finished, I held the pistol over the well and—I tried. I tried to let it go— but I couldn't."

I brushed my cheek against Bryce's whiskers, the tip of his nose chilling the bridge of mine.

"You frighten me," he whispered.

I pressed my forehead against his and closed my eyes. "I cannot change what I am."

Bryce touched his fingers to my cheek and traced them down to my chin. "That's not why I'm afraid. It's not because you're a Lunare, or because you're half-mad, or have that . . . gift—knowing what you shouldn't. It's not even because Grimstaad and the enforcers are coming for you."

"Why, then?" I breathed.

"It's because you've Viper. So beautiful, so dangerous. I can't stop worrying about you, how I'm going to keep you warm, fed, and get you to safety. And how long that 'safety' is going to be safe for you."

A short breath warmed my lips and his mouth fell upon mine. I felt nothing in this moment but warmth, the light of the world pressed against my lips. In my heart, I knew he loved me freely, with no malevolence or secrets. My partner, my ammorante, my sun.

"What happens now?" I asked.

"I take you to the Order, and then we go our separate ways."

I turned the pistol over in my hands, studying its crimson sheen against my pale skin. My hand wrapped around the grip and I turned to Bryce.

"No," I said firmly. "We will take *my father* to the Order. After he is safe—where you go, I will follow."

PART FOUR

We lived in an ugly world—men, always hurting one another, handing down conflict and strife to each other: a daisy-chain of cruelty.

Would it ever cease, or were we fated to harm each other forever?

33

A DREAM LIKE POSION

When we neared the foot of the mountains, I dreamed in hues of gray. The lush palette of cinquefoils, evergreens, and autumn leaves were left to days gone by, dirty rock and snow taking its place in my mind. I dreamed that my papa sang, his voice rising above mountain peaks, and my mother's voice joined his, rising in harmony to his hymns. I scanned the sky for a hint of their features—my mama's porcelain skin, the smooth curve of her wrist, her serpent bracelets resting against the warmth of her pulse. I searched for Papa's honey-rich smile, his robes, and his tomes. I sought, as well, any glimmer of Roland—a flicker of his dark hair or a wing, each so black it may carry a blue sheen against the gray sky. It had been days since Roland had revealed himself to me. Perhaps he was gone, entirely—a spirit faded from this world, gone to the next, and I would see him no more. Or perhaps his absence was fortunate, a lucky sign that my papa was holding onto life, and that Grimstaad and his enforcers remained far away. No omen of death.

Except me. Perhaps this was why I dreamed of both my Mama and Papa, together calling me from afar with their song. It was the song of mourning—a dirge.

Some kind of warning.

I awoke with a jolt and Bryce flinched awake. His hands, by instinct, curved around the hilt of his blade and he sat up—eyes wild and blue, his breathing rapid. I placed my fingertips at the edge of his chin.

"It was a dream, ammorante," I whispered. "Nothing more."

He exhaled, his pupils adjusting to the darkness, and he shook his head. He relinquished his blade and lifted my hand, bringing it to his lips. Kissing it gently, his gaze drifted afar; he was lost somewhere in the jagged rocks of the mountains.

"I felt it. Like poison . . . running through your veins." He shivered, weary, as the frozen ground stole life from both of us. "Don't know how or why."

"We are closer at heart," I whispered. "I'm sorry, ammorante. I did not know what it meant to be close to you, that I might bring you the darkness of my gift if we lay together."

"It's . . . terrifying, Viper. But maybe it will help us survive. If you dreamed it and I felt it like I did, then we shouldn't ignore it." He stood and began to collect our belongings. "Help me with this. I'll take your father. We should go . . . now."

∞

Dawn arrived early and brought with it little warmth or light. We did not stop to hunt and set no fire; I shared dried meat and berries from our satchels while the wind howled at us, biting our skin. I stayed close to Bryce as he dragged my papa. His mood turned black and he cursed while he pulled him along the frigid terrain. During a short break, he checked Papa's leg and swore loudly. My father's skin had turned as black and foul as his mood. My hope began to waver that we should ever come upon the gates of the Order.

We can't give up. I squeezed my eyes shut and steeled myself against the wind. *We must fight for this. Focus on the future.*

"Bryce." I squeezed his bicep. "After my father is safe,

where shall we go?"

"Don't know," Bryce grunted, working to force my Papa's body up a mossy incline. "Know a man in the north, owes me a favor. Might be able to get us on a ship."

"We would not stay here?"

He scoffed. "Can't."

"What about my father?" I asked. "And what of Pouelle? Did you not save them from being destroyed by the Deos Tactigit? You would be a hero in their eyes; they would protect us."

"I didn't save them," Bryce growled. "I marked them for death."

"How?" I asked, throwing my arms wide. "They are still alive because of you!"

Bryce frowned. "I suppose some of them might be. Most of them have probably scattered, starved, or been hung."

"Hung? By Grimstaad?"

"No, not him. Not directly, anyway. I thought Grimstaad was dead, until you told me otherwise. He would have been too wounded to ride out and perform the hangings. But his enforcers probably had orders to hang the banale and acted out of those."

"Bryce! If Grimstaad is hanging the farmers from Pouelle, they would *want him dead*!" I tugged at his arm, my mind alighting with hope. "We have to go back, once we take Papa to the Order! It's where we belong!"

Bryce shook his head vehemently. "No, Viper. We can't. There's nothing for us in Pouelle."

My brow hardened. "I do not understand. Roland told you to be a protector and to do right by others, did he not?"

"Viper, what I did in Pouelle, it isn't what he would have wanted."

I opened my mouth to protest, but behind us, my father groaned and writhed in agony. Our conversation halted abruptly as Bryce stopped, dropping the corners of the cloak he was using to drag my papa. I fell to my knees beside my father, taking his hand in mine.

"Papa . . . ."

My father made a strange sound, uttering clips of fevered words which I did not understand.

"Bryce!"

Lowering himself beside me, Bryce lifted the covering on my papa's leg. The stench hit me in a thick, rancid wave. I tasted the decay on my tongue. Heaving, I expelled the contents of my stomach.

"Easy." Bryce rubbed my back in slow circles, his palms rough but compassionate.

"I am fine," I said sharply. I spat into the grass, wiping my sleeve across my face. "We must keep moving. Give me the cloak. It is my turn to carry him."

I lifted my gaze to Bryce. Heartache and trepidation passed over the blues of his eyes. I stared into his face, examining the contours of his cheek, his nose. I felt his trauma hiding in the shadows of his features—valleys of horror revealing memories of the battlefield, men and parts scattered on the ground, a thick carpet reminding me of the shedding of wisteria petals in Cortellion.

Something was terribly wrong.

"I feel it," I hissed. "Tell me what is on your mind!"

Bryce shifted his gaze to the ground. "We can't keep going, unless I cut off his leg."

"What?" I cried, squeezing Papa's hand.

"It's too hard to keep moving him like this. We're going to freeze out here before we even set foot in the mountains. The leg's too rotten. It's the only thing I can do. Maybe we can carry him when it's off, but he might already be too far gone."

"N-no!" I bit my lip and turned away, brushing past him to hide my tears.

"It's the best we can do for him. And you can't be here when I do it. Bring me your father's herbs, take my tinder box and start us a fire—and then I need you to leave. Go far away, gather some water, and go hunt. I don't want you anywhere near this."

I tried, but failed to imagine my Papa with his leg missing, confined to a crutch and his staff for the remainder of his days. I stirred the embers of the fire and they jumped at me.

". . . I will do as you ask," I said to Bryce, feeling hollow, cold.

I turned back to Papa and whispered to him, humming the words of one of his hymns in the old tongue. His lips moved, mouthing the words as I sang them, and I focused my thoughts on our kitchen—the soft, white light spilling through our window while we kneaded the dough for piandia. I focused on pushing the thoughts from my heart into his. Papa sighed and I kissed the crown of his head.

"Everything will be well," I whispered. "Rest."

I waited until I was far into the trees to let my tears fall. Grasping the hilt of my blade, I wrung it tight. I refused to feel weak—vulnerable, like prey. Not when my father needed me. I silenced my tears and turned my attention to the hunt.

TRAIL OF DEATH IN MY PALM

I did as Bryce asked and moved far from them, spending my time trying to hunt. I walked for what felt like hours, trying to make myself useful, be strong, and do something to help with Papa's recovery—or, at least, aid in our survival.

Unfortunately, I was useless—in every manner. Snow blanketed the ground and I spotted no more roots, nor berries, to be foraged. I searched for rabbits, squirrels, even birds and insects, but the horizon blurred into a colorless, featureless mass beneath the veil of my tears—like a watercolor portrait in which the painter used too many dabs of his brush in the water so that the colors ran together. The stillness of the trees was maddening. I scanned the branches for movement, but they were all silenced by snow. Even the hanged men remained silent.

Frustrated, I felt the litha rising. Shadows from the trees' shadows swayed across the glistening grass. Too much. I was holding back too much—and I needed a release. I kicked at the ground, over and over exasperated, until my breath gave out and I shivered, resigning myself to return to our camp. Rubbing my arms for warmth, the twinkling snow and boundless sky made me feel small, alone. My cheeks stung as I allowed my tears to spill over my skin and turn cold. I sobbed and shuffled, empty-handed, to the spot I had last seen Bryce and Papa together. When I neared it, I found blood—a crimson stream across a canvas of white.

It was done.

I followed the harrowing trail, the scent of embers guiding my way. When the blood became thicker and a deeper hue of red, I found Bryce leaning against a tree shivering. Absent of his fur cloak, he looked up to greet me, his eyes bloodshot, sleepless.

"Was going to head out looking for you soon."

"There is so much blood," I whispered. I looked at my prints beside the trail and the world spun beneath me. "Did he . . ."

"He survived. He's sleeping right now and he's got enough vendrake in his veins that he'll stay asleep for a long time to come. Soon as the bleeding slowed, I took him to a cavern and seared the wound closed."

"You know how to do that?"

Bryce shook his head. "Hardly. Watched a field medic do it once. Prayed it would work. Looks like it did."

I felt the sting of hot tears forming in the corners of my eyes. Clenching my teeth, I blinked rapidly, forcing them away. My fingers curled into my fist, and I threw my shoulders back.

A viper would not cry. Not now. She must be strong.

"Take me to him."

Bryce tilted his neck back and stared at the sky. He panted, slumping against the tree, and swallowed a large breath of air. "In the morning. Once the stench has cleared."

I removed my cloak and placed it around Bryce's shoulders. The scent of bile clung to his shirt and I wrinkled my nose, turning away from him.

"Couldn't help myself while I was burying the leg," he said. "Like to wash up now that you're back, get some sleep. We'll start up the mountains soon as we can. I'll have to figure out how to carry him."

"I'm frightened Bryce," I said quietly. "You can barely lift your sword. And—what happens if the bleeding does not stop?"

Bryce looked down at his knees, scraping his toe against the grass. "Try not to think about that. Doesn't do either of us any good."

I closed my mouth and swallowed my feelings, forcing them to lie, unsettled, in my stomach. My eyelids fluttered closed and I counted my panicked heartbeats. *One-two-three-four, one-two-three-four.* I forced myself to take a deep breath and found my fingers clutching Bryce's pistol, finding comfort in its grip.

"I will do as you ask, Bryce—but you must do something for me, or I may lose my mind."

"What is it?"

"The woods are so still now. There is nothing to hunt, nothing to collect—nothing for me to do but wring my hands and worry. About Grimstaad, about us, about my Papa . . ." I choked on my last words.

Bryce's eyes flashed with their blue compassion. "What can I do to help?"

I slipped the pistol from my belt, turning it over in my hands. "Teach me how to use this."

His voice bent with hesitation, like a branch holding too much snow. "I'd rather not," he said, pressing his teeth into his lip. "But you're a wisp of a woman. Even with your blade, it's too easy to take you down. Not trying to offend, but you don't stand a chance against men who've trained for years."

I lay my hand atop his. I did not need my ilex to sense the embers of hope dying between us. They twirled like ash in the gray winter sky, falling as snow—lifeless as the dust. I patted his hand and sunned him with as much reassurance as I could summon into my fingertips.

"I understand, ammorante. You worry for me, but it is better for me to know than to remain naive. I do not like feeling so . . . helpless."

"Aye," he sighed. "I don't like it, but I'll show you."

He stood, retrieved his travel satchel, and removed from it a small tin box I had never seen before. It looked like his tinderbox, only smaller. He clicked it open; inside, it was full of small, square pieces of parchment thinner than leaves. A smaller wooden box, like a puzzle, rested inside as well. One corner of the tin was greasy with wax. Bryce put his hand into his satchel again, reaching deep inside. Cautiously, with great care, his arm emerged with an ivory-and-gray colored horn. From its size, I could not fathom which beast from which it may have come. The end of the horn was plugged with a cork, wedged tight. Bryce placed it gently beside the papers and the tin box.

"Come, Viper." He patted the ground beside him and my stomach clenched, curiosity and apprehension bleeding together. I felt as though I were a child again, studying my father's relics. I lowered myself beside him and he reached for my hands, turning my palms up, pushing them together. He placed the horn in them. I stifled a shudder at its cold, smooth polish against my skin. *Terrible.* This was something terrible. Something I should fear. The litha began to rise in my chest. I pushed my tongue against the roof of my mouth to plug the scream in my throat.

"Open it easy," Bryce said. "Slowly."

My fingers trembling, I maneuvered them around the cork and wedged it loose. It released with a small sigh and the smell of ore flooded my sense. It burned into my nose and mouth, leaving an acrid, tinny taste on my tongue.

It was the scent of death.

"Bryce, what is this?" I asked.

"Black powder," he said. "Pour a little in your hand."

I tilted the horn and a sprinkling of powder slid from it, falling into my hand. I rolled the tiny pebbles against my skin: a trail of death in my palm.

"Keep it away from fire; it'll kill you if it catches. You have to keep it away from water, too, if you want it to work.

That's why it's in the horn."

"What is it for?"

"Killing," Bryce said simply. "You use a cartridge, loaded with it, in your pistol. Then you point it at your enemy and hope he dies instead of you."

I furled my brow. "I do not understand."

"These pistols are dangerous. They can backfire, especially if you don't use them right, treat them with respect. One of the Deos Tactigit—a general named Harmin—he lost two of his fingers in a misfire. Did sloppy work, didn't load his pistol, and I don't think he ever cleaned it. I'm going to teach you to use it properly. Hate to see that happen to you."

I curled my fingers into my palm, hiding the black pebbles within. "Bryce, I'm not sure I want to do this after all."

"I don't want you backing out because you're scared. I'll show you. We'll roll a cartridge, fire it—and then you're going to make some more cartridges, while I wash up and shut my eyes."

He lifted a piece of parchment from the box and laid it flat on the lid. "Before we start, let's be clear. You only use the pistol here in the woods. Once we get in the mountains—your shot might bring a wave of snow down on top of us."

I nodded and he removed a piece of parchment and a wooden piece, like a small rolling pin, from his tin box. "Watch closely."

He folded the paper around the wooden piece, tying the bottom with a small piece of twine. From his wooden box he removed three small, silver marbles and dropped them in the cartridge, and a much larger one that reminded me of the gem in Suzette's brooch. He was careful in his movements, precise in where he tied the twine. He took my wrist and turned it; the powder in my hand trickled into the parchment. His fingers rolled deftly across the parchment in a series of complex folds, and he tied a final piece of twine to seal it.

"When you're done, dip your finger in the wax and

cover all the seams. Then, load it." I followed his motions, watching him seal the ends and all the creases in the greasy substances in the box.

"Now, you're ready," he said, his blue eyes heavy with exhaustion, a sad smile turning up the corners of his lips. "Hope you never need to do this, Lor."

"But if I do . . ."

"Keep the hammer half-cocked, don't get the pistol wet, and never—and I mean *never*—forget to remove it before you sit by the fire, when you've got a cartridge loaded." He loaded the cartridge into the pistol, cocked the hammer back, and placed it in my hands. The steel was cold and its chill burned into my skin. A blend of power and terror coursed through my veins as my fingers curved around the polished grip. Bryce lifted my arms until the pistol was parallel to my face, the point clearly aimed at a trunk a short distance from us.

His hands slid from my arms to my shoulders. "Stay calm, hold your arms straight, and aim for the chest or the head, if you think you can hit it. It's going to be loud. And it's gonna push you back when you pull the trigger. Keep your arms steady, wait for me to step back, and then pull the trigger."

Bryce moved away from me and I held my breath. The pistol and the black powder within seemed to seep into my veins. The weapon spoke to me in the sun's cryptic language— the one I never believed could be my own. The pistol winked at me and understanding what it asked of me, I released my breath and pulled the trigger.

A roar erupted from the weapon—a deafening trumpet's blare. It knocked me back, my fingers burning.

Oh, what beauty, oh, what death! My heart pounded with excitement, the corners of my lips turning upward as I breathed in shallow and uneven breaths, embracing this new power.

The power of life and death.

My ears rang and I gazed at the trunk. A splintered hole

Ynes Freeman

gazed back at me like the empty eye of the ouroboros etched
on Bryce's back.

ILIO SONOTU

It took much effort and error for me to remember all the folds and knots to create the cartridges, but I managed to complete two while Bryce bathed and slept.

He awoke after a short sleep, the sun high above us. We lay quietly beside each other on our backs. Still warm to the touch, I held Bryce's pistol above me, twirling it so that its barrel caught the sun: a spark of light igniting the edge. I blinked, my eyes stinging at its harsh glare.

"Viper." Bryce sat up. "Keep it out of sight. Grimstaad's bride or not, the enforcers see you with that, they'll snap your neck without a second thought."

"Mm." I nodded, half acknowledging him. I was entranced, still, by the feeling of firing my shot—the crack, the explosion, the kick. The power of life and death. The pistol's delicate metalwork sparkled between my fingers, scintillating like a sunbeam at the surface of a stream.

"Keep it on your leg, under your dress. I'll give you my sling, and we can make a slit in your dress so you can reach it."

"Mm."

"*Viper.*" Bryce lay his hand on top of the pistol, snuffing out its glow. I blinked, a flicker of ire sparking in my chest.

"I heard you." I glowered.

"No, you didn't. Put it away."

"Please, ammorante. Listen to me—and I will do ask you ask." I sat up and my braid fell over my shoulder, brushing his neck. I raised the pistol and pressed it, on its side, to his sternum. "This pistol, it is your pride, your blood, your honor, your wrath—your heart, ammorante. I am in awe that you would place it in my hands."

Wordless, he leaned in and kissed my forehead. I clutched the weapon and brought it to my own heart.

"*Ilio sonotu*, Alastair Bryce Corcoran," I whispered. The words spilled from my heart—deep, dark, devoted, like the moon to the night.

His lips parted and he sucked a breath between his teeth. Astonishment passed through him, warm as embers.

"Ilio sonotu," I repeated. "Do you understand?"

"Aye." He shivered. "Marriage vows."

"I know I am no longer Damica and that you are fated to die soon," I murmured. "But with this pistol in my hands, I get to choose. What, from the Damica I shall keep, and what I shall become. Who shall remain in my heart and mind—for all my days."

"Ilio sonotu, Laurel Aleandri," Bryce whispered. He kissed my eyes, his lashes brushing my cheek as his lips brushed the bridge of my nose. He cupped my cheek in his hand and drew me to him. My mouth connected with his and as we kissed, my mind flashed to the ouroboros on his back, its spine a perfect circle, teeth and tail becoming one in the same. This creature, this serpent—it moved with the grace of both sun and moon—caught between worlds, the gulch between life and death.

Ours was not a Damica wedding. But I was no longer Damica, and I was never a Maialinne, nor a Riognach, nor a Bethany. At best, I was a Suzette—but even she and I came from different worlds. She was fated to become a vedova, and I, a bride.

It was not a ceremony of the Order, or even what one would call a common marriage. My marriage to Bryce was one of the heart. The wind spoke our vows, the pistol pressed between our hearts was a promise—to share a life of blood and blade. The roots below us became the altar upon which we consummated our union—the sun, our witness. The withered leaves on the low branches of a tree shook, twirling around us. Bryce's gaze burned through me. His eyes the color of steel and sky; they shone like his blade in the sun. My braided hair fell over my shoulder. My blades struck against my thighs in a percussive rhythm—and I became one with him.

At night, my dreams held no more light, no more warmth, no more love. I lay with Bryce upon an icy patch of grass, the tiny, specter-like blades stealing thin threads of breath that passed through his lips. I pressed my ear to the ground; the earth growled back at me.

Something shifted in the wind, disturbing the peace of my sleep.

It did not welcome the living.

I lifted my head and raised it to the sky. A clear night, the stars were a scattering of dust across the tops of the mountains. They held a promise of life beyond our reach, always just a thread beyond our grasp. The moon was absent from the night, and I missed Her presence. I felt restless without Her—untethered as I wandered into a dream, jumping from my own world into the mountains.

Instinctively, I called for Roland.

"Blackbird?"

The earth groaned at my words—it was agitated, uneasy like me. I was alone in this land, my life fading, and I raised my chin to sing out my wedding vows—ilio sonotu—to the stars.

They were more than vows. In the dark, they were a battle cry, so that the night should know I will live. I shall not perish in the cold.

The earth echoed and roared in reply to my words, a

thunder erupting around me, moaning amid the depths of the underworld.

Mine.

I covered my ears and folded to my knees. The sound was awful—worse than the hanged men and their hollow, twisted rhyme. The word thundered into a crescendo and I righted myself, my stomach roiling with illness. My calves tensed and I erupted into a sprint. Clamped against my ears, my arms began to tremble. A scream clawed at the edges of my throat. I did not know what I was running from . . . until it appeared in front of me.

The scream burst from my lips.

It appeared as a centaur in darkness, pointed legs and broad chest raised in silhouette among the mountainside. A cry, shrill and awful, spilled from blackened lips. The pungent scent of sweat and fear mingled into an acrid brew, invading my senses. The creature's hooves clattered against the ground and I caught a glimmer of light in its hands. The soft warmth washed over its head and I saw, clearly, it was a horse and a rider—not a monster. But the knowledge did little to stop my legs from shaking. The rider shifted his lantern, the light bathing over his gloveless hand. It was pink and blistered, thin, black veins coursing through flesh like streams; his skin pockmarked with pulsing red bulges.

Grimstaad.

I reached for my pistol; Bryce's warning about using it in the mountains stilled my hand. My hand jumped to my blades, and I drew them and howled, my muscles tensing, braid whipping at my back. I planted my heels into the ground, gathering my power into the base of my foot, preparing to coil and strike. I raised my neck and called to the stars, but they winked at me from afar, unable to help. Grimstaad dismounted his horse. His eyes flashed upon me. Amber. Filled with hatred.

I was jarred from the mountains, thrown from the

dream.

Daylight. It flared like his horse. I blinked at the sky, the stillness of the woodland, heavy with snow, coming into focus. I shivered and sat up, examining my garments. I was drenched in a cold sweat beside Bryce. He slept lightly, his flaxen hair turning to gold in the early light, thin strands igniting like the intricate gold of his pistol. Bryce stirred in his sleep; the spines of his serpent peeked through his hair. I stared at my hands; they trembled against my will.

Deos Tactigit.

They were all dead. All except one. And I was glad for it. Nine generals, and I barely knew half of their names. Nine. Each and every one of them knew the atrocities that Darby Sloane inflicted upon my ammorante—and they had chosen to do nothing.

Vitis Grimstaad.

He had been one of those nine, and Bryce had suffered because of him. Grimstaad had stolen Suzette's future, scarring her face. My Papa would never be whole again because of his enforcers. The hanged men belonged to Grimstaad as well—to the Deos Tactigit.

Twist the ropes, make gallows for the Serpentine.

So much suffering.

It was not I who had been a rabbit: innocent, vulnerable—a beautiful creature to be hunted and devoured. I had been fated to be surrounded by serpents: my mother's jade bracelets, the snakes twining up my father's staff. Headmistress Elan matched me to Grimstaad because our hearts were full of darkness. We were meant to be a union of monsters. She had said it herself: *my gift paired well with death.*

Crawling quietly through the snow, I found and opened Bryce's travel satchel. Rummaging deep through its contents, I pulled each item out one by one and lay them in the snow. Roots, berries, trinkets—and I came upon the sling he had mentioned to me. I lifted my skirt, running my hands up my thigh. I slipped the sling around it, giving it a firm tug to ensure it would hold.

I found the tin box and removed a cartridge.

One. It was all I would need.

I ruminated on Bryce's words about Prince Brennan, why he had pointed this weapon at him, why he sent a steel ball ripping through his royal eye.

Like Damica Sofie, Bryce had laid down his life, his honor, to stop an abhorrent man from coming into power. I had come apart, too. Everything I believed—about the Damica, my headmistress, my litha, my gift—had been unraveled. I slipped the pistol into my sling. I did not have gallows for Grimstaad, but I had Bryce's pistol—his last vestige of the Deos Tactigit.

I took one final look at Bryce: his beauty, his blade. This man had chosen to rescue me—and I had become the new serpent on his back. I would not let Grimstaad take him, or what remained of my father. And after my father was safely delivered back to the order, I would cease to be Laurel. Like the hanged men, there would be nothing left to remember of her.

Grimstaad was hunting Laurel. He was not expecting to be hunted by Viper.

Laurel, Viper.

Viper, Laurel.

Damica, Lunare.

Bride, Assassin.

Life. Death.

Ouroboros.

I was a beautiful serpent twirling in a waltz, a dance of duality. No beginning, no end . . . a dichotomous continuum, fated to last forever.

An endless waltz of dust.

EIGHT IN THE FIELDS

This ends today.
I have gone to kill him.
Do not follow me.
I love you.
Take care of Papa.

The letter I left to Bryce was short, simple—written with soot and a stick on one of his parchment pieces. Even if he could not read my words, he would find my father, and through him, they would reach him.

I filled my travel sack with dried berries and meats before slipping the note under the collar of his tunic. He stirred lightly, and I took care to disappear into the trees before he woke. The ground took a sharp tilt so that my trek was uphill. The sun warming the top of my head, I trudged through a silent world, snow at my ankles. I panted and pumped my elbows, forcing my legs onward.

Onward, onward. By nightfall, Grimstaad would be dead and we would be free. *Free.* I would make certain of it. Papa would recover; we would climb the mountain without danger lurking just behind us; we would be able to hunt, rest, and wash properly, and we would pass through the gates of the Order. We would find our way . . . home.

Home. The Order would be home, if only for a short time. Bryce and I, together, would lift my Papa—holding him between us. If the Order turned Bryce away at the gates, I would take his hands and fill them with food and furs, and he would whisper to me where to find him. I would stay with my Papa only until he recovered and learned to walk with his staff, once more joining his fellow aeditiii and clericii in their hymns and work. And while his brethren rejoiced and slept soundly in the still of night, I would slip out of the door. Under the moon, I would use my ilex to find my way back to my Bryce, my husband-by-heart, seeking his warmth and love.

But I had to find Grimstaad first. Before any of this could happen, I had to learn how to use it to hunt Grimstaad . . . before he hunted me. When his enforcers grabbed me and choked the breath from me, they said Grimstaad had a *hunch* about where to find me. This hunch . . . it was as though he knew, somehow, where to look. It was *his* gift, as Deos Tactigit, and if a Lunare, such as myself, was so highly coveted in Trionfi . . .

Perhaps my ilex can to do the same.

I looked to the sun, its light broken by bare, winter-worn branches with a few withered leaves still clinging to them. I caught a glance at the moon—half present, like a loaf of bread sliced in two—Her pearlescence nearly invisible against the cerulean sky. Bare as they were, if I had been thicker into the trees, I might have missed Her entirely.

Onward. Onward.

I needed to see Her more clearly, and I did not have the luxury to wait until nightfall for Her light to strengthen me. What She was I had to accept; I would try to make use of it. I shuffled through the snow, stopping when I found a stream that was little more than a trickle. Sweat clung to the back of my neck; I lifted my braid and tucked it unto itself. My throat was dry from the efforts and exertion of trudging through the snow. I scooped the water into my hands and wet my lips eagerly.

The sun peaked at high noon by the time the trees cleared in front of me, and I had a full view of the sky, with both the sun and the moon present. I rested my back against a tree and sank into the snow. Twists of roots pressed into the bottoms of my thighs, and I felt a blush rise to my cheeks—my thoughts drifting to Bryce. The vows we made under the winter sky. *Sun and moon, side by side.* I unsheathed my blade and made a small tear into the side of my skirt, with enough give to slip my fingers within. The tension in my shoulders melted as my fingers grazed the frozen steel of Bryce's pistol. I closed my eyes, my lips parting as its cold bite penetrated my flesh.

We are the world. Sun, moon, and earth.

The back of my neck flared like fire, my ilex searing the image of the ouroboros into my mind. I gasped, my vertebrae twisting with cold and heat, and my eyelids fluttered open.

Gazing back at me was the face of a man I recognized. I had never seen him in person; I knew him only from my days in the Accademia. I had looked upon his hazel-colored eyes in my study-tomes. They were dull, uninterested, and sat beneath a swirl of ash brown ringlets. A silver crown rested upon his head, with two rows of rubies sitting within an ornamental lacework.

Prince Brennan.

In my vision, he was anything but the still-life I had grown familiar with in my studies; here, his hazel-colored eyes were brighter. They almost glowed orange in their center, and they shifted constantly. With a sweep of his decorated cloak, he surveyed his surroundings. My gaze followed his as we scanned a crowd of frightened faces—men, women, children, all on their knees, in calico blouses, patched trousers, and threadbare skirts.

A flash of gold glinted in the corner of my vision, and I turned. Both my hands snapped to my mouth and I dropped my head to my knees. Bryce. It was him! My Bryce, standing proud, handsome in crimson armor, with golden edges—just like his pistol. His face was absent of any beard and his flaxen hair was smoothed flat, tied with ribbon. He was handsome and well groomed. Arms crossed, he leaned against a wall and stared down at his pointed boots, Prince Brennan shifted his gaze to Bryce, a wrinkle of discontent causing the smoothness of his cheek to ripple.

Deos Tactigit. Pouelle.

We were in Pouelle with the farmers, the place where it had all begun.

"Oi! Corcoran!" Prince Brennan called out. "Which one of them should I do first?"

Bryce said nothing, continuing to stare at his boots.

"You awake, general?" Prince Brennan's scowl deepened. He narrowed his eyes and his lips squeezed into a pout. Behind him, an elderly man dressed in a black armor plate approached Bryce, and he draped his hand on Bryce's forearm. His glove bore the skeletal serpent of the Deos Tactigit.

This must be General Voralla. The one he spoke of; the one he killed.

Beneath a white beard, the elderly man's lips moved. "Please, Corcoran," he pleaded. "The young prince needs your encouragement. He idolizes you."

Bryce shook the general's frail hand loose. "Away an' wash the back of yer bollox!"

"*Language*, Corcoran!" General Voralla lectured. "You speak like a swine. Slow your tongue and form your words as we practiced."

Bryce sighed deeply and shifted his weight. "Fine. I'll say it as you like. *Leave me out of it.*"

Voralla shook his head. "I'm afraid you do not have a choice in this matter. His highness bestowed the honor upon you, of giving Prince Brennan his first kill."

The corner of Bryce's cheek turned up into a grin, and his chest shook with a rueful laugh. "'Course I don't have a choice."

Prince Brennan clenched his jaw, and he unsheathed an elegant blade from his side. "My patience is thinning, Voralla!

Make him do his duty!"

Voralla shook his head, lifting one heavy boot after the other, edging closer. Bryce straightened himself and uncrossed his arms.

"Calm yourself, Voralla. I'll do what you like." He rolled his neck from side to side, cracked his knuckles, and placed two fingers in his mouth.

He whistled at Prince Brennan. "Oi! Prince!"

"Aye, Corcoran?"

"Take your blade and stick it up your arse, ya right moran."

Prince Brennan clenched his jaw, his hazel-colored eyes hardening to stone. My ilex swelled in my chest. A rage had been simmering in the prince, one that had dwelled within him . . . for how long, I could not tell. It bubbled to a boil so quickly that I believed it may rip apart his skin. He raised his blade and the world seemed to slow. His sword came down recklessly, wildly across a group of farmers. He slashed at them without aim or purpose, and those he did not strike erupted into screams and ran. A spray of blood painted the prince's face, clinging to his ringlets. He threw back his head and laughed.

"What a thrill!" He grinned, panting. "Far more riveting than hunting. What say you, Corcoran?"

Bryce said nothing; he had not moved at all: arms crossed, staring at his boots. Voralla pursed his lips and shook his head, resigning himself to stand against the wall with Bryce. Prince Brennan sliced his blade across his wounded and the fallen alike, cutting through flesh and sinew and bone. I wanted to shield my eyes, but I forced myself not to look away. This vision had come to me for a reason, and I could not pull back and hide from it.

After a minute of hacking, Bryce uncrossed his arms, righted himself, and came off the wall. In an instant, his hand whipped to his belt and he drew his pistol from its sling. A thunderous *crack* rang out across the village, igniting a fresh wave of screams.

I whirled around and watched Prince Brennan fall. Bryce gripped his pistol, smoke billowing in a thick cloud from its mouth. The scent of ore hung heavy in the air.

Oh, ammorante. I wanted to run to him, to take the pistol from his hands, tuck it away and wrap my arms around him. We could lie in the fields, his head in my lap, while I stroked his hair, and sang softly to him.

Behind Bryce, Voralla gaped, blinked, stuttered as he tried to form words.

Hands trembling, Bryce lowered his pistol and tucked it in his sling. His blue eyes welled with tears while his gaze floated to the bodies before him, Prince Brennan crumpled and broken among the dead. Bryce breathed out, his gaze drifting over each of the survivors near him, a circle of frightened eyes. He shifted his attention back to the bodies. Voralla blinked rapidly, stumbling over his words.

"What have you done?" he asked shakily.

A tear spilled onto Bryce's cheek and he lifted his eyes to Voralla, a crease forming between his brows. His hand moved to his sheath. Voralla realized, as I did, what was happening.

"No!" His hands moved to the hilt of his blade.

I closed my eyes and turned away. I knew how this vision ended; Bryce had already told me. I expected to hear the guttural death-rattle of Voralla, and I waited a long time in anticipation of the sound of blade striking flesh and the frail man falling in his own blood. The world spun around me as I waited, dizzy and sick. But it failed to arrive. Instead, Voralla's voice cut through my mind.

"You are out of control, Darby."

Darby?

My eyes shot open and I found myself at the palace, standing by the door in a room decorated like Grimstaad's: a chandelier hanging from the ceiling, a four-poster bed with an abundance of pillows, tapestries decorating the walls, candlesticks on a writing desk. At the center of this room, two men sat across from each other at a round table. Although he no longer wore his black armor, I recognized Voralla from his white beard and time-worn features. The other man had auburn hair pinned into a pristine bun. I recognized him from the malice he carried in his eyes.

General Darby Sloane. The one who hurt my Bryce. The one Bryce killed, savagely, with a shovel.

Without soot masking his features, I could see he wore both age and scars; his nose bent slightly to one side as though it had been broken and did not heal properly. His face had been dusted in heavy makeup.

"I told you to stop preying on Corcoran. Show some restraint and good sense. He is one of our own—and your understudy, a man in your position cannot be doing this," Voralla lectured.

"I can do whatever I please," Sloane hissed. When I looked closely, it became evident that some of his features had been painted onto his skin: his left brow, and what appeared to be a small piece of his lip.

"Go back to your wife, Darby. You remember the struggle we had, convincing the headmistress to let go of Maggia—and give her to *you*. Think about your family. You have children, Darby. What will happen to them if King Armando finds out what you are doing—right under his nose, in his palace?"

"Are you planning to tell him?" Sloane pushed his chair back and leaned across the table.

Voralla sat up, rigid. "I am his highness's advisor. It is my duty. Do not forget your place, Darby."

"My place?" Sloane clenched his hand into a fist. "You're just an old man—a relic among the Deos Tactigit. I could drive a fist into your mouth, break all your teeth."

"I'd like to see you try."

Sloane pulled his arm back and the room swirled around me, pulling me out of Voralla's room and into a moonless night. I spun around; I was still at the palace, but outside, in what appeared to be a small courtyard—empty, abandoned. A raised archway led away from a babbling fountain adorned with mosaic tiles.

From behind the high arch—a thud broke through the peace. *Pain.* I ran across the courtyard, reaching the archway just in time to see Sloane drive his fist into Bryce's nose. I cringed and cupped my hand over my own nose.

Bryce spat on the ground and lunged for Sloane, but before he could reach him, a short, hefty figure emerged from the shadows, holding him back. A second figure of similar shape and size emerged and seized Bryce by the shoulders. The two laughed as they restrained him, pinning him against the wall. Sloane, grinning, drove a boot into Bryce's midsection. One of Bryce's captors gripped the archway; his index and middle finger were both missing.

General Harmin. Bryce talked about him when I was learning to make cartridges; he was the general whose pistol had misfired. Slone took another swing at Corcoran and all three men roared with excitement. I shut my eyes and turned away; I could watch no more.

The terrible voices and thuds of pain faded from my ears, and when I next opened my eyes, I found myself in an ornately decorated room, rows upon rows of benches, sunlight pouring through stained glass windows, casting shards of colored light across men in pressed jackets and trousers, women donning layered, extravagant gowns of all shapes and colors. We were in a throne room, sitting in the presence of King Armando and Queen Norina themselves. Bored and slouched in a plush seat, Prince Brennan sat beside the king. Three men, immaculately dressed in tailored jackets and trousers cinched at their calves, stood before King Armando.

Each bore the symbol of the Deos Tactigit.

His highness rose, addressing each man. "Generals Dane Thompson, Handel Greene, and Gavin Hughes. Trionfi owes you a great debt of gratitude. We commend your courage and swift action in crushing the insurgency in the west."

I scanned the audience and caught Bryce, seated with the other generals of the Deos Tactigit, in a row near the front, behind a group of nobles.

My heart froze. Seated to Bryce's right, Vitis Grimstaad sat with his arms politely clasped in front of him. I almost did not recognize him without his burns or the sneer of hatred plastered on his face. Beside him were seated the two generals I had seen with Sloane. Though their stature may have been smaller than that of their counterparts: from what I had witnessed in the courtyard, their strength was not to be underestimated. Each man was hound-like, with small eyes and matching noses. *Brothers. Perhaps cousins.* I could only speculate. One of them rested his face in his hand and I noted the missing fingers.

"This is rubbish, Elegin," Harmin spoke. "Those three had nothing to do with it."

"We should be up there," Elegin agreed.

"The Generals Kendall."

"Aye," Harmin said. "It was our kill. I found the Lunare. You snapped her like a twig."

"You remember how scared she looked?"

"She was a screamer."

"Aye. Would have liked to take my time with that one."

Voralla leaned over and lectured them, murmuring about respect and reverence for the king, and Harmin and Elegin ignored him entirely, furiously whispering and stifling their laughter. General Sloane chuckled quietly to himself. Grimstaad scowled, rolling his eyes at the spectacle.

"Pipe down over there!" Grimstaad hissed. "If you two didn't smell so foul, it would have been you up there instead of those dainty gentries."

A tiny peek of a grin creased the corner of Voralla's lip. Grimstaad heaved a sigh, rubbing at his temples. He crossed his arms. Scowling, he leaned over to Bryce.

"Why aren't *you* up there, along with those pretty boys?" he muttered. "I hear Slone's really taken a liking to you."

Sloane erupted into laughter, and Harmin and Elegin joined him. Voralla's smile disappeared and he sat still as a statue, head bent, hands in his lap.

Bryce stood up abruptly. Pushing past the generals, he strode down the aisle to a door at the back, throwing it open and exiting hastily.

The generals' laughter rang in my ears. A wave of white light blinded me, and when it cleared, I found myself back in Pouelle.

To my back, the charred remains of what had once been a peaceful farming town smoldered. In the far fields ahead of me, past the town's well, eight men's corpses were strung up, baking in the sun. Seven were whole, their arms outstretched and tied at the wrists. Their heads were lowered, limp. Birds beat their wings against each other, digging their claws and beaks into the bodies. One headless figure sat in the center of the others.

Bryce stood beside me, his armor gone. He gazed at the bodies stretched like scarecrows, the wind tugging at his golden hair. In his hand, his fingers grasped a clump of tangled auburn hair. Darby Sloane's head.

Bryce whipped back his arm and tossed the head across the field. A flock of birds shrieked after it, digging their forked feet into its side.

I scanned the bodies—eight in the fields. Voralla. Harmin. Elegin. The three gentries. Sloane.

And, Vitis Grimstaad. Head bowed, hair singed, smoke still rising from his skin.

The chaotic caws of the birds grew louder, louder. Feathers filled the sky, raining down like shadows.

Slowly, Grimstaad lifted his chin, his head rising, his eyes sharp, aware of what had happened—his broken body, his dead brethren. His hair fell across his face, burnt strands of different lengths sticking to him. His gaze locked on mine and did not leave.

I took a step back and screamed, my terror joining with the birds' calls. His eyes bored into my thoughts. I could not break the gaze. I covered my eyes but his remained with me— chuckling to himself, biding his time.

The birds continued to caw, bursting into a flurry of feathers and innards. A set of black wings leaped at me, beating at my face and I cried out, swatting my arms wildly.

Choking on feathers and decay, I blinked and sat upright in the snow. I was back in the world in which I belonged.

DEATH CLOSE TO MY HEART

I swatted at the snow around me, sputtering, still breathing the feathers.

"Come back!" I coughed. "Blackbird! Do not leave me!" The image of Grimstaad in the fields was seared on my mind—the flash of determination, the desire for retaliation, smoldering, like coal, in his eye. I shuddered, rubbing at my eyes to try to erase it—but it remained a part of me. Taunting me. Tormenting me.

I pulled my knees to my chest and rocked myself back and forth.

"Come back!" I cried. "Blackbird, please! Please! Do not leave me alone with *him*!"

I squeezed my eyes closed and tried to think about the darkness, to allow myself to be consumed by it. I touched my tongue to the top of my mouth, trying to taste the ore, and the blood of battle, the char, the ash. The beat of black wings echoed in my ears.

"Filia."

My eyes snapped open. "Blackbird!"

Roland perched on a low branch in front of me, his feathers catching the light.

"Where have you been?" I cried. "I called for you, and you did not come!"

"I have never left my brother's side."

I dusted the snow from my skirt and stood, craning my

neck to the sky. Sun and moon sat side by side, but the moon was faded, dim. She spoke no words, no comfort.

"I would like it, very much, for you to stay with me. To be by my side, always, too," I said to Roland. I reached into my skirt and thumbed the edge of my pistol. Slipping it from its sling, I held it flat in the palm of my hands, offering it to him. "Bryce and I: we spoke vows to each other; we made a promise of our hearts. Sun and moon: we are together, one."

Roland's black eye glittered, sharp, silent.

"You do not approve of our union?" I asked.

"I am here with you, filia, but I did not come to celebrate your union. Time has run out."

I pinched my brow. "What?"

Roland spread his wings wide and cawed, breaking the silence of the snow. *"Death is close to your heart."*

My body was swallowed by dread. Death close to my heart. He was the Blackbird: an omen. A shroud of death would be falling soon.

Grimstaad. I had to find him. I had to kill him before he found me. I rose quickly and stamped my foot in frustration, forming a hole in the snow. My vision told me nothing of Grimstaad—where to look, where he might be. Grimstaad had not even appeared until the end . . . and then the blackbird flew into my eyes . . .

I pushed my hands on my hips. "Why did you do it?" I cried. "Why did you fly at me and take me from my vision? I had just found Grimstaad. He was staring at me, in the field . . ."

"Yes. I am aware."

"If I had stayed, just a little longer, I would have seen where to find him."

"You are wrong."

"Blackbird, explain yourself!"

"You called my brother your sun, but this is a poor comparison. You cannot see or hear clearly in the daylight."

I sighed. It was true: I had trouble with my ilex without the moon to guide me. The sun's rays seemed to blind me with their harsh light.

"Roland, you are speaking in riddles. I do not understand."

One foot at a time, Roland sidled down the branch. When he reached the end, he hopped onto one below.

"Where were you when you had your vision?"

I twirled, motioning to the tree behind me. "Right here, at the roots."

"And what was in your hands?"

I gripped the pistol. "You already know."

"And in your heart?"

My eyelids fluttered closed. "Bryce." His name was warm in my mouth.

"Think about this." Roland spread his wings and cawed. *"It is your vision, your ilex. Best for you to learn how to read it."*

I wanted to retort, but I forced myself to stand quiet, pondering his words. My mama could read her suerradio with ease; I could not remember a time that she felt confused or uncertain of the messages revealed to her in tea leaves. She always found answers; they were clear as a bell. But not for me: not with my ilex, and certainly not with my litha. I was only the instrument through which to pull answers from others, but I could not read my own heart. I bit my lip with frustration, tucking the pistol back between the folds of my skirt. Bryce—his pistol and our vows so fresh in my mind, so deep in my heart— what did it have to do with my vision?

I recalled what papa said, why I had failed to detect that he had killed Prince Brennan. It was because I had not known to ask.

The vision was unclear to me because the *problem was with me.* It had told me nothing of Grimstaad because *I had not asked.* I had not held him in my heart when I was taken from one world to the next.

I threaded my fingers through my hair and tugged at it, crouching on the balls of my feet. "It's hopeless, Roland. I cannot sit here and learn how to use my ilex—all on my own, and in one day. I haven't a clue where I am going, what I am supposed to do, what I should be looking for, or how I should align my heart to connect with Grimstaad."

"Maybe you have already done so."

"How?" I lifted my gaze to the blackbird. "When?"

"When did you last sense you were in danger from him?"

I crossed my arms over my chest, slumping to my knees. There was the end of the vision: Grimstaad's amber eyes burning through mine—but I did not feel that held the answers I sought. I played both enforcer attacks over in my mind and shivered. Pain. Screams. Terror. I wondered how I had not died of fright.

It was the same feeling I sensed with the hanged men; I ruminated on the horror of stumbling into one of their corpses. Plugging my ears when they chanted at me, trying to hold back the litha. My shivering, the dread I had felt, my heart beating against my ribs . . . what aligned with it was my recent dream of the mountains. The earth moaning at me—restless, murmuring with its black voice. The thundering hooves, Grimstaad— emerging on horseback, coming to claim me. *Mine.*

I opened my eyes wide and gasped. The Lunare could sense ambushes before they occurred.

If we knew how to read the signs.

I had sensed an ambush once, too late. It was a near fatal mistake. If I were too late, again . . .

"I must get back! I must go back *now!*" I cried. "I knew he was coming—this morning, I sensed he was upon us—and I *left!*"

I scrambled to my feet, stumbling to right myself. "I left them, Roland! I left both of them alone with *him!*" I panted. "I thought it was a dream—but he was coming! He must be t*here*!"

Roland spread his wings wide, beating them furiously. *"Go, filia. Run! Go! Death is close to your heart."*

The terror that passed through me was impossible to describe—it was more ancient than even the old tongue. It was a language cold and unparalleled, and while I ran; I was no longer one with my body. I imagined myself rising over the mountains with Roland—a wayward night-moth, flapping her wings in search of light. The timbre of Roland's voice echoed in my skull. I wished to sob and press myself to his chest while he smoothed my hair, bathing me in the incandescence of his sad eyes.

I left them for dead. Bryce. Papa. I'm sorry. I'm sorry.

I silenced my thoughts and allowed only the wind to stir in my mind. I ran against a soft breeze and felt a vibration pass through my spirit. It was not obtrusive and fled quickly, leaving me only with a vestige of what it may have been. It hummed in my mind and stirred within my spirit—a faceless essence, somehow distinct and familiar.

Roland's sleek black body soared past me, weaving between the branches.

"What am I hearing, Blackbird?"

Roland did not answer me. I felt heavy, exhausted, and I wished that I could tumble into the grass, falling back to catch my breath. I felt confounded by Roland, frustrated by his silence. I tried to cling to the sensation I felt in my spirit. It was of no use. The feeling had already passed through my heart and fled. In my mind, I could still play the vibration. It sounded like the stones of the mountain rubbing against each other, deep underneath the earth.

Headmistress Elan had once taught us that the land and the wind were controlled by the spheres, heavenly bodies that spin in orbit, and that they created beautiful music when they rubbed together. I had never believed it, and I answered only to the moon, anyway. She, the only mistress to whom I was bound. And what I heard was not a beautiful sound. It was heavy—sorrowful.

The sun sank in the sky; still, I did not stop. The trickle of a stream chattered in my ear and knew I was drawing close. *Onward. Just a little farther.* I squeezed my fingernails into my fist to distract me from the rasp in my chest, my lungs, dry and burning from the cold. A trickle of sweat dripped down my brow, blinding me with its salty sting. Still, I pressed on.

I reached the tree upon which Bryce and I joined. He was gone, but his travel satchel was still open wide, his contents laid out in a tidy row—just as I had left them. I threw my head back and inhaled deeply, leaning forward to exude an enormous breath of relief.

I was wrong. Grimstaad was not waiting at our camp. It meant my ilex had been wrong—but in that moment, I did not care. There would be time, later, to figure it out. I wiped the sweat from my eyes and poked at the snow with the tip of my boot. Beneath a thin layer of white, I found a pile of sticks consumed by fire: ash thick, plush, and gray.

Fresh. Bryce had been there. He'd awoken and cooked after I left. I breathed in, and then out again, expelling my dread that had sunk heavy in my heart.

Everything is well. He is just checking on my father. I sighed. *In a few moments, he will return. We will pack our belongings, gather my father, and head up the mountains.*

My heart rattled with the last vestiges of fear, my legs shaking with both exhaustion and relief. A web of bright spots appeared in my vision and my skull vibrated. The sensation was quick, violent, abrupt—different from the litha, the opposite of litha.

I dropped to my hands and knees and the shaking ceased, the spots retreating. I pushed my tongue against the roof of my mouth. Dry and parched, I needed to wet my lips, soothe the burning in my throat. Cupping my arm over my eyes, I made my way toward the stream, one arduous step at a time. When I reached the water, I plunged my face into its icy flow. I took a large, painful gulp. The water stabbed my throat instead of soothing it, but still I drank ravenously, soaking the front of my blouse. I lifted my mouth and rubbed it with my sleeve, the chill of my wet garments sending a shiver through me. My stomach unsettled, I stood abruptly, steadying myself on the trunk of a nearby tree. From above, I felt a light brush on my shoulder and I whipped around, my stomach lurching to my throat.

I screamed.

A snow-covered boot bumped my shoulder gently, turning in a slow circle. A hanged man. One of Grimstaad's victims. The hanged man's boot bumped against my back.

My breath stopped in my throat and I pressed my palm to my heart, urging it to beat. To fill me with warmth. To free me of terror.

The boot tapped against me.

One boot. *One leg.*

The scent of bread pervaded my nose and I shrieked, the once-pleasant feeling from my childhood turning stale. The ground shuddered, spinning around me, humming. My mind spun, too, pressed like dough—all my words, all my thoughts smashed together.

My whole body trembled, my stomach turning over, my throat clenching shut. I could not look up. In my mind, I played the strange vibration I had heard in the woods in my mind again—echoing it over and over, slowing it, speeding it, matching it to a pitch and a timbre with which I was familiar.

Papa. It was him.

Roland had come to tell me: my father was dead.

CHASING FIRE
AND BLACKBIRDS

I was still screaming, kicking against the snow, when the enforcers found me. It took two of them to restrain me. They bound my hands and took my blades before forcing me to my feet, marching me through the snow while the sky devoured the sun. They talked among themselves, but their words were sand in my ears.

Papa. Oh, Papa. I did this. Me. It was my fault, entirely my fault. I had misunderstood my dream. I had misread the vision, asked the wrong questions. I focused my ilex not on survival but on love.

The enforcers' blue tunics darkened in the dusk; they pushed me forward up steep, snowy stones that eventually smoothed into an even-leveled hilltop. Like a small pyre, a bonfire raged in the clearing, flames twisting against the dying light of day. Four logs, one on each side, each with an enforcer seated at it, taking turns feeding a branch to the fire. My pulse throbbed against my neck and I lifted my eyes, my gaze darting quickly from left to right. *Seven.* Seven tarps jutting from the snow. Seven manes and tails flickering in and out of view through a cluster of pines. At the base of the trees, I spotted the spokes of a carriage wheel nestled among them.

The campsites that Bryce and I built paled in comparison. These men were not hiding; everything they did was visible, wide open among the expanse of the mountains. They had nothing to fear, no one to hide from, no wild desperation plaguing their eyes.

One of the enforcers released me hastily; I pulled my arm back from him. My other captor tugged at my elbow, forcing me to follow him. My first captor rose and lifted a corner on one of the tarps.

"General, we've got her."

The tarp jostled back and forth as if it were alive, woken by the enforcer's incantation. From the other side, a muffled voice barked, "Bring him, too. I want him there."

The enforcer folded the flap closed and moved away. He nodded to the men seated at the fire and one of them rose.

A gray-blue glove, the color of rain, swiped at the entrance of the tarp and threw it open. First a shadow stretched across the snow, and then the man within emerged.

Vitis Grimstaad. His skin was no longer ashen as it had been when I confronted him in the capital; he had regained his color, his skin pink and robust; it appeared rosy, healthy against his blue tunic. His hair and beard, too, had thickened. No longer emaciated, he loomed over me, lean and muscular. The anger he held in his eyes no longer smoldered, waiting patiently—hidden from view. It flared when he raised his chin. He was flushed with virility, dominance.

The enforcer pushed me into Grimstaad and I stumbled into his waiting arms.

Wordlessly, another enforcer dragged out a figure, bruised and bound, with two swollen purple eyes.

"Bryce," I uttered.

His nose bent at a peculiar angle and bled down to his mouth, which had been stuffed silent with a cloth. I sucked a breath through my teeth, terror and relief cycling through me, one after the other. Alive. He was alive. But, oh, my heart hurt seeing him . . . Grimstaad's prisoner, no different than me.

I cringed while Grimstaad ran his hand past my ear, stroking the side of my face with his fingertips. Claiming me, announcing I was *his*. He lifted my braid, smoothing his palm over its pattern. His lips pulled into a tight grin and he opened them slightly, making a strange sound, as if he were choking on his contempt. It took me a moment to realize it was laughter.

"My darling, faithful wife," he said.

I lifted my chin and cursed at him. "I am not your wife. I will never be your wife."

Grimstaad turned his knuckles toward me and cracked his glove across my face. I fell to my hands and knees, my ears ringing. My head searing, I stared into a veil of white. I could not decipher whether it was snow or moon.

From behind his gag, Bryce howled.

My cheek throbbed relentlessly, each burst of frigid air landing upon it, deepening its ache. I drew a gentle fingertip across my skin. A bulge had already begun to swell on the side of my face.

"You should have done what I asked. Looked again, within me. Told me I am still the patrolman I once was."

"You are not that man!" I took a deep breath and swallowed. The sound barely made it through my lips, forcing my heart and tongue to allow myself to form words. "You *murdered my father!*"

Grimstaad nodded, a ribbon of moonlight flashing across his top lip, painting his face an unnatural shade of white. "Yes, I'm sure it was quite a shock. I regret that I wasn't there to see your pretty face crumble when you made the discovery."

"You are enjoying this?" I pulled my lip back, exposing my teeth. "Suzette was right to tell you that you are hideous!"

Grimstaad scoffed. "Such venom for a Damica to hold in her heart. Your headmistress should have taught you better. Service. Obedience. Loyalty."

I choked on a sob, stuttering, digging in my mind for words vile enough to hurl at Grimstaad. I wanted them to cut him like blades. But no such words existed—so I spoke the language of the litha.

I lunged at him, wailing, beating my bound hands

against him.

I heard Bryce scream, cursing, pulling at his restraints. Grimstaad seized me, and he spun my body so that his tunic pressed against my back. He yanked on my braid and I cried out. Grimstaad turned his attention to Bryce, and I felt the bite of a blade against my skin.

"Loosen his gag," he ordered.

One of the enforcers pulled the gag from Bryce's teeth and he let out a terrible cry. Grimstaad tugged at my braid, exposing the length of my throat. His blade sank deeper into my skin.

"Corcoran, would you mourn my wife if she were to die? Do you think her sister-Damica would adorn her grave with flowers?"

"Let her go," Bryce growled. "You've got me. I'm worth more to you than she is."

"Tell me, Corcoran. What do you believe would be fitting for my wife? Bloodroot, perhaps?"

"Stop this!" I shouted.

Grimstaad flipped his blade and cracked the hilt against my skull. Blood oozed down my forehead, dripped down my nose, its salt and metal tainting my tongue. I dropped, my body surrendering its strength and Grimstaad caught me in his arms, his gaze cold as the mountainside.

"You will speak when I allow you to speak. You are *my* wife. And you *will* submit to me." He dropped me into the snow and I tumbled on my back. The bottom of a pointed boot glinted above me.

"No!" Bryce cried, his voice raw with pain, hoarse from desperation. "Grimstaad, no! You've got me! Leave her alone!"

One of the enforcers stepped in front of Grimstaad, nudging him back. "Oi! General! What are you doing? You'll kill her!"

"Take your hands off of me." Grimstaad scowled.

"She's Damica," the enforcer said. "I know she did you

wrong, but . . . look at her! Thin as a sheet. Kick at her guts and she might not give you an heir."

"Aye," Bryce gasped. "Let her go."

Breathing heavily, Grimstaad curled his hands into fists. Reluctantly, he drew back his boot.

"You're right," he said, placing his heel in the snow. "Her body is too precious for this punishment. However . . ." Grimstaad swung his leg back and drove the pointed toe of his boot into Bryce's ribs. "Yours seems to handle it just fine."

Grimstaad struck his boot against Bryce's chest, his torso, his groin, again and again—each blow causing him to wheeze with the exertion. I shrieked in horror. I tried to wedge myself between Grimstaad and Bryce, but my body was bound to the ground like stone. Sobs wracked my shoulders, my screams and protests falling silent, like thin raindrops on a howling fire.

"Pretty Corcoran. Darby's favorite," Grimstaad sneered. "I heard you resisted so much, the Kendalls had to come and hold you down for him. Such a fine young face. He just couldn't let you go. I've done you a favor, beating the pretty right out of you."

For the first time, my ilex and my litha both surged through me, at the same time. I shivered, each nerve in my body shrieking with Bryce's pain. My lungs became two stones in my chest, my breathing deep, long, and labored. A fresh trickle of blood dripped down my forehead and with shaky hands, I rubbed it away from my eye.

Do it.

I arched my back, gasping, choking on breath and spit. The litha roared within, rattling my ribs, threatening to burst my heart.

Make him suffer! Make him pay! The demon-whispers echoed in my mind, a violent throb pounding in my head.

My braid whipped my back as I lurched forward, pressing my hands against my eyes. It hurt. It hurt so badly. But underneath the pain, something else sprouted in my heart, a cool sensation. It felt like starlight spreading through my chest, a glimmering, tingling sensation that *peace could be mine*.

I could break him. I could *kill* him. My ilex was strong enough. The next time he laid his hands on me, I could dig my nails into his flesh and claw through his mind, tossing thoughts, memories, and secrets about like rose petals. I could rip his sanity to shreds.

Do it. Do it.

With both my ilex and litha flowing through me, it would not be difficult.

And it felt so right. So, so right.

Bryce moaned softly and fell silent. Grimstaad's boots thudded ominously on the ground toward me, his work with my ammorante complete. I steadied myself, forcing my breathing to slow. Squeezing my nails into the palms of my hands, my knuckles turned white.

Wait for it. Wait. I focused on my breath, the ache of my fingers held too tight, too long. I clamped down on my teeth and squeezed my jaw tight.

"Darling wife," Grimstaad growled. He removed a glove, revealing a bright, white dressing wrapped around his arm; small slivers of raw, blistered flesh peeked through the gaps. Hiis palms and fingers hid under a thinner glove, but the bulges of ruined flesh were prominent beneath it. My shoulders shook. My vision blurred with wild, angry tears.

Easy, easy.

Grimstaad tucked his glove neatly into his belt and reached for me.

"As for you." He lifted his hand to the side of my neck, stroking my flesh with the back of his hand.

Now!

With a low utterance, I lunged forward and grabbed his arm with both hands. I dug my nails deep into him, tearing into bandages and flesh alike. I pushed every horrid thought and feeling I could summon into him. The scent of charred flesh in Pouelle. The sound of Bryce's shovel thudding against Darby Sloane's neck. And: Suzette. The terror in her eyes, the shriek of horror as Grimstaad's blade sliced her face. I wanted that one seared into his skull.

Grimstaad cried out sharply, howling, writhing beneath my grasp like an animal.

Suffer.

I strengthened my hold on his arm, burying my fingers deeper into his tender, pink flesh. He growled and spat while I pushed my ugliest thoughts against him, trying to penetrate his heart. *Break!* I dragged the word against his heart like a knife and reached into his mind. My ilex flowed freely through him and I searched for memories, buried deep. Secrets, lost to time. Anything. Everything that I could rip out of him.

But my ilex turned up empty.

Grimstaad pulled free from my grasp and struck me with his fist. The blow sent me to my knees.

"General?" one of the enforcers called out to him.

"What?" Grimstaad rasped, between staggered breaths.

"I think . . . she was trying to kill you."

I looked up in time to see Grimstaad's fist connect with the enforcer's gut.

"You think?" He scowled.

My eyes burned with fresh tears. *I'm sorry, ammorante.* For all the power and terror and fear my ilex was rumored to have, it had proven to be . . . docile. I had felt it within, swirling with the litha. But, something about me was . . . broken.

Gently, I moved my fingers to the top of my head, touching the slick, oozing wound that dripped blood over my forehead.

Grimstaad had broken me. My gift was gone.

Litha, ilex both . . . they were useless; I was powerless.

I could not save us.

"Wicked Lunare." Grimstaad grabbed me by the waist

and lifted me, dragging me through the snow, behind the trees, past the horses and carriage. I thrashed and scratched at him as he carried me, but it did not deter him.

At the river's edge, where his enforcers captured me, he set me down and forced me to my knees. His fingers locked around my hair and he plunged my face into the icy waters. The chill struck my face immediately and without thinking, I opened my mouth and gasped. The river's silty water flooded my throat and I thrashed my arms, twisting and clawing in vain. Grimstaad pushed my head further down. The cold seared my head at its wound and while he held me under, my skin turned numb. The cold penetrated my skull, ceasing all thought, all feeling except my lungs—two red coals, screaming for air. As my vision began to dim, Grimstaad pulled me free of the water. I coughed and sputtered, expelling a mouthful of water into the snow. The meager contents of my stomach threatened to spill as well.

The thought of touching this man, sharing a bed with him, while Trionfi and its court, King Armando and Queen Norina—and my headmistress herself, smiling upon our union . . . it was more than I could bear.

"Why?" I wiped my mouth. My eyes stung with indignation. "Why do you want *me*?"

Grimstaad's fingers locked around my hair and he plunged my face into the water again.

Why? The chill of the water overtook me. I thrashed against Grimstaad, but his hold on me was steady. He had sent at least ten enforcers after me and had himself crossed the entirety of Trionfi to find me. *Why me?* He must have questioned Headmistress Elan. He may have interrogated Bethany. *There are other Lunare!* Why didn't he simply choose another?

Why? *Why?* The word threatened to consume me. I had avoided him in the dining hall. Spurned him in the palace. My litha caused me to attack him when he hurt Suzette.

Why didn't he ask Headmistress Elan to pair him with someone else?

I had run from him, led his enforcers to their deaths. I had tried to *kill him* with my ilex.

Why does he want me so badly?

When my lungs felt they would burst, Grimstaad pulled me out of the river. I retched, spitting up both bile and water. *Why?* I swallowed hard, rolling the word over in my mind. My whole body shook as I pieced together a possibility in my mind.

Grimstaad's lip twitched, and he smoothed his thumb over it to calm it. Even without my ilex, his answer was clear.

"I am not your first, am I?" I bit my lip hard and swallowed. "How many wives have you broken? Did you kill them, too? Hang them like my father?"

Grimstaad plunged me back into the river and I choked on the rest of my words. My screams bubbled to the water's surface. I wrestled to hold onto my senses, but I felt them slipping from me. I kicked and flailed my arms in the water, but each attempt I made against Grimstaad lessened in strength. My consciousness threatened to float into the depths and a gust of cold air suddenly hit my face. I gasped, trying to gulp down a breath, but my throat was sewn shut from terror.

"You will learn to stop asking questions," Grimstaad said flatly. "And simply *obey*."

He struck my back with a broad stroke of his palm and I sputtered, vomiting more bile than water. I crumbled into the earth and heaved, grasping for each breath of air. Grimstaad yanked both of my arms from under me, and he looped a length of rope around one wrist, then the other. He coiled the rope around both wrists and tied my hands together in a sturdy knot. He lifted me again and I hung limp over his shoulder—too weak, too broken to resist him. He carried me back, past the horses and pines. His enforcers stood up, clearing a space for us as we entered the camp.

Without a word, Grimstaad deposited me beside the

fire and shuffled, brooding, back into his tent. I lay on my back and watched the sky for a long time, smoke from the bonfire billowing in my eyes, the heat drying my soaking garments. The enforcers cooked around me and talked, and they laughed as though I were not present at all. Eventually they drifted back into their tents. Bathed in the light of a half-moon, I watched the stars and they watched me. The fire murmured. The moon shone. And faintly, I heard my name.

"Viper."

I turned on my side and found my ammorante, abandoned, as I had been, on the other side of the fire. Slowly he turned and his eyes opened—a crack of blue meeting my gaze. Besides his eyes, I could not recognize his face, it had been beaten and battered so severely. I tried to set my jaw and remain strong, but tears spilled over my lashes.

"Bryce." Arms bound, I inched on my side, twisting toward him.

"Stop," he uttered. "Save your strength."

"Why did they leave us out here?"

"Didn't want to waste a tent on it," Bryce rasped. "Figured we can't run."

I squeezed my hands together, shuffling my knees to inch closer to Bryce. "I thought they might have killed you."

"No," Bryce sputtered. "They would've killed me by now, if that's what they wanted. I'm worth too much to Trionfi to bring back as a corpse. Think they've got a different plan, to bring me to justice."

I shook my head. I could not imagine what plans Trionfi might have for a traitor—nor did I want to.

"What happened, Bryce? How did Grimstaad know about us?"

The fire crackled and I watched him struggle for breath behind the flames—each inhale a knife to his chest.

"They came up on me out of nowhere. Grimstaad, and six of his enforcers. I was cooking for your father when I heard the horses. I didn't know where you'd gone, and I went a bit mad, thinking they'd already got you. I drew my sword. Was ready to send them all to hell—or die trying." Bryce sighed, tenderly touching at his ribs while he tried to take a breath. "There was nothing I could do, and they already had your father. Found him before he found me. Probably found the trail of blood and tracked it to the cavern."

I pursed my lips, envisioning the blood-streaked snow I had followed when returning to our site, the spatters growing into thick blots the closer I drew.

"It was as bad a situation as it could be. Seven swords—against my blade. Knew I could take a few of them out, but after that, it'd be over for me. Grimstaad pushed through his men, told them to stand down. Looked me dead in the eyes. We were brothers-in-arms once. Fought side-by-side—before Pouelle. So, he says to me, 'You're not a fool. You don't want to die, and I don't want to lose more of my enforcers to you. All I want is the Damica. Give her up.'"

"I do not understand. How did he know I was with you?"

"Your father, for one." Bryce blew a breath of cold air into the sky. "But long before that, he'd been tracking us. Figured out I was involved when he found his first two enforcers dead."

"The ones you killed, the night we met?" I asked. "Anyone could have killed them! Banale! Wolves! How did he know it was you?"

"He knew. Before he was Deos Tactigit, or even an enforcer—Grimstaad was a trapper by trade. Hunting, making traps, tracking blood—it's all his game. You know the snares we made for the rabbits?"

I closed my eyes and sighed, the realization striking me. "He taught you."

"Snares and hangings are Grimstaad's signature. He recognized the knots. Probably looked at the bodies. The cuts were quick. Clean. No hesitation in them. My signature." Bryce shifted, fidgeting with the rope on his wrists. "Wouldn't take much for him to put the pieces together."

A tear spilled onto my cheek, rolling down the bridge of my nose before it was lost in the snow.

"So he told me to hand you over. Thought I was hiding you somewhere," Bryce continued. "I told him I hadn't a clue where you'd gone off to. Didn't believe me at first, but after some convincing, he accepted that I was telling the truth. Rolled his eyes, said you'd be back soon enough and he'd deal with you then. And then proposed we make a deal, end the violence so no one else had to die. He was tired of losing his men, and I . . . well, I had nothing to lose, by that point."

"You *bartered?*"

"Aye. Right there in the snow, blades out, fire still going. We talked about Pouelle. He told me, real quiet, he could understand Sloane and the brothers Kendall—everyone knew what they'd done." Bryce shifted and broke our gaze, a pain like poison, crossing his face. He cleared his throat. "Voralla's death surprised him. He was teaching me to speak properly, and he was planning to show me how to read, how to write with a quill—all of it."

Bryce squared his chin. "Said he never cared much for Voralla, or any of the others. 'Maybe we can settle this like men,' he said. We talked back and forth about your father—I told him he'd have a maelstrom to deal with back in Cortellion if he hurt someone from the Order. He promised to leave your father out of it, take him to a medic, see him to safety. For your part, Lor . . ."

Bryce paused, twisted his lips, and swallowed. "He told me he'd treat you like a proper wife, take care of you. Not like Sloane treated his Lunare. All I had to do was surrender; put down my sword and come with him."

A knot of confusion—betrayal—pulsed in my forehead. A scowl took control of my lips. "You agreed to this?"

"Of course I did."

I let out a guttural cry, thrashing against my bindings. My wrists glistened in the moonlight, slick with my anguish, my blood.

"How could you?" I hissed. "I would rather die than be his wife!"

"I'm sorry," he breathed, his voice heavy, weary from his wounds. "It was the best I could do for you. Grimstaad is a lot of things, but a liar's not one of them. He's Deos Tactigit—per vertui—honor among men, all of that."

I remembered what Roland had told me: *"My brother is many things, but a tradesman he is not."* I clenched my teeth. If only I had been there! Deos Tactigit, brothers-in-arms, per vertui . . . my ilex would have revealed Grimstaad's blackened heart for what it was.

"Bryce, he *killed my father*! I never would have believed him—not a word he said! Had it been your fate, I would have stuck my blade straight into Grimstaad's heart and let the rest of them cut me down."

"I'm sorry . . ." Shivering, Bryce breathed the word into the night. "That's why you're Viper, and I'm . . ." He smiled half-heartedly in my direction, a limp smile accentuated by his swollen lip and bloodied mouth. "Just a man who's in love with you."

He turned on his side. His furs had torn free of his back and gashes punctuated the thin linen of his shirt, blooms of red soaking the fabric. Moaning, he shifted, and amid his wounds I spotted a swirl of black—the glistening fang of the ouroboros peeking through a tear in his shirt. Its blood-streaked eye stared back at me.

"Bryce," I called. My voice trembled, cracking like a twig.

He shifted onto his back. "Aye?"

"How did Grimstaad know we are lovers?" I asked. "He knew we were traveling together, but I had paid you to take me to the Order. How could he have known? You can't get that information out of following tracks or examining corpses."

His features softened and he flashed a rueful smile. His grins, before, were boyish and wide, bright like the midday sun—but the look he flashed at me was tainted with the silver of the moon.

"Tell me." The command fell from my lips, smoldering.

Bryce fell silent for a moment. He heaved a sigh and said, finally, "You wrote that letter to me."

"*What?*"

I felt a lump of guilt bloom in my throat, and I pressed my tongue to the top of my mouth to keep a sob from escaping my lips.

It was my fault. My fault that my father was dead. Maybe Grimstaad was telling the truth—and he would have taken Papa to a medic. But once he found that letter . . .

My ears rang and my stomach began to churn. I could barely listen to Bryce's next words; they floated in and out of my ears.

"I surrendered to them. Dropped my blade in the snow, gave myself up," Bryce said. "They searched me, patted me down, took my blade, my coin purse, whatever they could find they thought was worth anything. The letter was in my pocket. One of them handed it to Grimstaad. He read it and . . . he snapped. Ordered his men to hang your father, wait near the body until you found it."

I threw my head back and screamed—arching my back, kicking the heels of my boots into the snow.

My fault.

I misunderstood all my dreams and I had left them alone, completely exposed, vulnerable—while I chased fire and blackbirds.

I love you.

Take care of Papa.

I did this. Me. All me. My fault. My fault.

I did not deserve to live—to call myself Lunare, to call myself Viper. I could not understand my gift; every time I had tried to use it, it spiraled out of control.

My Papa had died because of it.

But now, my gift was gone. I hoped that soon, I would be gone as well.

I remained on the ground, screaming, cursing at the moon. The howling was enough to rouse Grimstaad from his tent and he seized me by my braid, dragging me back under the tarp with him.

39

BEAUTIFUL SERPENT,
RESTLESS EMBERS

"Quiet!" Grimstaad growled. "You are keeping my men awake. We have a long day ahead tomorrow. All of us."

He stuffed a rag into my mouth to muffle my cries, then struck me across the cheek with his palm. He began to undress in front of me; turning his forearm to unthread the laces on his gauntlets. I screamed with my eyes as he placed them in the corner of the tent, removing his gloves and placing them beside them. His flesh was not the angry red I had seen in my mind: veins of black running through it, as I had seen it in the palace; it had taken on a much more innocuous color, a red and pink marbling, with flakes of white leaves still peeling.

He sighed. "I grow tired of your insolence. You *will* learn your place, wife."

Terrified that he would place his hands on me, I dared not make a sound. But he did no such thing. To my surprise, he looped his fingers around the bottom of his tunic and pulled it overhead. His face contorted with pain as he unhooked each clasp of his blouse, and his eyes combed down my body as he worked. He wheezed, the exertion bringing him great discomfort.

When he removed his blouse, my eyes widened. His burns spread over much more of his body than I realized. They were etched in waves across his stomach, reaching up his chest, grasping for his throat. Both arms were marbled in their entirety—peeling, shedding white, like a snake's skin.

He reached into his travel trunk and removed a tin of salve, sticking two fingers within and sliding them across his burned flesh. He shuddered, a small moan—relief—slipping through his lips. He pushed up his trousers and spread the salve across his feet, then up his legs, covering the burns crawling up his ankles and calves.

My terror dissipated and a wave of relief washed over me. He was in no condition to mate with me; he could hardly endure his own clothing in this condition. How was he able to make the journey across Trionfi? He could not have been taking vendrake to numb his injuries; it would have numbed all of his senses, as well. No—he was sharp, conscious, painfully aware of every aspect of his trek. Tracking us. Hunting us. I could not fathom the pain he must have endured . . . all for me.

We lived in an ugly world—men, always hurting one another, handing down conflict and strife to each other: a daisy-chain of cruelty.

Would it ever cease, or were we fated to harm each other forever?

What does he want with me? The question taunted me, burning like embers under my skin. Much as he enjoyed the hunt, the pain would have been excruciating. I looked away from him, repulsed. It was not his injuries that made him ugly. They were simply the result of some cruelty that had been handed down to him. Darby Sloane had inflicted it on Bryce, Bryce had inflicted it upon Grimstaad, and Grimstaad had inflicted it upon my father.

Why?

Grimstaad pulled another item from his effects: smooth, heavy, and bronze, he held it carefully, deliberately—meeting my gaze with his amber eyes. They held a spark of excitement. Eagerness, mingled with something else. Without my ilex, it was difficult to discern. Cruelty, perhaps. Satisfaction in something savage. He placed the item upright between us and I recognized it immediately as the candlestick I had struck him with in the palace.

I struggled against my restraints, choking on my gag as I tried to break free.

"Sit still!" Grimstaad hissed. "We are going to have a civilized conversation."

His threat was thinly veiled at best: *control yourself, or I will control you.* I clamped my teeth on the cloth in my mouth, sucking in as much breath as I could through the fabric. My heart beat so furiously against my ribs, I believe it may wear itself out and stop entirely.

He is going to retaliate. Break it against my skull. My life would slip from the crack in my head. He had gone through the trouble of keeping the candlestick, and carrying such a cumbersome, tedious object across Trionfi's harsh terrain—all in anticipation of this moment. To greet me with it. I clenched down on the gag and forced myself still. In his hands, this candlestick had purpose: a reason for standing between us that was more than a passing warning. He would use it at some point; I was certain of it.

The only questions in my mind were *when,* and *how.*

Grimstaad's gaze combed over my body as I attempted to keep my body from shaking. He sat still in front of me, his knees pulled to his chest.

Watching. Waiting.

After a long time, he cleared his throat and spoke.

"I had two wives before you," he said. "Annita was a governor's daughter. She earned me a title as captain—but she had her own ideas, her own ambitions. She didn't want children, didn't want a family."

Vicious, vile monster! He was taunting me—tormenting me with this game he was delighted in playing.

Grimstaad scoffed, wrinkling his lips into a grotesque expression. "What kind of wife is that? I told her it was dangerous thinking like that, carrying those ideas in her head. Four years after we were wed, she was pulled into an alley, stabbed to death. A shame—it may not have happened if she spent less time gallivanting around town with her silly dreams."

A lump swelled in the back of my throat as he spoke, and I swallowed it as he spoke his final words. Annita met a violent, disturbing demise—and *he believed she deserved it.*

"Lisabetta was better," Grimstaad continued. "She was a baroness—and we shared some of the same interests. I picked her because I was tired of attending dinners, having to endure all those miserable, status-hungry filia. Sitting beside me, batting their eyes, telling me how sorry they were to hear about Annita. I chose Lisabetta because she irritated me the least."

Grimstaad sighed—almost wistfully—and he shifted his weight. "It was easy to keep her happy. She liked money, silks—little gifts I collected while I was patrolling the roads. And she liked to watch my work with the banale. 'It's fun to watch them bleed,' she used to say."

Another monster. I felt a crease form between my eyes. *No wonder you liked her.*

Grimstaad smirked, chuckling to himself. "My work takes me on the road often, wife. You will come to accept this. You are not to speak to men, or be seen around them without my presence. You will wait for me—as long as it takes for me to return. With Lisabetta, I made the mistake of looking the other way. I let her run around, galivanting with other men. It was simpler that way, an arrangement that worked—while she was careful, discrete."

His expression soured. "Unfortunately, over the years, she became more brazen. By the time I became Deos Tactigit, the rumors were all over the court. She made a fool of me."

The hatred I recognized from our meeting at the palace flared in his eyes. "But it is no matter. One morning, she went out riding—and she never returned, alive. They say her horse threw her, broke her neck. Very sad. Don't you agree, wife?"

Hands bound, I pressed my bindings to my chest. My heart fluttered with terror in the presence of the candlestick and this hideous man, who delighted in the death of his wives. *Did he kill them?* I could not help but ask myself. The circumstances around their deaths he had left vague, open to speculation and terror.

He leaned in toward me, the candlestick sitting between us, and he cupped my chin in his hands. I winced at his touch, half relieved that I could not use my ilex to seek the answer to my question, and that I was blind to any other atrocities in his heart he had not revealed to me.

"Do you understand what your role is, as my wife? It is to *obey*. Nothing more, nothing less. Do what you are told. Annita and Lisabetta's deaths would have been entirely unnecessary if these women had just done what was expected of them."

He stroked my cheek with the back of his hand. Closing his eyes, he shuddered. My heart thudded with fright. He wanted me. He desired me—and his feelings ran deep.

Why? I would never obey him, never submit. He would have to be a fool to believe otherwise.

"Laurel Aleandri. So beautiful, so . . . much like *her*," Grimstaad uttered. "No one would have had to suffer, if *she* had just kept her promise at the start. But you Damica are all alike, aren't you?"

A small cry escaped my throat, muffled by my gag. *You Damica are all alike?* What was he saying?

Did he court another Damica?

Bound, gagged, and petrified—I could not ask him. With his ointment applied, Grimstaad drifted into a light slumber. Alone with my thoughts, with Bryce on the other side of the tarp, enduring the frozen ground and campfire smoke, I struggled to sleep—slipping into slumber, and then waking again with a snap. In this state, I waited the long night for dawn.

I awoke when Grimstaad pulled my gag from my mouth and tossed me out of his tent into a cold sun. The embers and moon had vanished in the chill of morning, and I looked desperately around for Bryce. He lay limp, perfectly still—exactly as I had left him. Terror squeezed my heart. Had he survived the night? A prickle of dread stung my throat and I swallowed.

"Ammorante," I mouthed, strands of my braid flicking against my bruises.

Bryce wheezed, turning his body to spit blood into the snow. His gaze fixed on me and he raised a concerned brow. The enforcers scurred about the grounds, gathering kindling, feeding the horses, washing—as if we were not present at all. One of them peeled back the flap of Grimstaad's tent and while they conversed, I turned to Bryce.

"Are you all right?" he rasped.

"I am fine. Grimstaad lectured me about his two wives and what he expected of me—but he did not hurt me," I whispered. "It is you who I'm worried about."

"Ack, Lor, I'll be fine." Bryce's upper lip pulled up into his blood-and-dirt-stained face, and he flashed me one of his boyish smiles.

The enforcers continued to busy themselves around us, several of them wandering back and forth from the stream with buckets. The fire hissed, spewing clouds of white smoke while they worked to extinguish it. They began to roll up their tents and pack their belongings.

"Where do you think they are going?" I asked.

"You'll likely head out with Grimstaad, and I heard them talking last night about taking me to La Grondaia," Bryce said.

"Where?"

"I won't be there with you after this. I want you to be ready." His voice broke and he shifted his body away from me, staring up at the sky. "Might be the last time I see the sun.

Think I'll enjoy it for a moment."

He fell silent and I watched the enforcers continue their work. One of them emerged from Grimstaad's tent. Stepping over Bryce's body, he paused when he reached me. Reluctantly he squatted down, balancing on the balls of his feet. He removed a small, flattened piece of bread from a satchel and held a corner to me.

"The general wants you to eat. Keep your strength for the journey ahead."

I held my bound hands to him and he slipped the bread between my fingers, taking his arm back quickly when I had taken the bread. *Frightened.* It must have horrified him, watching me try to use my ilex to try to kill Grimstaad; he did not want to chance to come too close. The enforcer moved to step back over Bryce but he stopped short, hesitating. He removed another piece of bread from his satchel and dropped it on the ground beside my ammorante.

"Even a traitor must eat," he muttered, and continued about his way.

La Grondaia. I etched the phrase into my mind. La Grondaia. La Grondaia. They did not kill Bryce. They were not planning to kill him—they were feeding him . . . and then sending him away to *La Grondaia.* The words sent a shiver down me.

Bryce took his hardened lump of bread and spread it apart. It opened like an envelope. He kneaded the dough between his hands, and were it not unleavened and stale, I might have believed that it was piandia. My mind flashed to the scent of dough in the kitchen of my home—the home to which I will never return—and the thrum of my father's hymns in the early morning light as we worked side by side, kneading flour and egg together.

The father who I shall never see again.

I picked at my own bread, biting my lip to keep tears from falling past my lashes.

"Bryce, what is La Grondaia?" I murmured.

"It's a prison," he said. "A place where Grimstaad and his men can do whatever they like to their prisoners, while Trionfi turns a blind eye. It used to be a mining quarry, but it's been abandoned some time now. If there are lots of them, Grimstaad and his men sometimes use it to hold the banale, before hanging them. I'm sure he'll turn me over to Trionfi for that, once he's finished with me at La Grondaia."

"I'm sorry . . ." I whispered, fresh tears streaking down my cheeks.

"It isn't your fault." Bryce said. "Grimstaad's fallen to madness. *Per vertui.* Hah. Never cared for him much when we were Deos Tactigit—but his one redeeming quality was his sense of honor. Seems he's given up on that. I should have done like you said—stabbed him in the heart, let the enforcers cut me to pieces, Viper."

My name on his tongue sent a shiver of strength through my heart. I gritted my teeth.

"I wish I could kill him," I uttered. "Stop him dead in his tracks. But . . . my ilex is gone. He hit me on the head and it just . . . stopped. I can't do anything."

"You still have the pistol?"

"Yes." A knot tightened in my forehead; I shifted my weight, a pang vibrating in my heart as I felt the sling weighing heavily against my leg. "He did not take it from me."

"Grimstaad had his men search me for it. I told them I threw it in the river," Bryce said.

"You may as well have." I sighed. "The cartridge I have is ruined. Grimstaad dragged me to the river and held me under, over and over. Every part of me was soaking wet . . . the powder, too."

"I've still got a cartridge," Bryce said.

I raised my chin. "You do?"

"Aye." He grinned. "Enforcers didn't know what it was when they found it. Stuck it back in my pocket. I'll try to get it to you."

"How?"

"Shh!"

Bryce craned his neck, and together we watched Grimstaad emerge from his tent. He strutted by each of his enforcers, scrutinizing their work. Clad in his gloves, the sun glinted off two ice-blue gauntlets while he stroked at his beard, deep in thought. He took several long, deliberate strides toward the remnants of the bonfire and cleared his throat.

"Our plans have changed," he announced. The enforcers halted their activities and turned to face him. "Take my effects out of the carriage. I'll be escorting my bride to our new home. Alone."

"Alone?" One of the enforcers protested. "Ah, General Grimstaad, I don't mean to question, but . . . she's a Lunare."

Grimstaad walked beside me and patted my head. "Hasn't she turned out to be such a lovely, obedient wife?" With one final pat to the head, he released me and approached the enforcer. With a loud crack, he struck the man across the face with his gauntlet. "I can't spend all my time answering your incessant questions. My bride and I need time to become acquainted."

A pair of enforcers nodded in affirmation and all of them dispersed. Several vanished behind the pines to gather the horses, and I remained seated across from the rest: one poking a stick at the dying embers while the other held a small harp to his lips and blew on it. The sound cut into my ears and I surmised that Bryce felt similarly about its ugly music; he twisted and groaned, his pain more pronounced. The bread in his hands lay on the ground, a small piece torn from it and ingested. But of the rest, he was too weak to partake.

"Heard they found Prince Brennan—finally. What was left of him, anyway," one of the enforcers remarked. "The farmers rolled him up in a sheet, took his body to a patch of dead forest—full of widowmakers—and burned him up in a clearing. They knew what they were doing. Some of our men eventually stumbled across the pile of burnt logs, but no one wanted to go dig through it . . . risk getting a tree falling on them, especially with snow starting to come down. But they found a few brave or foolish enough to do it, and that's where they dug up Prince Brennan's skull. Still had a ball lodged in it."

"Can't believe General Corcoran shot him," another enforcer said. "Think they'll hang him in Cortellion?"

"Hope so. They put on a good show around hangings. After all this time in the woods, a day in the capital knocking back drinks sounds like heaven."

The enforcer playing the harp removed it from his mouth. "Wait. How'd they know it was actually the prince, from just a skull and ball?"

"Aye, they didn't know at first. Not for sure," the first enforcer said. "Spent a long time trying to figure it out. But one of the men found a ring near the burn site—looked like it had Trinofi's crest. Took it back to Queen Norina and she burst into tears."

"Enough!" Grimstaad's barked through their comments. "You have one task, and it's not to sit around gossiping like a bunch of *filia*. Prince Brennan is dead, Corcoran killed him, and he is less than the remains of the earth that the earthworms have finished with. So shut your mouths and load him into the carriage. I will deal with him in La Grondaia once I've finished teaching my bride how to be a wife."

Though I wanted to scream, I remained silent. The candlestick still loomed in the back of my mind. If I screamed, if I struggled . . . it waited for me.

The enforcers scattered, some retrieving the horses and carriage, the others busying themselves with packing the last of the campsite. One of them moved to Bryce, forcing the tip of his blade into Bryce's back. "Up you get."

Grimstaad rested his hand on my shoulder and I

resisted the urge to yank myself away from him, fearing that any movement or act of defiance may cause him to order his men to take it out on Bryce. The carriage lurched heavily toward us. The painful squeal of a worn wheel sent a shudder through me. Grimstaad patted my back while sobs wracked my shoulders.

It was the end of my journey with Bryce. I would see him no more, except in my visions, my dreams, as I fell between worlds. But with my tears of sorrow, I cried, too, with relief. My heart could not endure another night of the beatings, hearing him groan and cry out as Grimstaad drove his boots into his side.

"You must allow me to bid him farewell!" I choked.

"A goodbye?" Grimstaad raised an eyebrow and scoffed.

"Please." Trembling, I rested my hand over Grimstaad's glove and looked deeply into his eyes. "I did not have a chance to say goodbye to Papa. Please, do me this small kindness."

Grimstaad tucked his lip into his mouth and I felt a sputter of breath rise from him, a frustrated sigh. His hand squeezed mine and he nodded.

"Do it quickly."

He guided me to the carriage, never removing his hand from my shoulder as he led me to Bryce, who was half-in, half-out the carriage door at the mercy of an enforcer's blade. Seeing us approach, the enforcer lowered his weapon and cleared away.

"Say your goodbye," Grimstaad growled.

I pressed my forehead against Bryce and breathed. Even in Grimstaad's hold, even under the veil of mourning, it was with Bryce that I felt safe. The fibers of his beard grazed my cheek, his breath warm in my ear.

"We always knew this is how it would end," he whispered. "I don't regret it—any of it. *Ilio sonotu,* Lor. I'm glad I met you."

Everything around me seemed to fall away—Grimstaad,

the carriage, the enforcers, the snow. All I could see, all I could hear was Bryce. My ammorante, speaking his last words to me. Never again would he sun me with his smiles, nor take me in his arms to comfort me. I would be alone with Grimstaad, and he would be dead. My throat clamped shut. Tears flooded my eyes and they spilled down my chin—fresh pain, like falling snow, blurring my vision.

"I'm glad I met you, too." I could barely speak the words.

Bryce raised his thumb to my eyes, wiping away the tears. "No more of this. It's time, now, for you to be Viper. Be strong; strike hard. Promise me. Now."

"I promise," I choked.

He lifted his chin, brushing his cheek against mine—and I felt the rumble of his voice against my neck.

"Oi, Grimstaad? Word of advice?" he called over my shoulder. I felt a lopsided smirk pull across his face. "I know you like them young, but if you keep cracking at this one's skull, she'll end up too childlike, even for you."

Grimstaad's expression soured into a humorless frown and his lips peeled back into a snarl. He pulled back his elbow and drove a swift fist into Bryce's gut. Bryce groaned and swore loudly, bending to one knee. His flaxen hair fell over his face and he buried his head against his bound arms, panting, taking deep breaths to steady himself.

"Bryce, no!"

I bent down to meet him and he thrust his lips against mine. A surge of salt and blood penetrated my mouth, tingling on my lips. He forced his tongue past my teeth and I jumped in surprise. He adjusted his jaw; his teeth shifted with purpose. An object—foreign to me—pushed past my lips, and he pinned it against my cheek. I blinked and pursed my lips, trying to keep it hidden. I closed my eyes and my mouth lingered on his a moment longer.

"Enough!" Grimstaad roared. He pulled at my braid,

yanking me back. My scalp aflame, I reached for Bryce to thread my fingers through Bryce's, but I was only able to brush the tips. Grimstaad threw me to one of the enforcers and he spun me around.

"Oi, no reason for a Damica to see this," he said softly. Leading me back from the carriage, he sat me at one of the logs by the extinguished bonfire. His hand came free from my shoulder and he returned to his group, leaving me with the embers, luminous like my pain.

I heard the thick crack of Grimstaad's gauntlet, Bryce heaving in pain.

With each strike, the serpent on my ammorante's back flashed through my mind. The smoldering, piercing eye of a snake. While Grimstaad brutalized my ammorante, I pulled my shoulders back. I pressed my teeth together to prevent a sob from escaping my lips and the corner of my tongue touched the object in my mouth. It was soft, enveloped in a pleasant taste: rich, earthy, sour on my tongue.

Piandia.

I passed the soft envelope of bread from my mouth to the palms of my hand. There was something hidden within. I dug my nails into the dough and it came apart easily in my hands. Underneath was a thick layer of tallow and wax. The scent of death pervaded my nose.

It was a cartridge.

The rattling of wheels captured my attention and I turned to watch Bryce, the enforcers, and the carriage roll away gently, without fanfare.

"Ilio sonotu," I murmured after it.

I spoke my vow not as a bride: my husband-at-heart gone. I had made my promise to Bryce and our vows had been fulfilled: blood and blade, life and death.

I spoke now as Viper. I pledged my vow—*ilio sonotu*—to *myself.*

Fate and chance. Serpent of death, venom and

vengeance. The ouroboros forever branded in my mind.

I was no longer Damica; I no longer wore moonstone at my throat. I wore a pistol and wielded death.

I was the *new* Deos Tactigit.

Per vertui. I would live with purpose, find some way to give my life meaning. Do *something* worthwhile—honorable— for those whose lives were cut short, with their promises of peace, comfort, and happiness unfulfilled.

I promised my heart to my mother, her jade serpents never powerful enough to bring her the happiness she sought.

I pledged it to my father, cherishing the memory of his hands kneading through dough early in the morning. I swore it to Roland: my blackbird, my soot-colored guide.

I pledged it to the hanged men: an answer, finally, to their ghastly call. I avowed it to the farmers in Pouelle: their wheat fields poisoned with the corpses of evil men, and then consumed by fire.

I was Viper.

I belonged to myself—and to all of them—until my dying day.

And they would never let me forget: the power to be found in bread.

40

A LAMB BROUGHT TO SLAUGHTER

I pushed the cartridge back into the bread and wedged it inside my mouth, the flavor of bread spreading across my cheek. Grimstaad, hands on his waist, watched the carriage clatter away until it disappeared entirely behind the trees. He turned and walked toward me, his silver boots crushing mud into the snow, each footfall quaking in my gut. His expression held steady, emotionless, as his rain-colored gauntlet collided with my temple.

I blinked, my vision white, glistening with stars. I did not realize I had fallen until I lifted my bound hands and found snow dusting the knots, my fingertips numb with cold. I blinked, the corners of my eyes dimming into a strange tunnel. The cartridge rested on my tongue, rattled loose from my cheek with the force of the blow. I pushed it to the top of my mouth, securing it in front of my teeth.

I need to stay awake.

I scooped a handful of snow and nuzzled it against my face.

Stay alert.

Grimstaad's shadow fell over me, darkening the snow. He plucked the edge of his sleeves, straightening his gauntlets. I shook my head and attempted to clear the stars. Forcing a frigid gulp of air into my lungs, I rolled onto my back.

"You just could not stop yourself." His voice was bent with his anger, like a ribbon pulled too tight. "I granted you one small favor, and you made a fool of me in front of my men."

He straightened his tunic and adjusted his belt. His neck cracked from side to side. He wrapped his hand into a fist around the hilt of his sword and yanked the blade free, the winter sun dancing along its edge. My heart pounded against my sternum; a breath caught in my throat.

Strike, Viper. Strike.

I pulled my leg to my chest and swung it at the side of his knee. The impact dropped him to one knee and he blinked, a blend of surprise and disdain surfacing in his amber eyes. I did not stop to stare. I sprang to my feet and ran, my braid whipping at my shoulders, my feet pounding as I struggled to maintain my balance with tied wrists. The rhythm of Grimstaad's footfalls did not punctuate mine. *Where is he? Why is he not chasing me?* I turned my neck, taking a backward glance at him. He had climbed back to his feet, but did not pursue me. Another prickle of concern nudged at my mind, but I dismissed it and continued to stumble ahead.

A moment later, my back erupted with pain and I fell into the snow. I wheezed, unable to draw a breath through my throat; my lungs felt as though they had been punched out of me. I heaved at the ground, writhing in my ropes. My leg brushed against the object which had felled me: a cold, fist-sized stone from the cliffs.

And finally, I heard Grimstaad's footfalls pacing behind me: a casual saunter to my frenetic dash. The ache from the stone spread between my shoulder blades and I remembered, sourly, what Bryce had told me of him. He was a trapper, a master of the hunt—he had a myriad of techniques at his disposal for how to capture his prey, stop it dead in its tracks.

A thin trickle of air passed through my throat. *He's coming for me.* He was coming to collect me, like one of his pelts. I had to do something—*anything*—to stop him. I lifted my head and forced my thoughts to slow. *Do not panic. Think. What would Bryce have me do?* I shook the thought from my head. *It was no good.* My ammorante had been a master of bladed combat, and I had no blades at my disposal.

I touched the blunt surface of the stone that had bludgeoned me. The scent of blood and ore flashed through my mind. *Like the battlefield.*

Roland. What would Roland have me do?

I wished I still had my ilex and could talk to him. Without it, I tried, as best as I was able, to hold his image in my mind: his jet-colored hair, his somber brown eyes, the soot and ash that clung to him—the hammer. Blackbird.

Blacksmith.

The fire from the campsite loomed a short distance from me. Grimstaad's glove clamped around my ankle and my heart lurched. Before I could hesitate, I lunged for the pit, digging my hands deep into the embers. They seared into my palms and I screamed, the heat sizzling deep into my flesh, igniting my nerves. It was worse than anything I had ever experienced—litha, nightmares, enforcers, terror. Embers and pain pulsed like a heart in my hands and Grimstaad's other glove gripped my calf. He dragged my body through the snow, locking his knees around my hips. I rolled onto my back and without hesitation or thought, I pressed the searing embers into his face.

He roared, his mouth twisting into grotesque shapes. The scent of charring flesh invaded my nose; whether it was mine or his, I did not know. He thrust his neck back and forth to shake me off, but I held tight against his cheeks, smearing the embers across his nose. My thumb found its way to his eye and I pushed against it with all the strength I could muster.

He reached blindly across his belt and yanked a hunting knife free, slashing wildly into the air. The blade ripped across my gown, cutting across my ribs. My blood flowed freely and I shrieked as the pain overtook me. I released Grimstaad, my hands throbbing as they fell. My body heaved with shivers, my teeth chattering as my blood pooled across my side.

Grimstaad turned from me, grabbing a fistful of snow to pack it against his face. He swore loudly when it touched his skin and slammed a knee into the ground. I tried, to no avail, to slow my trembling. Every part of my body throbbed with pain: my hands, the worst. I plunged them into the snow as Grimstaad had done for his face, uttering a curse as the throb turned to fire.

The pain died down and just as I climbed to all fours, Grimstaad slid his arms under each of my shoulders and dragged me. My ribs painted a crimson streak that meandered in the snow as the campfire faded from my sight. Grimstaad dragged me to the base of a thick tree, and I screamed as he slammed my back into its trunk. The force knocked my head against the tree, and the world turned on its side.

The stars returned to my vision—scintillating in the sun, I tried to count them but they winked, vanishing as I tried. I glanced around but I could not tell the sky from snow; blinking rapidly, I tried to make sense of my surroundings. All I could see was Grimstaad. He sneered at me with his red, pockmarked face, his arms doubled in my vision as he worked a rope around my waist.

"You Damica are all the same. Deceivers, all of you. Slaves to your headmistress," he growled as he worked, tightening the rope around me. "Now that our little game is over, why don't you tell me, Laurel Aleandri, what did she tell you to do to me? To grab hold of me when I came close, and use your gift to kill me?"

I shook my head, no. "She told me to serve you. For herself, the high court, and Trionfi," I choked. "She told me we would all be dead, if you did not win this war. If I did not do my part, to bend your prisoners, break their minds, siphon out their secrets. If I did not bear your children. I was nothing but a lamb brought to the slaughter."

"A lamb?" Grimstaad sneered. "You expect me to believe that any of you Damica are innocent? Helpless? No."

His arms continued to weave the rope around me. "You were promised to me. Sold. Sold like chattel. To *me*! It must be . . . *fate*."

Grimstaad snaked the rope behind the tree and looped it around the front. His amber eyes fixed on me and he threw his head back and laughed.

Monster. I wished he would stop talking, tie me to the tree, and do what it was he wished to do to me.

"You're all wicked, cursed creatures." Grimstaad cocked his head, his gaze combing over my body. "You're just like . . . *her*. She told me the same story . . . about how she was told to serve her husband, do her part. That she had no choice, either, about her marriage."

"What are you talking about?" I murmured.

A crest of bile rose in my throat. He was telling me something. Something of consequence. Without my ilex to aid me, I could not surmise what it was . . . only that it was something important. Something terrible.

"Clare," he growled. "She was supposed to be mine."

Clare? *My mother?*

No.

No, no.

I could not have heard him properly.

"Clare Aleandri, or Clare d'Arbenvale, as I knew her." Grimstaad tugged at the rope, working it into a knot. "I was nobody then—a lowly patrolman, and she was . . . Damica. Betrothed to another . . . Signore Claymonde, he was called."

Signore Claymonde? I had never heard Mama speak this name—nor had she ever spoken about Vitis Grimstaad. Perhaps this was an imagined romance in Grimstaad's mind. She had flashed him a smile, read his fortune—and he had misread her interest.

"I don't believe you," I gasped. "My mother never once uttered your name."

"Of course she would not. It was a shameful tryst, and

she was promised to another. We would meet in the moonlight in the barracks. We made promises to each other, that one day we would run away, start a life outside of Trionfi. But before that happened . . . I was called away from Cortellion. She promised she would wait for me. She was supposed to be *mine*." He scoffed, folding another loop of rope around the tree, and I winced as he tightened it around me.

Patrolman. A stiff coldness spread through my limbs, and I felt as though my body were no longer mine. The patrolman was who he wanted to be. Who he wanted me to find. The man who still had a heart. The man who still had my mother.

I began to shake. *That's why he wanted me.*

It had nothing to do with my ilex, or Trionfi, or a military victory.

He wanted to keep a piece of *my mother* with him. To punish. To break, for some misdeed he believed her to have committed. *Grimstaad always gets his man.* Bryce had once told me this. He was a hunter, a trapper . . . a master of nooses. He chased the banale and strung them up in the trees. All in the name of honor for Trionfi. Ridding the world of wrongdoing, one hanged man at a time.

A realization blossomed in my mind and my shivering grew more intense, violent jerks seizing me so that I was out of control. *That is the reason he hung my father.* There was little doubt in my mind: it was the kind of revenge he would revel in exacting. Righting a wrong. Out in the woodland, far from the protection of the Order . . . where no one but his own men were witnesses. The ground beneath me felt unsteady, and I struggled to stay upright.

"Murderer!" I wheezed, with what little breath I had. "My father was a good man. He did nothing to harm you!"

"You are naive, wife. His hands are dirty, too!" Grimstaad tightened a knot around me, his knuckles whitening. "He *stole* her from me."

The world spun beneath me, and my stomach lurched. I coughed and retched, trying to keep from vomiting. *Is any of this real?* I felt faint, weak—lost in delirium, had I imagined it all?

"When I returned from my travels to collect Clare, I discovered she no longer resided there; she lived with her husband. I rode to Claymonde's tenuta to find her, only to discover they had never wed. While I was away, the aedituus conspired with your headmistress and took her as his wife. When I found her, she was already with child. *You.*"

Grimstaad let the rope drop to the ground and cupped my chin in his hands. He squeezed my chin and I struggled to keep the cartridge in the corner of my mouth.

"I saw her in you . . . the moment I set my eyes on you in the palace. I knew you were her daughter—I was not going to let you get away. You are not slipping out of my grasp, Clare. *Not this time.*"

He stumbled to his tent and returned with the brass candlestick in his hands. Before my terror could spread throughout my body, he brought it down on my shin and I screamed. I writhed against the rope but it held me firm, steady against the trunk. The candlestick crashed against my leg again. I heard the snap, my bone crunching like a twig. Satisfied, Grimstaad nodded. He rubbed a fresh handful of snow against his face, then reached for his knife.

I hung my head and allowed myself to sink to the ground. It was over. He had won; whatever he was planning to do to me, I was powerless to stop. All I could do was pray for it to be over—quickly.

Daremi pacce.

Grimstaad lifted my arms and I offered them freely. His knife came down in the center of my bindings and I winced, waiting for him to swipe his blade across my fingers or wrists. But no such blow came to be. My bindings dropped into the snow. I gasped, holding my arms in front of me, the mar of the ropes etched up and down my skin.

Grimstaad groaned, lowered himself beside me into a crouch, and he gathered an armful of snow. I screamed as the icy slush hit my ribs.

"Hold this to your wound and pack it tight," he said.

I shivered and scooped more snow into my side. It bit into my ribs, stinging worse than the blade. Grimstaad watched me for a moment with his arms crossed over his chest. A slight grin pulled at the corner of his mouth. He had won. He reigned triumphant over Bryce, my father, my mother . . . and now, me. Bruised, burned, broken—I was forced into submission, wholly reliant on him to survive. He patted my head and traced his thumb across my lips.

"I'll be bringing you home on horseback for all of Trionfi to see. You will hold me, you will kiss me—and you will smile, wife. Do not bleed out before I have you treated."

He rose and turned away, his gait swift, proud. I held my hands in the snow and watched him go.

Fate and chance. They whirled together in a cloud of blurry thoughts, a kaleidoscope of gray. Mama had once been Grimstaad's lover. He disfigured Suzette; he had savagely murdered my father. He beat and tortured Bryce, his brother-in-arms in the Deos Tactigit, sentencing him to death.

Fate and chance. Turning over and over like my mother's serpent bracelets, weaving together in an intricate dance. This was the dance of all the Damica, the fragile duality of our gifts that we struggled to maintain—that which enveloped all past, present, and future, spinning together with an intricacy that I did not understand. I questioned whether any of the Damica, truly understood their gifts: the Verdetto, wielding truth and deception; the Vigore and their balance of strength and weakness. The Catene, the most feared, with their command over life and death. The Lunare, with the litha and the ilex: ah, such beautiful darkness. And the Fortuna—Mama, reading fate and chance in her leaves, telling others' fortunes while she remained blind to the future she had shaped for me.

Fate and chance. It always came back to fate and chance.

I slid my hand under my skirt and removed the pistol. It shone in my hands, glowing crimson in my palms. The golden accents winked at me and I bit my lip, thinking about my ammorante. I wrapped my hand around the holster. The coolness of the metal soothed my burns.

This was it. This was my chance. If I planned to kill him, it had to be now. I cupped a hand under my mouth and spit the bread into it. Fingers trembling, I slid the cartridge out and slipped it into the pistol.

In the distance, a horse nickered. I cocked the hammer back.

Easy. Steady.

Grimstaad's tunic flashed into my sight—a dull blue, almost gray like the sky. His eyes locked on me and his face distorted into a mask of shadow and hatred. He dropped his horse's reins and reached for his belt. As he pushed back his tunic, a glint of light blue metal caught my eye. A tremor of fear passed through my arms, hives rising on my skin.

"Deceivers, all of you." He whipped out his own pistol and pulled back the hammer with his thumb.

Taking a deep breath, I raised my pistol to his chest and squeezed the trigger. The world flashed white, and my back thudded against the tree. The trunk knocked the breath from my body. The horse whinnied and bolted away in the snow.

My ears rang with a high-pitched squeal; my eyes stung from smoke. Grimstaad's body stretched before me in the snow. Silently I twitched each of my fingers, blowing a breath of relief that they were still there.

I looked to the body—a hole burned into his tunic, Grimstaad's chest rose and fell with staggered breaths. His eyes, two colorless ovals, had relinquished his cruelty and spite.

I blinked and forced myself to swallow. My lips tasted of

blood and powder. I touched my fingertips to my cheek and they came away black, sticking with a mist of ore.

Grimstaad's breaths began to slow, turning slick, wet. I looked down at my broken leg, a red slush pooling around my body. I struggled to keep my eyes open. With tremendous effort, I lifted my head, scanning the trees.

A pair of talons rustled above me, the flash of a black wing greeting me. I inhaled deeply, my nose and mouth filling with the scent of iron. Hands throbbing, I released a wisp of cold breath and let the pistol fall.

"I am ready, Blackbird."

I surrendered my head to my chest, allowing his shadow to fold me into its darkness.

EPILOGUE

It was maddening, the snow.

It smelled like the mountains—freedom, fresh hope—but it rained down like ash: a constant, sticky patter clicking in my ears. Though I had sat at the foot of trees many times in the snow, I had never listened too deeply into them. I had leaned back and nuzzled the trees' broad, welcoming trunks, and they soothed me with their murmurs. But the tree to which I was tethered I could not hear and I imagined it slumbering: its old bones twinkling, swaying above me.

I hated the stillness: the manner in which it folded into me, slipping into every crease of my skin. Every twirling flake landing on my hair and each crystal that rested in my lashes beckoned the stillness to crawl up my body and nuzzle deep into my bosom.

The sun appeared behind a white haze. The trees glistened white. Grimstaad's body, still and silent—dusted with white flakes. I waxed and waned in and out of awareness. Each time I came to, the snow on Grimstaad's tunic gained more depth and breadth.

At some point, I must have stopped shivering. Blotches of blood, like crimson ink, soaked through my ribs, staining my bodice. A soft swirl of bloodied handprints tainted the snow beside me.

I stretched my arm before me. The backs of my fingers felt as cold and brittle as twigs. The hairs on my arms turned rigid. My eyelids fell, snow brushing my cheek.

Quiet, still. Pale as the snow, frigid at the wind.

I snapped awake. The tree still slumbered, its silence thick. Grimstaad's gauntlets were no longer visible beneath the snow. I looked to the sky; the peaks of the mountains were beginning to fade above the trees.

Night was falling.

I breathed in a light powder of snowflakes and let them melt on my tongue. My stomach moaned at me. My side, my leg . . . everything stung in white. Blisters bubbled up on my palms, a needling throb with a constant staccato rhythm. My head throbbed in a conflicting cadence.

My heart hurt so much it had stilled, slumbering like the tree.

I had never imagined there could be so many forms of pain.

I raised my eyes to the moon—She appeared as a small white semicircle hanging above the mountains, veiled by clouds.

I should have begged Her for release—to take my life, free me of suffering, let my breath fade and my life melt like a tender crystal, into the earth.

Instead, She winked at me through the treetops, tapping a message in shadow and light. I did not need my ilex to understand; She spoke a cryptic language, older than my ilex, and Her words rang clear in my ears.

We will rise again, together.

ACKNOWLEDGEMENTS

Derek Freeman, my husband, my Roland, and the love of my life: thank you for sticking with me over the years as this story evolved. You were there before this story was a story, and I'll never forget those times we'd drive around listening to "Forgiven" by Disturbed and talking through epic battle scenes. You were there for the inception of Roland, your "good" character in *Fable 2*, and Bryce, my "evil" character, who turned Roland to the dark side instantly, despite his best efforts to turn Bryce good. Thank you for the early days of adventure and for being there as I polished this story. You were the one who put up with my using you as a real-life mannequin ("Stand here and stare off into the distance. I need to see your eyes."), the one who sat at the table and watched videos about rabbit snares, and you used your Canadian superpowers to educate this native Texan about the snow. Thank you for being "the weird kid from Cortes": a very odd human who made me laugh during the most stressful parts of this process by dancing sprightly little jigs around the kitchen to black metal music. I love you forever and a day, bird.

Byron Freeman, my patient, silly, compassionate little boy. I started writing my first full draft of this story when you were only two years old. So many mothers told me I'd never be able to write a book with a child demanding so much of my time and attention. Well, sweet boy, you proved them wrong. You have always been incredible like that. Mom loves you more than I can say.

Leo Schmidt, rose of the otherlands, thank you, darling, for your pure and courageous heart. When I was in a crisis with this book and felt like everything was coming apart, you showed up for me. You screamed as loud as you could and used your sharp, pointy goblin teeth to bring me back from the dead. You get it on a soul level: books are sacred; words are hallowed. They are worth fighting for, worth dying for. And, most importantly, worth living for.

Kathy Larsen, my former colleague in the publishing trenches, my dear friend, and the absolute gold standard for editors. Thank you for the hundreds of comments on this book and for helping me take this from a good story to a great one. I am in awe of your skill. The dedication you have shown this book is astounding.

Eben Schumacher, you and I were on this journey together for a long time. I am so thrilled to have you guiding me now on all of the art for this project. A long time ago, I told you that you are one of the great healers of the world. That rings true now more than ever. Your ability to create beautiful illustrations gave me the resolve to see this through and put my best foot forward every day.

Valerie Schiffen, you watched my son grow up: fed him, played with him, tucked him into bed, and gave me the extra time I needed to complete the revisions to this book. Without you, it would not exist.

Georgina Key—beautiful friend, you were among the first to cherish Laurel's unique voice. Thank you for all the beautiful days filled with sunlight, art, music, and good company. The times at the Riverside Castle are special memories in my heart.

Jamie Portwood, my amazing, powerful friend with a soul made of fire. You have always believed in me, lifted me up, and been an amplifier for this book. Thank you from the bottom of my heart.

Tex Thompson, organizing and championing Writers in the Field means more to me than you will ever know.

Lois (Wetherington) Sullivan, what a joy it's been, trading so many pictures of fantasy forests and billowing gowns. I've missed you this past year, and I finished this novel with you in my heart (P.S., yours is coming, too).

Nyri A. Bakkalian, there is no one like you. We've come a long way since the days of sparrows in trees, and you are still in my heart, cherissima. Always.

Debbie Burns. *fires a thousand glitter cannons* You gave me the tools and the encouragement I needed to push through and get a completed first draft on paper. Thank you for founding Creative Central and Fiction Expedition, and for letting me be a part of them.

William (Bill) Wageneck, as group publisher, you were first my boss, then my mentor, and now my friend. You took me under your wing, taught me all the ropes in publishing, so that I could one day fly on my own.

Erin Hall, I will never forget our foray to the hibachi grill and then the Katatonia concert. Thank you for being an amazing friend and proofreader.

To the writers of Creative Central, Word Splurge, and the numerous literary endeavors I have embarked on over the years, thank you for being a part of my journey along the way: Jaumarro "Joy" Cuffee, Shannon McRoberts, Allison Hinkle, Kat Seto, Pearl Kilgore, Lesli Jenkins, NJ Sullivan, Leah Polumbo, Rachael Denessen, Mandy Trichell, Sianyn Leigh, Amanda Mills Woodlee, Dark Gary, Diane Prokop, Kathryn McClatchy, Melissa Algood, Sarah Tollok, Amy Bright, Rose Callahan, Theda Vallee, Andrea Coble, Hannah Vaughan, Patti Harris, Julia Jinkyong Allen, Elizabeth Gordon-Swain, Catherine Vance, Erin Lunde, Holla Watson, Tod Tinker, Sarah Hines, Kim Jury, Charlene Templeman, and countless others.

To my oldest friends, Peter Fata, Allen Fata, and John

Roth, thank you for being a part of my life and for your tireless and staunch enthusiasm over my book. Everett Bradshaw, thank you too, for being an early supporter.

A huge thank you to my mother, Elsa Malakoff, who used to listen to me read aloud to her. I am grateful to my brother, Morris Malakoff, for the stunning photography for my author photo.

Justin Gedak, thank you for putting your unique gothic touch on my author photo.

Robert Carl Ruble, I am so appreciative of you for designing Laurel's Lunare pendant.

And finally, I am forever thankful to my higher power. You are the stream from which all creativity flows. I know you put me on this earth to write this book for a reason, and I thank you for all the people I have met as I found my way through it.

ABOUT THE AUTHOR

Ynes Freeman is an award-winning gothic fiction author, and she is the publisher at Memento Vivere Press. Her work is beautiful, intense, and deep. She believes writing is the secret to immortality and that authors live forever through their books, changing the lives of people they will never meet. Her wish is for all creatives to believe in themselves and that their stories are worth telling. Under a variety of pen names, Ynes's work has appeared in *Everyday Fiction* ezine, *Primal Elements* (a poetry collection), *The Order of Us* (a Moms Who Write anthology), *Dragons Within,* and other anthologies. Learn more about her work by visiting @ynesfreeman on most social media.

Content Warning